"HERE WE ARE AGAIN."

PANTOMIME JOE;

OR,

AN ORPHAN BOY'S CAREER.

COMPLETE IN TWO VOLUMES.

VOLUME I.

ILLUSTRATED.

LONDON:

EDWIN J. BRETT, 173, FLEET STREET, E.C.

CONTENTS.

CHAPTER XLIII.

CHAPTER XLIV.

CHAPTER XLV.

CHAPTER XLVI.

CHAPTER XLVII.

CHAPTER XLVIII.

CHAPTER XLIX.

CHAPTER L.

CHAPTER LI.

CHAPTER LII.

CHAPTER LIII.

CHAPTER LIV.

CHAPTER LV.

CHAPTER LVI.

CHAPTER LVII.

CHAPTER LVIII.

CHAPTER LIX.

CHAPTER LX.

CHAPTER LXI.

CHAPTER LXII.

CHAPTER LXIII.

CHAPTER LXIV.

CHAPTER LXV.

CHAPTER LXVI.

CHAPTER LXVII.

CHAPTER LXVIII.

CHAPTER LXIX.

CHAPTER LXX.

CHAPTER LXXI.

CHAPTER LXXII.

CHAPTER LXXIII.

CHAPTER LXXIV.

CHAPTER LXXV.

CHAPTER LXXVI.

CHAPTER LXXVII.

CHAPTER LXXVIII.

CHAPTER LXXIX.

CHAPTER LXXX.

CHAPTER LXXXI.

PANTOMIME JOE;

OR, AN ORPHAN BOY'S CAREER.

"'HERE WE GO INSIDE OUT. HERE WE GO OUTSIDE IN!' SHOUTED YOUNG JOE."

PANTOMIME JOE;

OR,

AN ORPHAN BOY'S CAREER.

CHAPTER I.

SNOWY CHRISTMAS EVE—HOW THE MAN IN THE THICK COAT LEFT SOMETHING IN THE ROAD, AND HOW CLOWN AND PANTALOON TUMBLED OVER IT.

COLD, bitter cold. Snow everywhere, both in country and town. The fields looked like the tops of huge Twelfth cakes, in their snow-white coverings.

The roofs of the houses were also wrapped in the same flaky mantle, and every street, court, and alley had its share; only in the latter, perhaps, the snow was not quite so clean.

It was Christmas Eve.

About seven o'clock in the evening.

The church bells of Oldham, in Lancashire, were ringing a cheerful peal.

And the wind bore their music beyond the small town, with its busy factories and smoky chimneys, into the quiet, snow-clad country.

Along the lonely road a man, wrapped in a thick, warm coat, was making his way towards the town.

The snow lying thick in the path, his footsteps made no sound.

He seemed like some dark ghost, gliding along.

Looking neither to the right nor the left.

He carried something under his arm.

Something like a small coffin.

What could it be?

When he had arrived at about three quarters of a mile from the town, he stopped and peered anxiously up and down the road.

Not a soul was visible either way.

The lonely spot seemed to suit his purpose.

He then placed the something he carried on the snowy ground across the path.

So that anyone passing must either have seen it or stumbled over it.

Whilst thus engaged, the sound of voices approaching was heard.

Not speaking, but singing a very merry kind of chorus, in a merry manner.

The stranger in the thick coat lifted up his head and listened.

The tune was familiar to him, and the words also.

Just now, however, he must have been anything but happy, for "Tippitywichit" fell but mournfully upon his ear, and made him sigh.

As the choristers drew nearer, and the sounds became more and more distinct, the solitary stranger gradually receded, till he was no longer visible.

A very jolly little party they were, too, who were now approaching, consisting of no less important personages than the pantomimists engaged at the little theatre for the Christmas pantomime.

There were Joey Muggins, the clown, and Sarah Muggins, Joe's wife; Tom Trotters, the pantaloon; Charley Silver, the harlequin; Bill Wriggles, the sprite, and Carry Brown, the columbine.

They had just finished the last rehearsal previous to Boxing Night, and were all hastening from the theatre to Joe Muggins' lodgings to spend Christmas Eve in as convivial a manner as their circumstances permitted.

It had begun to snow again, and in order to enliven the walk, vocal harmony was suggested.

Accordingly they became harmonious at once, their voices echoing far and wide through the silent night.

They were in full swing with the " Tippitywichit " chorus as they approached the spot where the stranger had lately stood.

" Now then, boys," cried Joe Muggins, " give it mouth. Ri tol—tiddy iddy—tiddy iddy—ri tol tiddy iddy——"

The clown, who was—as he called it—giving all the mouth he possibly could (which was a good deal) to the chorus, suddenly ceased as he stumbled over something in the path, and fell sprawling on his hands on the snow.

" Hullo, Joey, what's up?" cried the pantaloon.

At the same moment he also caught his toe in the " something," and went down by the side of his companion.

" Here we are!" exclaimed Joe, cheerfully, as he sprang up with a pantomimic bound. " Get up, old un."*

As he spoke, he kindly assisted Trotters, by grasping him by the back of his collar, and hoisting him on to his feet.

" What is it?" inquired Tom; " seems to me as some un's been tying a string across the road to throw us over."

" It ain't string," returned Joe, " it's —hullo!" he cried, suddenly, as he caught

* A term usually applied to the pantaloon by the clown.

sight of the " something," and made a grab at it. " 'Ere it is; I've got it!"

" 'Alves!" cried the pantaloon.

" 'Alves!" cried harlequin and sprite.

" 'Alves!" joined in the columbine and Sarah Muggins.

" Well, we can't all of us go 'alves," returned the clown, with a good-natured grin, as he held the treasure—whatever it was—in his two hands.

" What is it?" inquired his companions, eagerly.

" We'll see," said Joe, as he placed the " something " down on the ground.

The falling snow had covered the top, and it was quite white.

" Looks something like a Twelfth cake, don't it?" suggested the columbine.

" In the shape of a coffin," added the clown.

" Oh, Joe!" exclaimed his wife, reprovingly.

" Well, it don't look unlike it," remarked the pantaloon and sprite.

This was perfectly true, it did not.

On the contrary, it looked uncommonly like a small coffin.

" Clear away the snow, Joey," suggested the harlequin, " and let's see what it is."

" That's jest what I'm a-going to do," returned the clown, as with his hand he scraped off the flaky covering from the top of the something.

An explanation of relief burst from the gazers.

" Why, it's only a basket after all," cried everybody; " a wicker basket."

" So it is," laughed Joe, " and as it's pantermime time, of course the clown collars the wicker."

With these words, Joe Muggins raised the article in question, and placed it under his arm.

" We'll investigate its contents when we gets 'ome," he said.

Then, pretending to be struck with a sudden panic common to clowns, he cried—

" Come on, old un, 'ere's a bobby round the corner."

The whole party laughed and set off briskly.

So eager were they to see what was inside the basket, that there was no more singing

But all wondered what it contained.

Ten minutes' sharp walking brought them to their journey's end.

The door was opened by Mrs. Nubbles, the landlady—a good-humoured-looking, matronly woman, with a rosy, comfortable face.

"Oh, 'ere you be, all of you," she exclaimed, by way of greeting.

"Yes, 'ere we are," returned Joe, in a tone of much exhilaration, as he stepped in with the wicker under his arm; "quite a party of us, ain't there? The fact is, Mrs. Nubbles, we're a-going to have a jolly evening amongst ourselves."

"That be right," returned the landlady, warmly; "the more the merrier."

"P'r'aps you won't mind joinin' us, Mrs. Nubbles?" said Joe, politely. "And when yer come up, yer'll bring the kittle with yer, cos," he added, with a comic wink of his eye, "I think it's very likely we shall want lots of 'ot water."

Mrs. Nubbles hurried away in a cheerful bustle to make the kettle boil.

Joe and his friends, looking like a set of Twelfth cake ornaments in their snowy garments, went upstairs.

At the same moment, the stranger in the thick coat, who had followed and watched them into the house, turned away from the door.

"I'm glad someone's found it," he muttered, as he hurried along the cold road.

CHAPTER II.

HOW THE MYSTERIOUS BASKET WAS OPENED—WHAT WAS FOUND IN IT— AN UNEXPECTED GUEST.

AS soon as they reached the apartment, Joe placed the basket he carried on the table, and having relieved his pockets of sundry bottles, poked up the fire.

The lamp was lighted, and the snug little room in a moment assumed quite a bright and cheerful appearance.

Sprigs of holly decorated the walls, and the scarlet berries, glistening in the rays of the sudden illumination, added to the cosy, Christmas-like aspect of the chamber.

"This is what I calls regler comfort-'ble!" exclaimed the clown, as he joined his friends, who had gathered round the table.

Of course, the principal object of interest was the mysterious basket that stood upon it.

"Open it, Joey, open it!" they cried, eagerly.

"All right; I'm a-goin' to," returned the clown, as he took a knife from the cupboard to cut the string that secured the lid. "But stop a minnit! Where's Sarah?"

Sarah had remained below stairs to relate the incident of the basket to her landlady.

"Come on, Sarah," he called from the top of the stairs; "we're all a-waitin' on the tip-toe of anxiety to know what's in this 'ere Christmas 'amper."

"I'm a-comin', Joe!" called his wife.

The next moment Sarah was heard ascending the stairs with Mrs. Nubbles, who carried the kettle, steaming furiously.

As soon as they had entered, and the kettle had been deposited on the hob, the last two arrivals took their places with the rest.

Anxious eyes looked down upon the wicker basket.

Joe flourished his knife, and was about to sever the string.

But he did not.

He paused suddenly, and said, inquiringly—

"S'pose we all give a guess what's inside afore I open it—eh?"

The whole party instantly became profoundly reflective.

"Now, then, time's up; fire away!" cried the clown, at length; "Mrs. Nubbles fust. What do you say it is, Mrs. Nubbles?"

"Fish," replied Mrs. Nubbles, after slight pause.

"Now, Sarah, what do you say?" continued her husband.

"Well, Joe," returned his spouse, with some hesitation, "I should think it was a

Christmas present—some sort—what, I really can't guess."

"I think it's hares," said the harlequin.

"Rabbits an' a bit o' pork," suggested the sprite.

"Goose," predicted Carry Brown, the columbine.

"Now, old un, what's your private opinion?" asked Joe.

Tom Trotters, whose confidence in baskets found by the roadside was, from the frequent sells he had experienced, of the slightest possible description, replied, briefly—

"A dead dog!"

The ladies uttered a slight shriek.

"Ugh! yer nasty ole man!" replied Joe, in a pantomimical tone of disgust.

"I've picked up three stunnin' Christmas 'ampers in my time," explained the pantaloon, "an' they all 'ad dead dogs in 'em but one, an' that 'ad a couple o' dead cats."

It was now Joe's turn to guess.

"I say turkey an' sausidges," he exclaimed, confidently. "Now let's see who's right!"

The knife flashed in the air, and came down upon the strings that secured the lid. The lid was raised.

A piece of red flannel was all that met the eager eyes of the party.

"O—h!" exclaimed everybody, in a disappointed tone—"o—h!"

"There's somethin' underneath, I'm sure!" said Mrs. Muggins, shrewdly.

"Right you are, Sarah!" returned her husband, as he turned back the scarlet coverlet.

If the party had a moment before expressed disappointment, they now uttered a simultaneous cry of horrified surprise.

It was not fish, or hares, or rabbits, or pork, or goose, or turkey and sausages, or even a dead dog, that met their astonished gaze—but the body of an infant!

For a moment a dead silence followed the startled cry.

They stood in speechless amazement, with their eyes riveted upon the tiny form.

At length Joe Muggins, whose emotions could no longer be controlled, exclaimed, with deep intensity—

"Well, I'm blest, so it is!—a babby—a real babby!"

"Are you sure it ain't a dummy, Joe?" asked the pantaloon, in an awe-struck tone.

"No, it ain't no dummy, Tom," returned the clown, seriously. "That's flesh and blood, as sure as we are."

"Poor little thing!" exclaimed Mrs. Nubbles and the columbine, pityingly.

"Is it alive?" asked Sarah, anxiously.

"Well, that's more than I can say at present, my gal," returned Joe. "I'll see, and while I'm a-seein', p'r'aps some-one'll uncork one of them bottles on the table yonder. I declare this 'ere little un's given me quite a turn."

The unexpected discovery seemed to have given everybody a turn, and all eyes looked anxiously towards the table where the bottles stood.

The harlequin performed the operation of uncorking.

Joe Muggins, in the meantime, turned his attention to the little stranger in the basket.

It was not stripped, neither had it been huddled into its narrow bed anyhow.

On the contrary, it was dressed, and covered round carefully with flannel.

But in spite of the precautions taken, the infant, from the bitter intensity of the weather, was icy cold.

This Joe discovered when he placed his hand gently upon his forehead.

The little face had a bluish, nipped look, and the eyes were closed.

"I'm afraid it's a case, Sarah," said the clown, shaking his head mournfully. "It seems to me to be froze."

"Well, suppose we take it out and see," suggested the good woman.

"Ah, yes, s'pose yer do," assented Joe. "If he is froze, the best thing'll be to thaw him as soon as possible. Yer'll do that better than I shall. Mind yer don't drop him."

There was no need of that caution.

In an instant Sarah Muggins had the baby out of his place of confinement, and snuggled up in her lap by the fire.

Joe recruited his nerves with a glass of Old Tom, and then returned to his wife.

"Has he begun to thaw yet?" he asked.

The kind-hearted nurse, having taken several sly peeps at her little charge, had come to the conclusion that it was not dead, and presently she was rewarded by a sigh, breathed faintly from the infant's lips.

"Oh, it's coming to—it's coming to !" she cried, joyfully.

"What, thawin' ?" eagerly asked Joe.

"I think so," answered his wife; "it's beginnin' to grow restless."

"That's a good sign," Joe responded, hopefully; "but I wish he'd burst out into a good cry. We should be sure he was all right then."

This wish had hardly been expressed, when the infant, whose partially-suspended animation had been restored by the genial warmth of Sarah Muggins' lap and the fire, evinced its willingness to oblige its benefactors by opening its infant mouth, and crying as loud as a child of two months could be expected to cry.

The sounds it produced were not very powerful, but they were highly satisfactory to all present, and relieved Joe from a load of anxiety.

It also suggested another idea to his wife, who exclaimed, compassionately—

"Bless its dear little heart! it wants something to eat."

Away rushed Mrs. Nubbles, and presently returned with a small saucepan, and a jug of milk, and a packet of something white, which proved to be arrow-root.

In a very few moments a teacup full of nutritious infantine soup was prepared.

The juvenile stranger, who appeared to be in excellent appetite, ate till it was tired, and then fell asleep.

Conviviality, and pipes, and Old Tom then became the order of the evening.

"Well," said Joe, as he mixed tumblers of hot grog for his friends, "who'd have thought of anythin' like this happenin'? It's quite romantic, ain't it?"

Everyone agreed that it was.

"There's only one point as is rather perplexin'," Joe continued, "and that is, now we've got 'im, what's to be done with 'im?"

The whole party looked thoughtfully in their glasses for an idea.

"Why don't you take him yourself, and make a little clown of him?" suggested the pantaloon, at length, to his friend Joe.

"Well, I thought I'd just give the rest of you a chance," Joe replied; "but, as it seems you don't care about it, dash my wig if I don't take the poor little creetur and be a father to 'im. What d'yer say, Sarah ?"

"Do, Joe, do," she answered, warmly, "and I'll be a mother to 'im."

"Then that's settled," cried the clown; "he's my private property from this minit. But stop, though," he exclaimed, pulling rather a long face, "here are we a-talkin' about 'im, and how do we know it ain't 'er all the time? It's just as likely to be a gal as a boy."

This seemed to perplex the worthy pantomimist extremely.

But, happening to turn his head, he observed a piece of paper affixed to a corner of the red flannel in the basket.

On this was written, in a good hand—

"*This poor child has neither father nor mother. Be kind to him, and Heaven will reward you.*"

"Hooray! it's a 'im; it's a boy, Sarah; that settles the point," cried Joe Muggins, triumphantly, after reading the notice. "I'll take 'im, and teach 'im all as I knows myself; and, as I was christened Joseph, after my illustrious brother pantomimist, the renowned Joey Grimaldi, so shall he be."

"And then there'll be old Joe and young Joe," remarked Tom Trotters.

This being settled, the glasses were refilled, and the baby's health was drunk with three times three.

It was Christmas morning before the merry party broke up, and Joe and his spouse were once more alone together.

"I wonder who it was ordered the poor little creetur' to be packed up in that basket and exposed to the cold and snow ?" Joe said.

"They must have been cruel wretches," said his warm-hearted wife, indignantly.

"No doubt of it," assented Joe, "but it don't matter now we've found him. "I'll do my duty by him, and make him a clown such as Grimaldi would be proud of if he could see him."

"I do hope you'll get on, Joe, and be able to send him to school," exclaimed his wife.

"I'm sure to get on, Sarah," returned Joe, hopefully, "and the boy shall go to a tip-top school when he's old enough. Though I did'nt have much eddication myself, he shall."

"Schooling's expensive," remarked Sarah, "and salaries are not great; and then," she added, with a sigh, "it ain't Christmas all the year round, you know, Joe."

"No, it ain't," admitted the clown, rather ruefully, as he thought of the long, "hard up" summer months, when pantomimes were out of season, and clowns were not wanted. "I wish it was."

But the cloud soon passed away from his round, jovial face, as he said, cheerfully—

"But never mind, Sarah; don't let's worrit about the future. It's my opinion as the same Providence as put that poor child in our way will give us a helping hand to support him."

With their minds full of these cheering prospects, Joe Muggins and his spouse sought their pillow in a very happy, contented frame of mind, carrying with them their newly-adopted son and heir.

CHAPTER III.

THE FIRST NIGHT OF THE PANTOMIME—A STAGE WAIT—OUR LITTLE HERO JOE MAKES HIS FIRST APPEARANCE ON ANY STAGE.

JOE MUGGINS, in his professional capacity, had mutilated the usual number of dummy babies.

But this night, in his dreams, he mixed up the real and the unreal in the most distressing manner.

All night long he seemed to be on the stage, acting pantomimes.

At one time he and the pantaloon were playing at catch-ball with his adopted son and heir.

At another he was turning a mangle with the infant Joseph under the rollers, black in the face.

Then again he dropped the baby on the ground, and sat down upon him so suddenly that he went off with a loud bang, like a pistol, and was picked up as flat as a pancake by the old un.

Joe started from his slumbers at last in a paroxysm of horror, and sat upright in the bed.

"I've squashed 'im! I've squashed 'im!" he cried, wildly.

"Squashed what, Joe?" asked a mild voice by his side.

"Why, the blessed babby—quite flat!" exclaimed the distracted clown, in an agony of remorse, as he looked over the bedside on to the floor, after the infant's mangled remains.

"I'm sure you haven't, Joe," returned the quiet voice, "for I've got 'im."

"Lor' bless me! so yer 'ave," cried Joe Muggins, in a tone of intense relief, as he found his wife sitting up by his side, feeding little Joey with some milk and water. "Well, I declare if I didn't think I'd been and sat on 'im!"

"You've been dreamin', Joe," said Sarah, laughing; "the baby's all right enough."

"So 'e is," returned her husband. "I s'pose I must ha' been dreaming—but it gave me a orful turn, it did!"

These nervous delusions—caused by over anxiety—however, soon passed off, and Joe and his wife spent a very comfortable Christmas Day at home.

Boxing Night came at last.

Joe Muggins was perfectly right in the first of his predictions.

In spite of the cold and snow, the theatre was crammed to suffocation.

If it could have held three times the number of people, it would not have been large enough.

"Tom, Tom, the Piper's Son, or the Naughty Boy that Stole the Pig," promised to be not only a great, but a tremendous success.

From the moment the curtain rose the applause commenced and continued.

Everything went well, and the audience were in ecstasies.

The "gorgeous transformation scene" had worked its multitudinous changes without a single hitch.

And now came on the great event of the evening, when the characters of the opening are transformed by supernatural power to the characters of the pantomime.

Our friends the pantomimists were all in full feather, standing in the wings,* waiting to make their appearance.

Charley Silver and Carry Brown, (known in the bills as Signor Carlo Sylvestro and Mademoiselle Carolina Brunetta), in their glittering dresses as harlequin and columbine.

Bill Wriggles (or the renowned sprite Wrigglecumtwister), in his tight-fitting costume, with its spiral rings.

Tom Trotters (alias Herr Trottmans), looking quite venerable as the pantaloon.

And last, not least, Joe Muggins (whom the bills announced in large letters as the great Joey Muggerini, the only successor to Grimaldi), newly chalked and painted, and looking, in his spotted dress, as fresh and lively as a clown should look at the beginning of a pantomime.

The fairy queen waves her wand, and in an instant the characters bound on to the stage before the audience.

"Hi! here we are. Merry Christmas to you all," cries he, as he turns a somersault and comes down on his feet, where he stands with his knees together, and his toes turned in in the most approved clown's fashion, pulling a succession of "mugs" at the audience, who are convulsed with laughter.

"Brayvo, Joey!" resounds from all parts of the house.

The introductory business being over, the business of the pantomime commences at once.

"I say, old un," says the clown, confidentially, as he shakes hands with the pantaloon, "what d'yer think?"

"I dunno," responds the latter. "What?"

"I've found a farden."

"Don't believe yer."

"Yer don't, yer wicked old man? Take that."

The pantaloon is knocked down, of course, by the injured clown, who picks him up by the waist of his trunks.

Harlequin, clown, and pantaloon then chase each other in a most bewildering manner.

At length they catch each other, and the three spin round like three living teetotums.

Suddenly they separate.

Harlequin nimbly disappears, clown and pantaloon come into violent collision and roll over, of course.

Up again in an instant, and, having formed a position with the harlequin and columbine at the back, coloured fires are lighted, and they are closed in,* amidst the cheers and laughter of the audience.

The first scene of the pantomime is over.

"It's all right, old gal," exclaimed Joe, exultingly, to his wife, as he came off at the wing; "this pantomime'll be a reg'lar triumph."

Mrs. Muggins, who always came to the theatre every evening, had brought little Joe with her.

The infant was snugly wrapped up in a shawl, and hugged up close to her.

Joe, whose paternal anxiety, in spite of its being the first night of the pantomime, could not be suppressed, pulled aside the shawl, and peeped at his adopted son.

"Keep 'im warm, Sarah; bless 'is little ten toes! keep 'im warm," he said.

The second scene was now on.

The band were playing away—one of the usual brisk pantomime tunes.

It was time for the clown and pantaloon to make their entrance again.

"On we go," shouted Joe, hilariously. "Come on, old un."

The scene progressed, during which clown and pantaloon start in the sausage business.

They at once do a roaring trade.

Yards and yards of sausages are made and sold to eager buyers, the proprietors not being very particular as to the ingredients they supply to their customers.

Already a fat boy and a policeman have been ground up in the sausage machine, to the intense delight of the audience.

They are waiting for another victim
A woman with a baby.

But the woman does not come.

The sausage machine is compelled to remain idle.

The scene begins to flag—there is a stage wait.

"What's up?" whispered Joe off at the wing.

---

* The side scenes, where the actors make their entrances and exits.

* A term used when a front scene is run on and shuts in another scene behind it.

"Property man's lost the dummy baby," whispers the prompter, in reply.

The spectators saw there was something amiss, and began to hiss slightly, just when the pantomime was going so well, too.

What was to be done?

Suddenly Joe remembered his baby.

Off the stage he rushes, and hurries up to his wife.

"Come on, Sarah," he cries, excitedly, "the property man's lost the dummy baby, so you must brig on Joe."

"What!" exclaimed Sarah, aghast. "To be ground up into sausage-meat?"

"I should think not," returned the clown, indignantly. "I ain't a-going to grind 'im, but the people are beginnin' to grumble at the wait, and the goose is flying about.* Come on, I won't hurt 'im."

But Sarah hesitated, and did not seem inclined to part with her charge.

"You'll be sure and not sit on him?" she said to her husband, in a tone of nervous apprehension.

"Of course not," responded Joe.

"Or throw him up in the air, or swing him round by one leg?"

"What a idea! Why, ye're growin' cranky, Sarah!" returned Joe, impatiently. "Hark! there go the hisses, and the pantomime 'll be ruined. Come on?"

With these words, he almost dragged the infant out of his wife's arms, and hurried on to the stage.

The hisses instantly ceased, and bursts of applause rang through the house as the shawl that enveloped the child fell to the ground, and discoved a real, live baby, in clean, white long clothes in the clown's arms.

"Here we are!" cried Joe, as he advanced to the footlights, and held up the infant, who opened its eyes and looked very much astonished, but didn't cry.

"Now, Mr. Simpson!" said the clown, turning to a milkman on the stage; "let's have the infant's supper; I've got the feedin' bottle in my pocket."

The applause was redoubled when the clown informed the audience that "It was his son and heir's fust appearance on any stage."

CHAPTER IV.

OUR HERO NARROWLY ESCAPES BEING GROUND INTO SAUSAGE MEAT—A VISIT FROM THE STRANGER IN THE THICK COAT.

SARAH MUGGINS stood at the wing with her hands clasped, expecting nothing less than that the child would go into convulsions with fright.

But as nothing of the sort happened, she was beginning to feel more composed when—the applause caused by the child's appearance having subsided—the pantaloon approached his partner, the clown, and said—

"We're out of sausidges."

"Oh, are we?" responds the clown. "Then we must make some more."

"That's a fine child you've got in yer arms," remarks the old un; "s'pose we make sausidges of him? He'd grind up beautiful."

"What! grind up my only son and heir!" shouts Joe, in pretended indignation. "Why, you hoary-headed miscreant, I've a great mind to——"

Here the clown made an expressive motion, as if he were about to hurl the innocent babe at the head of his unfeeling colleague.

A shriek, however, at the wing from Sarah recalled Joe to the fact that the child he held was not a dummy, and he did not throw him.

The pantaloon approached penitently, and protested he wasn't in earnest.

"Poor little creetur!" said the ancient hypocrite. "How old is he?"

"As old again as half," replies the clown.

"Bless his little gums, let me take nim

The audience are hissing.

a bit. I'm fond of nursing," remarks the pantaloon.

"Don't drop him, cos he's his father's hope and his mammy's joy," says the clown, as he places his adopted son in the arms of his partner.

"I'll be very careful of him," protests the pantaloon.

But at the same moment the latter treacherously hurries to the sausage machine.

Opening the lid, he is about to consign the infant Joe to destruction, when, unable to control herself any longer, Sarah Muggins rushes on to the stage.

"You wretch—you monster!" she cries; "give me my child."

After boxing the pantaloon's ears till they tingle again, and pulling his venerable nose till his eyes water, she snatches her precious charge from his sanguinary grasp.

It was now Joe's turn.

"Ugh! you atrocious old cannibal!" he cries, as he knocks the offending pantaloon down; "you ought to be ashamed of yourself."

Then, by way of retributive justice, Joe seizes his guilty colleague, and having pitched him head first into the sausage machine, commences turning the handle vigorously.

Thunders of applause and shouts of laughter followed these acts.

And when, in addition, a long roll of sausages, supposed to have been manufactured out of the old man's body, came gradually forth, the sensation was tremendous.

After this everything went smoothly, and the pantomime ended the first night of its representation triumphantly.

The audience were in raptures.

The manager was in ecstasies, and everyone else perfectly satisfied.

It had a long and successful run, as Joe had predicted.

Towards the end of its career the benefits of the pantomimists were severally announced.

Each one exerted himself to produce some extraordinary attraction in order to insure a full house.

Joe Muggins had the last night of the pantomime to himself.

Tickets went off briskly, and Joe felt pretty certain of a bumper.

It was on the night preceding this important event his wife met him at the wing.

"Somebody wants you at the stage door, Joe," she said.

"Who is it?" inquired the clown.

"A gentleman in a thick great coat," replied Sarah.

"Someone for tickets, I s'pose," was Joe's natural thought. "Didn't he give any name?" he asked.

"No, he only said he wanted to speak to you."

"I'll go down and see," said Joe. "I shall have time while the harlequin and columbine's doing their trip."

Accordingly, Joe went to the stage door.

Here he found a person wrapped in a thick, warm coat, the collar of which was turned up, and with his hat pulled so far forward over his eyes that he could not see his features distinctly.

"Mr. Muggerini, I believe," said the stranger, with a slight inclination of the head, as the clown made his appearance.

"That's me, sir," returned Joe, touching his wig with his finger by way of salutation.

"You're a very clever man, and a very good clown," the stranger continued; "and, as I think talent ought to be encouraged, I wish to take a few tickets for your benefit to-morrow night."

"You're very kind, sir," returned Joe; "how many?"

"You may give me ten box, if you please," the person replied.

Joe, who had taken the precaution to bring some tickets with him, counted out the required number, and handed them to the unknown, who gave him in exchange fifteen shillings.

"Sorry I can't afford to take more," he exclaimed, as he put the cards in his pockets, "but I'm not rich."

Joe expressed himself perfectly satisfied and very grateful.

The stranger then moved towards the door, as if about to depart.

But instead of going, he stopped, and, coming back, took Joe by the hand rather warmly.

"I forgot to wish you good night," he said, looking earnestly in his face, "and it's not likely we shall meet again, in this town at least, for I'm off to-morrow."

"What, before the benefit?" asked Joe, in surprise.

"Yes," returned the stranger. "I shan't use the tickets; I merely bought them to serve you."

Joe raised his lampblacked eyebrows in considerable astonishment, and the generous unknown then said, inquiringly—

"Your name is Muggerini, isn't it?"

"Ye-es, sir," replied the clown, after a moment's hesitation.

"Is that your real name?" he continued, rather more searchingly.

"Well, no, sir," returned Joe, with some embarrassment, "my legitimate appellation is Muggins—Joe Muggins, but as that don't look much in the bills, I——"

"Ah! I see, you transform it into Muggerini," interrupted the stranger, briskly; "a very excellent transformation, too. But a name matters little; whether Muggins or Muggerini, I've heard sufficient of you to know that you're a kind-hearted, charitable man. I shall see you in London some day, I feel certain. For the present, good bye, and God bless you."

Before Joe could recover from his surprise, the stranger was gone.

"I fancy he was alludin' to the infant as me and Sarah's adopted," he said to himself, as he returned to the stage. "I wonder how he knew about it, and who he is?"

The next moment the clown was on the stage again, immersed in the broad fun of the pantomime, and he thought no more of the stranger at that time.

The next night, Joe's benefit night, arrived in due course.

The theatre was, if possible, more crammed than it had been on Boxing Night.

The whole performance went off swimmingly.

Joe made a neat speech, in which he thanked his patrons for their liberal support.

The curtain fell, amidst red fire and cheers, and Joe Muggins went home at night almost staggering under the weight of his share of the receipts.

"Look 'ere, Sarah!" he cried, exultingly, as he counted out his money on the table; "didn't I say as that blessed babby'd bring us luck? Thirty pounds! why, it's a'most a fortin'!"

"So it is, Joe," exclaimed his rejoicing wife. "What a pity we shall be obliged to spend it, isn't it?"

"P'r'aps we shan't, ole gal," returned Joe, hopefully.

"I don't see 'ow we're to 'elp it," said Sarah, rather despondingly; "the pantomime's done now, and you've no other engagement to go to."

"Well, don't fret, my dear," answered her husband, soothingly; "thank goodness we've got a pound or two now to keep us goin' till something turns up. And somethin' will turn up too, I'm certain," Joe exclaimed, triumphantly, "for the sake of that dear child."

He pointed to the hearthrug, where little Joe, nestled in a warm blanket, was slumbering sweetly without cares, or aches, or pains, or anything whatever to trouble him.

Not even dreaming of the tricks and tumbles he was destined to perform, or the haps and hazards he would have to encounter in the future.

CHAPTER V.

SEVEN YEARS AFTER—PROSPEROUS TIMES—A COMIC CHRISTMAS PANTOMIME IN THE BACK KITCHEN SUDDENLY INTERRUPTED.

WE must now take a flying leap over old Time's head.

Some years have passed away since that eventful night when Joe Muggins tumbled over the mysterious basket on the snowy road.

But all Joe Muggins' hopeful predictions about the future have been literally fulfilled.

Joe Muggins, or, as he is now called, Mr. Joseph Muggerini, is now an established London clown.

"'POOR PUSS, POOR PUSS;' SAID THE CLOWN, CREEPING OUT ON 'THE TILES.'"

He has a good position in the profession, and has a house all to himself, his wife, and his adopted heir, in Bagnigge Wells Road.

But success has not turned their heads, or made Joe and his wife proud.

They are just the same simple-minded, kind-hearted people as ever they were.

The great change, however, is in the little infant we left slumbering in the blanket before the fire.

No one would ever take him to be the same individual.

He has grown up into a slim, active, pretty, saucy-looking, dark-eyed boy.

Very fond of his parents—as he supposes Joe and his wife to be—very lively and good-natured; as quick in his movements as a cat or an electric eel, and as full of mischief as—what shall I say?—well, as a clown.

He was the joy of old Joe's heart (I call him old to distinguish him from his son, though he was not forty years old), and the pride of his mother; and, I may add, a caution to all the cats in the neighbourhood.

Young Joe, with a view to his being thoroughly educated, had been sent to various preparatory schools since his third year.

He was consequently as well up in reading, writing, and arithmetic as boys usually are.

"Able," as old Joe often remarked with pride, "to give anyone change for sixpence."

The old clown had also gradually initiated his son into the mysteries of his profession.

And young Joe readily imbibed the instructions given him by his father.

If the truth must be told, he preferred standing on his head rather than trying to understand with it.

He could sing "Hot Codlins" and "Tippitywichit" (so the old man declared) as well as he could himself.

At throwing somersaults, bending his body back till he looked like an india rubber ring; walking on his hands with his heels in the air, throwing flip-flaps, and doing hand-springs, he was equal to any sprite of the period.

Not that our young hero had ever made his appearance on the stage since the night when he narrowly escaped the sausage machine on the boards of the Oldham theatre.

He contented himself with *private* performances.

And after his dad had gone out in the evening, he and a select few of his schoolfellows, who had a taste for dramatic pursuits, would act pantomimes in the back kitchen to their own great satisfaction and the intense delight of Matilda Jane, the maid of all work, who was always admitted to a private box on the dresser, where she sat to witness the performance.

Christmas was once more drawing on.

Our friend Joe was engaged to play clown at Sadler's Wells.

Being an important personage, the manager invited Joe to his house to dinner, and to hear the pantomime read afterwards.

Of course, Sarah accompanied him.

On this particular evening Young Joe had arranged with his juvenile brother pantomimists to have a good performance.

Very shortly, therefore, after the departure of the old folks, the *dramatis personæ* crept surreptitiously up to the door, and were admitted by Joe himself.

The number was limited, and consisted of Billy Buttons, the son of a tailor in the next street, who performed pantaloon—Master George Marrowfat, a juvenile hairdresser from the New Road, who did harlequin—and John Bangs, the son of a firework maker in the neighbourhood, who volunteered his services as sprite, and also found crackers and red fire for the general good.

Having no columbine, they were obliged to do without one.

Whilst these young but talented individuals were making their preparations, old Joe and spouse had reached their destination.

The dinner passed off, but sudden and unexpected business calling the manager away immediately after, the reading had to be postponed, and Joe and his wife returned much earlier than they expected.

On reaching the door of his residence, Joe let himself and spouse in with the latch-key. There was no light in the passage, and he was about to wonder why the gas had not been turned on as usual, when suddenly, a most extraordinary sound reached their ears from below. A confusion of voices, and a succession of bumps and thumps, as though some fierce encounter was going on in the back kitchen.

"Good gracious, Joe! whatever can be the matter?" murmured Sarah Muggins, apprehensively.

"It's burglars, no doubt, Sarah!" returned the clown; "they've watched us out and are come to rob the 'ouse. Wait a bit! Don't be frightened, my gal; I'll be down upon 'em!"

Joe crept into the parlour, and having armed himself with a stage sword, reappeared.

"Be careful, dear!" said his wife, in a timid tone. "Hadn't I better call the police?"

"No, I'll go down n the quiet fust, and see what it is," returned her spouse. "I'll astonish the vagabones' cocked 'ats if I get near 'em."

With these words the clown commenced descending the kitchen stairs as softly as possible, grasping the weapon he carried firmly.

Just as he got half-way down, there was a tremendous clatter in the back kitchen as though all the fireirons in the grate had suddenly taken fright.

At the same moment a bright red glare was distinctly visible underneath the bottom of the closed door.

"Good gracious, the 'ouse is a-burning!" ejaculated the clown, as he made a hasty rush towards it.

But suddenly he paused.

His experienced nose had detected the well-known odour of red fire.

In addition to which a barrel organ within at that moment struck up a lively tune.

"Burglars don't usually play organs or burn red fire," he meditated. "Dash my wig if I don't think it is my boy up to some of his little games!"

Sarah had by this time followed to the bottom of the stairs.

"Whatever is it, Joe?" she asked, anxiously, as she sniffed the sulphur.

She was answered by a mirthful shriek from Matilda Jane, on the other side of the door.

Young Joe's voice shouting out hilariously, in the most approved clown's fashion—

"Hi! here we are! come along, old un!"

Then followed another instalment of bumps and thumps, and a prodigious scuffling of feet, during which the organ played away with all its might.

"I know what it is now," whispered old Joe to his wife; "the young un's acting in there!"

"Never!" exclaimed Mrs. Muggins, in astonishment.

"It's my opinion that's what it is and nothin' else!" asserted the clown, in a tone of strong conviction. "Don't let's disturb 'em; let's go into the yard, and look through the winder."

Cautiously opening the door, Joe and his wife crept out, until, having arrived at the spot, the whole proceedings in the back kitchen became manifest.

Four boys, bearing a strong resemblance to a clown, pantaloon, harlequin and sprite in miniature, were at that moment doing a pantomimic rally.*

On the kitchen dresser sat Matilda Jane, with her mouth extended almost from ear to ear, screaming with laughter.

In the corner was an Italian organ grinder, who had been expressly engaged out of the street, and who was turning the handle of his instrument and grinning at the same time.

"Here we go inside out. Here we go outside in!" shouted young Joe, as they swung round.

"Well, if that don't beat everything as I ever see!" exclaimed Joe Muggins, almost breathless with surprise and, it must be confessed, admiration.

"Dresses, too, I declare, and wigs! And all made up in the reg'ler way! Wonderful!"

This was the first time the clown had ever seen his son and heir performing in character, and he thoroughly enjoyed it.

The youthful prodigy had drilled his young companions so effectually that they went through their work in a wonderfully business-like manner.

Young Joe had a perfect clown's dress, which he had persuaded Matilda Jane to make him; while the others had made various additions to their ordinary attire, to fit themselves for the characters they assumed.

---

* Swinging round rapidly with their hands joined.

The pantaloon's wig and beard were marvellous to behold.

Giving and taking the slap*; banging themselves down on the floor, and springing up again in an instant, as though they had been made of india rubber.

Old Joe stood looking outside, restraining any violent indulgence of his risible emotions, until his boy, in the character of clown, produced a pantomime poker as big as himself (which he had made and painted to look awfully hot), and chased the pantaloon round the kitchen.

"Look out, old un!" he cried. "I'll warm yer!"

This was more than his father could stand, and brought his excitement to a climax.

Dashing his fist through the window, in the excitement of his delight, he roared out—

"Brayvo, Joe! Brayvo, old un! Brayvo, Patchy! Brayvo, all of yer!"

The sudden crash of the glass, and the stentorian voice, created as sudden and startling an effect upon the parties in the kitchen.

The pantomime suddenly ceased.

The pantaloon, harlequin, and sprite bolted in various directions, like so many startled hares.

Matilda Jane dropped off the dresser, upsetting the candle in her fall, and went into kicking fits on the top of the organ.

The owner of the instrument, frightened out of his wits, made a desperate attempt to get into the oven, into which he thrust his head, where it stuck fast.

Young Joe alone stood his ground, and remained fixed in the centre of the kitchen, brandishing his pantomime poker like a hero.

"'Ere we are!" cried his papa, as he burst in in the dark.

Whizz! came down the formidable weapon within a couple of inches of the cheerful speaker's head.

The young professional had not recognised the paternal voice, and he had well-nigh wound up the performance by knocking his father's brains out.

He was, however, made acquainted with this fact, by the old clown suggesting that—

* The sleight of hand clapping together of the palms, adapted by the clown and pantaloon in pantomimes, when they slap each other's faces.

"He should draw it mild with the poker, cos it was him."

The candle being relighted, matters were soon explained.

Matilda Jane was brought to by half a pailful of water, which the juvenile clown kindly threw over her.

And a lighted cracker, fastened by a pin to the coat collar of the organ grinder, made such a terrific banging in his ears, that in pure desperation the terrified Italian dragged his head out of the oven so precipitately that he almost left his nose behind him.

But a shilling and a glass of ale quite restored the wandering minstrel, and he departed rubbing his nose, but altogether rejoicing.

"And now where's the other pantomimists?" asked old Joe of his son and heir, as he looked round with a good-natured, beaming smile on his round face.

This was more than young Joe could tell.

"They were here just now, dad," was the only explanation he could give. "I suppose they've taken fright, and hid themselves or run away"

"Let's see," said his father.

There was a prolonged search for the missing artists, which was eventually rewarded with success.

The harlequin was found, in a state of much trepidation, at the bottom of one of the drawers in old Joe's bedroom.

The sprite up the parlour chimney, shivering like an aspen, and as black as a sweep.

Whilst Bill Buttons (the old un) was discovered, at an advanced hour of the night, fast asleep in the dust-hole.

But they were soon relieved from all their fears.

And the good-natured Sarah, having washed them all round till their faces shone again, her equally good-natured husband had them all up in the parlour by the warm fire, and gave them a lump of cake and a bumping glass of currant wine, and a lesson in tumbling into the bargain.

The juvenile pantomimists went home in high glee, and one and all declared what a jolly evening they had spent, and what a rare old brick Joe Muggins was— and his wife too!

As for Joe himself, he was so thoroughly

delighted with the whole proceedings that he determined in his own mind to get his talented son on to the boards as soon as possible.

"It's a sin to keep him off," he said to himself.

"The public ought to know what a treat they've got in store for them.

"How can I manage it?

"I have got it!" exclaimed the old clown to himself, suddenly. "He shall play for my benefit, so he shall!"

CHAPTER VI.

IN WHICH OUR HERO TRIES HIS HAND AT MODELLING A MASK, AND TEACHES POPPY, THE CALL BOY, A LESSON—THE MANAGER IN A FIX—A CAT, AND A CAT-ASTROPHE.

DECEMBER had now arrived.

"Mother Goose, or Harlequin and the Golden Eggs," was in a forward state of preparation.

At the first rehearsal of the pantomime, Joe Muggins took his son with him.

Joe was as pleased as Punch to get behind the scenes.

Before he had been in the theatre half an hour, he had struck up an acquaintance with the master carpenter, the property maker, and was on very excellent terms with Poppy, the call-boy.

Young Joe was of an inquiring disposition, and was very curious to know the ins and outs of everything he saw.

He liked to watch the scenic artist as he mixed his colours, and applied them to the canvas.

But his principal delight was to stand by the side of Mr. Modelmug, the property maker, as he cast the moulds for the grotesque pantomime masks.

"What's that for?" he asked of the artist, as he was manipulating a mass of damp clay and plaster of Paris, and forming it into features.

"This is for the Demon King," replied Mr. Modelmug. "Now I've got to dry it, and then it will be ready for use."

"May I try if I can mould one?" asked young Joe.

"Certainly, if you think you can," answered the property maker, who was a good-natured man, and had taken a fancy to our young hero.

"Here," he continued, as he placed a lump of clay, similar to that he was using, on a stand before the boy, "I'm going to dinner. Try what you can do by the time I come back."

"I'll try," returned Joe, eagerly.

Joe, left alone, went to work at his task of modelling.

He found that it was not quite so easy as it seemed.

However, he had watched Mr. Modelmug narrowly, and he imitated him as nearly as he could, moistening the clay with water when it began to grow stiff, and coaxing it into shape with his fingers.

It was cold work, and made his hands ache.

But he persevered, and before very long he had manufactured a demoniac visage on a small scale, which he surveyed with considerable satisfaction.

"Now, then, I'll put it before the fire to dry," he said to himself, as he placed it before the glowing coke fire.

Whilst he was thus engaged, Poppy, the call-boy, who had missed him from the stage, looked in.

"Hullo!" he cried, "there you are! I thought you'd taken a flying leap down one of the vampire traps."*

"Oh, no," returned Joe. "I've been doing something better than that."

"What've you bin up to?"

"Modelling," Joe replied.

"Modellin', eh? What?"

"A demon king's head!" exclaimed Joe, as he pointed to his work.

"That!" ejaculated the youth, rather derisively. "D'you call that a demon king's head? It ain't 'arf a one!"

---

* Traps that open and close instantaneously with a spring, and used for supernatural appearances and disappearances.

"I know that," returned the youthful modeller, rather indignantly; "it's only in miniature."

"What a nose!" exclaimed the fast youth, pointing ironically to the steaming model; "d'you call that a nose? It looks more like a crab's claw. S'pose I was to pull it orff?" he added, with a mischievous grin.

Joe looked at him rather fiercely.

He was rather good at a joke himself, but the call-boy was a little too impertinent, he thought, and he answered determinately—

"If you were to pull off my model's nose, I should punch your head."

Poppy, without another word, pulled off the damp nose of the demon king.

Joe, without further remark, kept his promise, and punched Poppy's head, evidently much to his surprise.

Poppy was soon satisfied.

"You are spiteful!" said he, ruefully, as he rubbed his forehead, which the application of Joe's knuckles had made rather red.

"No, I'm not," returned Joe, "but you'd no right to spoil my work."

"Well, I suppose you don't bear no malice, do you?" Poppy inquired.

"Not at all," Joe answered.

"Then let's shake 'ands, cos I like you," said the precocious boy.

The lads shook hands, and Poppy, who seemed at once to forget all that had previously passed, said to Joe—

"Are you to do anythink in the pantomime?"

"No," replied Joe, "the only thing I shall do will be to see it."

"I thinks it'll be a stunner," remarked the call-boy; "your father can play clown to rights!"

"I know that," returned Joe, positively. "I mean to be a clown some day."

"Why didn't you get your father to interdooce you in the comic bisness as a juvenile Joey?"

"I never thought of it," Joe replied.

"It would'nt be 'arf a bad idea, would it?" continued Poppy, "you could call yourselves Ole Joe and Young Joe."

"I'll speak to dad about it," said our hero, who was more struck with the idea than he cared to confess to the call-boy. "I'm quite agreeable if he is."

At this moment the lad was loudly called.

"Wait a minnit!" he cried, as he hurried downstairs. "I'll be back as soon as I can."

"The manager wants you," said the master carpenter, as the boy reached the stage.

Away ran Poppy to the manager's room.

"Request Mr. Muggerini to come to me as soon as possible," said the manager.

Back went the call-boy to the stage, where the old clown was arranging the comic business.

"Please, sir, the manager wants to speak to you immediate," Poppy informed him.

"All right, my boy," returned Joe. "I'll be with 'im in 'alf a minute."

Having finished his explanation, the clown left the stage and proceeded to the manager's private apartment, whilst Poppy made his way once more to the property room.

"Good morning, Mr. Muggerini," said the manager, politely, as Joe entered.

"Good morning, sir," returned Joe. "You wished to see me?"

"I do. We're in a slight dilemma."

Joe looked at him for an instant, and then inquired what was the matter.

"Well, it's this. You know, in the comic business, you have a scene on the tiles."

"Yes, a very good scene it is, too; seems to me one of the best in the pantomime," Joe remarked.

"So I think, and that makes me especially anxious about it. You will remember in that scene you have to shoot a cat."

"Yes," said Joe.

"There's no cat, and it seems to me if there's no cat to shoot, it's impossible to shoot the cat."

"That's a moral certainty," answered Joe.

"What's to be done?"

"Only one thing as I can see," Joe replied; "we must get a cat. They're plentiful enough. I'll bet there's a couple of dozen ev'ry night molrowin' under my back garding winder!"

Joe laughed, and the manager laughed, and the latter said—

"You see, unfortunately, a real cat won't answer the purpose. What we want is some small boy who unites human intelligence with the agility of the animal in question. Do you happen to know such a one?"

Joe reflected for an instant, and replied—

"Yes, I do know one—and only one, and that's my boy! He's a merrikle of talent, and'd play anythink from a cat to a kangaroo."

"Would he?" exclaimed the manager, eagerly; "then he's just the boy we want."

"I should rather say he was," replied Joe, with evident pride. "He's more like a cat in the quickness of 'is motions than anythin' else, and as for intellec', you should only ha' seen 'im a-playin' clown in the back kitchin a few nights ago. It'd ha' done your heart good, I'm sure it would."

"Well, then, Mr. Muggerini," the manager continued, "perhaps you'll bring your son with you to-morrow. I should like to see him."

"You can see 'im this minit if you like, sir," returned Joe, briskly; "he's 'ere now."

"Is he? Bring him in," said the manager.

CHAPTER VII.

A BLOW UP IN THE PROPERTY ROOM—YOUNG JOE HAS A REHEARSAL.

"I'LL introduce you to the infant phenomenon in a minute, Mr. Manager," said the old clown, in a tone of much satisfaction, as he hastened to the door. Just as he threw it open, a tremendous bang like the report of a small cannon was heard, followed by a cry from the stage.

"Good Heaven! What's that?" exclaimed the manager, starting from his chair.

"Sounds like an explosion of gas!" said Joe.

A confused murmur of voices was heard, and one of the carpenters, looking very white and scared, and with his hair standing on end, rushed into the room.

"What in the world's the matter?" asked the manager, in a tone of alarm.

"Poppy and Master Muggerini's bin playin' with gunpowder and blowed up the property room!" gasped the man, breathlessly.

"What!" almost shrieked Joe, turning pale with horror; "my boy blowed up?"

Without waiting for a reply, the terrified pantomimist rushed from the room.

But he had hardly left the threshold of the door, when he was met by the master carpenter and Mr. Modelmug, accompanied by a crowd of professionals, in the midst of whom where the criminals in custody.

The property master led young Joe—the machinist held the call-boy by the collar.

In this order they entered the apartment.

Our young hero, to his father's great relief, looked very much the same as he always did, only, perhaps, a little pale with indignation.

The youthful Poppy, on the contrary, presented a somewhat grimy and woebegone appearance. His eyebrows and eyelashes had been singed off, and his hair frizzed by the explosion; whilst the powder had blown in his face and peppered it all over with minute black spots. Altogether he presented a slight resemblance to a half-roasted monkey.

"Now then, what is all this?" demanded the manager, sternly.

Mr. Modelmug stepped forward and briefly explained that during his absence at dinner-time, it seemed the two boys had been amusing themselves with lighting gunpowder in the property-room, and that the powder in the flask exploded and ignited another packet of the same explosive material, the result being that the skylight of the apartment had been blown out, and a large amount of damage done to the masks and properties.

The manager's brow grew dark, and he glared fiercely at Poppy, who looked particularly wretched.

"Very pretty! upon my word!" he exclaimed; "so my property is to be destroyed, and the lives of people endangered by your tricks, eh, you mischievous young monkey?"

"It wasn't me!" whimpered the call-boy; "it was him!"

He pointed to young Joe as he spoke.

"No, it wasn't!" replied the latter, boldly; "I told you not to touch the powder!"

"Oh, my! Oh! what a wicked crammer!" groaned Poppy. "Didn't you say, 'Let's make some fizgigs?'"

"You did, you mean!" answered Joe, rather scornfully; "and I told you I didn't call them fizgigs, but volcanoes."

"Well, and then didn't you say, 'We'll make some volcanoes and have a flare up?'" repeated the audacious Poppy. "You knows you did!"

"I know I didn't!" replied Joe, indignantly. "I said I wouldn't have anything to do with volcanoes, because I thought they were dangerous; and I told you to put down the flask."

"Oh! Oh! if ever I heard anythink like that!" protested the call-boy; "if he ain't a-tellin' lies as thick as peas!"

"'Ere, 'old 'ard—that'll do," exclaimed old Joe, as, with an unusually stern look upon his round face, he took the accuser by the ear. "You jest mind what you're sayin', cos it strikes me it's you as is tellin' the lies!"

"So it is, dad," affirmed his son, confidently. "It was while I was mending my demon king's nose, which he had pulled off, that he set fire to the powder."

"What!" cried the manager, furious at the aggravated offence; "did he dare to mutilate one of the masks?"

Horror seized upon everybody.

"Ugh! you unappreciative wretch!" almost shrieked Mr. Modelmug, as he sprang forward and made a grab at Poppy's other ear, which he almost pulled out by the roots.

"Oh, you perjured young villain!" exclaimed old Joe venomously, as he put the screw on to the ear he already held between his finger and thumb; "any boy as'd wantonly pull off an unoffendin' demon's nose, as never did him any 'arm, shows 'imself utterly devoid of all moral feelin'."

But however dead Master Poppy's moral feelings might have been, he proved that his physical sensibilities were in full vigour, by crying "Murder!" vociferously.

Far from eliciting sympathy, it increased the fury of the manager.

"Get out, you howling puppy!" he roared, as he sprang forward and seized the guilty but agonized call-boy by his coat collar; "you're discharged—begone!"

A sharp kick on the patched portion of Poppy's unmentionables sent the artful youth flying into the passage.

Orders were then given to repair the skylight, and in a few moments the room was cleared, and old Joe and young Joe and the manager alone remained.

"It's a mercy the fellow didn't blow up the theatre," exclaimed the latter; "but let's forget him, and come to business."

He looked kindly at our hero for an instant, and then said—

"I understand you're a very clever boy."

Joe looked at the manager, smiled, and glanced at his father, who gave him a nod and a wink just by way of encouragement.

"I can do a thing or two," he said, presently, with considerable modesty.

"Do you think you could perform the character of a cat?" the manager continued.

Joe, who had studied the habits and customs of this favourite domestic animal minutely, laughed, as he replied—

"I should think I could, too."

"Can you give me any idea of the position, tone, and actions of a cat?" was the manager's next question.

In an instant our hero was down on his knees, going through a series of feline evolutions.

"Purr—purr—pur-r-r-r!" he murmured, as he licked his forepaws and washed his face and ears after the fashion of a cat.

He then scratched out a few imaginary fleas.

After which he sprang on to the table, which, for the time being, answered the purpose of a roof.

"Miow! Miow! miow-ow-ow-ow! Oh, won't you come out to-night?" he exclaimed in that melancholy wail, in which wandering cats on the tiles are supposed to address one another.

After which he went through a variety of antics, ending with an imaginary battle between two antagonistic Toms, in which he "fizzed" and scratched, to the great amusement of the manager and the intense delight of his sire, who laughed till the tears rolled down his cheeks.

"That will do admirably," said the manager, at the conclusion.

"I told you he'd be all the way there, didn't I?" exclaimed the gratified clown, as he patted his son on the head.

"He's a very clever fellow, indeed," the manager admitted, "and he shall do the cat. That's settled, and all that now remains is to arrange about terms."

"Well, I shan't be heavy, as I'm on the establishment myself," returned Joe, magnanimously; "suppose we say three pound a week? I think that'll be fair to both parties."

The manager was perfectly satisfied with this arrangement, and old Joe went home to dinner in a perfect ecstacy.

"It'll be a capital introduction," he said to his son. "If you make a hit in the cat, which you're sure to do, I shall be able to have you in next year's pantomime as a sort of small clown along of me, don't you see?"

"Yes, dad," replied the boy; "it'll be young Joe and old Joe, won't it?"

"Ha, ha! of course it will," laughed his father, triumphantly. "Old Joe and young Joe; that'll be highly attractive, and a decided novelty."

From this brief conversation it will be seen that the idea suggested to our hero by Poppy was likely to be carried out.

CHAPTER VIII.

THE FIRST NIGHT OF "MOTHER GOOSE"—OUR HERO MAKES A SENSATION ON THE TILES, AND COMES DOWN SUDDENLY WITH A CRASH.

AGAIN Boxing Night had arrived. Again the theatre was crammed from the floor to the ceiling with anxious gazers, all drawn by the attraction of "Mother Goose."

The pantomimists were all ready dressed and in the green room, waiting for the transformation scene.

There were no strangers among them.

Joe Muggins was not a man to forget his old friends.

As soon, therefore, as he got to London, he never rested till he had brought his former colleagues after him.

By his recommendation they had been engaged at Sadler's Wells, and were now all together again.

Yes, there were clown, harlequin, sprite, and columbine, apparently quite unaffected by the knocking about of six years, just the same as when we saw them last on the stage of the Oldham theatre, not forgetting the "old un," who looked as brisk and lively as ever.

And there was now, in addition, young Joe in his cat's dress, with ears and a tail that moved when he pulled a string, looking so like the animal he represented that had a brother Tom met him on the tiles, he would hardly have detected the imposture.

"Don't he look a picture?" exclaimed old Joe, admiringly, to Tom Trotters, the pantaloon, as he pointed to his son.

Then, in a louder tone, he remarked, with a chuckle—

"I say, old un, there's a little difference between what he is now and what he was six year ago, eh? Don't you remember that night as we found 'im in the basket?"

"Rayther," returned the ancient and

"You'd have a difficulty to pack 'im up in it now."

"If I could," grinned the clown, "he'd make his way out in about two twos."

"Shouldn't be surprised at all," replied the pantaloon; "he looks as if he could."

"Lor' bless you," continued Joe, exultingly, "he's up to anythink; he's all gen'us and talent. If ever a boy turned out trumps he has. You should only see him do the red-hot poker business, that's all."

At that moment Sarah Muggins came into the green room with a needle and some strong thread, to make the cat's head secure by stitching it to the body.

This was soon done, and our young hero was pronounced complete.

Very shortly after, the call-boy came in to summon them to the wings for the transformation.

It was not Poppy, but a new call-boy.

Young Joe had generously pleaded with the manager that the former should be recalled, but all his appeals were met by a determined and peremptory "No."

Consequently, Poppy remained out of a situation, in the bosom of his family, where, being one of six, he was looked upon, now he brought nothing in, as an encumbrance, especially by his paternal relative, who was one of the carpenters at the theatre, a dissipated, drunken fellow, who beat his wife, and gave his children many more kicks than halfpence.

John Poppy cared nothing about his son, but his salary as call-boy had been ten shillings a week, and the loss of his situation was that sum less in his pocket for drink.

Consequently, he was furious.

Furious with his son, and furious with our hero Joe, to whom he attributed the dismissal of the former from his post.

His temper, naturally sour and morose, was inflamed and embittered by intemperance, and he vowed to be revenged on the innocent object of his displeasure.

"I'll serve him out," he murmured, "for takin' the bread and cheese out of my mouth, the lyin' young scamp. If I don't break his neck for him before the pantomime's over, my name's not Jack Poppy."

His plan was soon formed, and the scene of its operation was to be the roof where our hero was to go through his cat performance, and where it was expected he would achieve a great triumph.

The evil-disposed carpenter listened moodily to the praises bestowed upon our hero, who was a favourite with everybody, at rehearsal.

They added to his desire for revenge.

"Ugh!" he growled, "you may all nut 'im up as much as yer like, but I'll give 'im a drop as shall spoil 'is backbone, I know."

The scene offered a fatal facility for foul play.

The slanting roof extended from the flat scene* at a considerable height from the stage, and was supported by upright frames of timber, kept in their places by iron braces, which were fastened by strong screws to the stage.

John Poppy was one of the men appointed to assist in setting the scene.

His diabolical intention was to creep underneath at the last moment, and remove the screws.

The gambols of our hero on the tiles, he concluded, would throw the supports out of the perpendicular, and, he fiendishly hoped, bring the whole roof down with a crash.

*   *   *   *   *

The opening of the pantomime was over.

The pantomime characters had made their appearance, and everything was going on like clockwork.

Screams of laughter burst at every moment from the delighted audience.

Shortly, alas, to be changed into shrieks of another and more painful description.

But as this is of course unknown, every trick is loudly cheered.

Every witticism of the clown causes a fresh burst of merriment.

The roof scene comes on at last.

A hearty round of applause is elicited from the audience by its quaintly natural appearance.

It looks, at first sight, like a scene where there will be plenty of fun.

The clown's voice is heard without.

"Come on, old un!" is his injunction as usual.

They enter arm-in-arm, and are supposed to be looking for a lodging.

---

* The scene at the back.

The house with the tiled roof attracts their notice.

"I say, old un, I think this'll soot us."

"Knock at the door," says the old un.

Clown knocks.

Elderly woman enters.

Clown, by way of making himself agreeable, hugs her round the neck and kisses her.

"'Ow are ye, my dear?" he says.

Pantaloon, who has a habit of imitating his companion, tries to do the same, but gets his face slapped instead.

"Be quiet, old un!" cries the clown, reprovingly. "I am ashamed of you. Why don't you let the young lady alone?"

The old dame smiles at the artful Joey, who begins to bargain for the lodgings.

"'Ow much a week, ma'am?" he asks.

"Eight an' sixpence, sir," simpers the landlady.

"Very cheap indeed. I'll take 'em," says the clown, without hesitation. "Old un, give this good lady eight and sixpence, and then come upstairs to tea."

Clown goes into the house.

Pantaloon feels for the money, and of course can't find any.

"I'll pay you to-morrow, my love," he says, as he makes a decrepit rush to the door.

But the landlady stops him.

"Pay me first!" she cries threateningly.

"I shan't," returns the pantaloon, indignantly. "I'm a gentleman."

"If you don't, I'll call a policeman," persists the landlady.

"Call one," answers the pantaloon, in a tone of conscious rectitude. "What do I care for the police?"

A policeman, who is evidently waiting ready at the wing, walks on.

"I give this old villain in custody," says the landlady.

"I am an innocent man," declares the pantaloon. "Ask the milkman round the corner, if I ain't?"

The appeal is in vain.

"Come on," cries the policeman sternly.

The official is about to drag the falsely accused pantaloon to summary justice, when suddenly his colleague appears at the door with a teapot in his hand.

"Why don't you come upstairs? The bloaters are getting quite cold," he exclaims.

"Cos I can't," returned the old un, pathetically. "This gentleman in blue wants me."

The clown comes to the rescue boldly, having first thrown a teapot at the head of the gentleman in blue, and knocked his hat off.

"You let my little brother alone," he says, fiercely; "if yer don't, I'll tell my ma-a-a!"

"Don't interrupt me in my duty," cries the bobby, "or I shall take you too."

"Will you?" returns the clown. "Ketch 'old of 'im, old un, we'll take 'im downstairs and put 'im in the copper."

The public functionary is seized and carried into the house

Landlady follows, expressing emotion, and closes the door.

Clown and pantaloon, after a slight pause, during which they are supposed to have boiled the bobby, appear upstairs at the window taking their tea.

"Isn't this nice?" says the old un.

"Beautiful," admits the clown; "such a lovely prospect of chimbley pots."

"I'll trouble you for that bloater," says the pantaloon, politely.

The bloater is handed.

But before the pantaloon can take it, a fine cat (young Joe), attracted by the savoury smell, has crawled down the tiles and carried it nimbly away.

Great applause from the audience.

"Where's the bloater, Joey?" asks the old un, who has not observed the theft.

"I put it on your plate," affirms the clown.

"I don't believe you!" exclaims the pantaloon. "Where is it?"

"You've bolted it, you greedy ole man, you have," the clown cries; "I can see the end of it sticking out of your mouth!"

In an instant clown had his partner's head under his arm, and his mouth open, looking down his throat after the herring.

Not being able to find it, he, of course, knocks him down and picks him up again.

Tea being over, clown and pantaloon propose retiring to rest.

By way of preparation they put on a couple of large nightgowns and nightcaps over their daily attire.

Notice.—*With this number is given away a beautiful picture printed in colours entitled " HERE WE ARE AGAIN!" representing a comic stage scene in a Pantomime.*

"WHAT DO YOU MEAN BY RINGING MY BELL, EH, RUFFIANS?" HE DEMANDED.

It is summer time, and, being sultry, the clown makes a suggestion.

"It is very warm, old un," he says; "s'pose we sleep on the tiles; it'll be beautiful and cool there."

Of course, the pantaloon assents.

They bring out the bolster, blankets, and sheets, and make their bed.

"Good night, old un."

"Good night, Joey!" they exclaim mutually as they lie down.

There is a pause of silence, and then commences the melancholy music of cats.

"Miow - miow - ow - miow - ow-ow-ow !" wails a Tom-cat who appears on the top of the roof.

"Don't sing," requests the clown, mildly.

"I ain't a-singin'," replies pantaloon.

"Miow-ow-mol-row ? Oh, won't you come over the wall?" wails the Tom once more.

"There you go ag'in !" exclaims the clown, whose sleep is interrupted. "If you makes that noise ag'in, I'll give you somethin' for yourself."

"Oh, do come over the wall; miow-ow, fizz, pht !" goes the cat.

Clown sits up in a rage.

"I won't put up with it, you ole willin, I won't," as he tries to smother the pantaloon with the pillow.

Matters are adjusted, and they lie down again.

Cat descends tiles and walks over them.

They start up in alarm.

The cat nimbly escapes and sits on an adjoining chimney pot, where it washes its face and wags its tail to the great delight of the audience.

Little do they know that at that moment the villanous and revengeful drunkard is removing the screws that keep the supports in their places.

"Get the gun," cries the pantaloon.

Clown scrambles into the window and instantly returns with the gun.

The cat—young Joe—was still standing among the chimney pots, making a row that must have excited the envy of any real cat within hearing.

"Poor puss, poor pussy !" says Joe, as he once more creeps out on the tiles, and prepares his gun. "You are old Tom, I suppose."

"Why don't you give him a drop of old Tom, Joey?" says pantaloon.

"I'll give him a drop of another kind," says Joey, drawing back the trigger.

As he does so, he notices the roof is more shaky than it had been a moment before.

He whispers aside to his colleague—

"I don't think the platform's safe."

"Seems to waggle about a good bit," returns Tom, "but of course it's all right."

"I hope so," says Joe, "cos my boy's got to do his death struggle yet, and if it wasn't safe——"

"Oh, it's safe enough ; fire away."

Clown fires the gun.

It was now young Joe's turn to delineate the dying agonies of poor Tom.

As the bang is heard, he sprang up with a wild "miow," and rolled off the chimney pot.

"You've shot the cat," cries the old un.

But he had not killed it.

Young Joe, determined upon creating a sensation, reeled, struggled and kicked in his death agonies, till the audience applauded vociferously.

But the roof was growing more unsteady every moment.

Old Joe was beginning to feel awfully nervous.

"It'll go down, I'm sure it will," he murmured.

"Joe ! Joe ! 'old 'ard ! that'll do ! it ain't safe ! Cut it short, and die easy, that's a good lad."

But his son, in his excitement, did not hear him, and cutting it long, was dying hard—hard enough for twenty cats.

He rolled, and twisted, and writhed more furiously than ever.

Thunders of applause rewarded his exertions. But suddenly they are brought to an end.

A tremendous crash is heard, followed by a shriek of consternation from the audience, as the supports give way, and the whole roof (with those on it) falls to the ground.

The sudden transition from the extreme of delight to the opposite extreme of horror, produced an indescribable mingling of sensations amongst the beholders.

Some screamed, some fainted, some made a wild rush to the doors, but the majority sat still, and looked at the disaster in speechless dismay.

In the midst of which the front scene closed it in from their eyes.

CHAPTER IX.

IN WHICH THE CAUSE OF THE ACCIDENT IS EXPLAINED, AND JOE MUGGINS AND HIS FRIENDS TAKE THE LAW INTO THEIR OWN HANDS.

NO sooner had this taken place, than there was a general rush from the wings on to the stage.

Actors, supers, ballet girls, carpenters—hurried anxiously to see the result of the catastrophe.

Old Joe and the pantaloon, though much shaken with the suddenness of their fall, had received no material damage, and were immediately raised on to their feet.

But our young hero, the luckless cat, how had he fared?

Alas, the atrocious intentions of the cowardly plotter had been crowned with too much success.

The poor boy was insensible.

There were no writhings or contortions now.

He neither moved nor groaned, but lay perfectly still.

From his being enveloped entirely in his cat's dress, it was for the moment impossible to judge of the extent of his injuries.

Sarah Muggins, who had gone into the front to see the scene, and who had, when the accident occurred, rushed round in a paroxysm of terror, now hurried wildly into the midst of the assembled throng.

"Oh, Joe, you are alive, thank Heaven!" she cried, hysterically, as she threw her arms round her husband, who was supported by two of the carpenters attached to the theatre.

"Yes, I'm all right, Sarah," he answered, faintly.

"And the dear boy, is he?" She uttered a shriek as her eyes fell upon her son's motionless form. "Is—is he dead?" she continued, in an awe-stricken tone.

"Cut off his head, my girl, and see," was the clown's ominous reply.

This may seem, to non-theatrical ears, a rather strange way of ascertaining the truth.

But Joe alluded to the cat's head which our hero still wore.

In an instant Sarah had her scissors out of her pocket, and was cutting the stitches she had not long before made with her own hands.

When the head was removed, the face that presented itself was so pale and ghastly that a murmur of horror passed like an electric shock through the spectators.

And the mournful though whispered exclamation followed—

"He is dead!"

"No, no, not dead! don't—don't say that!" almost shrieked the distracted clown, who, with the tears rolling down his painted cheeks, looked a strangely grotesque picture of misery.

"My boy, my dear boy!" he moaned, as he fell on his knees and raised him gently.

At the same moment the manager, accompanied by a surgeon, approached the sufferer.

"He had better be taken into the green-room," said the latter, as he looked down upon the senseless form.

Many volunteers offered their assistance, but Sarah would allow no hands but her own to touch her pet.

"I'll carry him," she said, with a sob.

"How did this happen?" asked the manager of Joe, who did not follow to the green room, quite certain that his boy would be looked after since his wife was with him.

"I don't wish to make any unjust accusation agin anyone," he replied, deliberately; "but it seems to me as it 'appened through some gross neglect."

"Where's the master carpenter?" was the manager's next question.

"Here, sir," answered the machinist, as he stepped forward.

"How do you account for this, Mr. Benson?"

"I'm quite at a loss to account for it,

sir," returned the man, respectfully. "I am certain the supports were firm and fast, for I screwed up the braces myself. You can bear witness to that, Poppy?"

"Oh, yes," returned the latter, who was half drunk, and carried a scarcely-suppressed look of malignant exultation in his face. "I'll take my oath of that."

"That's what puzzles me," continued Benson, "how the supports could have given way. The screws I put in were enough to hold anything."

It seemed a mystery, altogether, that no one just then seemed able to account for.

Until a pale-faced lad from amongst the supers offered a suggestion.

"P'r'aps the screws might ha' bin took out ag'in, arter you screwed 'em in," he said, pointedly.

Everyone looked at the speaker.

Nobody at John Poppy, or they would have noticed that he seemed considerably disconcerted by this remark.

Before anyone could reply, another super came forward and said—

"That's jest what was done."

"Impossible," exclaimed the master carpenter, indignantly.

"Of course, it's impossible," joined in John Poppy, in a hoarse, bullying tone.

"No, it's not," repeated the super, positively, "for I saw the man who took 'em out."

"Who was it?" demanded the manager, fiercely.

"Why, there he stands," answered the lad, pointing to the guilty cause of the disaster, "John Poppy!"

"It's a lie; a base calumny!" shouted the drunkard, but turning very pale notwithstanding. "I never touched the screws."

"Yes, I saw you unscrew six, and put them in your jacket pockets; three in one, and three in the other," affirmed the super.

Before the confounded villain had time to reply, the exasperated clown had sprung upon him like a tiger.

He had forgotten all his bruises, and held him like a vice.

"Turn out the vagabond's pockets!" he cried, excitedly.

In an instant half a dozen pairs of hands were busy in search.

And each hand brought out a screw.

There was the exact number—six.

"What d'you say to that, eh, you diabolical murderer?"

The conscience-stricken wretch hadn't a word to reply.

His guilt had made him dumb.

"You've killed my poor boy, you have, you unfeelin' villain!" raved the incensed pantomimist, "and I'll kill you."

"What did he tell lies about my son for, and get him discharged!" growled John Poppy, doggedly.

"He did nothing of the sort," replied the manager, indignantly; "on the contrary, he begged very hard that I would take your son back again. But I refused. I've done with him and you too!"

"But I ain't," cried Joe Muggins. "I ain't begun with you yet, you atrocious brute!"

As he spoke, by way of beginning, the clown, who was a strong man, pitched into Mr. Poppy right and left.

And not only Joe Muggins, but the whole of his friends.

The harlequin, sprite, and even the old un, surrounded him like a flock of bees.

In about half a minute, he was knocked almost into a human jelly.

When the policeman came for him, he had to be carried off to the police station on a stretcher.

Our hero was not dead.

The surgeon, having examined the boy, discovered that he was severely bruised, and that one of his arms was broken.

He had come to his senses, and was shortly afterwards removed home in a cab.

The manager, when the confusion had a little subsided, led Joe and the pantaloon on before the audience, amidst immense cheering.

Then there arose loud cries for "the cat."

The manager explained that the latter had received injuries which, though not serious, would nevertheless prevent him from appearing before them again that evening.

Order was at length restored, and though the nerves of everyone had been pretty well shaken, the pantomimists braced themselves and continued their performance.

Young Joe had little sleep that night, and when he did doze, in his troubled dreams, he continued to enact his part in the pantomime.

CHAPTER X.

IN WHICH YOUNG JOE CREATES ANOTHER SENSATION—THE MAN IN THE THICK COAT AGAIN.

WHEN young Joe opened his eyes the next morning, after a restless night, it was to find himself very full of aches and pains, very hot and feverish, lying in bed with his left arm bound up between two splints, and his father and mother sitting anxiously by the bedside.

Joe tried to smile, but it was only a melancholy attempt, and he was obliged to give it up.

"Take it easy, my boy," said the old clown, soothingly; "the worst's over, and you'll soon be better."

Then, by way of cheering up the invalid, he said, in a gratified whisper—

"You made a hit, my boy, after all. It's in all the papers this morning."

"About the accident?" inquired our hero, faintly.

"Yes, of course that's in. But it ain't that as I means. It's the cat as I alludes to.

"The *Times* says, with respect to your performance, 'it was perfection;' and the *Telegraph* remarks as if you were sent to the cat show at the Crystal Palace, you would be sure to get the first prize."

Little Joe, whose inflamed arm felt as if it was on fire, moaned wearily.

But he said presently—

"What will they do at the theatre for a cat, now I'm ill?"

"I'm sure I don't know," returned his parent, shaking his head, solemnly; "it's a serious thing; very serious."

"I suppose they will find someone to do it," murmured the boy, with a sigh of pain, as he closed his eyes.

"I have my doubts on that point," said the clown, meditatively, to himself; "cats is scarce, at least cats like him. There's plenty of boys as could put on the dress; but could they imitate the actions of the animal? Certainly not."

At this juncture a soft knock came at the door.

It was the doctor and the manager, who had come together.

The former looked at the young invalid, and pronounced him to be going on as well as could be expected.

The latter also looked at him, and said to the clown—

"What are we to do for a cat to-night, Mr. Muggerini?"

"That's just what I was a-thinking when you knocked at the door," returned Joe; "someone must do it, and I'm sure I dunno who."

"Nor I," said the manager, in a perplexed tone.

Our hero opened his eyes, and said, in a weak voice—

"There's Poppy, that used to be call-boy. Let him do it."

"Poppy!" exclaimed the clown and the manager, indignantly, together; "Poppy be——"

They stopped short.

"Hold hard!" cried the former, "I was going to forget myself. But I can't abear to 'ear the diabolical name; I can't!"

The sick boy looked surprised.

"You are not aware, of course," explained the manager to him, "that it was Poppy's father who was the cause of last night's accident. He did it out of revenge for his son's discharge."

"But Poppy couldn't help that," pleaded the charitable sufferer; "it wasn't his doing. And besides, he's got five little brothers and sisters at home, poor and hungry. Let him do the cat. He's a clever boy, and will do it very well."

Joe Muggins and the manager looked at the young speaker with surprise.

"Well, my boy," said the latter, at length, "if you, who are the greatest sufferer, wish this, I don't see how I can refuse."

"I do wish it, if you please," little Joe replied.

"Very well, then; I promise you he shall do it," said the manager, "if only in compliance with your truly generous wish."

"Thank you," returned the young invalid, as he dropped asleep.

This point being settled, Poppy was sent for, much to his surprise at the unexpected good fortune, and instructed in the "cat's" business by old Joe.

It proved a fortunate event, too, for the entire Poppy family, as their paternal guardian got twelve months' imprisonment with hard labour for his vindictive act.

It was some weeks before our hero got round, but by the time the pantomime had run on to the fifth week of its career, he was entirely restored.

"I don't think as there's any good of your doin' the cat again," said his father; "I think you'd better turn your attention to clown, cos I means you to appear in that character on my benefit night."

Of course young Joe was delighted.

"I've arranged a pantomimic sketch as I think 'll be just the thing to please the public."

"What is it called, dad?"

"'All Sorts, or the Clown's Pie,'" old Joe exclaimed, with conscious pride; "that's a title, ain't it?"

"It just is!" admitted our hero, in a strong tone of admiration, "a capital title. You bring me out of the pie; that would be a jolly bit of fun."

"Just the very idea I'd hit upon," cried the old clown, with a delighted grin; and then continued—

> "When the pie is opened,
> I puts my hand within;
> And out I pulls a little clown,
> Fit to set before a king."

Father and son laughed for a long time over this excellent idea.

Young Joe from that moment went in at practice morning, noon and night.

The old clown watched his proceedings with great satisfaction.

"You're a-gettin' on, Joe, admirable," he remarked; "but there's one thing I must teach you."

"What's that, dad?"

"To take the leap."*

"I don't think it's very hard."

* A term applied to the flying springs that the clown and pantaloon take through shop-windows in pantomimes.

"Well, I don't say but there's many things as is 'arder," admitted his father, "but it wants care, or you're very like to damage your ribs. You'd better not try it, unless I'm with you."

Three mornings after, our aspiring young hero said to his parent, as he sat at breakfast—

"I can take the leap, dad."

"What!" exclaimed old Joe, almost choking himself with a piece of crust at the intelligence. "However did you learn that?"

"I practised it, dad, over the back of the sofa," explained his son.

"Yes; that'll do, as far as the leap is concerned," returned the clown, after an instant's reflection. "But that ain't all. You wants the window. It's the goin' through that clean as is the difficult part. You must have a window."

"So I had, dad."

"Did you? How did you get it?"

"Made it out of one of the large picture frames in the parlour," answered Joe, with the utmost animation.

"And how about the pictur' as were in it?" inquired his father, somewhat doubtfully.

Joe hung his head for a moment, and then replied, rather ruefully—

"I was obliged to cut it round the edges to let me through, dad."

"Oh, Joe," exclaimed his mother, reprovingly, "you've spoilt the portrait of your grandfather!"

"I only cut round three of the sides," exclaimed the boy, in extenuation.

"Well, it can't be helped," said his paternal relative, good-naturedly. "S'pose you comes and gives us a specimen how you goes through."

Young Joe cheerfully assented, and led the way to the parlour, followed by his parents.

Here they found a slight confusion in the furniture.

All the chairs had been placed one upon the other.

The table had been removed into a corner, and the top turned up out of the way.

Whilst the sofa, to the back of which the frame containing the portrait of the ancestral Muggins—a queer-looking old guy in a coat that seemed all collar— had been fixed to answer the purpose of a window, was dragged into the centre of the room, and placed lengthwise.

The old clown glanced for an instant at the general disarrangement, and then said to his son—

"Now then, let's see what you can do."

Joe retreated a few steps, and taking a run, shot through the frame like an arrow, and came down on the sofa, which creaked audibly.

"Brayvo! wery good! excellent!" exclaimed his father, admiringly. "You're a wery good boy, and I forgives you the pictur'.

"But, Joe," he added, mildly, "I don't think you'd better practise on the sofa any more, cos you might damage the springs, and I shouldn't like that, cos it's part of a sixteen-guinea soot."

The clown, as he spoke, sat down on the piece of furniture in question, and instantly disappeared.

The springs had already been damaged so effectually that he had gone through the bottom.

But these were trivial losses when compared with the gain that resulted from them.

At least so thought the worthy clown, who cheerfully paid for the necessary repairs without uttering a word of reproach.

At length old Joe's benefit night came.

The bill was an attractive one.

The pantomimic sketch of the Clown's Pie, with the additional attraction of two clowns, old Joe and young Joe, seemed to tickle the public taste immensely.

Every box was taken beforehand, and the forthcoming performance caused quite a furore.

A few days before the benefit, when the clown returned home from rehearsal, Matilda Jane, the domestic, said—

"Oh, please, sir, a gentleman's called since you've been out for a pound's worth of tickets."

"Of course you let 'im 'ave 'em, didn't you?" asked Joe.

"Yes, sir; I gave 'em to 'im myself," was the girl's reply.

"I s'pose he paid for 'em?" inquired her master.

"Which he didn't, sir," returned Matilda, "but he said as he'd leave the money for you at the stage door."

"Oh," ejaculated the clown; "ah," and then he added to himself, "I hope he will leave it."

After a short pause he inquired—

"What sort of a gentleman was he?"

"Well, sir," returned Matilda Jane, "I couldn't see his features very distinct, cos he wore his hat so much forrards, but what I did see of his face was very pale, and he wore a thick great coat with the collar stuck up."

This gave the cue at once to Joe's memory.

"I know who it is now," he thought to himself; "it's the same man as took fifteen bobs' worth of tickets of me for my benefit at Oldham six year ago. He said he might see me in London. I wonder who he is?"

Joe had once before expressed the same wonder.

Perhaps now he would learn.

The theatre was, in a short time after the opening of the doors, crammed to overflowing.

The performance went off in a highly satisfactory manner.

At length the grand feature of the evening came on.

"The Clown's Pie."

A very fine pie it was, too, made by Mr. Modelmug expressly for the occasion, full of all sorts of curiosities.

In this not only was our hero concealed, but at the last moment, his young friends Billy Buttons, Georgy Marrowfat, and John Bangs were pressed into the service, together with a pretty little girl named Polly Pritchard, who volunteered her services as columbine.

At the proper time, then, the old clown cut up the pie, and much to the delight of the audience he took out the miniature pantomimists one by one, between the prongs of an enormous fork.

The juveniles being liberated, performed a comic scene, which young Joe had arranged, all to themselves with immense effect.

The latter took his leap through a cab window in first-rate style.

And the last feat of all was performed by the old clown, his father, who, fastening a chain by an iron band to his waist, swung him round at arm's length, amid the cheers of the spectators.

But even this was to be sensational.

All of a sudden, as young Joe was

spinning round like a human catherine wheel with tremendous velocity, and just as the applause was at its height, a sharp click was heard.

The chain had snapped.

Old Joe found himself suddenly on his back, with the broken chain in his hand.

But little Joe was no longer at the other end of it.

In an instant he was up again, looking anxiously about for his son.

But he was nowhere to be found.

He seemed to have flown away into space, and to have disappeared altogether like a fallen star.

Joe Muggins was horrorstruck.

He rushed to the footlights, and entreated the audience in the stalls and pit to look carefully under the benches after his missing boy.

He next appealed to the boxes and gallery, imploring in the most urgent terms, if anybody there had found him, that they would " be kind enough jest to chuck him down on to the stage."

But as nobody had found him, nobody " chucked him down."

Sarah Muggins, utterly ignoring the audience in her anxiety, came rushing breathlessly on to the stage to her husband.

" What have you done with the dear boy, Joe?" she exclaimed, frantically.

" I dunno," groaned the bewildered pantomimist. "I'm afraid I must ha' chucked him clean out of one of the windows."

Under this terrible impression, without waiting to put anything on over his dress, the anxious clown rushed desperately out at the stage door.

He had hardly crossed the threshold when someone (he was too excited to see who) placed something (he was too nervous to know what) in his arms.

" There's the boy," said the someone. " He flew into the stage box where I was sitting, and I caught him in my arms. Take him."

" I'm all right, dad," exclaimed young Joe, as his delighted father hugged him to his breast.

" And here, Mr. Muggerini," cried the someone, as he thrust a sovereign into the hands of the pantomimist—" that's for the ten box tickets I had the day before yesterday. I like to pay my debts. Good night."

Before Joe Muggins could recover from his astonishment, the stranger was some distance off; but he could see distinctly that he wore a thick great coat, the collar of which was turned up.

Again the old clown muttered to himself—" I wonder whoever that man is?"

CHAPTER XI.

IN WHICH OLD JOE RESOLVES TO SEND YOUNG JOE TO SCHOOL—THE RESULTS OF PULLING A BELL.

THE pantomime at Sadler's Wells was over, but Joe Muggins and his friends were not now, as in old times, out of engagement.

On the contrary, a lucrative offer had been made to Joe to give a series of performances round the country, together with his talented colleagues, he having the entire management of the whole affair.

It became a question then what to do with young Joe during his absence from town.

The matter was discussed very seriously by Joe and his wife.

" I can't do without you, Sarah," said the former, " but I don't see how we could drag the boy about with us, on'y stopping a week in a place, too."

" Nor I either," admitted Mrs. Muggins; " it would only unsettle 'im. Besides, there's his edication."

" Ah, yes, to be sure there is," said Joe. " He ain't near finished off yet in his intellectual pursoots, and I wants him to know pretty well everythink as is to be knowed."

" I really don't think we could do better, Joe," his wife suggested, " than send him to some good boarding sahool, where he'd be taught well and looked after while we're away."

"Well, I don't think as we could," returned Joe, "so that settles the point. We must look out for a good classical academy, and put him there."

This being arranged, the old clown and his wife searched the advertisements in the papers perseveringly for such a school as seemed to offer the necessary advantages.

At last they found one that struck Joe as about the right kind of thing.

The advertisement ran thus—

SCHOLASTIC. — TO PARENTS AND GUARDIANS.—Parents and guardians desirous of placing young gentlemen at a first-rate scholastic establishment, are respectfully informed that there are vacancies for a few pupils at Doctor McSwisher's classical and commercial academy, situated in one of the most delightfully rural spots in the South of England. Extensive pleasure grounds, bath, gymnasium, and everything that can conduce to the health and happiness of the pupils on the premises. Terms, forty guineas a year. No extras. Payable quarterly, in advance. Address, Dr. Erasmus McSwisher, Tickle Toby Hall, Whoppington, near Tingleback.

"I think that'll be the very ticket," exclaimed old Joe, as he came to the end. "The terms is rayther stiff, certainly. But there! you must pay for a good thing."

His wife offered a suggestion.

"It seems a good school, Joe," she said, "but don't you think they're very hard upon the pupils there?"

"Hard! No; why should they be?" inquired her husband.

"I dunno," she answered; "but it seems as if they would be from the names."

"Dr. McSwisher, Tickle Toby Hall, Whoppington, near Tingleback," read Joe again.

"Well, certainly, it does seem to run in favour of corporal punishment. But it don't mean that. At all events, I'll drop the doctor a line, and see what he says."

This was done, and almost by return of post an answer was returned, so frank and genial that it quite won old Joe's heart.

"It'll do, Sarah; I'm sure of it," he exclaimed, warmly, as he placed the doctor's epistle before her.

Sarah was as pleased with the style of the letter as her husband.

And it was determined between them that their son should be conveyed thither without delay.

"I'll take 'im myself, Sarah," said Joe; "and then I shall be able to form a sort of a idea of the merits of the place and the doctor."

Our hero, at the first announcement, did not quite relish the idea of a boarding school.

It seemed to suggest long lessons and captivity, rather than pantomimes and freedom.

But his father explained to him that there were acres of land to roam over, and immense warm baths to swim in.

And this reconciled Joe to the prospect.

"I don't much like the ' Whoppington, near Tingleback,' though," he remarked.

"Oh, they're only names," explained his sire.

"Ah, well," thought the boy, "if Mr. McWhiskers whops me, or makes my back tingle, I can easily run away."

It did not take long to make the necessary preparations for our hero's departure.

Joe's box was well supplied, not only with his necessary wearing apparel, but with a large cake (almost a pantomime one in circumference), several pots of jam, and—last, not least—complete miniature dresses for the principal pantomime characters.

"We may want to do a bit of acting down at Whoppington, dad," he said, "and there's nothing like being ready."

At length, after a long journey by rail, old Joe and young Joe arrived at Whoppington, and in due time reached Tickle Toby Hall.

The mansion was surrounded by a high wall, and looked sufficiently appalling to inspire our hero with a strong wish to return instantly to Bagnigge Wells Road.

On the gate was a handsome brass plate, on which was inscribed, in bold characters, the name of the principal—

"Doctor McSwisher."

There was a solemn-looking bell-handle, depending from a thick wire on one side of the gate.

"P'r'aps we'd better pull it," suggested old Joe.

Young Joe at once did a pantomimic spring towards the solemn bell-handle, and having caught it, brought it down with a jerk that set the bell to which it was attached ringing as it had never rung before in its life.

This seemed to create a general consternation.

Windows were thrown up, and female domestics looked out excitedly, as if they thought the house was on fire.

An unseen but evidently ferocious dog began to howl and bark fiercely.

A small youth came hurriedly from a side entrance, making frantic efforts to fasten the forty-three small buttons of his page's jacket all at once as he came along.

Whilst at the same moment, the front door opened, and a thin, wiry-looking old man, in a dressing gown, having a very high-bridged nose, which supported a pair of spectacles, came down the steps in a fury of indignation.

In his hand he flourished an awful-looking cane.

It was the doctor himself, highly incensed at the alarm that had so thoroughly startled his household.

The little doctor, not perceiving anyone at the gate (old Joe having withdrawn behind the shelter of the wall to have a quiet laugh to himself, and young Joe having followed him), came hastily forward.

He and the youth with the buttons reached the gate at the same time.

"Who dared to agitate my bell in this way?" he shouted. "Who has presumed to disturb me in my scholastic labours in this atrocious manner? Forks, what's the matter?"

This was to the youth in the page's jacket.

"How do I know?" replied Forks, in by no means a respectful tone. "It wasn't me as touched it."

Whack, whack, whack! from the cane, and a yell from Forks.

"You ought to know, sir!" exclaimed his irascible master. "What do I keep you for, eh?"

"I can't do everythink all at once!" whimpered Forks, rebelliously, as he rubbed his back.

"Don't talk to me, sirrah! Open the gate and see if there's anyone there," cried the doctor.

The gate was opened, and Forks looked out.

"D'ye see anyone?" shouted the principal.

Forks opened his eyes very wide as he discovered Joe Muggins leaning against the wall, with his handkerchief thrust into his mouth till he was almost black in the face with his efforts to control his laughter, and his son standing by his side.

But the latter did not seem so mirthfully impressed.

There seemed too much of the "Whoppington, near Tingleback" about the proceedings to please him.

"Well, d'ye see anyone?" repeated Doctor McSwisher.

"Yes, sir."

"Who is it?"

"There's two on 'em, sir; a big un and a little un," explained Forks.

"Ask 'em what they mean," said the doctor.

"What d'ye mean, you two roughs?" demanded Forks, advancing sternly towards Joe Muggins and his son. "The doctor wants to know."

The old clown was so intensely tickled that he couldn't get a word out.

"Oh, my eye!" he chuckled inwardly. "If this ain't a prime comic scene, I don't know what is."

"What do they say?" roared the doctor, furiously.

"They don't say nothink," returned the youth with the buttons, "'specially the fat un, as does nothink but larf."

"Ho, ho, ho, ho!" roared old Joe, in his heartiest clown's tone.

"Do the scoundrels dare to laugh derisively at me?" exclaimed the irate little doctor, who heard the "ho, ho, ho!" distinctly.

"I'll let them know that I am not to be held up to public ridicule."

As he spoke, the indignant principal rushed out and advanced towards our hero and his father, looking as red and inflammatory as a turkey cock.

"What do you mean by ringing my bell, eh, ruffians?" he demanded, flourishing his "tingleback."

There was a slight pause, during which old Joe composed his features by a great effort, and then he replied—

"If you wants to know the real truth, my boy here pulled the bell, cos we wanted to get in."

A light seemed suddenly to flash across the doctor's mind, and he exclaimed—

"Is it possible that—yes—true—of course, I see. You are——"

"Mr. Muggins and son, at your service," answered old Joe.

The frown departed from the little doctor's brow.

The cane disappeared, as if by magic, beneath his dressing gown.

He smiled and appeared altogether quite a different being.

"My dear Mr. Buggins," he exclaimed, warmly, "your hand.

"I rejoice to meet you. Pray pardon me.

"I am persecuted by runaway rings; thought you were one. Accept my apology."

"Oh, I forgives you," returned Joe. "But allow me to say as my name is Muggins, not Buggins."

"Ah, yes, to be sure! so it is. I remember perfectly," exclaimed the little doctor, in a hurried manner.

"Muggins, I'm delighted to see you, my dear sir.

"And this is Master Bug—ahem!—Muggins, I presume."

"Yes, sir," answered our hero, to whom these words pointed.

"That's right. We shall be capital friends, I can see," he exclaimed, gushingly. "And so you—he, he!—pulled the bell, did you? Capital!"

"Yes," said young Joe, "I pulled it. I suppose it's there to be pulled, isn't it?"

"He, he! excellent! quite witty, I declare," grinned the principal.

"Your son's a very clever boy, Mr. Muffins."

"Muggins," corrected the clever boy

"True, I forgot," said the doctor shaking his head in a slightly bewildered manner.

Then recovering himself, he said, politely—

"Pray come in, Mr. Muggins. Mrs. McSwisher will be delighted to see you."

"Go ahead, then," exclaimed old Joe, "and we'll follow."

"Forks!" shouted the principal, "go forward and inform your mistress of our approach."

The small youth with the buttons led the way, and the rest followed.

As they advanced towards the house, young Joe took the opportunity to whisper to his father—

"I don't think I shall like Doctor Swisher."

"Well, he seems to me rayther a cure," his father responded.

"What a capital mask his face'd make for old Mullygrubs in the pantomime," Joe again remarked, as they entered the hall.

"Hush! perhaps he'll hear you," cautioned his parent, with a suppressed grin.

"This way," exclaimed the object of these remarks, as he threw open the parlour door.

Joe and his father entered.

CHAPTER XII.

IN WHICH OLD JOE RETURNS TO LONDON, AND YOUNG JOE REMAINS BEHIND AT WHOPPINGTON.

THERE was something about the interior of the large, rambling, chilly-looking parlour, with its gloomily-papered walls, suggestive of scientific research and severe mental application.

Two large globes stood on two separate tables before the windows.

An historical chart hung in a recess.

The books that lay on the table were either dissertations on natural philosophy or chemistry, varied with something of a lighter description in the way of "Elements of the Classics," and "Fractions Made Easy."

But nothing at all approaching the book of a pantomime was to be seen anywhere.

A melancholy-looking hour-glass reposed in impressive silence on the mantelpiece, as if to suggest to the beholder the tardy flight of time in that gloomy abode.

"HERE WE ARE!" CRIED YOUNG JOE, SLIDING RAPIDLY DOWN."

Altogether, everything had a depressing effect on our young hero Joe.

He had hardly finished his cursory examination of the surrounding objects, when the door opened and Mrs. McSwisher sailed in grandly.

If the doctor looked vicious and spiteful, the doctor's extensive wife appeared in Joe's eyes something almost too awful to be contemplated quietly.

The large, staring eyes; the stern expression about the mouth; the formidable beak, red as a lobster's claw; and the unusual bulk of the lady, impressed the juvenile clown very unfavourably respecting her.

"Arabella, my love," said the doctor, in his most affectionate tone, " Mr. Joseph —a—Bug——"

"Mug," interposed young Joe, correctively.

"True, so it is Mug. I had forgotten again. Thank you, my boy. Muggins —Mr. Joseph Muggins and son."

"Delighted to see you—truly delighted, Mr. Muggins," exclaimed the portly Arabella, through her nose, in a snuffling tone, that sounded dreadful to Joe's ears.

"And this is the young gentleman who has come to join us, is it?" she added, as sweetly as she could. "I'm delighted to see him, too. I am so fond of good boys."

"Then I think he'll be just about the kind of boy to soot you to a T, mum," remarked his father, in an explanatory manner. "I don't think there could be a better."

The amiable Arabella, affecting to be much interested at this announcement, looked down upon the young prodigy with her head on one side, like an old poll parrot.

Then, as if unable to restrain her natural feelings, she suddenly made a frantic dart at him, and clasped both his hands.

"Welcome, my dear child—welcome to Tickle Toby Hall! I'm sure you'll be very happy here. All our pupils are so. We are, if I may use the expression, quite a happy family."

Forks entered at that moment with a bottle of sherry and a plate of biscuits, murmured "Walker" to himself, and retired.

"You'll take a glass of wine, Mr.—— —Dug——"

"Mug," from Joe.

"I beg your pardon—Muggins."

"Well, I don't care if I do," answered old Joe. "My boy'll have a glass, too, I dessay."

Without waiting for a reply, he filled a couple of glasses.

"Good health, Doctor Whisker."

"Swisher, if you please—McSwisher," corrected the principal, looking as though he would like to correct young Joe at once.

Old Joe and young Joe drank their wine. Then the former said—

"I thought, as I was a-goin' to place my boy under you, it'd be as well to bring him down myself, just to see what sort of a place he was comin' to."

"Quite right—very proper, Mr. Dug —Bug—Muggins—very."

The old clown emptied his glass, and replied—

"Look here, Mr. McLicker——"

"McSwisher," sweetly interposed Arabella.

"McSwisher, I don't pretend to be an educated man; I'm only a professional."

"Oh, indeed!" exclaimed the principal and his wife, quite eagerly. "What, the medical, or the legal, or——"

"Legal be blowed! I'm a clown," exclaimed old Joe, indignantly.

"So am I," chimed in his son and heir, with conscious pride. "We're both clowns; they call us old Joe and young Joe."

"Clowns!" echoed the astonished and, if the truth must be told, inwardly disgusted pair.

"Yes, clowns," returned the pantomimist, almost in a tone of defiance. "None the worse on that account, I suppose?"

"Ha, ha! of course; I see," sniggered the doctor, who perceived his visitor's displeasure. "You belong to the Grimaldi school?"

Old Joe's transient display of temper subsided in a moment, and he smiled beamingly.

"That's more like it," he cried. "You've hit it this time. Well, as I was a-goin' to remark, I've taught a few in my time—not history or geography, or anything of that sort, but tumbling."

"Very abstruse science to teach, I should think," remarked the doctor.

"Very," assented old Joe, "because you wants your brains in your back and your arms and legs—anywhere but in your head. Here, Joe," he cried, suddenly, "just give these here good people a specimen of your talent."

In a moment, young Joe was going in for all he knew—tumbling, walking on his hands, turning somersaults, and throwing flip-flaps, and handsprings, to the great delight of himself and his father, and the scarcely-concealed horror of the doctor and his spouse.

"Wonderful!" exclaimed Doctor McSwisher, with a very wry face, as our hero concluded his performance.

"Incredible!" echoed the doctor's wife, holding up her hands in amazement.

Old Joe patted his clever son on the head, and said to him, in a low tone of approval—

"That was first-rate, my boy; and now, if you like, you can leave me to say a few words to the doctor and his missis. Suppose you has a turn at the splits in the hall."

Young Joe, who was not sorry to leave the gloomy apartment, slipped quietly out by the door.

The moment after, he was exercising his limbs on the door-mat.

His parent once more resumed his conversation with the principal and his spouse.

"You've just had a specimen of what my boy can do," he said. "Well, all I've got to say is, as I taught him what he knows, and I wouldn't wish for a more willinger pupil. I never had to use any of what you calls corrective measures with him. He sucked in all he had to learn jest like sugar."

The clown poured out another glass of sherry and drank it off, after which he went on—

"You see my youngster's allays bin used to have his liberty, and he might feel his school dooties rather confining at first."

"Oh, he'll soon get used to that," said the doctor; "our way of teaching is so full of interest; our pupils love their lessons almost more than their play."

"Do they, indeed?" exclaimed Joe, in a tone of surprise. "That is wonderful.

Not as I quite believes as my boy will You see, having been used in the habit of exercising his limbs, he's uncommon active, and has got little peculiarities as might surprise them as didn't know him."

"Um, ah, yes! I see!" ejaculated the doctor, shutting one eye, and looking profound, as though wondering what these little peculiarities might be.

"I suppose he—a—stands on his head occasionally?" said Mrs. McSwisher, inquiringly.

"Ho, ho!" laughed the pantomimist, "I should rather say he did. He ain't been christened Pantomime Joe for nothing—not he! I'll back you finds him oftener on his head, or walking on his hands, than you will on his feet."

"Ah—um—exactly," returned the doctor, reflectively; "it's quite inverting the natural order of things, though," he murmured to himself, "and might induce a vitiated taste for such practices in the other scholars."

"But that ain't all," continued old Joe, who was becoming more and more good-humoured every moment at the recital of his son's little peculiarities; "he's uncommon fond of playing ride-a-cock-horse on the banisters. Lor' bless you, he can descend from the top of the stairs to the bottom like a flash of lightning or a apparition."

The principal glanced viciously at his wife, who returned his look with one of equal expression.

"In short," the old clown summed up very cheerfully, "I should recommend you, if you've got any furniture as is good for anything, to keep your eyes on it, especially the couches and chairs, because Joe's particular good at breaking chair-backs and knocking out sofa bottoms, not forgetting the pictures, which he's remarkable clever at jumping through."

"Good gracious!" exclaimed the principal and his wife, in a kind of horror; "you surely don't mean to say he jumps through pictures?"

"As sure as I'm a-standing here," returned the pantomimist, with a flush of honest pride upon his face, "he's jumped clean through his venerable grandfather, as hangs in the parlour at home, over and over again."

"I'm very glad you informed us of

this, Mr. Hug—I mean Muggins," repeated the doctor, with scarcely-restrained perturbation. "I see your son will require a—um—strict supervision."

"He jest wants you to keep your eye on him, that's all," returned the clown, "and you'll find him a very good, well-disposed boy. And if the young gentlemen should feel disposed to get up a little pantomime among theirselves at breaking-up times, Joe will show them how to do it to rights."

The doctor took an emphatic pinch of snuff, and his wife blew her nose sharply by way of reply.

The conference was at an end.

"I suppose I'd better pay you the quarter's money in advance," said the old clown, as he took out his pocket-book.

The features of the principal relaxed, and he smiled assentingly.

The money was paid, and the receipt given.

"Well, now I think I'll just have one more glass of sherry, and then I'll be going," said the clown.

The wine was poured out.

But before Joe Muggins could raise his glass to his lips, a prolonged yell and a burst of laughter from without caused him to set it down untasted.

"Good gracious!" exclaimed the doctor and his wife, "whatever can be the matter?"

Old Joe seemed to have a strong suspicion, for his mouth curled up into a smile, as he said—

"I shouldn't wonder if it was my boy indulging in one of his little peculiarities."

In order to ascertain whether this idea was correct, he went to the door and threw it open.

As he did so, the boy in a page's dress darted hastily through another door in the distance and became invisible.

The coast seemed perfectly clear.

But the yells continued, and the next moment a couple of distracted cats came flying down the stairs with their tails tied together, and disappeared into the lower regions.

This was followed by a loud clatter overhead, as though a pail had been overturned; and the voice of Betsy, the housemaid, exclaiming loudly—

"Oh, you mischievous boy! See what you've done!"

At the same time, a torrent of soapy fluid from above fell with a loud splash on to the oilcloth.

"That's him," cried the old clown, grinning all over his face; "he's up to one of his little games, as sure as my name's Joseph."

The doctor and his wife stood aghast in silent horror, which was by no means diminished when the housemaid Betsy came hurrying down quite in a panic.

"Oh, if you please, ma'am, the new young gentleman has been and upset the pail, and the water is running everywhere," she cried, excitedly.

"And my best carpet will be utterly ruined!" snuffled the matronly Arabella; "go and get the mop instantly."

Betsy disappeared as though her life depended on her speed.

"It's no good making mountains of mole hills," remarked old Joe, in a mollifying tone, "it's only a little water, as will dry up, and no harm done after all." Then, going to the foot of the stairs, he called out—

"Heigh! hullo! Joe."

"Heigh! hullo!" Joe replied, in a lively tone, from above.

At the same instant a boot appeared, and then a leg, in its progress of descent from the second flight.

"He's at it," cried the old clown, in a tone of great exhilaration; "he's doing the aerial descent.

"Here he comes," he shouted, as his son and heir skilfully turned the curve of the banister and came in sight.

"Ugh!" shrieked the doctor and his wife, in a paroxysm of nervousness, "he'll be dashed to pieces."

"Get out!—dashed to pieces," returned the old clown, scornfully; "not he; he's as right as ninepence."

In proof of this young Joe, with his arms and legs extended, came gliding down the mahogany handrail with the rapidity of a sky rocket.

"Here we are," he cried, sliding rapidly down and winding up by throwing a somersault on to the oilcloth matting, and almost startling Betsy, who had just appeared with the mop, out of her wits.

Old Joe gave his protégé a hug of delight, and then approaching the scared domestic, whispered a few words of consolation into her ear, accompanied by a donation of half-a-crown, which seemed to cure her immediately, and sent her upstairs all smiles and giggles to mop up the water.

The doctor and his wife, however, found it exceedingly difficult to control their indignation.

They both looked as dark and lowering as two thunderclouds.

Even old Joe fancied they did not seem quite so delighted as he thought they ought to have been.

But it was now time for him to return to London.

"Good-bye, my dear boy," he said, as he kissed his son and heir affectionately. "Mind and learn all as you can, and as you're at school, p'r'aps it'd be as well to draw it a little mild with your acrobatic performances."

He led young Joe away a step or two, and added, in a lower and more confidential tone—

"But mind, whatever you do, keep up your tumbling, 'specially your hand-springs and flip-flaps, cos they're necessities for a clown—and remember Christmas'll come round ag'in in course of time. Good-bye, Joe."

A warm embrace followed between the old clown and the son he loved as dearly as his own life.

The door was opened, and the former walked out to the gate.

The gate swung open on its hinges, and closed again with a hollow clang.

"Good-bye, my dear boy!" called old Joe once more, as he waved his hand through the railings.

"Good-bye, dad, dear!" called young Joe from the top of the steps. "Give my love to mother."

The next moment Joe Muggins was out of sight on his way to the station, and young Joe found the doors of Tickle Toby Hall closed upon him.

CHAPTER XIII.

IN WHICH FORKS INTRODUCES HIMSELF TO OUR HERO—AN INTERESTING CONVERSATION SUDDENLY INTERRUPTED—AN ABRUPT EXIT—AND A COMIC SCENE IN THE GLOOMY PARLOUR.

IN order to commence at once in the right way, and let the new pupil know where he was and who he had to deal with, the principal, as soon as he had him to himself, opened the door of the gloomy parlour, and said, sharply—

"Go in there, and wait till you're sent for."

Joe, feeling rather depressed in his spirits, threw a somersault into the room, in order to cheer himself up a bit.

"Understand me distinctly, Master Bug—Muggins," growled the doctor, indignantly—"I prohibit tumbling—remember that!"

With these words he slammed the door, and retired to hold a conference with his better half respecting the new arrival.

"I don't know what to think of this boy," he said, as soon as they were alone together, screwing up his lips doubtfully.

"His connections are low—decidedly low," snuffled the fair Arabella. "The idea of a clown is really—a—disgusting!"

"Well, it shan't be my fault if I don't cure Master Muf—Bug—confound the name! I can never recollect it — Muggins of his little 'peculiarities,' as his illiterate parent terms them."

As he spoke he drew forth the cane from beneath his dressing-gown with a swish, as if he had been drawing a sword.

"If this new boy attempts anything in my establishment of a tumbling or acrobatic nature," exclaimed the doctor, as he flourished the elastic weapon in the air, "he'll find he hasn't come to 'Whoppington, near Tingleback,' for nothing."

The idea was altogether so humorous that the principal and his spouse grinned at each other like a pair of ogres.

"You are so droll, Erasmus," snuffled Mrs. McSwisher at length.

"At all events, my dear," replied the doctor, "I flatter myself I know how to manage boys, and in order to start well with this new arrival, I shall give him a sound caning at the earliest opportunity."

Our young hero, in the meantime, ignorant of his preceptor's kind intentions towards him, remained in the gloomy parlour.

It seemed to him awfully dreary.

Having nothing else to do, he read the titles of the books on the table, examined two lizards, preserved in spirits of wine, and a petrified toad on the sideboard, and then, to relieve his mind, he stood on his head on all the chairs in succession.

After which, he walked round the room on his hands.

Whilst he was thus engaged, he heard a sharp tapping at the window.

He immediately dropped on to his feet, and looked out.

The boy in the page's jacket, with his nose flattened against the pane, met his gaze.

The latter nodded and grinned in an intensely friendly manner, and motioned to the prisoner within to open one of the windows, which reached to the ground and moved upon hinges like a glass door.

The suggestion was instantly complied with.

The way of communication being opened, Forks, who was a youth of the most free-and-easy description possible, at once commenced the conference.

"You're come to stop here, ain't you?" he asked.

"Yes," returned Joe, briefly.

"Your name's Muggins, ain't it?"

Joe nodded.

The other grinned.

"Muggins!" he repeated, with evident relish. "It ain't 'arf a bad name—a'most as good as mine is."

Our hero thought his visitor a trifle too fast, but he only inquired—

"What is yours?"

"Forks—Tom Forks," returned his companion, readily. "I've got two names."

"So have I. My other name's Joe," explained our hero.

"Joe Muggins?"

"Yes."

There was a slight pause, and then Joe continued—

"Is this a happy family?"

"'Appy family!" grinned the page boy. "What a rum question. Why?"

"Why, because the stout lady with the red nose, Mrs.—a—what's her name?"

"Mother Swisher," said Forks.

"Ah! yes, Mrs. Swisher—she said it was."

"Well, that may be her opinion," returned the page, "but," he added with a grin, "I don't think as she adds much to the amount of happiness herself. But I thinks the pupils makes theirselves pooty jolly amongst one another. I should say as you'd get along with 'em first-rate."

"I hope so,"returned Joe.

"How much pocket money do you have?" was the page boy's next question; "because a good deal depends on that."

"Sixpence a week, and I've got plenty of money in my purse besides that," Joe answered.

"Oh, that's the sort," exclaimed Forks, with enthusiasm; "you'll do. You'll be amongst the head boys. Old Sally comes regular every Wednesday and Saturday. Don't she sell prime tarts, neither? Oh, crikey!"

The small youth smacked his lips at the remembrance of these luxuries, and then remarked—

"I've been a-looking at you through this here window once before to-day. I say, can't you tumble about a bit?"

"I think I can a little," replied Joe, modestly. "See!"

As he spoke, he threw several somersaults backwards and forwards, and then walked across the room on his hands.

"Bravo, bravo!" cried the youthful page, clapping his hands in an ecstasy of admiration.

"Who taught you to do that?"

"Why, dad, of course," answered Joe.

"What, that old cove as brought you here? Is he your dad?" inquired Forks, in a tone of astonishment.

"Yes, he is," returned our hero, indignantly; "and please don't you call him names, because I don't like it."

"Oh, I begs your pardon," said the page, apologetically. "And can he tumble?"

"I should think he could, too," replied Joe, warmly; "he's a clown."

If Forks' hair had been long enough, it would have stood on end at once at this announcement.

As it was not, however, it kept where it was, and he echoed—

"A clown! What! a real clown as acts in the pantomimes?"

"Yes," returned Joe. "I act too."

"What, on the stage?"

"Yes; I've been acting this last Christmas at Sadler's Wells."

"And what did you act there?" continued Forks, with breathless interest.

"Cat and juvenile clown on dad's benefit night," explained our hero, and added—"I went on the stage when I was quite a little baby. That's why I am called Pantomime Joe."

The wonder and admiration of the page-boy at these astounding revelations was something tremendous.

"I say," he said, earnestly, "I should like to be a clown better than anything. Will you teach me to tumble?"

"Oh, yes," returned Joe, with the utmost readiness, his eyes sparkling, and feeling that he had found at least one congenial spirit in that apparently uncongenial abode; "I'll teach you as often as you like."

"I'll have a lesson as often as I can," said Forks. "We shall have to do it on the quiet, because the doctor's as cantankerous as Old Scratch. He don't understand nothing about the fine arts. Tumblin' would be very far beyond the reach of his intellects."

"Dad told me to keep up my tumbling," said Joe, "so I shall tumble every day, whether he likes it or——"

The young speaker ceased abruptly, as he observed his listener's round face contract with a sudden expression of horror, and his twinkling eyes become fixed in a kind of fascinated stare, which was evidently directed at some object over his shoulder which he could not see.

He turned round, and found himself face to face with the stern doctor himself.

The principal had entered softly, and heard the latter part of the conversation, and now stood there, stern and awful, with compressed lips and knitted brows, peering at him through his spectacles like some elderly scholastic demon.

"So, Master—Bug—Pug—Muggins," he exclaimed, in a terribly ironical tone, "you'll practise tumbling, whether I like it or not, will you? Very good."

Our hero, who was by no means so appalled as he might naturally have been expected to be, answered simply—

"Dad told me to tumble, and I must do as he tells me."

"No, sir; I am master here," returned the doctor, fiercely, "and I order you not to tumble. Disobey me if you dare."

He then fixed his eyes on the fascinated youth in the buttons, who, in the course of his conversation with Joe, had gradually edged himself into the room.

"Forks," he ejaculated, with awful brevity, "step this way."

The voice of the master broke the spell.

Forks glanced at the cane that quivered in the principal's bony hand, and remained where he was.

"Come here, sir. Do you hear?" repeated Dr. McSwisher.

"Not if I knows it," muttered the youth, as he made a desperate rush towards the window.

But, unfortunately, the latter had swung to and was closed, and in passing by the small table on which the terrestrial globe rested, and which stood in front of the window, his toe caught in one of the branch legs, and he shot forward, and went crashing head first through one of the lower panes.

The table was also upset, and both that and the globe fell with a bang to the ground.

Forks fell on his hands and knees on the gravel walk outside.

"Stop, you scoundrel!" shouted the enraged doctor.

"Don't you wish you may get it?" muttered the small youth.

He was on the right side to run away, and he availed himself of the chance by scrambling on to his feet and bolting at the top of his speed, glittering all over with splinters of broken glass like an icicle.

Our hero was left alone with the doctor and his cane.

"Pick up that table, sir," cried the doctor, savagely.

Joe obediently picked it up and stood it on its legs.

"Now replace the globe," exclaimed the principal.

Our hero was not quite so successful in his next attempt.

The frame had been cracked by the fall, and when he lifted it, there was an immediate dissolution of partnership amongst the fragments.

The frame remained in Joe's hands.

The globe once more fell plump to the

ground, but this time on the doctor's toes, who roared like a bull.

"Ugh! you've crushed my corn, you young villain!" he raved.

"I couldn't help it," protested Joe, who, even at that critical moment, was thinking what a capital comic scene the whole of the preceding incidents would make for a pantomime.

But matters rapidly grew more serious, for the furious doctor, having nursed his toe for a few seconds, came limping forward, brandishing his cane in an awfully ominous manner.

"Now, sir," he cried, "I shall make an example of you. Hold out your hand."

Our hero, not seeing any particular reason why he should perform this act, especially when there was a cane hovering in the air ready to drop down upon it, very naturally objected.

"It wasn't my fault that the globe was broken," he argued.

"Don't talk to me, sir!" roared the infuriate principal. "Hold out your hand."

But Joe still declined.

He began to see that he should have to bring his own activity and skill into play in opposition to the rage and strength of the wrathful preceptor.

Joe was as active and nimble as a cat, and he thought to himself—

"I'll fancy this is a comic scene. I'm the naughty clown at school, and there's the schoolmaster waiting to thrash me."

"Here we are!" he exclaimed, suddenly, as he began to dodge the doctor.

"I'll let you know I'm here," cried the latter, as he stepped forward.

Swish went the cane.

But it did not descend on our hero's back.

It simply inflicted a tremendous crack upon the globe.

The region of Central Africa suffered considerably.

Joe had slipped on one side, and was now behind the doctor.

Swish, swish, swish! went the cane at random.

But it only struck the air.

When the irritated principal looked round for his prey, he discovered him on the other side of the room, with the table between them.

"Do you intend to stand still, you confounded Merry Andrew?" he shouted.

"Not to be beaten for nothing," returned Joe.

Such an event as a pupil objecting to receive as much "tingleback," or "tingle-hand," as the doctor chose to administer, had never before occurred to him in his experience.

He was perfectly aghast—furious.

He made a hasty rush after his juvenile defier.

But Joe dodged him round the table with perfect impunity.

He slashed at the youthful dodger with his formidable cane across the mahogany.

But the latter wisely drew back, and the blows fell harmlessly on the "Elements of the Classics" and "Fractions Made Easy."

Roused beyond endurance at being thus successfully thwarted in his designs by a mere child, the principal, who was an active, wiry man, sprang on to the table, and towered over his young pupil like a Colossus.

"Now, sir!" he said, fiercely. "If you don't stand still, I'll flay you alive when I get hold of you."

"I don't intend you to get hold of me," Joe thought to himself; and consequently he did anything but stand still.

The principal wheeled round and round on the table, waiting for an opportunity to take a leap and swoop down upon his prey.

Our hero divined this, and thinking it would be as well to be prepared with some weapon of defence, he glanced round for something available.

What would he not have given then for the red-hot pantomime poker he had at home?

But there was not a glimpse of anything of that cheerful description in that gloomy parlour.

And the furious doctor was dancing round like an ancient monkey on the table, ready to drop upon him at a moment.

Suddenly Joe's eyes fell on the petrified toad.

It was not by any means a comfortable-looking missile, certainly not ornamental.

But it was hard and heavy, and had a certain skull-cracking, eye-bunging, rib-tickling quality, that made it exceedingly useful just at that time.

Our hero seized it at once.

"Put that valuable relic down, sir," shouted the doctor, raising his cane, and preparing to spring.

Joe, instead of obeying, drew his arm back and took as good aim as he could at the speaker's head.

The action was expressive, and increased the desperation of the principal, who perfectly understood it.

With a yell of rage, he gathered himself together, and leaped from the table.

At the same instant, Joe let fly with the petrified toad at the doctor's head.

There was another loud crash heard.

The valuable relic had missed its intended mark, and flown through the window.

A second pane was fractured, instead of the doctor's skull.

The doctor himself lay on the carpet, growling like an angry bear over its prey.

And where was our hero?

Lying crushed beneath him?

Not a bit of it.

He had darted nimbly under the table out of harm's way, and had become invisible.

At the same time Mrs. McSwisher, who had been alarmed by the crashing and banging in the parlour, and thought murder was going on there, came hurrying in at the door, followed by Betsy the housemaid and Jane the cook, in a great state of apprehension, to see what was the matter.

"Good gracious, Erasmus! What are you doing?" almost shrieked the startled Arabella, as she descried her husband huddled up on the ground, struggling desperately with nothing.

"Don't talk, but act," gasped the little doctor, excitedly. "Get me a rope, quick! I've got him—the young ruffian!"

"Got what?" inquired his spouse, who, seeing nothing answering the description, had a slight idea her husband was going out of his mind. "Got what, Erasmus?" she replied.

"Why, this abominable, tumbling, jumbling, infernal Pug — Bug — Muggins!" he exclaimed, breathlessly. "I can't hold him much longer. A rope. Quick!"

"My love, you're mistaken," snuffled the fair Arabella; "I see nothing at all."

"No more do I, mum—nothink," affirmed the housemaid.

"Nor me neither, mum," added the cook.

"Don't stand chattering there like a parcel of idiots, but fetch a rope!"

"Well, but look," exclaimed his spouse.

The excited man glared down through his spectacles, and to his great astonishment found nothing.

"Bless my heart alive!" he ejaculated, in profound astonishment; "I could have have sworn I had him. Help me up."

The bewildered principal, having been assisted on to his legs, commenced an excited detail of our hero's misdemeanours.

"The young rascal has destroyed my globe, smashed my windows, and defied my authority, Arabella—my authority!" he exclaimed, indignantly.

"Where is the young wretch?" Arabella exclaimed.

Diligent search was made in the cupboard, behind the curtains, under the sofa, and up the chimney.

But no signs of the culprit.

He had quietly slipped out through the broken pane.

The doctor looked savage, but at the same time baffled and perplexed.

He had thought to teach the new boy a lesson, and it seemed as though the new boy had taught him one instead.

Tingleback appeared quite powerless upon one who hopped about like an electric eel.

CHAPTER XIV.

IN WHICH OUR HERO ENCOUNTERS A FEROCIOUS ANIMAL—HOW HE QUIETS HIS FOE AND ASTONISHES DOCTOR MCSWISHER.

OUR hero having got clear of the parlour, found himself in the front garden.

There was the iron gate and the bell handle to which he had clung so gleefully a short time before.

This brought his father to his mind, and he felt half inclined to clamber over the gate and make the best of his way to the railway station. But he soon altered his mind.

"Dad wants me to learn all I can," thought he to himself, "and as he's paid the money for me, I won't run away. I should like to get out of this garden, though."

He walked along till he came to the end, where there was a wall.

"I suppose the playground's over there," he reflected. "I don't hear any of the boys' voices. They haven't come out of school yet. I wonder where Forks is. Forks—Forks!" he called, softly.

There was no reply.

The small youth's faculties were at that moment absorbed in the interesting operation of peeling potatoes in the scullery, and he did not hear the summons.

"I think I could climb that wall," said Joe to himself, as he contemplated the branches of a fig tree that were nailed against it.

To think, with our hero, was to try.

In a moment he had clambered up, and was seated astride on the top.

It was, then, the easiest thing in the world to drop down on the other side.

This he accordingly did, and found himself in a yard, at the end of which was a narrow passage, bounded by a door.

"That's the playground, I suppose," he thought. "I'll see."

But, at the first step he took, an enormous mastiff sprang from out his kennel, and, uttering a terrible growl, opened his formidable jaws as though he would have swallowed him there and then.

This was Caractacus, the guardian of the Tickle Toby domains, who was kept to protect the premises, and who had a horror of beggars and strangers.

The only probable reason why the animal did not at once make a meal of the new boy was that his chain prevented him from getting at him.

But the chain was long, and the brute made frantic efforts to reach our hero, standing on his hind legs and showing his fangs, as much as to say—

"Oh, if I only could, wouldn't I?"

Joe felt rather startled at this unexpected foe.

It seemed as if he had just got out of the frying-pan to fall into the fire.

To reach the door of the house he must pass the dog, and that the length of the animal's chain prevented.

To add to his dismay, too, in addition to the howling of the dog without, there suddenly burst upon his ears a howling of a different description from within.

This proceeded from the luckless Forks, on whom the irascible doctor had just pounced, and on whose diminutive carcase the dreadful Tingleback was in active operation.

These sounds gradually died away.

But our hero stood still in the yard, held at bay by the mastiff, who seemed resolved, if perseverance and tugs would accomplish his purpose, to break his chain and devour the intruder.

Joe's position seemed even to himself anything but pantomimical.

It was, on the contrary, extremely imminent, especially as one of the links of the chain was beginning to yield to the frantic efforts of the dog.

Joe, who had observed this, began to feel very uncomfortable.

"If the chain breaks," he said to himself, apprehensively, "it will be all up with me. That big brute will bite my head off, and then what'd poor dad do?"

It did not at that moment occur to him to inquire what he should do himself without that useful member of his body.

But a moment or two later he said, ruefully—

"I couldn't very well play clown without any head on my shoulders!"

In the meantime, Caractacus kept up his howlings and tuggings.

Joe looked up wistfully at the wall.

But it was six or seven feet high, and there was no fig tree on the side on which he stood.

To climb over it again was utterly impossible.

And the link was opening wider and wider every instant.

The mastiff seemed to know it too, and increased his efforts in proportion.

Suddenly an idea flashed across our hero's mind.

"I've got it!" exclaimed Joe; "I've often done it on the stage, and I'll do it here."

In an instant our hero turned his jacket inside out, and put it on with the collar stuck up.

He then pulled his cap tightly down over his face.

Next he quietly put himself into the proper position by tucking his legs up in the air, and supporting himself on his hands.

And he was not an instant too soon.

He had hardly assumed this posture when snap went the chain.

With a tremendous growl, and widely-extended jaws, the fierce animal sprang with one bound to the spot where a moment before the new boy had stood.

But to the great surprise of Caractacus, the boy seemed to have disappeared, and his place to be supplied by some strange animal, the like to which he had never yet beheld.

A wonderful nondescript animal, with a black head and light pink paws, with two limbs sprouting up in the air, hopping about as composedly as if he had been only a poodle instead of the fierce creature he was.

Caractacus was evidently taken aback—floored.

He walked round the nondescript, and patted it gently with its paw as if to see what it was made of.

Joe instantly retorted by lowering one of his feet quickly, and giving Caractacus a sharp kick on his muzzle.

It was a rash act, perhaps, but it had a good effect.

It convinced the dog that the strange animal before him was dangerous, and not to be assaulted with impunity.

Accordingly, Caractacus dropped his howling and his tail at the same time, and squatted down on the ground, looking at the nondescript with a kind of doubtful interest.

The sudden cessation of the noise enabled Joe to hear the doleful wailings of the unfortunate Forks, who, having received his own share of Tingleback and our hero's into the bargain, was coming to give vent to his feelings in the coach-house.

He came into the yard hastily and slammed the door after him.

"I won't stand it no longer," he blubbered. "I'll let ole Swisher know who I am. I ain't a-goin' to have my back converted into a gridiron and my joints damaged in this here way. Wait till he goes to town next time, and if I don't tie a string acrost the lane and chuck him on his nozzle, my name ain't Tom."

"Forks!" shrieked a distant voice from without.

"Ain't a-comin'," shouted the youth back.

"You have got to finish peeling the 'taters and clean the winders," continued the voice.

"Shan't peel the 'taters nor the winders neither," bawled the indignant urchin; "cus the winders! cus the 'taters! cus every——"

His voice died away suddenly, as his eye encountered the picture of the mastiff seated on the ground, and the strange object hopping round him.

"Whatever is it?" he muttered to himself, his grief yielding at once to his curiosity.

He walked forward a few steps to examine the unusual figure, not for an instant guessing who it was.

"Well, that is a rum sort of article," he said, in a soliloquising tone. "What is it, Crac, eh, old boy?" he asked of the dog.

Crac, thus appealed to, uttered a low whine, as if to express his utter ignorance.

THE DOG WAS EVIDENTLY SURPRISED."

But Joe, who had recognised the voice of the page boy, said in a low tone, such as a clown under difficulties might have used—

"Hollo, Forks! Here we are!"

Forks almost fell on his back with amazement.

"Oh, my eye, Master Joe, is it really you?" he gasped.

"Yes, it's me," Joe replied, cheerfully, and sung—"Ri tol tiddy iddy — iddy iddy—ri tol tiddy iddy—ri tol day!"

The youth with the buttons forgot all his troubles instantly in his wonder and delight.

"Well, you lick me regular holler, you do!" he exclaimed. "What is your little game?"

"To save myself from this fierce brute here," our hero replied; "he broke his chain, and if I hadn't done this, and puzzled him, he'd have gobbled me up long ago."

"Oh, Lor'!" exclaimed the page, in a breathless tone of wonder. "Well, if you ain't a perfect miracle, there never was one."

"See how I can do a frog," said Joe, as, suiting the action to the word, he doubled his legs up behind his neck, and hopped across to the kennel, into which he sprang, and turning round, popped his head out, and exclaimed—

"Here we are."

Forks grinned from ear to ear, and applauded vehemently.

"I must learn to do the frog," he said. "Will you teach me?"

"Yes, of course," replied Joe.

"But you ain't a-going to keep on being a frog for long, are you?" asked the boy.

"No," returned our hero, "I've had almost enough of it; it's rather tiring to keep your legs stuck up in the air like this."

"I should say it was," assented Forks.

"If you'll get that dog out of the way, I should like to stand on my feet once more for a change," said Joe.

"All right, I'll soon manage him," replied the page. "Old Crac's a jolly good-natured old cove when he knows you."

"But when he doesn't?" interposed Joe.

"Oh, then he's a Tartar, and no bones about it," Forks admitted.

The small youth seized the chain, but before he could lead the animal away, a loud burst of shouting in the playground announced that school was over, and immediately after Doctor McSwisher emerged from the side door.

His search after his pupil having been unsuccessful, he began to think he must have run away.

"Forks," he cried, "harness the horse to the car——"

The principal stopped suddenly.

"What are you doing with that dog?" he demanded, sternly.

"Nothing," returned the youth, who had not forgotten the "Tingleback," sulkily.

"Why is he loose?"

"I dunno," muttered the page; "I suppose it's cos he ain't tight."

"Don't be impertinent, sirrah," growled the doctor, as he approached the dog, and picking up the chain, examined it.

"Someone has been tampering with this chain," he exclaimed, looking fiercely at Forks.

"I ain't been a-tramplin' on it," returned the youth.

The principal uttered an indistinct blessing on the head of the small domestic, and then approaching the kennel, stooped down to look at the piece of chain that was attached to it.

"This chain has been broken," he muttered to himself. "Did the dog break it or——"

At this juncture, he happened casually to glance inside the kennel, in which our hero in his frog-like posture was snugly concealed.

It is possible, had he remained quiet, the doctor would not have noticed him.

But Joe's pantomimical instincts suggested that this was far too good an opportunity for a little bit of fun to be neglected.

He accordingly made a playful bob with his head at the doctor's nose, exclaiming at the same time in a sharp dog-like tone—

"Bow, wow."

"Ugh! Oh!" shrieked the startled doctor, as he fell instantly on his back; "help, help!"

The playground door was instantly besieged by juvenile heads, looking eagerly over the top.

There was their preceptor, huddled up nose and knees together on the ground, shouting for assistance.

But our hero kept inside the kennel, and nothing else was to be seen.

"What's the matter?" asked the boys one of another, in a tone of wonderment.

Forks, in a state of intense delight that baffles all description, crept forward and motioned that he had some most important intelligence to communicate.

"Oh! crikey, such a jolly lark," he whispered; "let us in."

The door was hastily opened, and the small youth admitted into the playground.

In an instant he was surrounded by the scholars, who almost dragged him out of his jacket in their thirst for information.

"What is it?" they cried, eagerly.

"It's the new boy!" explained Forks.

"What's his name?"

"Joe Muggins!"

"Ho, ho! what a name!"

"Oh, but his father's a clown—a real clown," continued the youth, impressively.

"What, a clown that performs at theatres?" inquired the juvenile throng, on whom this piece of information took a great effect.

"Yes, of course," returned Forks, "he acts in pantomimes, and so does his son. He acts too! He does juvenile clown and cats, and he's called Pantomime Joe; and oh, my eye! can't he tumble neither! He's performing a frog now."

"A frog! Where?" inquired all the boys at once, with intense eagerness.

"Why, in the dog kennel," answered Forks, with an explosion of mirth; "he's turned his jacket inside out and pulled his cap over his face, and almost frightened old Swisher into fits."

"Oh, what a jolly lark!" cried the young listeners.

In an instant there was a rush back to the gate.

Half a score of eager faces were once more eagerly peering over the top.

"Murder!" shouted the doctor, who still lay on the ground afraid to move.

But the frog was invisible.

At this juncture, however, the side door opened, and out rushed Mrs. McSwisher and the domestics in a body.

"Good gracious, what's the matter now, Erasmus?" cried the red-nosed Arabella.

"Murder; the dev—I mean something dreadful there, in the dog kennel," groaned the principal, as he pointed distractedly with his finger, to the great delight of the youngsters on the top of the door, who were up to the joke.

"Dear me, what can it be?" exclaimed Arabella; "look, Betsy."

The housemaid, with evident trepidation, peeped in, and uttered a shriek.

"Oh, mum! please, mum; there's something black there."

"Oh, nonsense, Betsy," cried her mistress; "it's your fancy; it must be."

As she spoke, she advanced to the dog kennel and looked in herself.

"Boo!" cried our hero, bobbing out his head playfully, as he had done before.

Back flew Mrs. McSwisher, shrieking in her turn, as she stumbled over her prostrate husband, and almost crushed him flat in her fall.

"Ugh, my ribs!" yelled the doctor.

At the same moment our hero, following up his innocent little joke, emerged from his place of concealment, and hopped round the discomfited pair.

At the sight of the strange animal with the black head and pink paws, terror seized upon the housemaid and cook, who added their shrieks to those of their master and mistress.

Suddenly, however, Betsy burst into a laugh and exclaimed—

"Oh, missis, it's Master Puggins!"

"Muggins, if you please, Betsy!" cried Joe, as he released his legs, and pulling his cap from his face, sprang up once more in his natural position.

"Here we are," he cried, cheerfully; "don't be frightened; it's only me."

A loud shout of admiration from the spectators on the top of the door caused the doctor to look up.

In an instant the cause of the alarm was explained.

"So, sir, it's you, after all, is it?" he exclaimed, as he fixed his eyes in a wrathful but perplexed manner upon our hero.

"Yes, sir, it's me," replied Joe, complacently.

The principal did not strike him.

He only shouted—

"Get off that door, you boys."

In an instant the heads disappeared, and the principal, turning to Joe, said—

"This is most extraordinary conduct,

Master Bug—Muggins. Didn't I tell you I forbade tumbling?

"A very pretty example you're set-ting——"

A ringing shout from the playground rendered the rest of the doctor's speech inaudible.

"Hurrah! Three cheers for the new boy, three cheers for Pantomime Joe! Hurrah! hurrah! hurr-a-a-a-ah!" cried a score of youthful voices.

"Confound it!" muttered the principal; "this fellow will inoculate the whole school."

Scarcely knowing what he was doing, Doctor McSwisher seized our hero spitefully by the collar, and hurried him into the house.

Ten minutes after, the large bell in the playground rang, and the pupils were then summoned to attend in the schoolroom.

CHAPTER XV.

IN WHICH DR. MCSWISHER ADDRESSES HIS SCHOLARS, AND ISSUES AN EDICT AGAINST TUMBLING—OUR HERO PUTS JEMMY MUDDLE UP TO A PLAN OF DODGING THE DOCTOR.

DOCTOR MCSWISHER had spent the intervening ten minutes in reflecting what would be the best way to treat his new pupil.

At first he thought he would administer a severe dose of Tingleback.

But as he had already vented his spleen upon Forks, his passion had cooled down, and he altered his mind.

Instead of applying corrective measures, he resolved to address his scholars in presence of the new boy. He would warn them against all tumbling or acrobatic feats in the strongest terms.

If, after that, any were found disobedient, let them look out.

When our hero was marched into the schoolroom by the doctor, he found the whole fifty scholars seated in order at their desks.

The assistant masters, Mr. Fluster Fogem and Monsieur Jules Bonbon, were also seated at theirs.

Doctor McSwisher stalked along the room, leading Joe in one hand and grasping his cane in the other.

Having ascended to his desk, which was on a raised platform, around which the pupils stood to say their lessons, he gave it a sharp smack, according to custom, and cried—

"Order!"

There was a dead silence.

"Now, young gentlemen, listen to me," commenced the principal, glaring imperiously through his spectacles at the rows of faces before him; "allow me to introduce to you a new pupil, Master Joseph Bug—Muggins. Stand forward, Master Muggins."

Joe stepped briskly forward as directed, and quietly put out his tongue at the same time.

A suppressed smile gleamed on several youthful countenances in consequence.

The doctor observed the smile, and took occasion to allude to it.

"I perceive," he continued, "the name excites your risible emotions, but I can excuse that. Muggins *is* a peculiar name; the boy also who owns it is given to little peculiarities. Observe him well; look at him."

Fifty pairs of eyes were instantly fastened upon our hero.

The latter, not at all abashed, did a clown's squint, and pulled such an unmistakably comic mug at his schoolfellows that the whole of the fifty boys went off at once into an uncontrollable fit of laughter.

The doctor, little imagining what our hero, whose back was towards him, was up to, was not displeased at this.

He took the burst of merriment as a compliment to his own sarcastic remarks, and continued, in the same tone—

"The father of our new young friend is a professional——"

"A clown, isn't he, sir?" asked several voices, eagerly.

"Yes, young gentlemen," replied the

principal, emphatically, "a clown, who performs in stage pantomimes, and earns his living, I believe, by grimacing and tumbling."

"Here we are," murmured Joe, throwing his mouth into all sorts of shapes, to the intense delight of the spectators.

"Silence, sir!" exclaimed the doctor, rapping the desk with his cane, and continuing—

"I am sorry to say this new boy has acquired from his parent habits of a highly vicious and dangerous character. Tumbling and putting his limbs into all kinds of extraordinary postures seem to be his constant employment."

"Oh my! how funny!" remarked Joe, in the peculiar tone in which clowns speak.

"Will you be quiet, sir?" shouted the doctor.

The juvenile pantomimist closed his lips for an instant.

The principal went on—

"Tumbling and posturing, and such Merry Andrew tricks, may be all very well on the stage, but I beg distinctly to state that in an educational establishment they cannot of course be tolerated for an instant."

"Ri-tol-tiddy-iddy, ri-tol-day!" sang Joe.

Doctor McSwisher started up in his seat and banged away at the rail of his desk with appalling vehemence.

"Be quiet, sir!" he shouted. "If you dare to annoy me with any of your 'ri-tol-tiddy-iddies' here, I shall make you a severe public example at once."

Our hero relapsed once more into silence, and amused himself and his audience by screwing his mouth from side to side, and squinting awfully.

The pupils were of course convulsed, without any apparent cause.

"Order! order!" cried the doctor, sternly. "We have had sufficient laughing for the present; let me have no more of it. Strict attention, and serious countenances, if you please."

Bang, bang, went the cane.

At this ominous sound, of course every one tried to be serious.

But the attempt—thanks to our hero, who persisted in "pulling mugs" with all his might—was an utter failure.

In vain the boys bit their lips and pinched themselves, in order to control their emotions.

Involuntary explosions of mirth were continually taking place.

At length one particularly weak-minded youth, with a round, heavy, fat face, went off with such a sudden and loud explosion of laughter that the doctor's wrath could no longer be controlled.

"Come here, Muddle!" he cried, gazing sternly at the culprit through his spectacles.

Poor Jemmy Muddle was naturally a very dull boy.

In fact, he was the dunce of the school.

He tried to learn, but his memory was so deficient he could remember nothing.

It was needless to say he and Tingleback were daily acquaintances.

But he was a thoroughly good-natured boy, and though he was often the scapegoat of his schoolfellows, and the victim of their little practical jokes, he was a general favourite.

All the boys were sorry when they heard the doctor's summons.

They knew what was coming.

So did he.

But he was so used to the cane that he took it as a matter of course.

"Oh, Lor'," he muttered to his next companion, as he got out of his seat, "in for it again. I wonder how many cracks I shall get this time?"

"Now, sir," demanded the doctor, when the luckless James reached the desk, "what were you laughing at in that idiotic manner, eh?"

There was no reply.

Jemmy was no sneak, and would have been cut to pieces, rather than get another boy into trouble.

"Hold out your hand, sir!" exclaimed the principal.

But as the doctor was stepping from his desk, the instrument of torture caught in one of the rails, and was jerked out of the master's hand to some distance.

While he was waiting for it, our hero bent down over the side of the desk, where he was stationed, and whispered—

"Stuff your handkerchief up your sleeve, and when he hits, slip your hand forward, and let the cane fall upon your jacket. I'll 'take the slap' for you. He'll never know."

Poor Jemmy, slow as he was at comprehending most things, understood this piece of advice at once.

In an instant he had crammed his handkerchief up his sleeve.

But he had unfortunately two hands to be operated upon, and only one handkerchief to protect them.

What was to be done?

"Take mine," whispered Joe, as he hastily dropped his handkerchief over the side of the desk.

By the time the principal had recovered his cane, the culprit was ready for him.

"Now, sir," said the doctor, in a freezing tone.

Jemmy held out his hands alternately.

The cane descended.

Smack, smack, was heard.

"Again, sir," cried the remorseless doctor.

The operation was repeated.

Smack, smack, was heard as before.

"Now go and sit down again, and let that be a caution to you not to laugh again."

The doctor was satisfied that he had most cut the poor boy's hands in half.

The culprit was also satisfied.

Joe's plan had been perfectly successful.

The stuffed jacket sleeve had received the blows.

Joe's nimble hands had "done the slap," and the doctor's cane had not touched Jemmy Muddle's hands at all.

"Now, young gentlemen," cried the principal, "what I have finally to remark is this—and I beg you'll bear it in mind, all of you—I expressly forbid anything in the shape of posturing or tumbling. Anybody found standing on his head, or attempting to walk on his hands, or to stretch his legs beyond natural limits, will render himself liable to immediate and severe castigation."

Bang, bang, went the cane on the desk, as a means of enforcing his words.

He then turned to his assistant masters, Mr. Fluster Fogem and Monsieur Jules Bonbon.

"I expect, gentlemen," he said, "you will be vigilant, and report every acrobatic case that attracts your notice. Now, young gentlemen, you are at liberty."

With a sweeping flourish of his cane, he descended from his raised desk and stalked grandly out of the schoolroom.

No sooner had the master disappeared, then there was a general rush made towards our hero.

Joe found himself popular among his schoolmates at once, partly from the account Forks had given of his prowess, and partly from what they had seen him do with their own eyes.

Jemmy Muddle, who had been discreetly sitting with his head in his desk, where he was supposed to be shedding penitential tears, as soon as he heard the door close on the doctor, looked out from his retreat, and exclaimed, quite cheerfully—

"Cock-a-doodle-doo!"

He then joined his companions.

There was such a confusion of voices, and such a scuffling to get near the new boy and shake him by the hand, that at first nothing could be heard.

"Jolly chap!—brick!—trump!" were amongst the principal words that could be detected.

Gradually, however, the crowd dispersed, and Joe found himself surrounded by six of the leading boys.

Doctor McSwisher's was only a preparatory school, and the eldest pupil was not more than twelve.

These were Harry Merriman, one of the eldest scholars—Tom Tattler—Ben Brisk—Charley Dimond—Will Warner, and last, not least, Jemmy Muddle.

There was also another, but he stood aloof from the rest, looking rather suspiciously at our hero; neither speaking to, nor offering to shake hands with him.

This was Simon Sly, the second oldest boy in the academy, who was of a prying, treacherous disposition, and who had earned for himself the unenviable appellation of Sneaking Simon.

But no one seemed to take any notice of him.

"Come on, Joe," said Harry Merriman, after the first introductions were over, "let's come out in the playground, shall we? We don't want old Fogem or Frenchy to hear what we say."

"All right," replied Joe, readily. "Come on."

Our hero, accompanied by his six schoolfellows, who seemed on as good terms with him as if they had known him for months instead of a few minutes, went at once into the playground.

CHAPTER XVI.

IN WHICH SIX OF THE LEADING PUPILS FIND OUT THEY HAVE SEEN OUR HERO BEFORE.

"AND so your father really is a clown, is he?" asked Harry, as a leading question.

"Yes, that he is," returned Joe, warmly. "He's the best clown in London; the papers say he's about equal to Joey Grimaldi."

"But he doesn't go by the name of Muggins, does he?" inquired Tom Tattler, who did not remember any clown of that name.

"Oh, no," explained Joe, proudly. "He's called in the bills, the great Joe Muggerini."

"What!" cried the whole six boys, at once. "Was it he who was clown at Sadler's Wells this last Christmas?"

"Yes."

"Then I saw him."

"We all saw him," burst in a torrent from the lips of the young speakers.

"He can play clown, too," remarked Jemmy Muddle, admiringly, when the excitement had died away a little. "I never laughed so much in my life as when he pulled the bobby in half. And can't he make rum faces, too? He twists his mouth about just as you do."

"Yes, dad taught me to mug," said Joe.

"And are you going to be a clown, too?" asked Ben Brisk.

"I am a clown already," replied our hero, with conscious pride.

"What, have you ever acted in a pantomime, then?" inquired the boys in a breath.

"Of course I have. I acted first when I was only two months old," explained Joe.

"I should think you must have been good at tumbling then," remarked Jemmy Muddle, with a grin.

"I don't remember my first appearance," laughed Joe, in reply.

"Oh, never mind your first appearance; that was nothing," exclaimed Charley Dimond. "Babies can't act clown."

"They 'take the slap' though, sometimes," remarked Joe, wittily.

The boys laughed at the little joke, and Will Warner said, inquiringly, looking eagerly at young Joe—

"Where did you act last?"

"I played at Sadler's Wells, in 'Mother Goose,' this last Christmas," said young Joe, proudly.

"Lor'!" exclaimed the six boys, with another burst of astonishment. "What did you act?"

"The cat in the roof scene."

The lads crowded round our hero, as if they would have devoured him at this piece of information.

"Did you, though?"

"Was it really you?" was the question.

"Yes, it was, indeed," returned Joe. "But I only acted it on Boxing Night, when the scene fell down and I broke my arm."

"That was the night we were there!" cried his companions. "How well you did it."

"I thought it was a real cat, only it was rather too big," said Ben Brisk.

"It was quite as natural as a real one," protested Will Warner.

"Quite as natural!" echoed Jemmy Muddle, indignantly. "It beat all the real cats that ever I saw into fits."

"It was lucky you weren't killed when the scene fell," said Harry Merriman.

"I thought I was," returned our hero; "but I soon got over it, and I'm all right now."

"How jolly glad I am you're come," exclaimed Jemmy Muddle, with a burst of gratitude. "Didn't you save me from old Mac's Tinglehand?"

"How did you manage that?" inquired the lads, who had partially seen the "handkerchief trick," without quite understanding the process.

Jemmy explained the means by which he had escaped his punishment, to the immense delight of his young listeners.

"Hurrah!" they exclaimed, triumphantly. "No more Tinglehand after this; a couple of handkerchiefs apiece is all we want to dodge the doctor. Hurrah!"

"We can have some jolly larks now you're come," said Harry Merriman. "I say!" he suddenly exclaimed, "couldn't we get up a pantomime?"

"Certainly," returned Joe, with enthusiasm. "It's just what I should like better than anything else."

"But who's to write it?" asked Ben Brisk, doubtfully.

"I will," returned our hero, "and get it up as well. I've got a capital title— 'Harlequin Old Bogey; or, The Brave Boys of Whoppington.'"

"Bravo! bravo!"

"But we shall want masks."

"I can model."

"But how about the scenery?"

"I can paint it."

"You are a clever chap. But the dresses?"

"I've got them already."

"You have? Where?"

"In my play-box."

"Hurrah!" exclaimed the eager enthusiasts. "We'll have a pantomime. You must teach us to tumble."

"I'll teach you all," returned Joe, benevolently. "But the doctor!" he said, drawing his mouth aside with a clownish affectation of dismay. "What will he say?"

"Oh, bother the doctor!" cried the boys. "Who's he?"

In proof of the sincerity with which the question was asked, the six determined speakers were the next moment defiantly standing on their heads in a row against the playground palings.

Whilst our hero, not to be out of the fashion, stood on his head in front of them.

It happened that just at this moment Forks was in the dining-room laying the cloth for dinner.

The window of this room looked out upon the playground.

Consequently, as the youth in the buttons paused for a moment to refresh his faculties by a glance without, the six young gentlemen, with their heels where their heads ought to have been, caught his sight.

It had such an immediate and exhilarating effect upon Forks' spirits that he instantly rushed away into the playground, and stood on his head by the side of the young gentlemen.

This was doubtless a liberty on the part of the "generally useful" boy.

But he was so true and staunch to those of the scholars he liked, and did them so many good turns, that they looked upon him almost as one of themselves.

Consequently, when he joined the party and threw up his heels in the air like the rest, nobody was at all astonished at the proceeding.

But there was one of a different disposition altogether, who observed what was going on.

This was Master Simon Sly.

The latter, from his prying, sneakish disposition, was avoided generally by his schoolmates.

When the friendly seven accompanied the new boy into the playground, not one of them had asked Simon to join them.

Consequently he remained behind, rather sulkily, in the schoolroom.

Being, however, curious to know what the "united band" were doing, he looked through the window.

There he saw them acting in direct defiance to Doctor McSwisher's commands, and standing on their heads.

Instead, however, of laying aside his sulky moroseness and joining in the fun, he thought it would be a chance not to be lost of proving what a good boy he was.

So he quietly crept out of the schoolroom and went in search of the doctor.

The principal was, according to his usual custom, taking a constitutional walk in the garden, which ran along by the side of the playground, from which it was separated by the palings.

The little doctor was extremely well pleased with himself, and the energetic measures he had used to secure the obedience of his pupils.

"There is nothing like being decided! Nothing!" he chuckled to himself, as he walked briskly along the gravel walk, muffled in his great coat, with his hands in his pockets; "decision is necessary in a school, and——"

A burst of joyous laughter mingled with "hurrahs" rose from the other side of the palings.

The doctor little guessed the cause of the expressions of mirth, and he continued to himself—

"Boys like to be dealt with firmly; they are all the happier for it. A master who is not firm ought to——"

At this moment footsteps behind him attracted his notice.

Turning round, he saw hastily coming towards him, with a cautious expression on his features, Master Simon Sly.

No sooner did the principal catch sight of him, than he guessed at once he had something important to communicate.

So he said—

"Well, Simon, what is it?"

"If you please, sir," answered Simon, "some of the boys are tumbling."

The doctor's eyebrows flew up almost to the top of his forehead with surprise and indignation.

"Eh, what? Tum—tumbling?" he exclaimed.

"Yes, sir," returned the sneakish Simon. "I think the new boy's teaching them, and after what you said, I thought I ought to let you know."

"Right, Simon," ejaculated the principal; "quite right. I'll tumble 'em! Wait till I get my cane!"

Away rushed the doctor for the dreadful Tingleback.

Having found it, he paused for a moment to look out at the dining-room window.

There, to his horror, the truth of Simon Sly's report was fully confirmed.

There were the seven youths on their heads, and our hero, Joe, evidently taking the lead in the rebellious act.

But this was not all—Forks, the daring Forks, was also there, standing on his head with the rest, and no cloth spread r dinner.

Not a single knife laid.

The doctor turned pale with rage, and shed to the door.

"Arabella!" he shouted. "Come ere directly, Arabella!"

"Good gracious me! Whatever is the matter?" exclaimed the lady, hurrying in in a flutter of alarm. "I declare this is a perfect day of excitement! What is it now?"

"Ha, ha!" laughed the doctor, in a spiteful and rather hysterical tone; "tomfoolery and hanky panky's the matter, ma'am. There's only seven of 'em at it at this moment!"

"At what, Erasmus?" demanded the lady, considerably scared at her spouse's excited manner.

"Tumbling, Arabella!" shouted the doctor, fiercely. "Look at that harrowing sight!"

He pointed to the window.

Mrs. McSwisher looked.

"Good gracious! So they are!" she exclaimed. "And Forks, too, I declare!"

"The atrocious young miscreant!" cried the principal. "I see how it will be; this abominable habit will spread like a contagion. We shall all catch it, I suppose, before long, Arabella; you and I—ha, ha!—shall be found standing on our heads!"

The lady uttered a slight ejaculatory shriek at this fearful supposition.

But the doctor did not hear it.

He had rushed from the dining-room, cane in hand.

"I'll teach them to set my authority at defiance," he grunted, as he hurried along; "and as for that rascally Forks, I'll break every bone in his atrocious body!"

In the meantime, the seven—or rather, we may say, including the boy-of-all-work, the eight—stood on their heads and clapped their heels together triumphantly.

Joe now stood before them, giving directions.

"Number one, keep your body up!" he cried.

"Number two, don't stretch your hands out so far!"

"Number three, you're all right!"

"Am I all right, Master Puggins?" shouted Forks, who was number seven and who was playing a lively tune wit the soles of his boots; "this'll do, won' it?"

Whack, whack, whack! Swish, swish, and loud howls from the youth in the buttons announced the fact that Doctor McSwisher and Tingleback had reached the spot.

Forks lost no time in dropping on to his feet, and darting like lightning across the playground, yelling and rubbing his limbs, to the schoolroom door, by means of which he disappeared.

The seven amateur posturers also quickly assumed their proper positions, and looked at Joe inquiringly, as much as to say—

"Here's a pretty go! What's to be done now?"

Joe whispered quietly—

"Don't be frightened; if he tries Tinglehand, do the handkerchief dodge."

The doctor regarded the seven culprits sternly for a moment. Then he said—

"Did I not, in the strongest and most emphatic terms, forbid everything in the shape of tumbling?"

"If you please, sir, it is not called tumbling to stand on one's head," explained Joe, briefly.

"I call it so," returned the principal, eyeing our hero like an ogre through his spectacles, "and I shall punish you all for your disobedience. Follow me!"

The doctor, flourishing his cane, led the way to the schoolroom.

"I'm sure to catch it first," said our hero to Harry Merriman, as they went along. "Lend me your handkerchief, and take the slap for me, will you?—and I'll do the same for you."

The handkerchief was instantly given, and Harry inquired—

"How am I to take the slap?"

"Like this," returned Joe, as he dropped his hands and clapped them together. "That's the way the clowns do it in the pantomimes. You watch me and do as I do. Tell the rest to do the same. We must lend one another our handkerchiefs."

Harry briefly communicated this to his companions.

As they reached the schoolroom door, Simon Sly came sneaking from it.

"Oh! won't you catch it!" he exclaimed, with an ominous grin at the young culprits.

"Get out, you sneak," said Harry Merriman. "I suppose, if the truth was known, you told the doctor. If we find you out, you shall pay for it."

On entering the schoolroom, they found the assistant master, Mr. Fluster Fogem.

"How is it, sir, you are not more vigilant?" demanded the principal, sternly, of the usher.

Mr. Fogem, who had Latin and Greek at his fingers' ends, and who had been quite lost in one of his favourite classic authors, looked up from his book in a somewhat bewildered manner.

"I was not aware the young gentlemen were misconducting themselves, sir," he replied.

"They have been inverting the laws of nature, Mr. Fogem, by standing on their heads!" explained the pedagogue.

Mr. Fogem looked rather foggy himself, and Doctor McSwisher, turning to our hero, straightened his cane, and said—

"Now, sir, hold out your hand."

Joe, in the most cheerful manner possible, extended his hand four times successively.

Four times did the formidable Tingleback go swishing through the air.

With what result, the reader will readily imagine.

Joe, having received his punishment, slipped his handkerchief into Harry Merriman's hand, and then threw himself on the ground, where he affected to writhe in agonies almost unendurable.

Harry was the next to suffer, after which he too fell prostrate and writhing on the floor, by the side of his companion.

In like manner did the remaining five, Joe quietly "taking the slap" for all.

It was with intense satisfaction the doctor beheld the seven victims, all groaning together on the ground.

Never had Tingleback been so effectual.

As for poor Jemmy Muddle, so fearful was the punishment he appeared to have received, that he howled lamentably, and declared he should have a "locked jaw."

"Let this be a warning," exclaimed the principal, emphatically, as he stalked away; "no more tumbling."

The door was no sooner closed than the six sufferers sprang up.

Joe turned three somersaults in succession, and walked on his hands across the room.

The rest, not being able to do anything else in the tumbling way, boldly repeated their former feat of standing on their heads.

Having thus proved their independence, they stood on their feet again, and crowding round our hero, Joe, whom they looked up to by common consent as their leader, shook him warmly by his hands.

At the same moment Forks, with very red eyes, came in with the bowl in which the pupils washed their hands before dinner.

"Did you catch it?" asked Harry of the small boy.

"Didn't I neither?" whispered the latter in reply. "I dodged the doctor, but Mother Swisher dropped on to me with the rolling pin. She cotched me on the funny bone. Oh! my eye, it was awful!"

The boys sympathised with the youthful sufferer.

"Never mind, Forks," whispered Joe in his ear. "We are going to get up a pantomime, and you shall act a part in it."

"What, a real pantomime?" returned Forks, in an ecstasy, "and me to act in it? Oh, crikey! what a lark."

From that moment, the anguish caused by the rolling pin was forgotten.

His funny bone ceased to trouble him.

Forks was himself again.

CHAPTER XVII.

DINNER AT TICKLE TOBY HALL—OUR HERO INDULGES IN A LITTLE COMIC BUSINESS, WHICH NEARLY LEADS TO SERIOUS CONSEQUENCES.

SHORTLY after the great bell rang for dinner.

Fifty hungry boys came in, in single rank and file, and took their seats.

Our hero, not having had any place assigned to him, remained standing.

The doctor, observing this, said—

"Why don't you sit down, Muggins?"

"Because I haven't been told where to sit, sir," replied Joe.

The reply was satisfactory to the doctor.

It pleased him to see the new pupil obediently awaiting his orders, instead of choosing a seat for himself.

"You will sit between Merriman and Tattler," said the principal, after a moment's reflection, "and let me hope that the castigation you have received will suggest to you the propriety of behaving yourself circumspectly. I am very particular about behaviour at meals. You can now take your seat."

Our active hero accomplished this feat without causing the least confusion.

He simply placed his hands on the shoulders of his friends, Tattler and Merriman, and hoisting himself up with a nimble jerk, dropped neatly into his place.

Mrs. McSwisher, who was serving the pudding, dropped her knife and fork in dismay.

She thought the new boy was going to turn a somersault over the table.

Finding, however, this was not the case, she picked up her carving utensils, and went on serving.

Joe, being seated, made a clown's face for the especial benefit of his friends, and sat quietly on his seat for a moment or two.

Presently Forks brought him a slice of something in a plate, the like of which Joe did not remember ever to have seen before.

The something was covered with some glutinous substance of a dark brown colour.

"Here you are, Master Joe," said Forks, as he set down the plate before him.

"What's this?" asked our hero, rather suspiciously, in a low tone.

"Pudden," replied Forks, in a whisper, with a suppressed twinkle in his round eyes.

"And what's that brown stuff?" Joe next inquired.

"Treacle," exclaimed the small youth, mysteriously; "it's supposed to be condoosive to health."

Joe said no more, but began to eat.

Cautiously at first.

But the pudding was by no means to be despised, and our hero liked it very well indeed, and began to eat with more confidence.

It was almost as good as a pantomime to see him.

"NUMBER ONE KEEP YOUR BODY UP," SAID JOE.

He cut his pudding into such extraordinary shapes, and pulled such wonderful mugs every time he put a piece into his mouth, that "the seven" had the greatest difficulty to avoid going off in bursts of laughter.

"Now I'm going to draw old Cocky Wax," said Joe, in a whisper, to Harry Merriman.

In an instant a countenance, supposed to be that of old Cocky Wax, but which bore an astonishing resemblance to the doctor, was cleverly delineated in treacle upon our hero's plate.

He held it up cautiously, that his companions might see it.

The effect was great.

To poor Jemmy Muddle it had almost proved fatal, for a lump of pudding which he was in the act of swallowing stuck in his throat, and produced alarming symptoms.

"Good gracious, Muddle, what are you making those hideous grimaces for?" demanded Mrs. McSwisher, in a vixenish tone.

The hopeless subject of this inquiry returned no answer.

His eyes were starting out of his head, and he was growing black in the face.

"Good Heaven!" shouted the doctor, "he's choking. Slap him gently on the back."

Half a dozen fists from his alarmed companions on their schoolfellow's back (and anything but gently) saved Jemmy's life and caused him to disgorge his lump of pudding.

"Let that be a lesson to you, Muddle, not to take such large mouthfuls," said the doctor, sternly, after the excitement had somewhat subsided; "voracity is detestable, and makes boys dull and stupid."

The dull boy affected to look penitent, and for a few moments all was quiet.

Pudding being concluded, meat followed.

Joe, having finished his repast, made a small pantomime figure with his handkerchief, which he fastened upon the forefinger of his right hand.

There was a large knot for the doll's head.

And two smaller knots for its hands.

He then caused this mimic sprite to perform such mirth-moving antics that in a very few moments the entire six of Joe's friends were cramming their handkerchiefs into their mouths to avoid an explosion, which would have drawn down upon them the doctor's wrath, if not some more Tingleback.

Forks caught sight of the little figure, and it required almost superhuman efforts on the part of the youth with the buttons to maintain the necessary gravity his duties demanded.

"I say, draw it mild, there's a good cove!" he murmured, pleadingly, to Joe as he passed; "I know I shall burst in a minute if you don't."

"Oh, rooey, tooey too!" murmured Joe in return, in quite a Punch-like tone.

This was too much for the small youth with the buttons, who went off at once, and dropped the plate he carried.

At the same moment the "united seven" also went off, and became convulsed and shaking like so many jellies.

Jemmy Muddle seemed more moved than any of the others.

It happened too, unfortunately, that he sat in the most convenient position to catch the doctor's eye.

The principal grew fierce and crimson as the sounds of subdued mirth caught his ear.

He stopped carving and looked round the room sternly.

His spouse also looked round with a frown upon her features.

It seemed to the doctor that his pupils were possessed by the spirit of disorder.

"Whatever is the matter?" he exclaimed, in a tone of profound indignation. "I demand to know the cause of this outrageous conduct?"

This, instead of appalling the delinquents, only aroused their cachinnatory tendencies.

Jemmy Muddle, the luckless Jemmy, in his efforts to restrain himself, made a most unearthly noise in his nose.

The doctor pounced upon him in an instant.

"You're certainly not choking this time, Muddle," he exclaimed, looking as black as thunder.

The unfortunate James almost wished he had been.

"Stand out, sir," exclaimed the principal; "I find I must teach you another lesson."

"He richly deserves it, I'm sure," joined in his amiable partner.

"No, he doesn't, ma'am," exclaimed Joe Muggins, briskly, looking round; "it was my fault."

The doctor and his wife turned their eyes in a perplexed and irritable manner upon our hero.

"What do you mean, sir, by your fault?" demanded the former. "Do you deny, or does Muddle mean to deny, that he made a most unnatural snorting just now?"

"No, sir," returned Joe, "he wasn't snorting; he was laughing, but I made him laugh."

"What were you doing to make him laugh?" the doctor asked, fiercely.

Joe held up his pocket handkerchief, with the three knots still in it, and replied—

"I found my handkerchief in my pocket, tied up in this way, and I put my finger so, and my other finger so, and waggled it like this."

As our hero spoke, he inserted his fingers, as he had previously done, into the knots, and put the figure once more through its performance.

"Oh, rooey tooey too, rooey too!" exclaimed Joe, with all the professional coolness of a Punch and Judy showman.

"That was all I did," said Joe, innocently, as he explained; "isn't it funny?"

The entire fifty of Dr. McSwisher's pupils, who had witnessed our hero's performance with the knotted handkerchief, gave their unanimous assent, bursting into a simultaneous laugh.

The doctor and his wife, who did not see the joke at all, stood glaring along the tables at the rows of grinning juveniles, scarcely knowing what to do.

It was impossible to thrash the whole fifty.

It was impossible to punish Jemmy Muddle for snorting like a pig, after the new boy's candid explanation.

So it ended in the doctor's withdrawing from his determination.

"I did intend," he said, grandly, "to have punished James Muddle for his unseemly conduct. However, as Master Bug—Pug—Muggins has given a mitigating reason for the same, I shall overlook it this time. But I take occasion to caution every boy against tying knots in his handkerchief in future. If I find any such knots, rest assured I shall *not* pass it over."

Dinner being over, Mrs. McSwisher said grace in a very snuffling tone, and the young gentlemen rose and left the dining room.

The seven immediately united together like a swarm of bees.

Joe seemed to have become a great object of admiration, in proportion to the peril in which his facetious pranks had placed them.

It happened to be Wednesday, and consequently half holiday.

There was, therefore, plenty of opportunity to arrange plans for the future.

"I hope you'll sleep in our dormitory, Joe," said Harry Merriman.

"There's a spare bed in it," said Tom Tattler.

"It's the jolliest room out of the lot for larks," suggested Ben Brisk, "and the window looks into the yard."

"Where the dog is?" interposed Joe, with a grin.

"Yes," answered Charley Dimond, "but old Crac's a good-natured animal enough when you know him."

"But the best of being in the room that looks into the yard," explained Will Warner, "is that we can haul up anything that Forks gets for us by a string. Don't you see?"

"Oh, the heaps of tarts and the bottles of pop we have sometimes!" exclaimed Jemmy Muddle, smacking his lips. "It would do your heart good."

"I hope I shall be in your room, then," returned our hero, earnestly. "We shall be able to rehearse the pantomime there without anyone being the wiser."

"Mind, not a word to that sneak, Simon Sly," cautioned Harry Merriman. "I believe it was he told the doctor about our tumbling."

"I shan't say a word," returned Joe.

"If he gets hold of it, good bye to our pantomime," said Tom Tattler.

After a few more remarks, our hero suddenly remembered that his play box must have arrived, and thought it would be as well to look after it.

"There's a plum cake in it as big as the top of a tub," said Joe, "fit for a pantomime."

The mouths of the seven began to water instantly.

Jemmy Muddle's especially.

"Go and get it, Joe," he said, eagerly. "Go at once, or perhaps Mother Swisher will find her way to the inside first."

"Oh, there are other things beside cake," said Joe, proudly.

"What things?"

"Lots of jam—three pots of raspberry and one of marmalade; besides hard-bake, oranges, apples, and nuts, and all the pantomime dresses."

The excitement increased.

"I say, Joe, I wouldn't stop another minute if I were you," counselled Harry Merriman.

"No, come on," exclaimed Jemmy Muddle, whose alimentary organs were intensely affected at the prospect of the luxuries. "I'll help you carry the box."

"And eat what's inside after, won't you, old fellow?" laughed Joe.

"I believe you," returned the rest.

The next moment our hero, accompanied by his friend Jemmy, was on his way to the parlour door to claim his property.

CHAPTER XVIII.

HOW OUR HERO APPLIES FOR HIS PLAY BOX, AND HOW HE DON'T GET IT—WHAT HE SAID AND DID, AND WHAT FORKS HEARD AND SAW.

JOE, having reached the portal, tapped boldly.

"Come in," cried the sharp voice of Mrs. McSwisher from within.

Our hero entered.

A savoury odour of dinner and port wine pervaded the atmosphere.

The doctor and his wife were in the midst of their repast.

The former, who, with his white napkin tucked under his chin, was paying great attention to a plate of soup when Joe entered, simply looked up for an instant at him through his specs, and continued his soup as before.

"What is it, Muffins?" inquired Mrs. McSwisher.

"If you please, ma'am," said our hero, without taking any notice of the mispronunciation of his name, "I should like to have my play box."

"Eh? What's that? What does he want?" asked the doctor, with his mouth full.

"His play box," replied his wife, indignantly; "the idea of making such an application at this unseasonable moment —in the midst of our dinner, too, above all other times."

"Umph!" grunted the principal, "tell him to go away."

"You can't have it now," returned Mrs. McSwisher. "Come again in an hour."

There being no resource but to wait, Joe retired, and at the end of the stipulated time, again presented himself at the parlour door, at which he tapped.

No answer being returned, he opened the door softly and looked in.

The dinner had been cleared away.

The doctor and his wife were comfortably nodding in their respective arm-chairs, with their glasses of wine beside them on the table.

They were taking their customary forty winks after dinner to assist digestion.

"I think they're asleep," said Joe, putting his head out at the door and speaking to his friend Jemmy, who was waiting in the passage.

"Wake 'em," counselled Jemmy, briefly but decidedly.

"How?" thought Joe, as he softly entered the parlour.

He reflected a moment.

Then an idea struck him.

The heads of the slumberers were thrown back, and their noses were conveniently raised in the air.

Both were snoring melodiously.

On the mantel-piece were several pieces of paper, screwed up ready for lighting the gas or a candle.

"I'll soon wake 'em," said our hero to himself, as he seized upon two of the papers.

Cautiously creeping under the table till he was between the doctor and his wife, he raised his hands, and taking a good aim, tickled both their noses at the same time with the ends of the twisted papers he held.

The effect was instantaneous.

A loud sneezing dispelled the dreams of the sleepers.

By the time the scholastic pair opened their eyes, Joe had crept back under the table, and was standing placidly on the other side.

"Bless my soul, there's that boy again!" grunted the doctor, between his sneezes, as his eyes fell upon our hero.

Mr. McSwisher, after rubbing his eyes, asked—

"What does that boy Puggins want here?"

"I want my play box, if you please," Joe explained. "You told me to come again in an hour."

"Oh, bother the play box!" grumbled Mrs. McSwisher, annoyed at being disturbed in her nap, and rubbing her nose vehemently; "you're in a great hurry, I think."

"I want to get something out of it, ma'am," replied our hero. "You needn't trouble yourself to get it. I can carry it if you tell me where it is. Master Muddle will help me."

This was an unfortunate remark of Joe's, and caused the doctor to say, irritably—

"This is some of that Muddle's doing; he is a boy addicted to gluttony, and has urged our new pupil to make this untimely application."

The voracious individual alluded to heard these remarks as he stood outside, and prepared to bolt.

But Joe assured the doctor that his application for his box was entirely his own idea.

"I thought, as my playthings were in it, I could have it like the rest of the boys," he said.

"Oh, well, you can have your box," snuffled Arabella, tartly; "but I invariably make a point of examining the contents of such receptacles before giving them up. The injudicious fondness of parents leads them, too often, to cram them with articles highly injurious to youthful stomachs, and I, therefore, use my discretion as to what my pupils may eat, and what they may not eat."

Jemmy Muddle groaned inwardly as he heard the words of the prudent lady.

All his fond visions of raspberry jam and marmalade—to say nothing of the nuts, oranges, apples, and hardbake—melted away into thin air.

"She wants to eat them herself, the greedy red-nosed pig," he muttered, despairingly.

Joe was about to explain that there was nothing in his box that would hurt anyone, but Mrs. McSwisher checked him abruptly.

"I am the best judge of that," she said, in a decided tone, as she rose and rang the bell.

Betsy the housemaid responded.

"Bring Master Pug—Muggins's play box here, Betsy," said her mistress.

"Yes, mum," replied the maid.

There was a lapse of a few minutes, and presently the scuffling of feet announced the approach of the article in question.

The housemaid, assisted by the small youth in the buttons, appeared lugging the play box along.

"It's jolly heavy," murmured Forks, as he and his fellow-servant deposited their burden in the parlour. "I wish you may get what's inside, Master Joe," he whispered; "but I has my doubts."

The box was corded and locked, and the key attached to the handle.

"You can remove the rope, Betsy," said Mrs. McSwisher, as with a pair of scissors she at once detached the key with her own hands, and seized upon it.

Joe's eyes followed it wistfully.

The cord was speedily untied.

The key was placed in the lock and turned.

The lid was raised.

"Good gracious!" exclaimed Arabella, as her eyes fastened upon the contents.

Nothing but oranges met her gaze.

The kind-hearted Sarah Muggins had not stinted her son and heir.

"I declare," exclaimed Mrs. McSwisher, "here are enough oranges to stock a fruiterer's shop."

"Oh, but there are lots of other things underneath," explained Joe.

"Unpack the oranges, Betsy," ordered the scholastic matron, sternly.

Six dozen ripe, juicy specimens of this interesting fruit glistened on the table.

"Don't they smell lovely?" murmured Jemmy Muddle to Forks, as they watched the proceedings through the crevice of the partly open door.

"Delicious!" admitted Forks; "but I thinks as a sniff's all you'll get."

The oranges being removed, there appeared an equal number of apples.

These being also taken out of the box, two large bags of nuts, three pots of jam, and a brown paper packet containing hardbake, next revealed themselves.

"Out with them," exclaimed the doctor, gruffly.

These articles being disinterred, the next object that dawned upon the sight of the beholders was the plum cake, which Sarah Muggins had flattered herself was rather a model of what a cake ought to be.

"Mercy on us!" ejaculated the doctor and his wife, "what a size!"

"Ain't it a fine un?" murmured Jemmy Muddle, in a kind of ecstasy, through the crevice of the door, as the cake was lifted out.

"Reg'lar stunning!" assented Forks.

"It's almost fit for a pantomime, isn't it?" Joe exclaimed, in a tone of enthusiasm.

"Fit for a pantomime!" returned the disgusted doctor. "Hang me if I know what it's fit for. I never saw anything like it in the shape of a cake, in all my life."

"I'm not going to eat it all myself," said Joe, modestly.

"Eat it all yourself!" echoed the principal. "I should think not."

"I'll take care of that," chuckled his spouse, in an undertone to herself.

"At a moderate computation," continued the master, "I should say there was enough trash in that box to make the whole school ill."

These remarks seemed rather ominous to Joe.

So they did to his two friends Jemmy Muddle and the small but "actively industrious" youth in the buttons.

"You see if old Swisher don't stick to the lot," whispered the latter.

An inward groan and a muttered execration from the former expressed the state of his feelings.

"Anything else?" inquired the principal at length, somewhat ironically, as he glanced into the box.

"Nothing else to eat," answered Joe.

"What's that at the bottom?" demanded the doctor, suspiciously, as his eye fell upon sundry parti-coloured articles of wearing apparel.

"Oh, they're the pantomime dresses," exclaimed our hero, enthusiastically.

"Pantomime dresses!" repeated the scholastic pair, aghast with horror. "Whatever induced you to bring such things here?"

"I thought perhaps I might want them," Joe replied; "dad said they would be useful if we got up a pantomime at holiday times."

"I allow no such tomfoolery here, sir," sternly remarked the irate doctor, as he made a snatch at the articles in question.

They were beautifully made, and exact copies of the usual pantomime costumes on a small scale.

"That's the clown's dress," exclaimed Joe, as he pointed to the white body and trunks,* ornamented with bright scarlet and blue spots and stripes; "I wear that."

"The idea!" ejaculated the matron.

"That's the old un's," continued Joe, as he indicated the pantaloon's garments; "and this is for harlequin."

As he spoke, our hero caught up the elastic skinlike shape, glittering with spangles, and held it aloft.

"Oh, my! how beautiful!" ejaculated Betsy the housemaid.

Joe felt quite grateful to the girl for her expression of admiration.

"Pshaw!" growled the doctor, morosely, "this is not a theatre, but a temple of education; we want no clowns' dresses here, nor harlequins' either. Take away this rubbish," he cried; "in my opinion, the best thing would be to put it on the fire."

"Dad would be sure to make you pay for it if you did," said Joe, boldly. "Rubbish as it is, it cost more than ten pounds, and there are two sprites' dresses besides, and the wigs."

"I shall take charge of them, Master Muggins," said Mrs. McSwisher, in a decided tone; "and when you go home for the holidays, you can take them with you."

---

* The short, baggy breeches worn by clowns.

Our hero wished sincerely in his heart that that joyous period had arrived.

But it was then far distant, so he put as good a face upon the matter as possible, and said—

"I suppose, if I can't have the dresses, I may take the box and the other things?"

"Decidedly not," returned the scholastic lady, knitting her brows sternly.

Our hero did not at all understand this refusal, and he replied—

"Why not? Mother bought them for me, and they're mine."

"I am your mother, sir, while you are here," exclaimed the matron, grandly.

"No, you're not," muttered Joe, bluntly. "I wouldn't have such a mother."

"But I tell you I am, sir," insisted the lady, "and I shall see that you do not make yourself ill by gorging yourself with these deleterious combinations. I shall distribute them as I consider most prudent."

"But I want to share them with my schoolfellows," argued Joe, staunchly.

"You will obey Mrs. McSwisher's orders, Master Bug—Muggins," thundered the doctor, in an awful tone, that curdled the blood of the listeners outside, and caused them to beat a hasty retreat.

"When you wish for a piece of cake, or a portion of jam, come and ask me," said the red-nosed matron, "and if I think proper, you will have it. You can take an apple or an orange now, to begin with, if you like."

"No, I don't like," returned Joe, indignantly; "you've no right to keep the things from me at all, and I shall write to dad and tell him——"

"You'll do what, sir?" shouted the doctor, turning purple with rage.

"Write to dad," repeated our young hero, at the top of his voice, "and you'll soon hear what he says."

In a paroxysm of fury, the principal made a rush towards Joe.

The latter dived under the table, like lightning.

The doctor pitched head foremost into the box.

Before he could recover himself, the young pantomimist had darted out, and rejoined his friends in the playground.

"The young imp!" groaned the scholastic gentleman, as the housemaid and his wife assisted him on to his feet. "I wouldn't receive any more boys like him for a hundred guineas a year."

"Betsy," said Mrs. McSwisher, as she placed the pantomime dresses and wigs in the hands of the domestic, "lock these things in the clothes press; I will replace the other articles myself."

The housemaid departed, full of admiration at the boldness of the new boy, and encountered the youth in buttons, who was lingering outside for any information he might be able to pick up.

"What have you got there, Bet?" he asked.

"Pantomime dresses and wigs," answered the girl. "Such beauties! they belong to Master Duggins."

"Have you really, though?" exclaimed Forks, in a tone of intense interest. "Let's look at 'em."

"Come upstairs, then," said Betsy, hastily, "because I've got to put them away in the clothes press."

"What, won't the old uns let him have 'em?"

"No."

Forks and the housemaid hurried upstairs, and the former was permitted to feast his eyes on the spotted and spangled wonders Betsy held in her hands.

"They are stunnin'," exclaimed the small youth.

Popping on the wig, he then made a clown's face, in imitation of Joe, and cried "Here we are!" to Betsy's great amusement.

Having thus gratified his curiosity, Forks retraced his steps downstairs.

The parlour door was still ajar, and with that natural thirst for information that characterized him, he paused a moment to hear what was going on inside.

"There's a awful smell of cake and oranges," he thought; "I wonder whether the old one is having a taste."

Approaching the door on tiptoe, he listened.

"The oranges are delicious," said Mrs. McSwisher, who was sucking at one like a leech.

"The cake is by no means despicable," chuckled the doctor, in a mumbling tone, as though his mouth was full; "in fact, it's rather nice."

Forks, unable to resist, peeped in.

There, sure enough, the principal and his wife were regaling themselves to their hearts' content upon the good things the new boy had brought with him.

The indignation of the youth in the buttons was stirred to its depth.

"Well, if that ain't a bit of diabolical villany, nothink ain't," he muttered.

"Will you try a little marmalade, love, on a slice of cake?" asked the affectionate wife.

"Well—a—I think I will; just a little, Arabella," replied the doctor, smacking his lips.

The lady cut two ample slices of cake, and overspread them thickly with the luscious compound.

"Oh! you pair of greedy guts!" murmured Forks to himself.

"That which is highly injurious to youthful stomachs," said Mrs. McSwisher,

with a grin, "we of mature age may indulge in with impunity, and even with advantage."

"Precisely, Arabella," returned the doctor, winking his eye knowingly and seizing upon his piece of cake.

But ere he could get it to his lips, the youthful Forks exclaimed through the crack of the door, in an awfully hollow tone—

"I'm a-lookin' at you—oh!"

At this awful announcement the principal and his wife dropped their jam in dire confusion, and fell back in their chairs as if petrified.

Long before they could collect themselves sufficiently to inquire into the cause of the mysterious sounds, the youth with the buttons was out of sight.

CHAPTER XIX.

IN WHICH A PLOT IS FORMED FOR THE RECOVERY OF OUR HERO'S PROPERTY—A TRAITOR IS SUSPECTED AND PUNISHED—HOW SIMON SLY WAS MADE TO PAY HIS BILL AND A LITTLE OVER.

FOR some time after our hero's return to the playground, with the account of his unsuccessful mission, the countenances of Joe and his companions were gloomy and downcast.

It seemed hard to be done out of their expected feast, and Old Sally had not yet appeared with her tarts to cheer them.

Whilst they were meditating as to whether it would be advisable to get up a rebellion, storm the parlour, and carry off the play box and its contents by force of numbers, the head of the actively industrious youth appeared above the door which was in a snug corner of the playground.

"Hi! here, Master Joe," he whispered, hastily; "I wants you half a minute."

Joe turned to the gate; Forks unlocked it, and admitted him to the other side.

"What do you think?" asked the boy, breathlessly.

"What?" asked our hero, in return.

"Why, old Swisher and his wife are a-gobblin' up your cake and jam like old boots; I see 'em at it jest now."

"Are they, though?" exclaimed Joe,

his face flushing indignantly. "That's too bad."

"I should say it was, by long chalks," returned the small boy. "No wonder they wouldn't let you have it, when they wanted it themselves."

"I will have it, though," exclaimed Joe, determinedly; "you see if I don't."

"I would if I was you," said Forks, encouragingly, "only don't say as I told you hanythink."

"Certainly not," our hero assured him. "Do you know where they will put the box?" he asked.

"In the parlour cupboard, certain," Forks said.

"All right," answered Joe.

As soon as the latter returned to the playground, the six crowded round to hear the intelligence their companion had just received.

Great was the indignation that burnt in their youthful bosoms as they listened.

Jemmy Muddle's wrath was of far too fierce and boiling a quality to admit of description.

"Let's go all at once and smother the

greedy old alligators with raspberry jam," he cried, chivalrously.

"Come on," exclaimed Joe, who was ready for anything. "I'll lead you."

But this daring suggestion, much as it was applauded, was overruled by Harry Merriman.

"No, no; we can't do it that way," he said. "I've got a better idea than that. Come here, and I'll tell you what it is."

The seven retreated to a corner of the playground, and Harry related his plan.

"We'll wait till night, and when all's quiet, we'll go down quietly and walk the whole lot upstairs into our room. I'll warrant there won't be much left in the morning."

This proposal was received with much applause.

But presently Tom Tattler said—

"Suppose they lock the parlour door?"

"They never do," answered Harry.

"They might now, and the cupboard as well, knowing what there is in it," suggested Ben Brisk.

"Break 'em open," exclaimed Jemmy Muddle, desperately. "Burglary and nuts, smashed locks and hardbake for ever."

"I'll break 'em open, and if I can't do that, I'll knock in the panels but I'll have my things," exclaimed our hero, determinedly.

"We'll stick to you, Joe," protested his six friends; "fight to the last, and no quarter."

"Very well, then, that's settled," said our hero, shaking hands with them all round; "it shall be done to-night."

"To-night!" echoed the conspirators.

At this moment Will Warner pulled Harry Merriman by the sleeve, and pointed.

The cringing form of Simon Sly was seen creeping away from the spot where they were standing.

"Did he hear anything?" said Harry, apprehensively. No one knew.

They had all been so interested upon their plans, and so excited, no one had been conscious of his presence, if even he had been there.

"If he has got the slightest idea of our intentions, he's safe to blab," Harry remarked.

"Let's ask him," suggested Joe; "we shall be sure to know by his manner whether he's guilty or not."

"Very well, so we will," returned Harry, who forthwith called, "Heigh! Simon, here!"

Simon shrugged his shoulders, and pricked up his long ears slightly, but kept on his way, pretending not to know he was being called.

"There are none so deaf as those that won't hear," said Tom Tattler, with a significant shrug.

"I'll wake him up," exclaimed Jemmy Muddle, and then he shouted, "Now then, Sneaking Simon, don't you know your name?"

The sneak stopped, and turning round, put on an expression as though snarling at them.

"You needn't call names, Master Muddle," he called back; "you had the cane for that last week, you know."

"Never mind last week," returned Harry Merriman; "come here, we want to speak to you now. If you don't come to us this minute we shall come to you."

Thus admonished, Simon Sly came slowly towards them, with his eyes roaming furtively from side to side, and looking every inch of him the sneak he was.

As soon as he reached the seven, Harry Merriman hooked his finger in his button hole in order to secure him, and fixing his eyes upon him steadily, said—

"You were standing close to us just now."

"Was I?" returned Simon, with an innocent affectation of perfect unconsciousness.

"You know you were," growled Jemmy Muddle, ferociously.

"If you know I was, why do you ask me?" retorted the sneak, with a somewhat ghastly smile. "I'm sure I don't remember."

"At least," joined in our hero, "if you were near us, you know what we were talking about."

"Oh, that I don't; I'm sure I don't. I didn't hear a single word," protested Simon; "not half a word."

"I suppose you didn't tell the doctor that we were tumbling either, eh?" went on Harry Merriman.

"Me tell the doctor? I never told the doctor anything," affirmed Simon, excitedly.

"Oh, what a crammer, Master Sly," cried a voice behind him.

Turning round, there appeared the form of the youthful Forks, who had just admitted old Sally with the tart basket, and who had come forward to announce the fact.

The guilty Simon turned pale, but still protested his innocence.

"Betsy told me," continued the small boy, "as she saw you from the window go to the doctor, as he was a-walkin' in the garden, and tell him as these young gentlemen and me was a-tumblin'; in consequence of which we got whopped all round."

The evident embarrassment of Sneaking Simon was sufficient proof of his guilt without anything further.

"Take that," cried Harry, as he twisted him round, and administered a sound kick behind.

"And that," said Tom Tattler, as he obliged him with another.

"Here's something for a keepsake," cried Jemmy Muddle, as he gave him one in the ribs.

"There's a trifle to keep your back warm," called out Ben Brisk, as he administered his punch.

Other blows, bumps, and kicks dropped in rapid succession.

"Here's a little un in gratis," chuckled Forks, as he quietly stuck a pin in his calf.

Simon Sly howled like a beaten cur, and was glad to limp away and hide himself in the schoolroom.

He muttered, however, threats of vengeance as he went that proved he had heard more than he confessed.

"You'll break open the parlour cupboard and get the cake and jam, will you?" he murmured between his teeth. "We'll see."

Our hero and his friends being well supplied with pocket money, were very good customers to old Sally.

Sneaking Simon soon discovered, from seeing through the window so many youthful jaws in active exercise, that the woman with the tarts had arrived.

Simon had a great love for tarts.

He would have emptied old Sally's basket, if he had had the chance.

But though Simon's purse was known to be well stocked, and though he had a good share of pocket money like the rest of the boys, few ever saw him part with any coin.

He was a miser as well as a glutton.

He was ready enough to eat as many tarts as he could get "on tick."

But he seemed to have a natural horror of paying for them.

He was already a considerable sum in old Sally's debt, and as he never attempted to pay off any of his old score, but kept on eating fresh tarts, of course the debt grew larger.

After the retributive justice he had just received, he felt nothing would so restore his bodily energies as a good blow-out of pastry.

He knew the seven would be sure to be surrounding the old woman, and he dared not venture near them himself.

"If I go, they'll be punching and kicking me again like a lot of ruffians," he argued, mentally; "and yet I must have some tarts. How shall I manage? I know, I'll send."

Opening the schoolroom door, he beckoned one of the younger boys.

"Here, Dawson," he called, "I want you."

The boy approached.

"Go and get me a shilling's worth of tarts of old Sally, will you?"

"Where's the money?" Dawson asked.

"Oh, that'll be all right," returned Simon. "Tell her to put them down to me, and I'll settle with her next week."

This was his invariable promise.

But the settling week never came.

"Go on," he continued, seeing the youthful messenger hesitated; "if you don't go pretty quickly, I'll wring your ears for you. If you bring me back the tarts, I'll give you one for your trouble."

On the strength of this bribe, the boy hurried away to the old woman.

"Shilling's worth of tarts for Master Sly, if you please, Sally," he said.

Sally put twelve tarts in a bag, and then said—

"A shilling, if you please."

"He didn't give me any money," said Dawson. "He says you're to put it down to him, and he'll settle with you next week."

"Ah, that's what Master Sly always says," returned the dame; "he owes me a matter of eight shillings already, and I'm only a poor woman, and can't afford to give long credit."

"Of course not!" exclaimed Harry Merriman and his companions, who were gathered round; "it's a shame! He's got heaps of money saved up; why don't he pay?"

"Don't let him have the tarts unless he sends the money," remarked Jemmy Muddle, who was hard at work upon an apple turnover.

"I really don't think I can," said old Sally.

"We won't let you," cried the seven. "You shan't be cheated."

"Go back to Simon Sneak," said Harry Merriman to the young messenger, "and tell him old Sally says she can't let him have a single tart until he sends nine shillings."

Away ran Dawson back with the message.

Simon Sly turned quite yellow with rage.

"I won't pay a farthing," he growled, spitefully.

"She won't let you have the tarts, then," suggested Dawson.

"Ugh, the suspicious old fool!" muttered the indignant glutton. "I suppose some of the boys have been telling her I shan't pay, haven't they?"

"I don't know," answered Dawson, cautiously; "but the old woman says she must have her money; no money, no tarts."

Simon hesitated, and at length his appetite overcame his stinginess, and he took out his purse.

There was plenty of money in it.

"Here's half a sovereign," he said, as he tendered the coin reluctantly; "you'll have to bring me back a shilling change, mind."

The messenger hurried away joyously.

"Here's the money, Sally," he said, "and I want a shilling change."

"Quite right," returned the old woman; "there's the tarts. I'll give you the change in a minute."

She held forth the bag to Dawson, but Harry Merriman intercepted it.

"Stop," he said. "Don't be in a hurry; I'll take charge of this."

"But Simon's waiting for it," said the young messenger, nervously.

"He'll have to wait, then," returned Harry. "Never mind the change, Sally,"

he continued, addressing the old woman, who was holding out the silver coin; "we'll take it out in tarts. Let's have another shilling's worth."

Sally grinned and counted out the requisite number.

"Now then, boys," cried Tom Tattler, "gather round."

A crowd of small pupils soon assembled, to whom Harry Merriman distributed the juicy morsels in turn.

The youth in the buttons was standing near, watching the proceedings with much interest.

"Hullo, Forks," cried Harry; "do you think you could manage to eat a tart?"

"Well, I daresay I could if I was to try werry hard," grinned the actively industrious youth.

"Here you are, then."

Forks caught the tart that was thrown to him very skilfully in his mouth, and bolted it with evident relish.

"Now, my boy," said Harry Merriman, to Dawson (who had had two tarts for his share), "you can take the empty bags to Master Simon Sly, and say Sally's very much obliged for the ten bob, but being sold out with the tarts, he shall have the two shillings' worth he so kindly paid for in advance on Saturday."

A shout of applause followed this message.

Dawson grinned apprehensively.

"He'll pull my ears," he said.

"If he does, we'll pull his off," cried Jemmy Muddle.

Simon Sly was not only furious, but the loss of the tarts drove him well-nigh to despair.

However, he dared not go out to complain.

He dared not retaliate upon his messenger's ears.

He could only put his head in his desk and mutter bitter threats.

Threats which he fully intended to carry out.

The afternoon passed off as usual, and evening came, and at eight o'clock the pupils retired to rest.

As Joe sincerely hoped he might, he was appointed to occupy the spare bed in the room overlooking the yard.

Consequently "the seven" were together.

"THE DOCTOR PITCHED HEAD FOREMOST INTO THE BOX."

"Isn't this jolly?" exclaimed Jemmy Muddle, after Mr. Fogem, whose duty it was to see the young gentlemen to bed, had departed with the light.

Everyone agreed that it was.

What pleasant chats, what larks, what feasts, what pantomime rehearsals they would have there, and no Sneaking Simon to turn traitor and inform the doctor against them.

CHAPTER XX.

IN WHICH THE CONSPIRATORS HEAR A SIGNAL AT THE WINDOW—FORKS GIVES THEM SOME VALUABLE INFORMATION—ELEVEN O'CLOCK!—TIME!

THE important event of the night, however, had yet to take place.

This was, of course, the recovery of Joe Muggins's play box and its contents.

"I suppose you're still in the same mind?" asked Harry Merriman of our hero, whose bed was next to his.

"I believe you, I am too," returned Joe. "I'm more in the mind than ever to have what belongs to me, that is," he added, "if you're ready to help me."

"Of course we are," protested his companions.

"What time do the doctor and his wife usually go to bed?" asked our hero.

"Between ten and eleven," answered Harry Merriman. "They're generally on the full snore by that time."

"Of course nothing can be done till then," Joe remarked. "I wish it was half-past ten."

It was then only half-past eight.

More than two hours would have to elapse.

Everyone in the room was pledged to take his full share in the adventurous enterprise, so that, in case of discovery, all might stand equally guilty.

It did not take very long to settle the programme of their operations.

By nine o'clock all this was decided upon.

The moments flew by.

Half-past nine had chimed—ten o'clock had struck on the Whoppington church clock.

Suddenly a shower of gravel came with a swish against the window overlooking the garden.

The conversation ceased, and all listened.

"What's that?" inquired Joe, as a second shower rattled against the glass.

"That's Forks' signal," said Harry Merriman, as the noise at the window was repeated a third time.

"For what?" again asked our hero.

"That he wants to speak to us," said Jemmy Muddle.

"Shall I answer him?" asked Tom Tattler.

"Yes, do," returned Harry. "See what's up."

The window being opened softly, Tom peeped cautiously out.

Beneath the window, half hidden by the shrubs, appeared the form of the small page boy.

"What is it, Forks?" inquired Tom Tattler, in a whisper.

"I wants to tell you something very important," whispered the youth in the buttons, in reply. "Chuck out the rope."

In an instant a rope, not thick but strong, was lowered.

Forks placed his foot in a noose at the end, then, grasping the rope, he cried, softly—

"All serene; hoist away!"

The rope was immediately hauled up by seven pairs of willing arms.

The small youth seemed to glide up the wall like a human caterpillar, and pop in at the window as if by magic.

The window being closed, Forks was instantly surrounded by the seven, who, as they stood with their blankets wrapped round them, looked not unlike a party of white Indians.

"Now then, what's the news?" they asked.

"Sneaking Simon's been a-blabbing again," answered the boy.

"Blabbing what?" re-echoed the party.

"Somethink as I suppose he heerd this arternoon," said Forks.

The boys looked at one another in the dark.

"He did hear, then, the dirty, lying sneak!" exclaimed Jemmy Muddle.

"What has he been saying?" asked Joe.

"Hadn't you young gentlemen got some idea into your heads of trying to get the cake and jam out of the parlour cupboard to-night?"

"I should rather say we had," returned Joe, with energy; "we're not only going to try; we mean to succeed."

"Not a single apple, orange, or even nut's to be left behind," exclaimed Jemmy Muddle, determinately.

"Well, then, blest if that out-and-out sneak, Simon Sly, ain't been and blowed the whole affair to old Swisher and Mother Red Beak."

"He has?" cried the seven, breathlessly.

"Yes," returned the small youth, emphatically. "I seed him a-sneaking downstairs to the parlour arter the young gentlemen had gone to bed, so I says to myself, 'I'll jest keep my eye on you.' Accordingly I listens at the door, and there I hears my gentleman a-layin' it all down to the doctor and the missis as clear as new-laid eggs."

"And what did the doctor say?" asked the boys.

"Why, he patted Sneaking Simon on his nut, and said he was a good, honest boy, as was to be trusted, and wished there was more like him. Then he give him a horange and a slice of your cake, Master Joe, and told him to go to bed."

"And was that all that passed?" inquired Joe.

"Oh, no," answered Forks. "Arter Master Sly had gone out of the parlour, I heard the doctor say to his wife, 'So they're coming to take forcible possession of the jam, are they? Very good, Arabella; they shall have it to their hearts' content. I'll give them such a dosing, they shall never be able to look at a jam pot without shuddering for the rest of their lives.'"

"What did he mean?" asked the listeners, eagerly.

"Listen and I'll tell you," returned the small boy. "Well, arter he'd said this, I was sent for. When I got into the parlour, old Swisher says to me—

"'Forks, go to the chemist's and get me half a ounce of tartar emetic.'

"'Yes, sir,' says I, and off I goes.

"Arter I'd got the stuff, I thought there'd be no harm in axing what it was used for. So I says to the gentleman behind the counter, as served me—

"'What's tartar emetic used for?'

"'To induce vomiting,' says he.

"'I suppose you mean by that it's to make people sick, don't you?' says I.

"'Precisely,' says he, with a grin all over his face, and half way down his back; 'there's enough in that packet to make all the boys at Tickle Toby Hall bring their hearts up.'

"'Thank'ee,' says I, and away I comes back with the emetic, and gives it to the doctor.

"'That'll do,' says he; 'you can go.'

"When I went out of the parlour, I left the door ajar, and stopped to see if I could discover what he was a-goin' to do."

"And did you find out?" asked the boys, eagerly.

"Rather!" grinned Forks. "The doctor went to the cupboard and brought out a pot of your marmalade—yours, Master Joe—and emptied the whole half ounce of tartar emetic into it, and then Mrs. Swisher stirred it all up together with a spoon."

"The nasty beasts!" cried Jemmy Muddle.

"I suppose they want to make us all sick?" said Joe.

"That's it," replied Forks, with an assenting nod.

A murmur of indignation passed through the assembly.

"I rather think they'll be disappointed," remarked Harry Merriman.

"Of course they will," returned the small boy; "it ain't likely as you'd go and eat any of the jam as they've doctored. That's why I come to tell you of the villany."

"You're a good fellow, Forks, and we're very much obliged to you," exclaimed the seven, gratefully.

"And, after all," suggested Joe, "it will turn out for the best in the end, for as they think we're going to fall into the trap they've baited for us, they're sure not to interrupt us."

"Right you are," exclaimed the youthful page, exultingly; "it'll be as easy as kissing your hand."

"Oh, crikey!" he continued, snapping his fingers with delight, "won't it be a sell for old Swisher and Mother Red Nose? While they think that you're a-pitching into the tartar emetic pot, you'll just walk off with all the rest of the swag and leave that where it is for them as likes it."

There was a general burst of mirthful congratulation at this, and Joe said to Forks, inquiringly—

"You're sure they didn't put any of the tartar emetic into any of the other jam pots?"

"Quite sure," Forks replied, "because I heard the doctor say as there was no call to do the lot, because one dose all round would be enough for the lot of you."

It now wanted but a few minutes to eleven.

Presently the clock struck.

"Time!" cried our hero, as the last stroke died away.

"Time!" echoed his companions.

They hastily put on their trousers, and then, according to previous arrangement, Joe quietly left the room and went out upon the landing to listen.

All was perfectly quiet.

"Is it all right?" whispered Harry Merriman, who had followed in the distance.

"As right as ninepence," returned our hero. "Old Swisher and his wife are fast asleep, and playing such a pretty tune on their noses."

"Snoring?"

"Yes. Come on."

The word was passed into the bed-room—

"Come on!"

The united band crept cautiously out.

Seven juvenile conspirators, in their trousers and shirts, and with nothing on their feet but their stockings, stood on the landing in the dark.

Forks had taken off his boots and followed.

"I'm a-goin' to be one in this," he whispered.

"All right, so you shall," returned Joe; "you deserve your share."

Then he said—

"All ready?"

"All."

"Forward, then. Hush!"

As silently as ghosts the boys glided one after the other down the stairs.

Will Warner remained at the top of the flight, to give notice in case of any alarm.

Charley Dimond was posted at the bottom to convey any intelligence that might be necessary to his brother conspirators.

The rest then approached the parlour door.

"Let me open it," said Forks. "I'm used to the handle and shan't make no noise."

In an instant, without a sound or a crack, the door swung back on its hinges.

And the boys stood in the parlour.

CHAPTER XXI.

IN WHICH, AFTER SUNDRY MISHAPS, THE BOX AND ITS CONTENTS FIND THEIR WAY UPSTAIRS, WHILST SNEAKING SIMON HAS HIS FEAST TO HIMSELF IN THE PARLOUR CUPBOARD.

"IT'S dark enough, isn't it?" remarked Jemmy Muddle.

"We'll soon have a light," said Harry Merriman, as he took a piece of candle from his pocket.

A lucifer was struck, and the candle lighted.

At first it shed a dim ghostly glimmer over the large room.

But it speedily burnt up, and disclosed the cupboard which was to be the field of their operations.

"Come on!" whispered Joe, eagerly.

They approached the cupboard.

The key stood invitingly in the lock.

"Here goes," said our hero, as he turned it.

The door opened.

The cupboard was large enough to hold the entire party.

The six conspirators entered.

"Here we are!" exclaimed our hero, in a subdued clown's tone. "How are you to-morrow?"

"Yes, here we are," joined in Jemmy Muddle, smacking his lips as he glanced up at the shelves; "how are you the week after next?"

The sight that met the eyes of the young foragers was charming.

There were the oranges and the apples, the bags of nuts, and the packet of hardbake.

And by their side the gigantic cake and the three pots of jam.

The third pot, the doctored one, stood invitingly open.

Into this our hero dipped his finger, and bringing it out again covered with jam, pulled an intensely comic mug, as he said—

"Now then, who's for a taste? Come on, Jemmy; come on, Forks, open your mouth."

There was a general grin at the facetiousness of the idea.

"No, thank'ee," said the former.

"Not for Joseph," said the latter.

"You won't have any, then?" continued our hero, extending his finger to his companions.

"Not if we know it," was the reply.

"Very good; declined with thanks," laughed Joe, as he scraped his finger against the edge of the pot and returned the compound to its original receptacle.

The empty box stood on the ground.

"We'd better pack the things in that," suggested Harry Merriman.

"Won't it be rather heavy to carry?" said Joe.

"Besides, we might drop it," remarked Ben Brisk.

"Of course we might, and wake old Goggles and Mother Swisher," said Jemmy Muddle. "I've got a better plan than that. Look here!"

As he spoke, he produced an empty pillow case.

"Let's put the oranges, apples, and nuts in here," he said, "and I'll carry 'em over my shoulder."

"Bravo, Jemmy, a capital idea; so we will," said Joe.

"Go on, then. I'll hold the bag open."

By the united efforts of five pairs of hands, the oranges and apples were speedily transferred to the interior of the pillow case.

"That's right," chuckled Jemmy; "now the nuts."

These quickly followed.

"Now, then, who'll carry the cake?" asked Joe.

"I will, like a brick," responded Forks. "Here; we'll tie it up in the table cloth."

This was accordingly done.

"I'll take one of the jam pots," said Joe.

"And I'll take the other," said Ben Brisk.

"And I think I can manage to carry the hardbake," joined in Harry Merriman.

"And what's to be done with the box?" asked our hero. "We shall want that to keep our pantomime props.* in."

"Then upstairs it goes," cried Tom Tattler; "I'll carry it."

This being settled, each one picked up his respective load.

Nothing—not a nut—was left behind.

Nothing but the pot containing the marmalade and the tartar emetic, which stood in solitary loneliness on the cupboard shelf.

"Forward," whispered Joe.

The conspirators, with their treasures, moved towards the parlour door.

"Now, then, the sooner we get upstairs the better," said our hero. "Come on; tread light."

In a moment they had passed out of the parlour and stood in the passage.

A moment more, and they were at the foot of the stairs.

"Is all quiet?" they asked of Charley Dimond, who remained there on guard.

"Quiet as mice," he answered.

They were about to ascend, when a hasty warning from Bill Warner, who was on the landing at the top, made them pause.

"Hist! hist!" he whispered, and instantly came hurrying down.

"I heard a door open," he said, hastily.

"The doctor's?" eagerly asked the conspirators.

---

* Short for "properties"—by which is understood the various articles used in pantomimes—such as masks, sausages, carrots, turnips, fish, &c., &c.

"I can't say," he answered; "but I'm certain it was a door."

Everyone was silent.

A stealthy step, descending from one of the upper flights, caught their ears.

It did not seem like the doctor's step.

Who could it be?

No one could guess.

"Out with the light," cried Joe.

Forks extinguished it by crushing the wick betwixt his finger and thumb, enduring the blister it raised like a young Spartan.

Again they listened.

Cautiously, slowly, but surely the footsteps were coming nearer.

"We'd better get out of the way," murmured Harry Merriman; "it's too bad to be stopped now."

"Just as we'd managed it all so nicely," remarked our hero, in a vexed tone.

"I won't give up the nuts and oranges," growled Jemmy Muddle, determinately. "I'll be crunched first."

There was a recess in the wall at the foot of the stairs, large enough to receive the adventurous party.

In this they shrouded themselves.

The person, whoever it was, who was approaching, carried no light, but kept steadily on his way.

Creak, creak, creak, went the staircase as he descended.

"Phew!" he murmured, as he reached the bottom of the stairs. "I've got down at last, and no one any the wiser. I'm quite safe. After what I told the doctor, he'd never suspect me. If I can only get inside the cupboard, what a jolly feast I shall have."

It would have been better for the speaker if he had kept his opinions to himself.

As it was, he betrayed himself and his designs.

"Simon Sly," murmured the eight watchers, as he crept forward in the dark towards the parlour.

"Oh, my eye!" exclaimed Forks, "he is an out-and-out sneak, and no mistake."

"I wish him luck of all he'll find," chuckled Jemmy Muddle.

"He'll be just in time for the tartar emetic," suggested Joe, with a suppressed laugh.

"Oh! ah! so he will," murmured the rest, who in their momentary excitement had almost forgotten the "doctored" jam. "I hope it'll do him good."

"Won't it be too strong, though?" said our hero, apprehensively. "Not finding anything else, he'll be sure to empty the pot, and it may kill him."

"Not it," cried Jemmy Muddle, "it'll only turn him inside out like; and serve him right too, the dirty sneak; it'll teach him a lesson."

Suddenly Harry Merriman said—

"I should like to see what he's up to."

"It wouldn't be a bad idea to lock him up in the cupboard, would it?" said Joe.

"No, capital. Let's lock him up by all means," exclaimed the rest.

They cautiously crept back to the parlour door.

Master Simon Sly had just lit a night light, with which he had taken the precaution to provide himself, and was letting himself into the cupboard.

As soon as he entered, the band of youngsters, feeling themselves quite safe, quickly stepped in at the door.

They heard, with intense satisfaction, Master Simon's exclamation of disappointment as his eye failed to discover any traces of the cake, oranges, apples, and nuts he expected to find.

"I'm done," he exclaimed, "those greedy boys have been here before me, or else the doctor's taken them upstairs with him. What a beastly swindle."

Suddenly, however, his eye fell on the pot of marmalade.

"Here's something," he exclaimed, as he seized upon it eagerly and looked in.

"Orange marmalade," he ejaculated.

"It isn't full, but there's enough for one."

Smacking his lips, he dipped his two fingers in and sucked them afterwards with avidity.

"Isn't it delicious?" he murmured to himself.

"I hope it will do you good," said Harry Merriman, quietly, as he softly closed the cupboard door, and turned the key.

Leaving Sneaking Simon to empty the fatal jam pot, the conspirators returned to the recess where they had left their spoil.

Having once more loaded themselves, they ascended the stairs.

They had reached the top of the flight in safety, when suddenly a new and unexpected casualty occurred.

The pillow-case which Jemmy Muddle carried, being somewhat old and worn, suddenly gave way at the bottom, and out poured a stream of oranges and apples in dire confusion.

Bump, bump, bump, they went as they rolled down the stairs.

"Oh, Lor'! oh, Lor'! what an awful row," murmured the youth in the buttons, as he stood aghast on the landing, listening in horror to the descending shower of fruit.

Bump, bump, bump!

"Confound it!" exclaimed Harry Merriman, in an agony of apprehension; "old Swisher's safe to hear this, and then——"

Rattle, rattle, went something else at this moment.

"What now?" cried the seven.

"It's the nuts," groaned Jemmy; "the pillow case has sprung a leak, and the whole lot's dropped out."

The latter accident was worse than the former, for the nuts went rattling down the stairs on to the oil cloth below in a torrent, making the silent house echo again.

For an instant the young conspirators stood motionless—breathless.

Every moment they expected to hear the doctor's sharp voice.

"Go on with the cake and jam," whispered Joe, hurriedly, to his companions; "get them into the bedroom if we get nothing else."

This order was instantly executed.

"Well," murmured Jemmy Muddle, "if that old prig of a doctor does come, all I hope is he won't have his shoes on. I should like the soles of his feet to have the full benefit of the nuts."

But the doctor gave no signs of making his appearance.

In a moment or two the party returned from the bedroom.

"The cake and jam's all right," said Tom Tattler; "they're safe in the box, stowed miles away under the bed."

"That's the ticket," exclaimed Jemmy Muddle, in a tone of relief, "and now how about the oranges and apples, and the nuts?"

"I don't see the fun of leaving them behind," said our hero.

"No more do I," joined in Harry Merriman.

"I vote we light the candle, and pick them up; it won't take long if we all go to work."

"No, no; out with the matches."

The candle was relit, and in a few moments every runaway apple and orange was recovered.

"But the nuts!" cried Jemmy Muddle, anxiously.

"I'll soon get them together," exclaimed Forks, as he made his appearance with the housemaid's broom.

This proved effectual, and in a very short time the Barcelonas and Brazils were swept into a heap and restored to their bags.

By half-past eleven the whole party were snugly seated in the dormitory, feasting to their hearts' content upon the luxuries they had secured with such determination.

Having eaten as much as they wished, the remains of the feast were locked up in the box and lowered from the window to the ground.

The small youth in the buttons followed, and contrived to remove it to the boot-house, in a remote corner of which he stowed it away, concealing it from prying eyes by piling some old timber against it.

CHAPTER XXII.

WHICH EXPLAINS HOW THE TARTAR EMETIC AGREED WITH SNEAKING SIMON —AND PROVES THAT OUR HERO HAD A GOOD HEART IN HIM, IN SPITE OF HIS TUMBLING PROPENSITIES.

"WELL," said Joe, after he and his companions had wished their assistant Forks good night, and drawn up the rope and closed the window, "now we've had our feast, perhaps it would be as well to see how Master Simon Sly is getting on downstairs."

"Oh, he's doubled up with the gripes

by this time, I'll bet," chuckled Jemmy Muddle, who was inveterate against the sneak. "Serve him right, too."

"Yes; but we only meant to teach him a lesson," argued Joe, charitably; "not to kill him outright. I propose we go down and listen. You know we left him locked in. Let's go and see how he is."

"He's hardly worth the trouble," yawned the boys, who were crammed full of cake and nuts, and were sleepy, "but, if you like, we'll go."

"Yes, I should," Joe replied.

The parlour door was soon reached.

Awful groans were heard proceeding from the cupboard.

Sneaking Simon was evidently receiving the full benefit of the mess he had so eagerly swallowed.

"Oh, ain't the emetic giving him pepper!" murmured Jemmy Muddle.

There was no doubt that it was giving him pepper.

He was in terrible pain, and fearfully sick.

"We'd better unlock the door, I think," said our hero; "I shouldn't like him to die in the cupboard."

"You can do as you like," said Harry Merriman; "but it strikes me Master Simon ain't one of the dying sort."

"No such luck," muttered Jemmy Muddle.

"I mean to unlock the door, at all events," persisted our hero.

He accordingly walked softly across the parlour and turned the key in the lock.

"Oh! Oh! Ah!" groaned the tortured Simon, from the inside.

The noise he made was so piteous that it excited our hero's compassion.

"Who's there?" he asked, pretending not to know.

"Oh! Oh!" groaned the sufferer.

Joe slipped back to his companions.

"Give me a match," he said to Harry Merriman.

Harry gave him a few.

Joe returned, and striking one, opened the cupboard door and peeped in.

On the ground, curled up, nose and knees together, lay Master Simon.

By his side was the almost empty jam pot.

So severe were his sufferings that he did not appear even to notice the light.

Our hero put the cupboard door gently to, and returned to his friends.

"He seems awfully bad," he said; "I've half a mind to wake the doctor."

"Oh, leave him alone," counselled the rest; "he'll be all right to-morrow."

"I'm not so sure about that," returned Joe.

"I fancy he'll be all wrong, if something isn't done. Show me the way to the doctor's bedroom."

This step appeared so terribly rash to Joe's companions that there was a general murmur of surprise.

It seemed to them very much like thrusting his head into the lion's mouth.

But our hero was firm.

"Let's all come," he said. "If we give the doctor this information, he will never believe we have had anything to do with the disappearance of the cake and things, and, of course, we shall never split upon one another."

"Of course not," exclaimed the six.

"It's not a bad idea, after all," said Harry Merriman, suddenly.

"When old Mac goes downstairs, he'll find our friend Simon doubled up in the cupboard, with the jam pot by his side, and, of course, he'll look upon him as the guilty party, not us."

"Of course; he'll think Sneaking Sim's bolted the lot," exclaimed Jemmy Muddle, rubbing his hands together with delight.

"I'm one to go with you to tell the doctor," said Harry.

"I'm another."

"So am I."

"And I."

"So we are all. Come on."

The door of the doctor's chamber was quickly gained.

The deputation paused and listened.

Melodious gurglings and snortings from the throats and noses of the scholastic pair were distinctly audible.

"Shall I knock?" asked Joe.

"Yes, fire away."

Tap, tap, tap, from Joe's knuckles.

No answer.

Bang, bang, bang, from our hero's fist at the panel.

"Eh, bless my soul!" exclaimed the doctor, startled from his sleep. "What' the matter?"

"It's thieves, Erasmus; I'm sure it

is," snuffled his spouse, who evidently had her head under the bedclothes.

Tap, tap, repeated.

"Who's there?" sharply demanded Doctor McSwisher.

"We are, sir," exclaimed the seven, all at once.

"Good gracious! what do the boys want at this hour of the night?" muttered the principal, half asleep. "What's the matter?"

"If you please, sir," said Harry Merriman, "there's such an awful groaning somewhere downstairs, we can't go to sleep, and we thought we'd better tell you."

"Awful groaning?" retorted the doctor, who having been suddenly aroused from his slumbers, had forgotten the trap he had laid. "What can it be?"

"It isn't the cat, sir," remarked Harry Merriman.

Suddenly the principal recollected what he had done.

The groans were no longer a mystery.

"I'll get up and see what it is," he called; "you can go to your rooms."

The doctor got out of bed shivering, for it was a cold night.

The seven heard him strike a light.

"Get up, Arabella," they next heard him cry, "we've caught the atrocious despoiler. Get up directly!"

Murmuring and snuffling, Arabella rolled herself out of bed.

In a few moments the scholastic pair were partly dressed.

"Stop!" cried the doctor. "Where's my cane?"

The question was sufficient to quicken the movements of the waiting party without, who hastily beat a retreat.

The door opened, and the doctor, holding the lamp in one hand and his cane in the other, came forth, followed by his wife.

Both were muffled in their dressing gowns and nightcaps, and presented a highly interesting appearance.

The seven anxiously watched them down the stairs.

"Come on," whispered Joe to his companions. "Let's follow and see all that happens."

Accordingly they once more crept downstairs.

The McSwisher couple had entered the parlour, and approached the cupboard door. Here they paused.

Seven juvenile heads, which they did not see, were protruded into the apartment, anxiously looking after them, and watching their movements.

"There's no doubt about it, it's Bug—Pug—confound the name!—Muggins," said the doctor to his wife.

"I have no doubt of it, Erasmus," snuffled the lady, with a shiver.

"I'll lay my life," continued the principal, grasping his cane viciously, "we shall find Muggins and Muddle, and—a—probably Tattler, in the cupboard."

The seven nudged one another, and the doctor continued—

"Gluttony is deeply rooted in that boy Muddle, as deeply as tumbling pervades the faculties of the new pupil Bug—Muggins; I'll try what I can do to cut it out of——"

"Oh! oh! oh!" from the interior of the cupboard, suddenly cut short the doctor's speech.

"Ha! ha!" he cried, exultingly; "retributive justice has overtaken the delinquent."

"Oh! ho! ho! help me, somebody," groaned the delinquent in question.

"I'll help you," muttered the pedagogue, clutching his cane fiercely; "hold the light, my dear, open the door, and give me plenty of elbow room."

The cupboard door was thrown open.

The doctor drew back his arm to strike.

But it fell powerless by his side.

Neither the new boy, nor Muddle, nor Tattler were to be seen.

Nothing but the trustworthy, well-behaved Master Simon, lying on the ground pale and ghastly, and writhing in agony.

"Good gracious," gasped the astonished couple, "what is the meaning of this?"

"What are you doing there, Master Sly?" almost shrieked Arabella.

"I'm dying! Oh! oh!" groaned poor Simon, kicking his legs, and writhing in the extremity of his anguish. "Send for the doctor."

"Why, surely you haven't been tasting the jam in that pot, Simon?" said Mr. McSwisher, in a well-assumed tone of horror, pointing to the earthenware jar by his side.

"Oh, yes, I have !" groaned Simon. "I've swallowed ever so much of it. Oh! what a wicked boy I am."

"You are a wicked boy," replied the doctor; "but you will receive your punishment. You may consider yourself a corpse; no doctor can do you any good; the pot you have emptied contained poison for rats!"

The presumed corpse gave a melancholy howl, and plunged violently as the emetic gave him an extra twinge.

At that moment Mrs. McSwisher cast her eyes on the shelves.

"Erasmus !" she exclaimed, with a sudden shriek, "look."

The doctor looked in a rather bewildered manner through his spectacles in the direction indicated by his spouse's extended finger.

"Why !" he gasped, "where's the—a—cake ?"

"And the apples and oranges ?" cried his wife, eagerly.

"And the raspberry jam ?"

"And the nuts ?"

"Oh, oh !" groaned Simon.

Swish, swish, went the cane on that part of the sufferer's body which was at that moment most conveniently disposed for the reception of Tingleback.

"No wonder the fellow's ill," cried the indignant principal; "he seems to me to have devoured everything in the cupboard."

"But the other jars and the box, where are they ?" whispered the chagrined Arabella.

"He's swallowed them as well, I think," vociferated the doctor, furiously.

And then followed another fierce application of Tingleback.

But matters had now become very serious.

The violent effects of the emetic he had swallowed had so thoroughly overpowered the unhappy victim that he no longer uttered a cry. He was really in a dangerous state.

But the incensed doctor and his amiable partner did not seem to notice this.

"You pilfering villain !" cried the former.

"You abominable glutton !" snuffled the latter.

"I'll teach you to——"

Again the cane was raised for chastise-ment, when our hero exclaimed, in a hasty whisper, to his companions—

"We mustn't let them kill him."

And banging open the door, he sprang forward into the room.

The six instinctively followed.

"Don't hit him again," cried Joe, agitatedly; "he didn't take the things."

The doctor and his wife, almost startled out of their wits, rolled against one another, and remained in that position with their eyes and mouths open, glaring at their unexpected visitors.

It was some little time before either could speak.

At length the principal contrived to gasp out—

"If—a—he didn't take them, who did ?"

"I did," answered Joe, boldly taking all the blame upon himself.

"I helped, too," said Harry Merriman, immediately.

"So did I," cried Jemmy Muddle.

"We all helped," joined in the rest.

The boys stuck together like a small band of juvenile veterans.

Doctor McSwisher was so utterly confounded, he knew not what to say or do.

"So you all helped, did you ?" he exclaimed, in an irritable, nervous kind of way. "Ha, ha! Upon my word, you're a very strange set of boys—very strange."

"The things belonged to me," said our hero; "and as I felt I had a right to have them, I took them."

"We all took them," echoed the six, courageously.

"Ah! yes; exactly !" faltered the doctor, "and—ha! ha!—pray what have you done with them ?"

"Eaten them," answered the boys, with one voice.

"Jolly nice they were, too," exclaimed Jemmy Muddle, recklessly; "especially the plum cake."

The doctor glared at the last speaker, and made a mental note of his audacity.

But he did not deem it prudent to resent it just then.

"You had better retire to your beds, young gentlemen," he said, in a grand tone, to cover his perplexity. "I will speak to you upon this subject to-morrow."

"Simon Sly had nothing to do with us," explained our hero; "nor did he have any of the cake, or apples, or oranges——"

"Or hardbake," joined in Harry Merriman.

"Or nuts," cried out the daring Jemmy Muddle.

The doctor pointed with his cane to the door, and growled, spitefully, between his teeth—

"Go to bed."

The seven exclaimed—

"Good night, sir! Good night, ma'am!" and walked out in a cluster.

"The world's coming to an end, I think," growled the doctor, as they disappeared. "And now, what's to be done with this fellow?"

This was in allusion to Simon Sly, who lay perfectly motionless in the cupboard, the door of which was wide open.

So motionless was he that the scholastic pair became alarmed.

"Simon! Master Simon, my dear boy," snuffled Arabella, tremulously, "do say something."

But Simon uttered not a word.

The doctor, in a paroxysm of alarm, stooped down and raised his head, and dropped it again suddenly.

His eyes were fixed, his countenance was livid, and there was froth upon his lips.

"Good Heaven!" cried the principal, in a tone of terror; "he's in convulsions —dying, perhaps."

Mrs. McSwisher uttered a shriek.

"Don't die; don't, there's a good boy," she cried, excitedly. "It wasn't poison; you'll get better."

At this announcement the sufferer half opened one eye, and groaned.

"Tell Betsy to light the fire and put on the kettle immediately," shouted the doctor. "I'll make him a little warm brandy and water. Let Forks go instantly for Doctor Drenchem. In the meantime we'll get him to bed."

All this was accomplished, and Sneaking Simon was carried by the preceptor and his wife to his room.

The doctor came, and the result was that the patient did not die.

But it was some days before he could leave his bed, and when he did, he walked about looking as white as a ghost.

By some extraordinary piece of forgetfulness, Doctor McSwisher never investigated the matter of the missing cake and oranges.

Perhaps, considering all things, the principal thought it would be as well to let the matter drop.

At all events, our hero and his friends heard no more of it.

CHAPTER XXIII.

IN WHICH IT IS DECREED THAT OUR HERO AND HIS FRIENDS ARE TO LEARN TO DANCE—THEY START FOR THEIR FIRST LESSON—SNEAKING SIMON ALSO STARTS, BUT GOES RATHER TOO FAR AHEAD, AND GETS HIS IN ADVANCE.

TIME passed on, and the state of affairs was altogether satisfactory at Tickle Toby Hall.

It became gradually apparent to Doctor McSwisher and his wife that the new boy, Joe Muggins, was not by any means the dangerous character they had at first acquaintance taken him to be.

On the contrary, he proved to be a very promising pupil—quiet at his lessons, and good-natured and amiable amongst his schoolfellows.

His only fault was his pantomimical propensity for tumbling.

In spite of all the doctor's threats, Joe would persist in standing on his head and walking on his hands at every possible opportunity. Nor was this all.

The contagious example spread like wildfire through the school.

And now there was scarce a boy, from the oldest to the youngest—not excepting Forks—who could not (thanks to our hero's instructions) stand on his head, throw somersaults, do the splits, almost as well as he could himself.

As for the small boy with the buttons, he practised so perseveringly that our hero promised to get him an engagement as sprite at the first opportunity.

"A MOMENT MORE AND THEY WERE AT THE FOOT OF THE STAIRS."

Sneaking Simon did not take kindly to tumbling.

In fact, he was the only boy, out of the whole of the doctor's fifty pupils, who preferred standing on his heels rather than his head.

His excuse was that his brains were delicate, and that standing with his heels in the air made his head ache.

So he went on his own way, sneaking and telling tales, as usual.

But no one liked him—no one cared to associate with him.

It was about this time that Forks, who seemed to have a wonderful knack of knowing anything that was going on, looked one day hastily over the playground door.

"News, news!" he cried, his countenance expressing vast importance.

"What is it?" asked our hero.

"Call our lot together," returned Forks; "come inside here, and I'll tell you!"

Joe gave a peculiarly sharp whistle, which was understood amongst them as a signal, and in a moment the united six came running up.

Forks unlocked the door, and the party hastily slipped through.

"Now, then, what's the news?" they asked, eagerly, as soon as they were on the other side.

"You're all a-going to learn dancing," said the small boy.

"Dancing!" echoed the six.

"Yes!" returned Forks, "up at Miss Tabitha Teachwell's. She keeps a boarding school for young ladies, about a mile from here; and you're a-goin' there every Wednesday afternoon, so as you can be taught your steps, and have the young ladies for partners."

This idea seemed altogether very agreeable to the young gentlemen.

"That's jolly!" cried Harry Merriman; "there'll be the walk there——"

"And the walk back," joined in Tom Tattler.

"And the larks on the road," added Joe.

"To say nothing of the larks with the young ladies," suggested Forks.

"Are they nice girls?" asked Ben Brisk.

"I believe you they are too," responded the youth with the buttons, in a tone of strong admiration. "Such beautiful curls as they've got too; all hanging down their backs, like corkscrews."

"I suppose we shall have cake and wine between the dances, shan't we?" asked Jemmy Muddle, who had a weakness for such things.

"Well, I really can't say," repeated Forks, with a grin; "but you're sure to have a breaking-up party, and there'll be lots of good things flying about then, you may be sure."

This intelligence caused considerable excitement amongst the boys.

Nor was this allayed when, that very afternoon, they were summoned into the parlour, to be fitted by Mr. Pinchtoe, the shoemaker, with a pair of pumps each.

This important transaction being got over, Mrs. McSwisher addressed the youngsters.

"Now, young gentlemen," she said, "it being the wish of your parents that you should be instructed in the Terpsichorean art,* I have made arrangements with Miss Teachwell, of Roselip House Academy, a friend of mine, to teach you; you will therefore be ready to start, at three o'clock every Wednesday afternoon, for her establishment."

There was a great deal of washing of faces, and scrubbing of nails, and brushing of hair, and a strong odour of bears' grease, on the eventful Wednesday.

And when at length the seven were ready, all dressed in their best things, they looked so smart and prim, that even Mrs. McSwisher felt inclined to be proud of them.

Just as they were ready to start, Master Simon Sly came creeping downstairs, dressed in his best things.

"Hullo!" cried Harry Merriman, in a tone of surprise, and anything but welcome, "what are you up to, with your Sunday clothes on?"

"I'm going to Miss Teachwell's to learn dancing, like the rest," replied Simon, rather sheepishly.

This was a drop none of the seven were prepared for.

To have a sneaking telltale, like Simon Sly, amongst their little party, was a wet blanket at once upon all their prospects of enjoyment.

* The art of dancing.

"You?" they exclaimed at length, with evident disgust in their countenances; "what do you want with dancing?"

"I suppose I've as much right to be taught as any of you, haven't I?" he inquired, with some indignation.

"No, you haven't," returned Jemmy Muddle, emphatically; "a chap that won't tumble has no right to dance."

"I dare say I shall be able to dance as well as you, Master Muddle," said Simon, pettishly.

"Oh, yes! you look as if you would," returned Jemmy.

"I say," he added, turning to his companions with a grin, "won't he look well trying to do the sailor's hornpipe?".

The seven burst into a laugh, much to Sneaking Simon's annoyance.

At this juncture, Mrs. McSwisher came out of the parlour, accompanied by M. Jules Bonbon, the French master, with his violin in a bag under his arm.

"Now, young gentlemen," she said, "I expect, as you are going into the society of young ladies, that you will assume your very best behaviours; I shall expect to hear a satisfactory account of your conduct from Monsieur Bonbon, who will accompany you."

This was not altogether agreeable to the youngsters.

What with the presence of the French master and Sneaking Simon, it seemed as if the fun they had promised themselves would be rather limited.

"Never mind," whispered Joe to his friends, consolingly; "we must make the best of it, and get what larks we can, and be satisfied."

As soon as they got out of the school gates, M. Bonbon said, with a strong French accent—

"Now, young gentlemen, me and Master Simon shall go on first, and you will follow after us behind."

"All right; go ahead, Frenchy!" muttered Harry Merriman.

It was a fine, bright day early in April, and as they proceeded, the boys' spirits became so exhilarated with the walk that a little tumbling was proposed.

In an instant they were hard at it.

When M. Jules looked round casually to see how the pupils were conducting themselves, they were all walking on their hands, with their heels in the air.

"Aha!" shouted the Frenchman, shaking his fiddle at them, "dat is very wrong, very; you must valk on your feet as ve do, and not lag behind."

His rebuke put a stop to the tumbling, but the boys lagged behind nevertheless.

When they were about a quarter of a mile from the place of their destination, M. Jules, who was a long way ahead, was suddenly scared by loud shoutings, intermingled with screams of terror.

M. Bonbon grasped his violin convulsively, and stood still.

Master Sly skulked behind him, and caught hold of his coat tails.

"Vat is dat noise?" said the former, apprehensively.

"I don't know, I'm sure," returned Simon, in a timid tone, "unless it's a mad bull."

"A mad bull," almost shrieked M. Jules. "Oh, *ma foi!* ve shall be toss up in ze air on his horns. Oh, *helas!* vat shall ve do?"

He had hardly asked this question, when from a turning in the road there rushed about a dozen young ladies, accompanied by their governess, in the wildest terror and confusion.

These were pursued by some eight or nine country lads, who were insulting and pelting them with stones.

Poor Miss Finnikin, the governess, was quite as frightened as any of her young charges, who crowded round her, and whom she knew not how to protect.

Seeing a gentleman standing in the road, accompanied by a good-sized lad, the agitated female rushed towards them.

The twelve young ladies followed their governess, and in an instant the Frenchman and his companion found themselves surrounded by a group of young boarding school misses shrieking for help.

Neither M. Jules Bonbon nor Sneaking Simon were remarkable for courage.

But perceiving that, instead of a mad bull, the cause of their alarm was only a body of rustic ruffians, the French master became chivalrous at once.

Grasping his violin, and puffing out his cheeks fiercely, he exclaimed, in a dauntless tone—

"Get away, get away, you *mauvais garçons,* you bad boys, or I shall knock all your heads out of your brains with my fiddle !"

An ironical "Haw, haw !" of rustic laughter and a shower of stones soon answered this threat.

Amongst the missiles was a brickbat, which knocked off M. Bonbon's new hat.

This was of far more consequence to the Frenchman than the lives or limbs of the twelve young ladies.

"Oh, *mon chapeau !* my beautiful new hat vat I buy for ten shillings and sixpence !" he cried, despairingly.

But when the daring yokels began to play football with Monsieur Jules' tile, he became frantic.

"*Sacré !* you young villains !" he shrieked, as he rushed, regardless of conquences, into the midst of the throng. "I shall be the death of you !"

But he reckoned without his host.

The rural ruffians surrounded him.

In vain he struck wildly with his fiddle.

At the first blow it went to "immortal smash" on one of the country boys' thick heads.

They kicked his shins with their hobnailed boots.

They tore off his coat tails.

They punched him in the ribs and pulled his hair.

And when at length he recovered his *chapeau*, it was smashed as flat as a pancake, and minus its crown.

During this encounter, Master Simon Sly remaining shivering and shaking in the midst of the young ladies, who clung to him desperately as their only hope.

"Oh, do pray save us from these dreadful boys ?" pleaded a dozen rosy lips and white, scared faces.

"I can't," whimpered Simon, who was as pale as any of the girls, and shaking like a jelly. "Let me go! I don't want to get killed; ma would never get over it if I was."

This palpable cowardice disgusted many of the young girls, frightened as they were, and one pretty dark-eyed miss, with beautiful curling hair, said, indignantly—

"Oh, let him go; he's only a great coward after all. We shall be just as safe without him as with him."

In an instant every fair hand relinquished its grasp of Simon.

He was free to go.

And he lost no time in taking advantage of his liberty.

But he was not to get off so easily.

He crawled into the ditch by the road side, and was sneaking along on his hands and knees, hoping to get by unnoticed, when the rustics, tired of assaulting the Frenchman, who was reduced to a perfect wreck, caught sight of him.

"Eh, where be thee sneaking off to ?" cried one burly young rustic.

In an instant the sneak was hoisted out of the ditch by the seat of his unmentionables, and kicked from one to the other till he reached the middle of the road, where M. Bonbon sat weeping and execrating in French.

"If you touch me, you ill-mannered boys, I'll tell Doctor McSwisher," he exclaimed, in a breathless tone of terror.

A roar of laughter answered this portentous threat.

"Eh, he do look like a Swisher," cried his captors. "We'll swish thee."

In an instant his legs were knocked from under him, and it is possible he might have had every rib in his body broken, had not a loud shout near at hand arrested the attention of the juvenile ruffians.

It was the seven, accompanied by Forks, who had been despatched after them with their dancing pumps, which they had forgotten.

The youth in the buttons, having performed his mission, evinced no disposition to return.

But, being free beyond the bounds of Tickle Toby Hall, he determined to make an afternoon of it, and to accompany the young gentlemen to Roselip House.

The sight of their French master and their sneaking schoolfellow Simon on the ground, but especially the twelve terrified young ladies and the governess, who stood huddled together as if panic-stricken, added to the menacing attitudes of the group of rustic ruffians that were spread across the road, explained to the new comers the state of affairs pretty clearly.

And they took the precaution to arm themselves with a stone apiece as they advanced.

They came running up at full speed, our hero, Joe, taking the lead.

As soon as they reached the spot, before they interchanged a syllable or asked a question, the young girl with the dark curls, who had previously spoken, exclaimed—

"These brave boys will help us, I'm sure they will."

If anything had been wanting to inspire the seven with a particular desire to distinguish themselves, it would have been such an expression of confidence, from such a pretty pair of lips.

The united seven, or we may include Forks, and say the united eight, looked fiercely at the assaulting party of yokels.

The yokels, in return, looked with dogged insolence at the new arrivals.

Our hero was the first to speak.

CHAPTER XXIV.

A DESPERATE CONFLICT, IN WHICH THE SEVEN COME OFF V'CTORIOUS—OUR HERO ENCOUNTERS THE STRANGER IN THE GREAT COAT FOR THE SECOND TIME.

" WHAT are you doing here?" he asked of the country lads, boldly.

"What's that to thee, young bantam cock?" was the contemptuous reply.

"If you call me a bantam cock," returned our hero, determinately, "you'll find I can fight like one."

"So can I," shouted Forks, at the risk of sacrificing his buttons.

"He, he, he!" laughed several of the yokels, derisively; "look at little breeches."

This deadly personal insult was more than the small youth could endure.

For an instant he glared at his insulters, and then, having nothing better at hand, he hurled the bag containing the pumps at their heads.

The bag missed the objects aimed at, but Sneaking Simon caught it on his nose instead, and added his plaintive howls to the general confusion.

"What have these fellows being doing?" cried the seven, simultaneously.

"They have demolish *mon chapeau*, my beautiful hat, they smash my fiddle; they tear off my coat tails, ze villains!" roared M. Bonbon.

"They kicked me in the ribs, and now my nose is flattened," moaned Master Sly.

"They have insulted us," cried a dozen sweet, shrill voices, that came from the group of little beauties, from whom the rustics separated our young heroes.

"How dare you?" demanded the seven, imperatively.

"They wanted to kiss us, the rude things!" exclaimed the little miss who had spoken before, her dark eyes flashing with passion.

"That wretch tried to kiss me," shrieked Miss Finnikin, pointing her parasol indignantly at a chuckle-headed lout, as though she would have liked to have poked it in his eye.

"It's a lie, thee old fright, I didn't," retorted the party accused.

"And if we had kissed 'em all round, what be it to you—eh?" grinned several of the rustics, with their usual insolence.

Forks had taken the opportunity of informing the seven that the young girls in the road were Miss Tabitha Teachwell's pupils, and Joe replied, fiercely—

"It's a great deal to us, and we're not going to let you insult young ladies as you like."

"Oh, indeed, ain't you, cocky bantam?" cried the one who had previously applied this term to our hero.

"No, I'm not, pudding head," said Joe.

"I should think not," joined in Harry Merriman.

"No, no," echoed their companions.

"Down with the atrocious ruffians!" shouted the diminutive Forks, standing on tiptoe, and feeling like a giant, as he clenched his small fists.

"Punch their heads," growled Jemmy Muddle, mentally picking out the pudding-headed bumpkin as the object of his attack when the contest should begin.

"He, he, he!" roared the rustics, at this playful idea.

"Let's try and break through them," whispered Harry Merriman to Joe.

"Certainly; we shall then be between them and the young ladies," assented our hero.

"Come on, Tom! Come on, Jemmy!" he cried. "Now then, all together."

With a ringing shout they rushed forward, striking out with all their force.

It was quite a charge on a small scale.

And a successful one too.

The party attacked were taken so suddenly, that they wavered—and eventually gave way.

The pluck of the youthful seven had broken the line.

The young heroes were now next to the fair cluster of lilies and rosebuds they sought to defend.

"Don't be frightened," cried the boys, hastily, but with chivalrous gallantry, to the young girls.

"We'll thrash these clodhoppers," exclaimed Joe, addressing, without particularly intending it, the dark-eyed little maiden who had previously expressed her indignation at the daring conduct of the rustic persecutors.

She answered him with a bright smile and a rosy flush, as she replied, encouragingly—

"I'm sure you will; you look like a brave boy."

This so inspired our hero, that he felt he could have demolished the entire foe single-handed.

And he shouted to them, defiantly—

"Now, then, do you intend to go about your business, and leave these young ladies to continue their walk?"

"No, we don't; we mean to have a kiss all round first," was the insolent reply, that elicited a slight shriek from the girls and Miss Finnikin.

"Then we'll make you," cried the gallant seven.

"Get ready, all," shouted our hero. "Come, Simon, don't you be out of it."

"I wish to goodness I was," groaned the sneaking cur, as he still kept his seat on the ground.

"Get up and do something," exclaimed Jemmy Muddle, as he assisted him with a terrific kick behind, that almost hoisted him up in the air.

But Simon either could not or would not imperil his precious self.

A groan of execration burst from the lips of the seven.

"Well, he is a great coward," exclaimed the girls, indignantly.

"Charge!" cried our hero. "Stones first."

The seven discharged the missiles they had picked up, with more or less effect.

After which, they rushed in upon the ruffian crew.

The determination with which the attack was made rather astonished the rustics.

The latter had been impressed with the popular but false idea that, because their opponents were well dressed and gentlemanly, they could not protect themselves.

They soon, however, dropped this erroneous notion, when their plucky antagonists came to close quarters.

Blows fell like rain, and several of the rustics had their heads cut by the stones.

Black eyes and bloody noses were pretty equally distributed on both sides.

But the country lads were more in number than their adversaries.

Being ten to eight.

Neither M. Bonbon nor Simon Sly took any part in the affray.

They had crawled to the side of the road to avoid being trampled on, and there they sat helplessly.

The one bemoaning his *chapeau* and his fiddle. The other his nose and ribs.

The ruffian crew, too, were generally superior in size and strength to their assailants.

And their heads, moreover, being pretty thick and not having much in them, they were not greatly affected by the knocks they received.

After the first surprise was over, they recovered themselves, and fought with the dogged brute courage of young bulls or bulldogs.

"I am afraid they're too much for us," whispered Harry Merriman to Joe, who was by his side.

"Don't give in," Joe replied, breathlessly, as he danced round his opponent nimbly, avoiding his heavy blows and dropping in one occasionally where he could.

"I don't intend to," returned Harry, who had received a cut on his forehead, and into whose eyes the blood from the wound was trickling; "but I can hardly see."

"How are you getting on?" asked Joe of Jemmy Muddle.

"Like a house on fire without the engines," returned Jemmy Muddle, who was making great efforts at the pudding-headed youth he had selected, and who gave him all his work to do.

The latter seemed to have no feeling whatever.

And Jemmy was almost as tired of punching as of being punched.

He already had a black eye and a cut lip.

"I must upset him somehow," thought Jemmy.

He accordingly backed his opponent till he was conveniently in front of Simon Sly.

Then, gathering all his strength, he bent down and rushed forward, full butt, with his head in Pudding-head's chest.

The youth staggered back and fell with a tremendous crash over Master Simon.

The blow was decisive, and he laid in the road on his back gasping.

Jemmy, having thus got rid of his adversary, went in vigorously for the relief of his schoolfellows.

Being heavy and somewhat clumsy in his build, he was perhaps, in size and weight, the most formidable of the seven.

Whilst, from not being particularly sensitive, he was more on a par than any of companions with the thick-headed young ruffians by whom they were surrounded.

He accordingly lent his help wherever it seemed most necessary.

Popping in a blow here and there where he saw it was likely to be of service.

Forks, who, from the look of his jacket, seemed to have been turned inside out, was still fighting like a youthful lion.

Seeing he was overmatched, Jemmy quietly knocked his antagonist's legs from under him, and gave the small youth time to breathe.

The tide of victory was just on the turn, and it is probable a few moments more would have decided it, when the contest was suddenly put a stop to by an unexpected arrival.

This was a gentleman in a chaise, who, seeing what was going on, checked his horse with a loud—

"Hallo, there!"

The combatants ceased, all but two, and turned to look at the stranger.

The two boys who did not leave off fighting were our hero Joe and his rustic opponent.

And they, without taking any notice of the gentleman in the chaise, continued the battle like a couple of young terriers.

The new comer was speedily put in possession of the cause of the encounter by Miss Finnikin and the young ladies.

"The young ruffians!" exclaimed the gentleman, indignantly. "I'll soon put a stop to this."

But there was no occasion for his assistance.

The battle had already come to an end.

Joe had upset his antagonist at last, and the rest of the rustics, taking alarm at the sight of the gentleman in the chaise, hurried from the spot as quickly as possible.

"Bravo, Muggins! Bravo, Joe!" cried his companions, triumphantly, as they surrounded him.

"Muggins — Joe," murmured the stranger, thoughtfully, "that was the name. Can it be the same?"

Walking the horse forward a little, till he reached the group of boys, whose features all more or less bore witness to the struggle they had gone through, he said, good-naturedly—

"You've had rather a hard battle, haven't you, my lads?"

"Yes, sir," replied Joe, who was spokesman, "but I think we've beaten off the enemy at last."

"That's right," returned the gentleman. "I congratulate you on your victory; you're a very brave set of boys, and deserve it."

The speaker looked scrutinisingly at our hero for a moment, and then, beckoning him to approach, said, in a confidential tone of inquiry—

"I think we've met before, haven't we?"

"Have we?" returned Joe, looking at his questioner, and fancying he remembered having seen him somewhere; "where was it?"

"Your name is Joe Muggins, isn't it?" asked the stranger, without answering the boy's inquiry.

"Yes," answered Joe.

"The son of the great Joseph Muggerini, who played Clown at Sadler's Wells Theatre last Christmas?" continued the gentleman, eagerly.

"Yes, yes; that's dad," returned our hero, eagerly, his heart warming towards the speaker, but still not identifying him thoroughly; "do you know him?"

"Well, yes; slightly," answered the other; "I usually take a few tickets for his benefit."

"Oh!" exclaimed Joe, who began to recognise the person addressing him.

The latter, with a smile twinkling in his eyes, which was all our hero could see, since his coat collar was stuck up, and his hat pulled down low over his forehead, said—

"Don't you remember flying into the private box, when the chain broke one night at Sadler's Wells Theatre?"

"Oh, yes," cried Joe, vividly, "I remember; it was or dad's benefit night, and it was you who caught me."

"It was," laughed the stranger; "and I suppose you're at school here—eh?"

"Yes, sir," replied Joe, with a curiously comic smile, owing to one of his eyes being nearly closed by the knuckles of his antagonist.

"Getting on well with your lessons?"

"Capital," returned our hero.

"That's right; learn all you can."

The horse began to move on.

"I suppose you'll be in town, at Christmas, for the pantomime?" the gentleman asked.

"Certain," said Joe.

"I shall look out for you then," cried the stranger, as he drove off.

"I wonder who he is," thought Joe, "and why he wears his coat collar stuck up on a fine, warm day like this."

Harry Merriman and his companions were surrounded by the young ladies during this brief dialogue.

The former had explained to the governess that they were on their way from Tickle Toby Hall to Roselip House, for the purpose of taking their first lesson in dancing.

"Dear me," exclaimed Miss Finnikin, holding up her hands in dismay; "is it possible?"

The boys looked at one another, and could not help smiling, as well as they could, at the rueful spectacles they presented.

There was not one of them who had not got a black eye, or a cut lip, or a swelled nose, or some other species of pugilistic ornament on his features.

"We don't look very fit to dance with young ladies, do we?" remarked Joe, as he joined the party, and glanced affectionately out of his one eye at the pretty little girl with the curly locks.

"I think you do," said the latter, warmly, as she extended her hand to our hero; "I like brave boys."

Her young companions expressed themseves to the same effect.

And Miss Finnikin said to the youngsters—

"You had better come along with us. I am sure Miss Teachwell will be so much obliged to you for the service you have done us."

To this proposal the seven willingly assented.

But at this juncture, Monsieur Jules Bonbon came limping up.

"Oh, it is no good for ze young gentlemans to go to dance. They cannot dance without music, and my fiddle is smashed to little bits," he exclaimed, in a despairing tone; "they must come back."

"We don't want you, monsieur," replied Harry Merriman; "you and Master Simon can go back if you like, but we wish to take our dancing lesson."

This proposal being unanimously received, the party set forward to Roselip House.

After behaving so gallantly in their defence, the young ladies could not do less than honour their defenders by taking their arms.

Accordingly, they proceeded in this manner, to their great satisfaction.

Our hero accompanied the little, dark-eyed girl, whose name was Fanny Fairchild.

Forks walked along on tiptoe by the side of Miss Finnikin, as proud as a small peacock.

Whilst the cowardly M. Jules and his companion, Sneaking Simon, at whom none of the girls would look, came creeping along behind them.

CHAPTER XXV.

HOW THE SEVEN MADE FRIENDS WITH THE YOUNG LADIES AT ROSELIP HOUSE —AND HOW THE YOUNG LADIES PROMISED TO ACT IN THE PANTOMIME.

IN a short time, the united party of young ladies and gentlemen arrived at their place of destination.

Miss Teachwell was very much concerned at the vivid account which the governess gave of the perils from the ruffianly country boys which she and her young charges had escaped, owing to the bravery of Doctor McSwisher's pupils.

Miss Tabitha was filled with wonder and admiration as she listened to their deeds of prowess, and at the determined manner in which they had put the bumpkins to flight.

The young heroes were cordially welcomed by the worthy lady, who shook hands and thanked them all in turn, not excepting Forks, who carried the bag of dancing pumps under his arm, and whose features were so battered and punched that he was only to be recognised by his buttons.

"Poor, dear fellows!" exclaimed the good-natured schoolmistress, as she gazed at the varied mixture of black eyes and swollen noses that prevailed generally; "it's quite a mercy they were not killed by the rustic savages; the law ought to take notice of it, that it ought!"

But, alas! the law was in a bad state at Whoppington.

The entire police force being represented by two solitary and very inefficient bobbies, who never took anyone into custody, and who were never, by any chance, to be found when wanted.

It was, therefore, more than probable that what ought to have been done by the law never would be done.

The young heroes were all marched off to the comfortable kitchen, where their wounds were carefully attended to.

Miss Tabitha, in a kind and motherly way, superintended and assisted in these operations.

Bruises were fomented with warm water.

Cuts were bound up with sticking plaister.

Poultices of scraped briar root were laid upon the black eyes.

By the time they were all finished, the atmosphere was quite fragrant with the mingled odour of friar's balsam, *eau de Cologne*, and odoriferous pomade, with which the sufferers' contusions had been anointed.

At length they all assembled in the schoolroom, which was the place appointed for the dancing saloon, and where the young ladies were anxiously awaiting them.

Of course each of the girls had fallen in love with her own particular juvenile hero.

And each juvenile hero reciprocated the compliment by falling in love—boy fashion—with the young ladies respectively.

"There," cried Miss Teachwell, as she ushered them in; "now, before we do anything else, you must all have a piece of cake and a glass of wine.

"I'm sure you require it, and I'm quite sure you deserve it."

Away hurried the good lady in search of these refreshments.

The moment the door closed, there was a general rush on the part of the girls towards their gallant young cavaliers, whom they surrounded like a swarm of bees.

The seven, it must be confessed, did not at that moment present altogether as interesting an appearance as they might have done.

In fact, what with plaister and bandages, their natural features were scarcely discernible.

But in spite of that, they were all quite cheerful, and laughed as they peered at one another as well as their damaged optics would allow them.

"What a set of one-eyed gunners we

look, don't we?" remarked Harry Merriman, with a smile, intended to be comic, but which caused him to assume an appearance of weeping.

"That we do," assented his companions. "If it was the fifth of November, here we are seven as ugly-looking Guy Fawkes as any one could wish for, all ready made."

But the young ladies wouldn't hear of any such remarks.

"Never mind your looks!" they cried; "you're all brave boys, and got your knocks and lumps in our defence, and we like you all the more on that account."

That was so flattering to the young heroes — Jemmy Muddle especially — that the latter shouted, in a fit of enthusiasm—

"Hurrah! three cheers for the pretty girls of Roselip House!"

This was chivalrously responded to.

"Hurrah! hurrah! hurra-a-a-h!" rang through the schoolroom.

And then, in their gallant excitement, the young heroes kissed the rosy lips of the aforesaid pretty girls.

And the pretty girls seemed not at all to dislike the proceeding.

It only seemed to make them blush and smile and to look prettier than ever.

In a few moments they were all firm friends, and as much at home as though they had known each other all their lives.

Presently there was a tread of footsteps and a jingling of glasses heard outside.

The door opened, and Miss Tabitha's smiling face appeared as she led the way, followed by Martha, the domestic, carrying a tray glistening with decanters and wine glasses.

Forks, whose eye had been bandaged up with great care by Sukey Brown, the scullery maid, followed with a handsome-looking cake.

"Hurrah!" once more shouted the bruised but gallant juveniles.

"Now then," exclaimed Miss Teachwell, who seemed, instead of being stunned by the furore, to enjoy it extremely; "come, all of you, and refresh yourselves."

The cake was cut, and the wine poured out, the young gentlemen politely attending to their fair companions.

Miss Teachwell then said to our heroes—

"I think, after what you have undergone this afternoon in defence of these young ladies, you will not be much in the humour for dancing; I therefore propose that we postpone our lesson until next half holiday, and that you remain here to tea instead."

Again the boys hurrahed joyously, and the hospitable schoolmistress, having drunk their healths in a glass of sherry, retired to order the preparations for tea.

As soon as she was gone, the young ladies and gentlemen clustered together, and chatted and laughed and joked to their hearts' content.

Our hero, Joe, had taken a great interest in the dark-eyed girl who had so particularly noticed him, whose name was Fanny Fairchild, and who, with her arm in his, never left his side.

It suddenly struck the latter that, in the pantomime they intended to get up, they would want fairies, and that no better fairies could be possibly found than the pretty pupils of Roselip House Academy.

Accordingly Joe suddenly left his fair companion, and beckoning his schoolfellows aside, he hastily suggested the idea.

Of course it was eagerly assented to.

"Capital! First rate! The very thing!" they all agreed.

"Let's ask them if they will join us," said Harry Merriman. "You explain matters, will you?"

This was to Joe, who willingly agreed to do so.

"Now, young ladies," said our hero, when they returned to the girls, who wondered what they had been talking about by themselves, "I've got a secret to tell you."

"A secret?" exclaimed the latter, eagerly. "Oh, how nice! What is it?"

"Let's all sit down, then, and you shall hear," returned Joe.

In an instant everyone was seated.

Our hero paused impressively for a moment, and then said—

"We're going to get up a pantomime."

"A pantomime!" echoed the girls, with one voice, in astonishment.

"Yes," returned Joe, in a tone of profound importance.

"What, a real pantomime, such as they perform at the theatres at Christmas?" eagerly inquired Fanny Fairchild.

"Yes," Joe answered again.

All the young ladies were in the habit of visiting the theatre at holiday times, and all knew perfectly well what a pantomime was.

But still they were quite surprised at what they had heard

"But where are you going to get it up?" asked Miss Lydia Lester, a pretty girl, with long fair hair and blue eyes, who had attached herself to Harry Merriman.

"Doctor McSwisher's, Tickle Toby Hall," Harry answered.

"But how can you get up a pantomime?" asked Miss Fairchild, incredulously. "You would want a stage, scenes, dresses, and pantomimists for that."

It astonished Joe to hear his fair companion talk about these things, as though she knew all about them, but he replied, with a kind of proud confidence—

"We shall have all these."

"What, then, are you going to have actors and actresses from London?" inquired Miss Charlotte Berry, innocently.

"Oh, no," responded the seven, laughing at the idea. "We're the actors, and you are the actresses."

"I'd rather play Columbine than a fairy, if I may," said Fanny Fairchild, in a confidential whisper, to Joe.

"Would you? Then you shall be Columbine, if you like," Joe answered, and added, gallantly, "and a very pretty Columbine you'll make, too."

Fanny smiled and blushed a little, and Joe continued—

"I'll teach you the business."

"I know it," she answered, quickly.

"Know it!" echoed our hero, in surprise. "How did you learn it?"

"From my father," Fanny answered; "he taught me."

"What, then, is he a pantomimist?" replied Joe, eagerly.

"Yes, he is a harlequin, and performs in the London theatres."

Before our hero had time to express his surprise, the little girl continued, inquiringly—

"I suppose, if I do Columbine, you'll be the harlequin, won't you?"

Joe looked at the pretty dark-eyed speaker rather wistfully.

"I should like to, very much," he said, hesitatingly, "but——"

While he was reflecting, his fair companion said—

"What is your line of business?"

This question restored our hero to himself in an instant, and he answered, grandly—

"I'm a clown."

"A clown!" echoed Fanny, in amazement. "Can you really act clown?"

"I should think so," Joe replied, "and I can tumble, and sing 'Hot Codlins,' besides. Dad taught me."

"Is your father a clown, then?"

"Yes; he was clown at Sadler's Wells, last Christmas."

"What, the great Joey Muggerini?"

"Yes, that's my dad," cried our hero, with enthusiasm.

"Oh, my papa knows your papa, then, quite well," returned Fanny, with equal animation.

These facts tended greatly to increase the friendship of the juvenile sweethearts.

In fact, the mutual confidence that had grown so rapidly between Doctor McSwisher's young gentlemen and Miss Teachwell's young ladies was something remarkable.

"And so you can tumble, can you?" asked Fanny, presently.

"Tumble!" echoed Joe, with conscious pride. "Certainly, we can all tumble, can't we?" he continued, addressing himself to his companions.

"Rather," they replied in concert.

"See," cried Joe.

And suiting the action to the word, he turned several somersaults in succession, and walked across the room on his hands.

The example was infectious.

Instantly the entire seven were walking on their hands, with their heels in the air.

In the midst of the exhibition the door was pushed open gradually, and a pale face, with a lump of something white in its centre, looked in.

The face was that of Master Simon Sly, and the white lump was Master Simon Sly's nose, which had been strapped up with plaister, and just then looked not unlike a turnip radish.

"WHAT IS THAT NOISE?" SAID JULES BONBON."

CHAPTER XXVI.

IN WHICH MASTER SIMON SLY IS TREATED WITH THE CONTEMPT HE DESERVES—HE ASKS FOR CAKE AND WINE, AND GETS MORE THAN HE LIKES.

SOME of the young ladies caught sight of this apparition, and uttered a startled scream of dismay. The head was hastily withdrawn.

At the same moment, the voice of Miss Tabitha was heard outside.

"What are you doing there, sir, prying about?" exclaimed the good lady, sharply.

She had been very distinctly informed of the cowardice of Master Simon and M. Jules Bonbon, and Forks had moreover taken upon himself to describe the former as a prying sneak.

"Why don't you go inside?" she continued to the sneaking youth, as he stood cringing and rubbing his hands nervously one over the other. "I don't like creeping boys, that peep through cracks and keyholes."

"I didn't know whether I might go in, ma'am," snivelled Simon, who felt very uncomfortable at the prospect of meeting his schoolfellows and the young ladies after the rank cowardice he had displayed.

"Oh, of course you may go in," cried Miss Tabitha, in a tone that proved how little she thought of him; "or, at least, I won't have any prying, or peeping, or listening in my house."

The seven had heard the voice of the schoolmistress, and at once assumed their proper attitudes.

When Miss Teachwell ushered in Master Sly, they were all standing on their feet.

"I've brought in this young gentleman," said the preceptress, emphatically. "I found him standing outside on the mat peeping, so I thought I had better bring him inside."

Low murmurs of contempt were audible from the seven.

As for the young ladies, they curled up their rosy lips and turned up their pretty noses at the coward.

Some went so far as to hiss him.

Master Simon, with his back up, and looking furtively out of the corners of his eyes, sidled up to the table and placed himself in a chair, as near as possible to the cake and wine.

But Miss Teachwell took no more notice, and was talking and laughing with the rest of the party.

"She's forgotten me; she must have forgotten me," he murmured to himself. "I want my share as well as the rest; I'm sure I've had as much exertion as anyone else."

But as no notice appeared to be taken of him, he resolved to help himself.

He was about to do this very cleverly, when suddenly Miss Teachwell, without appearing to do so intentionally, removed the wine and cake to a sideboard at some distance, and completely frustrated his plans.

The seven, however, had been watching him, to their great delight.

They knew the gluttonous character of their sneaking schoolfellow, and could fully enter into the joke.

"I say," whispered Merriman to his friends, "doesn't Master Simon Sly look happy?"

"Very," laughed our hero; "especially about the nose."

Of course this made everyone laugh.

"We may as well amuse ourselves with him," suggested Joe. "Instead of wine, let's give him a drop of another sort."

"What sort of a drop do you mean?" asked the girls, curiously.

"We'll show you," whispered our hero in reply.

"You must draw him into the trap, Ben, when we've laid it."

"All right," returned Ben.

It was uncommonly simple, this trap, and one quite familiar to most schoolboys, being simply the decoying an innocent victim to the extreme end of a form on which several are sitting; then, at a signal, all but one rise suddenly, and the form, overbalanced by the victim's weight, instantly tilts up, and the victim is dropped on the floor.

Presently, Miss Teachwell seemed about to remove the cake and wine on the sideboard.

This was too much for Simon, and he groaned aloud.

"Whatever is the matter with you, sir?" asked the preceptress, turning round sharply. "What are you groaning for in that manner?"

"You've forgotten to give me any cake and wine," whimpered the afflicted youth, dolefully.

"No, sir," returned Miss Tabitha, sternly. "I have not forgotten you, but I have heard such a bad account of you generally, that I do not intend you to have any."

Simon Sly blubbered outright.

The girls and the seven laughed so much to themselves that they too shed tears—tears of mirth.

There had been a little previous consultation amongst them.

Another nice little plot against Sneaking Simon had been hastily formed.

And they now proceeded to carry it out.

Several of the seven and the young ladies approached Simon, who was weeping bitterly to himself.

"What's the matter?" asked Fanny Fairchild, in a tone of pretended commiseration, although she felt inclined all the time to pull the plaister off his nose.

"I haven't had any cake and wine, and I've as much right to have some as anybody else," snivelled Simon.

"Oh, poor fellow!" exclaimed all the girls at once, "that's dreadful."

Simon, believing that he had excited their pity, moaned more piteously than ever.

"Oh! he does look very bad indeed, doesn't he?" remarked Charlotte Berry.

"What's to be done?" asked Lydia Lester.

"Get me a piece of cake and a good, large glass of wine," murmured the sufferer, rolling his eyes round him with pretended anguish.

"So I will," cried Fanny Fairchild; "I'll go and ask Miss Teachwell. Who'll come with me?"

"I," volunteered Joe, magnanimously.

Away went the pair.

The rest proceeded to lay the trap.

"Oh, don't sit here all by yourself," said Charlotte Berry; "it's so unsociable. Come and sit on the form with us, won't you?"

"I don't mind," snuffled Master Sly. "But I thought you didn't want me, perhaps."

"Oh, yes, we do; we're going to play at forfeits presently. Come on."

There was a general rush to the form.

All the places were instantly taken, except one.

That one being a small space at the extreme end.

"Where am I to sit?" asked Simon, in a wailing tone, looking extremely wretched; "there's no room."

"Oh, yes, there is," cried Miss Berry, who sat nearest the end. "Get up higher," she called out, pretending to push her companions closer.

There was no more room than before.

"I can't sit here," grunted Simon.

"Sit on your thumb," cried out one of his schoolfellows.

"I can't sit on my thumb. Don't be stupid," he replied.

Charlotte Berry caught him by the arm and pulled him into his seat.

"There, that will do nicely," she said.

At this moment the door opened, and Miss Fairchild appeared with Joe, carrying a slice of cake and a glass of wine on a tray.

"See," she exclaimed; "I've brought you your cake and wine."

Simon's eyes brightened at the sight of the luxuries on the tray.

"Give it him, if you please," said Fanny to our hero. "Poor fellow! he looks as if he wanted something."

Joe advanced; Simon extended his hand, but ere he could reach the cake, Fanny's silvery voice exclaimed—

"Sneak!"

All sprang to their feet with a sudden bound.

Up went the form in the air, and down went Master Sly on the floor with a tremendous bang, the form toppling over upon him.

"Oh, my funny bone! Oh! oh!" he yelled.

Of course everyone pretended to be very sorry.

At the same time they were all dying with laughter.

Simon had fallen into the snare with such beautiful simplicity.

He was picked up by the seven, who kindly pretended to rub his funny bone, but who jostled and poked him in the ribs till he was almost frantic.

"Be quiet," he roared; "and give me the cake and wine. If you don't, I'll tell the doctor you've been tumbling; I saw you through the doorway."

At this terrible threat they pretended to be very much frightened.

"You'd better give it him," whispered Harry Merriman.

Joe instantly obeyed.

Simon Sly seized upon the cake and wine like the glutton he was.

The latter he placed on the table by his side, and contemplated the former.

It looked very tempting, and there was a large piece of candied citron near one side.

Simon was particularly fond of this preserve.

He began to eat greedily, taking enormous mouthfuls, and chewing fast as though his life depended on his haste.

Suddenly he stopped, and turned very red in the face, and opened his mouth.

"Good gracious!" cried his companions, "what's the matter?"

"He's bit on his tooth," suggested one.

"Swallowed a plum stone," cried another of the boys.

"An almond gone the wrong way, perhaps," exclaimed a third.

"Oh, yes, he's evidently choking," cried the young ladies;" "slap his back; pray do."

Instantly a dozen hands were hard at work, slapping Master Sly wherever they could get a chance.

"I ain't a-choking," roared the sneak at length, as he burst through the throng of sympathising friends; "I'm on fire inside."

"Send for the engines!" shrieked the young ladies.

"Fetch the pumps!" shouted Jemmy Muddle.

"Oh, oh, oh!" howled Simon, who was dancing about like a maniac or a wild Indian, puffing and blowing furiously to cool himself.

"Have a drop of wine?" suggested Joe.

Simon rushed to the table, seized the glass, and dashed the contents down his throat.

But this did not relieve him, for no sooner had he swallowed the draught than he screamed out—

"It isn't wine at all," and staggered out of the room.

A loud yell of derision from his companions followed him.

"What have you been giving him?" asked Charlotte Berry.

"A dose of cayenne pepper and red ink," explained our hero, Joe, "and we hope it will do him good."

A roar of laughter followed this explanation.

"What, did you sprinkle the cake, then?" asked the girls.

"No, I cut a hole in it, and having filled it up with pepper, I covered it up with a nice, large piece of candied citron," said Joe; "because I knew he'd bite that first."

"I think he got the lot," laughed Harry Merriman.

"And the red ink?" inquired Ben Brisk.

"I poured out of a bottle that stood on the kitchen shelf," said Joe; "there was no wine, and I didn't like to disappoint him."

There was a great deal of laughing over this.

When Master Simon crept in to tea, he looked very pale, and answered very sulkily to the numerous kind inquiries as to whether he was better.

He felt a trick had been played him, but he said nothing about that.

He only resolved to serve out his tormentors at the earliest possible opportunity.

As the young gentlemen were later in returning than was expected, Miss Teachwell wrote a note to Doctor McSwisher, stating what had happened, and highly commending the courageous manner in which his pupils had defended her young ladies from the insults of the country yokels.

The doctor was completely staggered when the party of heroes made their appearance.

He had never seen so many black eyes, cut lips, and swelled noses in his life.

But after the note he had received, he could not blame the boys.

And besides this, there was M. Jules Bonbon, the French master, with his torn coat, his dilapidated *chapeau*, and his smashed fiddle, to bear witness to the fierce encounter in which they had been engaged; and he muttered to himself—

"If this is learning dancing, the sooner it's stopped the better."

CHAPTER XXVII.

CONSULTATION ABOUT THE PANTOMIME—THE LIGHT UNDER THE DOOR.

A WEEK or two after the events we last recorded, the lights had been extinguished in the bedrooms at Tickle Toby Hall.

But the pupils—the seven, at least—were not asleep.

On the contrary, they had never been more wide awake in their lives.

They were now about to hold a council respecting the grand pantomime they were going to produce.

They were all sitting up in their beds, with the bedclothes drawn snugly around them, for the night was chilly.

"Forks ought to be here," said Harry Merriman.

"Certainly," answered the rest; "why isn't he?"

The actively industrious youth was so necessary now to the operations of the young gentlemen, that they could hardly stir a step without him.

And Forks himself took such an interest in the proceedings, and was so thoroughly trustworthy, and, moreover, was likely to prove such an excellent sprite, that they quite looked upon him as one of the dramatic company.

It was by no means the fault of the small page that he was not amongst them.

He was detained by certain household duties he could not escape.

Presently, however, his well-known signal—a handful of mould thrown up at the window—was heard.

"Here he is!" cried the boys, eagerly.

In an instant the seven were out of bed, the window softly opened, the rope lowered, and Forks drawn up.

"Here we are once more!" exclaimed the small youth, as he was dragged in. "I should have been here before, but Mother Swisher wanted her boots brushed because she's going out early to-morrow."

"All right; better late than never," said Harry Merriman. "Now, then, to business."

Joe, who was spokesman, opened the conference.

"As the young ladies at Roselip House have promised to join in with us——"

"Very nice young ladies they are, too," remarked Jemmy Muddle, parenthetically; "'specially Miss Pickles."

"Order!" exclaimed Harry Merriman. "It's business now."

Silence being restored, Joe continued—

"There's no reason why we shouldn't have a first-rate pantomime."

"Hear! hear!" from the seven and Forks.

"The first thing," remarked Harry Merriman, "is to settle when we're to act the pantomime, and, then, how we shall be able to act it. I mean how to get the doctor's permission, which won't be easy, since he doesn't like pantomimes, I fancy."

"No," returned our hero, decisively, "that's the last thing we must settle."

"Oh!" ejaculated Harry, in surprise.

There was a slight pause, and then Ben Brisk said—

"What's the first thing, then, to be done, Joe?"

"Well," replied our hero, "first we'll settle who's to play the comic characters."

"Very well, then, let's settle that at once," said the boys.

"I suppose I'd better do clown," Joe went on.

"Yes, yes, of course."

"Then I think Jemmy Muddle ought to be pantaloon. Will you be the old one, Jemmy?" asked Joe.

"Yes, I should like to," eagerly responded Jemmy; "we shall get along together like a house on fire. I'll be the old un."

"All right! Then suppose Ben Brisk does Harlequin."

"I'm quite agreeable," returned Ben, quickly, "especially as Miss Fairchild is to be the Columbine."

"Yes," interposed our hero, with dignity, "but you'll please to remember that Fanny's my sweetheart."

"Oh, of course, that's understood," returned Ben. "I'm engaged to Lucy Sparkle, and I don't want two."

"Very well, then, the comic business is settled."

"No, it ain't," exclaimed Forks, abruptly. "How about the Sprite?"

"Oh, ah, I forgot that," cried Joe; "of course you'll do Sprite, Forks."

"I believe you I will, too," returned Forks, triumphantly. "I'll let the British public see what a sprite ought to be!"

Harry Merriman then said—

"But, Joe, as we can't all be clowns, or pantaloons, or harlequins, what are the rest of us to do?"

"Oh, there'll be plenty of parts in the opening of the pantomime," Joe replied. "There'll be the demon king, and the wicked baron, and the wicked baron's servant, and a lot of other characters besides. We shall all have to play in the opening."

"Oh, that's all right!" exclaimed Harry and the others. "We shouldn't have liked to be out of the fun."

"I should think not," replied our hero, warmly, and then continued, "The first thing now to be done is to write the pantomime."

"You promised to do that," exclaimed several voices.

"So I will," answered Joe. "I have written some already, and I've got the rest pretty clear in my head."

"What a clever nut you've got of your own," remarked Forks, admiringly.

"Let's see; what was to be the title?" asked Harry Merriman.

"Harlequin Old Bogey; or, The Brave Boys of Whoppington," answered Joe. "There'll be the cruel Baron Bogey."

"That's good to begin," cried the boys.

"Then there'll be the Demon Tingleback!"

"Ha, ha!" laughed the seven; "that's better."

"Yes, good name for a demon, isn't it? Well, then, there's Funky Fum, the baron's servant, who is frightened, and everything."

This last name was received with great applause.

"Three cheers for Funky Fum!" exclaimed Jemmy Muddle, exultingly.

But they suddenly remembered where they were, and repressed the cheers.

"I haven't quite fixed upon all the names yet," continued Joe, "but I will to-morrow, and in a night or two I shall have the pantomime scenes, business and all, written down in a copy book. Then I'll read it and tell you all what characters you're to play."

"And how about the stage to act upon?" asked Ben Brisk.

"We must fit up a stage with planks, on the schoolroom desks," returned Joe.

"And the scenes?—we must have scenes," suggested Harry Merriman.

"Of course," returned Joe; "we must buy some calico and paint them. I think I can manage that; I've often watched the artist at the theatre."

"You'll be all right with the masks and props,* won't you, Joe?" said Jemmy Muddle.

"Oh, yes, I'll take care of them," answered our hero, triumphantly. "What would a pantomime be without good masks and properties?"

The little party grew quite enthusiastic over these prospects, and presently Forks offered a remark—

"I s'pose you'll want some place to paint the scenes in and to make the properties, won't you, Master Joe?" he said.

"Well, yes, Forks, I suppose we shall," Joe replied. "I was only just then thinking which would be the best place."

"Well, I think the back of the coach house would be as good as any. Then, as fast as they're done, you could roll 'em up, and stow 'em upstairs overhead, in the room where I sleeps, and the properties as well."

"So we will, then. That will be just the thing," said Joe. "I suppose we can get paint and size and whiting in the town?" he inquired.

---

* Short for properties.

"Oh, yes, any amount of it," responded Forks.

"Very well, then; as soon as I've written the pantomime, we'll commence at once."

"And if you should happen to be short of calico," proffered Forks, "I dessay I can put my hand upon a few of Mother Swisher's sheets; I should think they'd come in uncommon handy for drop scenes, sewed together."

This tickled the boys' fancies, and they burst into a hearty laugh.

But it was instantly checked by Harry Merriman, who cried, in a hasty whisper—

"Hush! danger. Light under the door."

Every voice was hushed instantly, and all eyes were at once turned in the direction indicated.

The rays of a lamp or candle were distinctly visible.

CHAPTER XXVIII.

FORKS' ESCAPE BEING FRUSTRATED, HE IS SUDDENLY STRUCK WITH AN IDEA —ARRIVAL OF MR. FLUSTER FOGEM—HARROWING CASE OF SOMNAMBULISM.

"WHO can it be?" whispered Joe. "Is it the doctor, or one of the masters?"

"Whoever it is, I think the sooner I'm off the better," suggested Forks. "Come on and let us down."

"Here's the rope," said Harry Merriman.

The light was still where it had first appeared.

But by some unlucky chance, the window that had, up to that time, always opened easily, now stuck fast and refused to move.

The murmuring of whispered voices without, too, caught the ears of the boys.

"Here's a pretty go," muttered Harry Merriman.

"Hark," now whispered Tom Tattler; "I think there's someone speaking outside. Listen!"

Everybody listened.

But no one could hear what was said. Only they fancied they detected the voice of Master Simon Sly.

Cautious footsteps were then heard approaching the door.

To open the window was now impossible.

"I'm afraid you're caught, Forks, old boy," murmured Joe to the page.

"Seems like it," returned the latter, philosophically. "Well, it can't be helped. Stay, though!" he suddenly exclaimed, "I've got a idea."

"What?" hastily inquired the boys.

"All of you get into bed. But don't lie down," said Forks, hurriedly. "Then, if anyone comes in, pretend you're nervous at something white as you've seen walking about the room—gammon it's a ghost, d'ye see? Leave the rest to me."

The boys hastily crept into bed.

The actively industrious youth, with much expedition and decision, stripped off his trousers and jacket.

"Here," he exclaimed, "catch hold of these here togs."

As he spoke, he thrust his garments into Joe's hands, much to the astonishment of the latter.

"Stow them away under the bed clothes," he whispered, hastily; "someone's a-coming."

It was a considerable mystery to the seven, to know what was Forks' motive in stripping himself to his shirt in the manner he had.

But there was no time to waste in surmises, for at that moment the door opened slowly, and there entered, carrying a candle in his hand, the English resident assistant, Mr. Fluster Fogem.

It was a kind of relief to find that it was he, and not the fierce doctor.

To the great surprise of the master, he found every boy sitting up in bed, nose and knees together, with the clothes gathered round them.

Mr. Fogem stood for a moment gazing at their faces, which was all that was visible.

Every countenance (thanks to Forks' suggestion) wore a look of alarm.

But the small youth himself was nowhere to be seen.

The usher thought, naturally, that it was his unexpected presence had produced these symptoms.

"What are you all doing?" he asked, sternly.

"We were startled out of our sleep, sir, by a strange noise," said Harry Merriman.

"Oh, indeed," returned Mr. Fogem, in an ironical tone, as though he did not quite believe what was told him. "A strange noise, eh? Well, what sort of a noise was it?

There was a slight pause.

The precise kind of noise had not been determined upon.

At length Jemmy Muddle replied, haphazard—

"It was a dreadful kind of ghostly noise, sir."

"And pray, what do you mean by a ghostly noise, Muddle?" asked the master, still sarcastically.

"A noise like ghosts make, sir, when they walk," explained Jemmy, whose ideas on the subject were rather indefinite, and who was almost sorry he had spoken.

"That won't do, sir," returned the tutor, fixing his eyes rather venomously on the speaker. "In the first place, ghosts are spirits, and make no noise at all. And, in the second place, they never walk, they glide."

"That was just it, sir," returned our hero, Joe, quickly, coming to his friend's assistance. "There was something white gliding here, up and down the room, and we all thought it was a ghost. Didn't we?"

Everyone responded—

"Yes."

Mr. Fluster Fogem shook his head.

"So, then, I suppose I am to understand that you are alarmed at the supposed presence of a ghost in the room, are you?"

"Yes, sir," replied the boys.

"Scared almost out of your wits with terror, eh?"

"Yes, sir," they repeated.

"I never felt in such an awful funk in my life," protested Jemmy Muddle, shuddering vehemently, and affecting to bury his face in the bedclothes.

Mr. Fluster Fogem peered round at the pupils out of his half-closed eyes (he was very near-sighted), and then said, impressively—

"Now, listen to me, young gentlemen; if you are in the state of terror you describe, how was it you laughed so heartily just before I came in, eh? It is not usual to laugh under such circumstances."

There was a dead silence.

The question was difficult to answer.

At length Harry Merriman said—

"I think you must have been mistaken, Mr. Fogem; there was no laughing here."

"I beg your pardon, sir," returned the master; "I heard it distinctly with my own ears."

"It wasn't any of us," replied Jemmy Muddle, boldly; "we were all asleep."

"It must have come from one of the other rooms," suggested Joe Muggins.

"No," exclaimed the assistant, positively; "it came from this room, and my conviction is that the story of the ghost is all a sham, and that there is one, if not more, of the boys who ought to be in their own dormitories concealed here. I shall search."

Accordingly, Mr. Fogem commenced his investigations, beginning at the beds nearest the door.

He looked under and over them, and on each side, and so on until all had been examined.

But no stray boys could he discover.

Neither were there any unusual protuberances under the bedclothes, implying that someone was hidden there.

Save where the occupant of each bed lay, all was smooth and unruffled.

Mr. Fluster Fogem paused, and scratched his ear reflectively.

It seemed very strange to him.

So it appeared to the seven, who wondered what had become of the actively industrious youth.

Had he got up the chimney?—or had he the power of making himself invisible?

The former of these ideas seemed to have struck the assistant, for he walked to the fireplace and looked up, but could distinguish nothing.

"Very singular," he muttered to himself, "very! I'm confident there's someone here somewhere."

At the end of the room stood a press

in which the clothes of the young gentlemen were kept.

"Ha!" he cried, as the rays of the candle fell upon it, "it is not impossible he may be there."

He approached the press.

The hearts of the spectators beat quickly with mingled anxiety and curiosity.

"I wonder who it will turn out to be?" thought Mr. Fogem, as he placed his hand on the brass knob. "Will it be Jones, or Simpkins, or Wigsby? I'm inclined to think Jones."

He turned the handle and flung the door of the press wide open.

Then, holding up the candle, he looked in.

Suddenly he uttered a startled exclamation, and recoiled a step, as a diminutive object in white attracted his notice.

"Bless my heart alive, what's that?" he cried.

The small object was in his shirt, standing bolt upright, and appeared to be doing something very diligently which Mr. Fogem could not clearly make out.

"It is a boy, undoubtedly," he murmured to himself; "but it isn't Jones, or Wigsby, or—good gracious!" he suddenly exclaimed, as he recognised the actively industrious youth, "it's the boy that cleans the boots."

Yes, there stood Forks in his shirt, with his eyes fixed, looking as quietly awful as he could look, and engaged in polishing an imaginary boot.

"Good gracious, is he in a fit?" gasped the master.

The boys, hearing these exclamations, sprang from their beds and crowded to the spot.

The sight of the small youth, and the clever way in which he was acting his part, so tickled his friends that they felt inclined to roar with laughter.

But they restrained themselves, and Harry Merriman suddenly exclaimed—

"I know what it is; he's walking in his sleep."

"Ah, yes; probably so," returned Mr. Fogem, who felt convinced this was the fact.

"That's it, sir, depend upon it," joined in Joe. "He fancies he's in the boot house, cleaning boots; look at him!"

Forks at this moment turned up his eyes to such an extent that nothing could be seen of them but the whites.

Mr. Fogem uttered an ejaculation of dismay.

"Never saw anything so awful in my life," he murmured. "He's a somnambulist."

Forks stepped from the press, and breathing on the imaginary boot, brushed away at it harder than ever with an equally imaginary brush.

Then, in a low, solemn voice, he said—

"I must give this 'ere a good polish, cos it's Mr. Fogem's, and he likes his boots to shine."

"Wonderful!" cried the tutor. "And to think, now, that he doesn't know either what he's doing or saying. I think I'd better wake him up."

"Oh, no, sir; don't wake him—pray don't!" entreated the boys. "Sleepwalkers often go mad when they're startled out of their sleep suddenly."

"Ah, yes, I've heard so," returned Mr. Fogem; "but something must be done. It won't do to leave him here."

"If he's left to himself," said Joe, "it's most likely he'll go quietly enough as soon as he's finished his work."

The quick-witted young actor took this as his cue.

And having given Mr. Fogem's phantom boot a final touch, and examined it carefully all over to be sure it was perfectly brilliant, he went through a little pantomime of corking up the blacking bottle and putting his brushes together.

After which he murmured to himself—

"There, now I can go to bed."

Then with slow and measured steps his tiny form marched itself off and disappeared out of the door.

There was a moment's pause, and then the assistant master said—

"I don't wonder at your being startled, young gentlemen, for I declare the sight I have seen has given me quite a turn myself. Get into bed and go to sleep."

The clever performance of Forks had quite imposed upon Mr. Fogem, who had not the least doubt that the boy of all work was addicted to somnambulism.

The admiration of the seven at their young coadjutor's presence of mind was something tremendous.

"What a plucky chap he is, isn't he?"

exclaimed Harry Merriman, when they were once more alone.

"And the idea of old Fogey Flusters being so green as to believe he was asleep," grinned Jemmy Muddle, in an ecstasy; "ho, ho!"

Their admiration had not died away when a handful of mould came dashing up at the window.

"There he is," cried the seven.

Out they sprang from their beds.

The window condescended to open again now.

Seven heads were popped out in an instant.

Beneath stood the actively industrious in his shirt.

"Chuck us down the togs, please," he whispered, hastily; "it's rather cool without 'em."

"I should think so," returned Harry Merriman. "Here they are."

Forks caught the garments.

"I think I floored old Fogey, didn't I?" he grinned, exultingly.

"You did it splendidly, old fellow," cried the seven. "Good night."

"Good night."

Five minutes after everyone was in the land of dreams.

CHAPTER XXIX.

IN WHICH THE PREPARATIONS FOR THE PANTOMIME GO ON SWIMMINGLY—AND AN ACCIDENT HAPPENS THAT THREATENS DISCOVERY.

IN the course of a few days our hero Joe, according to his promise, had finished the pantomime, and written it out fairly in a copy book.

I am not going to assert that it was entirely the fruit of Joe's own imagination —it certainly was not; but it was very well put together, and when he read it to his young companions they were delighted, and declared it was everything that a pantomime should be.

"So it ought," laughed Joe, candidly. "I think there's a bit of almost all the pantomimes that were ever written in it."

After this the pantomime was cast,* and the parts copied out and distributed.

Each of the seven went about with his respective character neatly stitched in a cover of brown paper in his pocket.

On the next dancing lesson day, those of the young ladies at Roselip House who were to play speaking characters had their parts also given to them.

Matters being thus far settled, it only remained now to get everything ready for the performance.

The coach house having been fixed upon as the scene of their operations, it was the duty of the small boy with the buttons to let two or more of the seven privately through the playground door

by means of the key, of which he always had possession.

This could be easily done, and when once on the other side of the gate, and the gate locked, they were comparatively safe.

It was Forks also who procured the necessary materials from the town of Whoppington.

Calico, plaster of Paris, pipeclay, size, paint, whiting, and paint brushes arrived periodically, and were stowed away in the coach house.

The scenery was the first thing to which their efforts were directed.

Probably these efforts were not quite so successful as the artistic touches of Messrs. Telbin and Grieve, but Joe went to work with energy, and his companions thought he produced marvellous results.

There was the dark and gloomy abode of the Demon Tingleback, with green and crimson snakes twining round copper-coloured pillars.

Then came the castle of Old Bogey, the Baron, which had an arched gate and portcullis, and iron bars to the windows.

Next the cottage of Dame Trot (with a thatched roof and any quantity of hollyhocks growing in the garden), where Wilhelmina, the Fair Maid of Whoppington, lived.

After this the fairy dell, which was

* The characters assigned to the various performers.

principally remarkable for its fountains, which spurted up very blue water out of very white lily beds.

Lastly came the grand transformation scene, which was a dazzling combination of all kinds of colours, thrown up with strips of bright foil paper, in front of which a brilliant star was to revolve.

All this being accomplished, and stowed away upstairs in the sleeping apartment of the youth with the buttons, the next thing was to paint the scenes for the comic business.

These consisted of a butcher's shop, with a baker's adjoining.

A pawnbroker's and a public house.

A marine view and a railway station.

These were also finished and removed as before.

About this time sundry sheets were unaccountably missing. No one seemed to know anything of them.

"It's very strange, Betsy," remarked Mrs. McSwisher one day to the housemaid, "where those sheets can have gone to; I miss six pairs. Have you any suspicions?"

"Oh, no, mum, indeed I haven't," protested Betsy, vehemently. "I only know as I washed and wrung 'em, and hung 'em on the line."

"Someone must have got over the wall and stolen them, I'm afraid," snuffled Mrs. McSwisher. "This is really very serious; sheeting is expensive. If I lose any more, I must really call the attention of the police to the premises."

Little did the matron guess that the small boy who waited daily at table was the culprit.

Little did she dream that her missing sheets were lying snugly packed away under Forks' bed, neatly stitched together, with a demon's cave, a baron's castle, and a railway station painted upon them.

The properties accumulated rapidly.

As fast as they were made and painted, they were carried up to the usual storehouse, Forks' sleeping apartment, over the coach house, until, at length, the small youth was completely surrounded by heaps of pantomimical carrots and turnips, cabbages and flat fish, loaves and sausages, with the addition of a dead cat and dog, stuffed, of course, and a baked potato can.

To these were added several policemen's staves, and a never-to-be-forgotten red-hot poker.

Our hero, Joe, was now hard at work at the masks.

And wonderfully well he made them too.

Every mask, more or less, resembled someone on the establishment.

Old Bogey was a striking likeness of the principal.

Dame Trot might have been recognised anywhere, by her nose, as Mrs. McSwisher, the principal's wife.

The Demon Tingleback found a fitting duplicate in Mr. Fluster Fogem.

While Funky Fum, the baron's cowardly servant, was the image of M. Jules Bonbon, the French master.

Last, not least, there was a mask for the Greedy Boy in the comic business, which was an exact copy of Master Simon Sly.

When they were all painted and varnished, they looked so ludicrously natural that the seven shouted with genuine delight.

As for the words of the pantomime, they were known so perfectly that any one of the actors could almost have said them backwards.

It was a capital opportunity on dancing days, after the lesson was over, for a little private rehearsal in Miss Teachwell's schoolroom.

M. Jules Bonbon, having lost his violin, was no longer required.

And Master Simon Sly got so fearfully ridiculed by his companions and the young ladies, that he suddenly discovered that dancing didn't agree with his health, and therefore discontinued his lessons.

So the young conspirators had no one to interfere with them, and the pantomime gradually assumed quite a complete form.

Everyone knew his exits and entrances, and every scrap of the "business," so thoroughly that he could have performed it at any hour of the day or night.

All they now wanted was the necessary dresses, and these, by the assistance of the young ladies and their good-natured governess, Miss Teachwell, to whom they confided the secret, were being made at Roselip House.

"'YOUR NAME IS JOE, ISN'T IT?' ASKED THE STRANGER."

Just about this time, however, an event happened that had almost put the anti-pantomimical doctor on the scent of what was in contemplation.

One afternoon Jemmy Muddle, who was never very bright at the best, but whose brains were now completely full of "Harlequin Old Bogey," made fearful blunders in his English History.

He gave the most wild and frantic answers to the questions asked him.

William the Conqueror was the first Roman emperor; Queen Elizabeth was the only son of Mary, Queen of Scots; Henry the Eighth was murdered in the Tower, by order of his grandmother, Richard the Third.

These, and other absurdities, begotten of poor Jemmy's bewildered brain, oozed from his lips, to the great disgust of Mr. Fogem, who, after enduring the infliction as long as he could, hauled the delinquent up to the doctor's desk, and made his complaint.

"Oh, he won't answer your questions, won't he? We'll see," growled the doctor, grasping his cane.

Jemmy's handkerchief crept up his sleeve, in the usual manner, instantly.

"Now, sir," cried the doctor, "attend to me."

Jemmy attended.

"Now answer me, and mind what you're saying. What was the title of William the Conqueror before he ascended the English throne?"

Poor Jemmy scratched his head hopelessly.

"Go on, sir!" shouted the doctor.

"He was shot in the brain by an arrow, sir," faltered Jemmy.

"Oh, was he?" exclaimed the doctor, sarcastically. "We'll try again."

"Who was the oldest man that ever lived?"

Jemmy paused.

"Quick, sir! quick!" cried Dr. McSwisher.

"Old Bogey," returned Jemmy.

"Old Bogey!" roared the doctor, fiercely. "What the deuce do you mean, sir—eh?"

Slipping from his seat, he seized the unhappy muddle-headed youth by the collar.

"Now, sir, the oldest man, directly!" he cried, as he shook the culprit by the collar violently.

"Funky Fum," gasped Jemmy, hopelessly.

The rest of the boys looked on in silent amazement, scarcely knowing whether to laugh or pity their comrade.

Doctor McSwisher simply glared at his victim, and echoed—

"Funky Fum! The fellow must be mad."

At this precise moment a small manuscript, stitched together in a brown paper cover, jerked out of Jemmy's jacket pocket by the violent shaking he had undergone, fell to the ground.

CHAPTER XXX.

IN WHICH JEMMY MUDDLE REHEARSES HIS PART BEFORE THE DOCTOR.

THE eyebrows of the principal went up suddenly to the utmost extent they could go with astonishment.

So did the eyebrows of Mr. Fluster Fogem, the assistant master.

So also did those of M. Jules Bonbon, the French professor.

The extraordinary words the doctor had just heard had completely mystified them.

The principal, with a perplexed frown on his face, wiped his spectacles, and read the strange inscription again.

And then he exclaimed — looking sternly at the proprietor of the singular MS.—

"What in the name of common sense is the meaning of this, sir?"

Jemmy looked very vaguely at the doctor.

His senses—common or uncommon—appeared to have gone out for a stroll and lost themselves, and he made no reply. There was a dead pause.

"Here's a pretty mess!" murmured Harry Merriman.

"Awful, isn't it?" ejaculated Tom Tattler, in reply.

"Will he tell?" whispered Ben Brisk.

"Not he!" returned Joe Muggins.

This was true. Poor Jemmy was staunch, and would have endured any amount of Tingleback rather than get any of his schoolmates into disgrace.

Just then, however, he was so horrified at the accident that had occurred that his mental powers were all in a fog.

"Now, sir," shouted the doctor, who was growing fierce and impatient, and brought the cane down on his desk with a terrific slash, "are you going to answer me?"

"Y—es, sir!" exclaimed Jemmy, jumping half way out of his bluchers at the startling sound.

"Very well, then, explain quickly. What is this nonsensical gibberish?"

The principal pointed sternly to the MS. in the brown paper cover as he spoke.

Jemmy Muddle shut one eye and peered at it curiously with the other, evidently at his wits' end what to reply.

"Now, sir, what is it?" again demanded the incensed doctor.

"Please, sir, it's F—unky Fu—um!" faltered Jemmy.

"Funky Fum!" exclaimed the pedagogue.

"Funky Fum!" repeated Mr. Fogem.

"Fonkee Fom!" echoed the French master, in his foreign accent.

"And pray, sir, what is the meaning of Funky Fum?" inquired the principal, glaring down ferociously upon the hapless James. "Is it Chinese?"

"No, sir," returned the latter; "it's English, I think."

"English, is it?" repeated Doctor McSwisher; "then perhaps you'll have the goodness to read it."

As he spoke, he held out the MS. to the culprit.

Jemmy had now to a great extent recovered his self-possession, and having made up his mind for a good thrashing, he resolved to behave like a hero.

He therefore glanced significantly at his companions, who stood in mute expectation of what was coming, and then, instead of taking the stitched pamphlet the doctor was offering to him, he said, complacently—

"I don't want the book, sir, thank you. I know it all by heart."

This piece of intelligence was something so extraordinary, that the doctor dropped his cane, and positively staggered back.

The assistants also narrowly escaped falling off their seats.

It was the first time upon record that poor Jemmy had ever been guilty of knowing anything by heart.

It took several moments before the principal and his satellites recovered from the shock of this astounding announcement.

At length the doctor, drawing a long breath, exclaimed—

"So you know it by heart, do you, Master Muddle?"

"Yes, sir," responded Jemmy, quite briskly.

"I know it every bit, business* and all."

This term was of course quite unintelligible to the doctor, and he said, gruffly—

"If you know it, let us hear it," adding, sarcastically, "it will be quite a novelty in your case."

Jemmy cleared his throat, and at once commenced his part in the pantomime.

"Curtain rises, discovers exterior of the Baron Bogey's castle. Music. Enter Funky Fum, the Baron's servant, his face pale and hair erect, as though frightened. Starts every now and then nervously. After looking off at the wings,† he advances to the front and sings."

Jemmy stopped suddenly and said, inquiringly, to the doctor, who was glaring at him through his spectacles—

"Shall I say the song, sir, or speak it?"

The idea of a boy who was supposed to be deficient in the usual amount of intellect not only speaking, but singing, was a fresh surprise.

"Sing it, if you can," growled the doctor. "Ha, ha!" he laughed, ironically; "the idea of Muddle singing. That's good, very good, ha, ha!"

"Ho, ho!" joined in Mr. Fluster Fogem, in a sepulchral tone.

"He, he, he!" piped M. Bonbon.

---

* This means the pantomimic action of the part as distinct from the dialogue.

† Side scenes.

Jemmy, nothing daunted at the sneers of the masters, pulled a sly mug at his brother pantomimists, that set them all on the grin, and then threw himself, heart and soul, into his part.

He withdrew to a certain distance, and then, imagining himself on the stage, made his entrance.

It was worth something to see how he shivered and shook (according to the character he was representing), and how frightened he looked.

As there were no wings to look off at, he cautiously peeped into each desk as he passed.

He let the last desk shut with a heavy bang, and pretending to be dreadfully alarmed, started back, and stood trembling so violently, but so naturally, and with such strange contortions of his features, that the entire school roared again and again.

"Order!" angrily shouted Doctor McSwisher.

"Order for Jemmy's song!" echoed Ben Brisk.

"Who said that?" demanded the principal, angrily.

Nobody knew, for Ben was crouching down behind his companions, and was out of sight.

After running his eyes along the line of boys, the doctor turned once more to the pantomimic James, and said, in a tone of authority—

"Go on, sir."

Jemmy, who had never left off, but who had been shivering and shaking to his heart's content from the moment he had commenced, advanced towards a row of imaginary footlights,* where, after a few more comical contortions, he commenced—

FUNKY FUM'S SONG.

"A master I have,
    And I am his man;
To save him I try
    All that I can;
Wherever he goes,
    At his heels I must run,
I shiver and shake,
    And my name's Funky Fum.
Shivery shakery; quivery quakery,
Oh, oh, oh, oh! my name's Funky Fum.

My master's a baron,
    A baron is he;
Such a monster ferocious
    You never did see;
His hairs are like bristles;
    His teeth he employs,
Does this dreadful old Bogey,
    To eat little boys.
Shivery shakery; quivery quakery,
Oh, oh, oh, oh! my name's Funky Fum

Our castle's a den,
    And whoever gets in
Must think himself lucky
    To get out again;
There's such corners and holes,
    Such dark cellars and traps,
Full of ugly dead shadows,
    And swarms of live rats.
Shivery shakery; quivery quakery,
Oh, oh, oh, oh! my name's Funky Fum.

I shudder all day,
    And I shiver all night;
And I can't get away,
    Cos he holds me so tight;
But the first chance that offers,
    Far off will I run,
For old Bogey's lodgings
    Don't suit Funky Fum.
Shivery shakery; quivery quakery.
Oh, oh, oh, oh! my name's Funky Fum."

At the termination of this explanatory ditty, Jemmy Muddle plunged at once into a characteristic comic dance, in the course of which he performed such extraordinary evolutions that the whole of the fifty scholars were in ecstasies, and cried, "Bravo!" and clapped their hands with all their might and main.

In the midst, however, of this grotesque exhibition, the doctor's voice was heard.

"Stop that tomfoolery!" he cried, imperatively.

The representative of Funky Fum ceased instantly.

Once more silence reigned throughout the schoolroom.

The doctor then continued, sternly—

"From what I can understand of the intellectual composition to which you have treated us, Muddle, it appears to me to be something of a pantomimical character."

"That's just what it is, sir; you've hit it exactly," returned Jemmy, briskly. "It is the opening of a pantomime."

Joe Muggins and the rest of the seven were aghast at his imprudence, and tried to telegraph to Jemmy, by signs, to be more guarded and less confidential in what he said.

But, in his eagerness, he did not observe these signs.

"Oh, it's the opening of a pantomime,

* The row of gas lights that run along the ground, in front of the stage.

is it?" repeated the doctor, showing his teeth viciously.

"Yes, sir. And a capital one it is too, sir," answered Jemmy, who was, somehow or other, under the delusion that the principal was rather delighted than otherwise with his efforts. "The part of Old Bogey's first rate; so is Funky Fum, if you'd like to hear a little more."

"More, sir!" shouted the doctor, his eyes flashing fire through his spectacles. "No. I'm sufficiently disgusted as it is. Did I not expressly forbid the introduction of any such miserable rubbish into my establishment? Did I not do so, sir? Eh?"

Jemmy Muddle looked considerably crestfallen at this, and scarcely knew what to reply or what to expect.

But the principal soon enlightened him on the latter point, by exclaiming—

"You know I did, sir, as well as you know that you are transgressing my positive commands, and that you deserve the penalty of such transgression. Step this way; I shall make a public example of you, for the benefit of all the rest."

Poor Jemmy had so often been made use of in this useful manner that it was nothing new to him.

He therefore simply pressed his coat sleeve with his hand, to assure himself that the handkerchief he had placed there was in its right position, and was about to approach the desk, when our hero Joe, unwilling that his friend should be punished unjustly, stepped forward in front of him.

"If you please, sir," he said, firmly, "it is not Master Muddle's fault that he knows the song he has just sung, but mine. I gave him the part, and I taught him the tune, and how to sing it. So if anyone must be punished, it ought to be me."

Doctor McSwisher drew back his head, and pulling down the corners of his mouth, gazed fiercely at Joe.

He did not like to be thwarted when he had resolved to administer a good dose of Tingleback.

And this he had just now firmly resolved to do in the case of Jemmy Muddle.

But as he could not very well castigate one without the other, he resolved that the culprits should share the chastisement.

"I shall punish you both," he said, in a decided tone. "You, Muggins, for teaching your schoolfellow such nonsense, and him for allowing himself to be so taught."

It was at this moment the principal discovered, for the first time, that he had dropped his instrument of punishment.

After looking about in all directions, he saw that it was lying on the ground under one of the desks.

"Bring me that!" he cried to one of the junior boys.

The junior, with fear and trembling, obeyed the order.

"Now then!" exclaimed the doctor, as he once more grasped his favourite weapon, "step this way—Muggins first."

"It's all right, old fellow," Harry Merriman whispered to Joe as he passed him. "I've clipped the cane at the end, and slipped in a piece of horsehair. It's quite certain it'll split."

Joe heard this intelligence—not that it mattered much to him, since he felt pretty confident of being able to cheat the doctor by the handkerchief trick.

He advanced therefore boldly towards the principal.

The doctor adjusted his spectacles, and extended his arm with Tinglehand at the end of it.

Not a few out of the fifty lookers-on shuddered inwardly, and felt as though cold water was at that moment being poured down their backs.

"Now, sir," exclaimed the principal, in an awful tone.

Joe held out his hand. Down came the cane on the handkerchief.

Smack! went Harry Merriman's hands under the desk at which he sat.

"Again, sir," cried the doctor.

The operation was repeated, and with the same result.

It took four blows to satisfy the ferocious principal, who had struck spitefully, as hard as he could.

He smiled a ghastly smile as Joe turned away, feeling quite delighted at the thought of the anguish that he had inflicted.

At the same time our hero had not felt the cane at all; in proof of which he pulled an excruciatingly comic mug at his friends as he went back to his place.

It was now Jemmy's turn.

He was quite a veteran at corporal

punishment, and held out his hand as bold as brass, as if it was rather a pleasant sensation than otherwise.

"Move this way," cried the doctor, waving his cane in an awfully practical and terrifying manner.

Poor Jemmy Muddle moved his hand as directed.

Up and down went Tinglehand in a most vigorous style.

"Slap, slap, slap, slap, slap, slap!" counted Harry Merriman, as he clapped his hands under his desk, and at the sixth the horsehair in the cane took effect, and Tinglehand split from the top to the bottom.

The doctor, who little suspected the cause of the effect, was delighted at this incident, as it seemed to prove how awfully severe the punishment he had inflicted must have been, to have made such havoc with the instrument of torture.

He glanced at the victims, and chuckled inwardly, as he observed that they both had their heads in their desks.

"Ha, ha!" he thought, "I think I've cured them of pantomimic nonsense."

Delusive idea.

Could he have looked through the lid of the desks, he would have discovered, to his horror, that the spirit of pantomime was as full of life as it had ever been in the hearts of the supposed sufferers.

Both Joe Muggins and Jemmy Muddle had performed the handkerchief trick successfully, and were at that precise moment making clown's faces, and squinting at one another with all their might.

CHAPTER XXXI.

IN WHICH A GRAND DISCUSSION ON THE PANTOMIME QUESTION TAKES PLACE IN THE COACH HOUSE, AND THE PLAN OF PROCEDURE IS FINALLY ARRANGED—THE HOLE IN THE WALL AND THE EYE.

TIME passed rapidly on, and the Midsummer holidays were fast drawing near.

Everything had been long since prepared for the forthcoming pantomime.

It lay all ready for action, like Robinson Crusoe's canoe; and as that only wanted water wherein to launch it, so the pantomime only wanted an opportunity for its performance.

There was a grand consultation on this important subject, one half holiday, in the coach house.

The seven were present. Forks also.

Our hero, Joe, opened the proceedings.

"One thing's very certain," he remarked; "if the pantomime's to be done at all, it must be done before we break up for the Midsummer vacation."

"Midsummer!" exclaimed Will Warner. "That's not exactly the proper time for pantomimes, is it?"

"Not quite so proper as at Christmas, certainly," returned Joe; "but if we don't do it then, it's very likely we shall never do it at all."

"Oh! Oh! Oh!" exclaimed his companions, in strong accents of reproof. "Don't say that, Joe!"

"Well, at any rate," Joe continued, "I shouldn't be able to take any part in it."

"Why not?" asked all the boys at once, eagerly.

"Why, because I shall be wanted at the theatre in town for the pantomime there," Joe answered.

"Oh, ah, so you would," exclaimed the seven, rather ruefully; "we forgot that."

"I should have to leave school at the end of November at the latest," continued our hero, "as they always have three weeks' rehearsal at the least, on the stage, for the comic business of a pantomime in London."

A cloud seemed to pass over the features of the youngsters at the idea of losing the leader and stage manager.

"We should make a mess of it, I'm afraid, without you, Joe," said Harry Merriman.

"Yes, I think it'd be a case of pickles myself," assented Ben Brisk, despondingly.

"Pickles!" exclaimed Jemmy Muddle, vehemently; "we couldn't do it at all. Where's our clown to come from?"

There was a pause of silence.

Without Joe there was none.

Under these depressing circumstances the faces of the assembly lengthened considerably.

At length Forks exclaimed, magnanimously—

"Look'ee here, young gents; rayther than the pantomime should be a frost, I shouldn't mind doin' clown myself."

But this proposal was not received with the gratitude it deserved.

Tom Forks, with all his talent and tact, was not considered a fitting substitute for Joe Muggins.

"No, no, no!" exclaimed the boys simultaneously; "we'll have Joe for clown, or else no one!"

"Well, I didn't mean no offence," said the small youth, whose feelings seemed rather hurt at the cold water that had been sprinkled upon him. "I thought I'd make the offer; not that I'm by any means certain I could accept it," he added, consequentially, "cos I might be engaged for sprite at a London theatre myself."

The small boy puffed himself out like the frog in the fable as he uttered these words, and a shout of laughter was the reply.

"You do sprite at a London theatre?" echoed Ben Brisk and Harry Merriman, derisively; "you'll have to eat a few more plum puddings before that comes to pass, Master Tom."

Master Tom looked indignant, and retorted—

"What do I want with plum puddin's? I'm the best tumbler of the lot—arter Master Joe, o' course, and he said he'd get me an engagement—didn't you, Master Joe?"

"Certainly I did," Joe replied, "and so I will if I can."

"There!" exclaimed the youth with the buttons, triumphantly, greatly comforted by his young patron's assurance. "I shall be in a London theatre yet."

"Of course you will," replied Harry Merriman, adding to himself, "when you get there."

"But all this has nothing to do with our pantomime," remarked Joe, coming back to the old subject; "and the long and the short of it is, if I am to play clown, it must be before the Midsummer holidays."

"Certainly; of course; we'll have the pantomime then," exclaimed everybody.

"It's quite ready," continued Joe; "the proscenium and scenery painted—dresses complete—masks and tricks made and varnished, and all perfect in their parts."

"Hear! hear! hear!"

"We shall want a carpenter to fit up the stage," Joe went on.

"I've made it all right with Bob Nailer," interposed Forks; "he's a reg'lar trump, he is—as knows all about theatres, and he'll knock up a stage in no time."

"Bravo, that's the sort!"

"I'll write to town, to Jack Bangs," continued Joe, "and he'll send me down as much red fire and fireworks as we want."

"Capital, capital!" responded the eager listeners.

"And now comes the great difficulty," said our hero, impressively.

"Ah!" ejaculated everyone, fervently.

"The next great difficulty is how we're to manage the doctor."

"Bother the doctor!" growled the six.

"I think we do that, occasionally," continued Joe, "but in this case we want to prevent the doctor from bothering us."

"Lock him in his room," suggested Harry Merriman.

"And Mother Red Nose—what's to become of her?" asked Tom Tattler; "she's as bad as the doctor."

"Lock her up with him."

"And old Fogem and Bungbung, the assistants?" inquired Ben Brisk.

"Put 'em into the coal cellar!" cried Jemmy Muddle, determinately, "and turn the key."

Joe burst into a laugh.

"The ideas are all capital," he said, "but I'm afraid we should find them rather hard to carry out."

Gloom instantly settled down on every countenance.

"But we mustn't despair," continued our hero, hopefully; "we must think of some other plan."

The countenances brightened up instantly.

"Can anyone suggest a new idea?" Joe asked.

"Give 'em a dose of summat as'll send 'em to sleep for a week," proposed Forks, brilliantly.

"Good, good!" cried the boys, eagerly; "what shall we give, and how shall we give it?"

Forks was at a standstill, and didn't know.

Nobody knew.

"I'll ask Dick Mullins, the doctor's boy," cried Forks, with a sudden idea; "he's wonderful clever at mixtures. His poison for rats and wermin's something marvellous."

"But we don't want to poison anybody, you know," said Joe.

"No, no, of course not," returned Forks. "I understand that. All we wants is something as'll make people sleep, so as nothing won't wake 'em. The only difficulty will be to get 'em to take it arter we've got it."

"That's just what I was thinking," remarked Joe; "I'm afraid the sleeping draught won't do any more than the coal cellar."

"Oh, dear! Oh!" almost groaned Jemmy Muddle, in his anxiety. "Can anybody tell what will do?"

"Stay!" exclaimed Joe, suddenly, "an idea has just come into my head, which I think will really answer the purpose."

"Hurrah!" shouted the seven, "let's hear what it is."

"Well, then," Joe replied, "it's this; suppose, two days before the breaking up, the doctor should receive a letter from town——"

"Yes, yes."

"From some important person, stating that he had heard a great deal of Tickle Toby Hall, and what an excellent school it was—how clever the pupils were——"

"At tumbling and standing on their heads!" interrupted Jemmy Muddle, with a grin.

Laughter, and cries of "Be quiet, Jemmy!" "Let's hear!" "Go on, Joe, old fellow!"

"And how kind the master was," Joe continued.

"Ha, ha, ha!" laughed the boys.

"Who said Walker?" murmured the actively industrious youth.

"Well, what then, Joe?" they asked.

"Then," proceeded our hero, "the letter might go on to say that this im-portant personage had three boys whom he was desirous of placing under the care of that worthy couple, Doctor and Mrs. McSwisher."

"Ho, ho! Yes; go on!"

"That the important personage could not spare the time to come to Whopping-ton to see the doctor and his wife, but would feel much obliged to the doctor and his wife if they would go to London instead to meet him."

"Yes, yes!" ejaculated the boys, eagerly, as they began to comprehend the drift of the idea.

"Of course," Joe went on, "both Doctor and Mrs. McSwisher would start off to town by the first train, and leave us here quietly to ourselves to fit up our stage and act our pantomime."

A ringing and triumphant cheer burst from the seven, as the speaker concluded.

"That will do, Joe," they cried, vociferously; "it's sure to do; couldn't be better!"

"But, then," said Harry Merriman, "there will still remain the two masters. What are we to do with them?"

"Oh, we must get rid of them somehow," replied Joe.

"I've got a hidea for them," remarked Forks.

"What is it?" inquired the rest, eagerly.

"Well," returned the small youth, "it's almost the same as Master Joe's hidea, but this is what it is. Mr. Foggy and Mounseer Bungbung are both on 'em dead nuts on the two Miss Tomkinses. I knows this because I've heard 'em talking about 'em and often seen 'em kiss their hands to them when they passed."

"Who are the Miss Tomkinses?" inquired the seven.

"They're pupils at Mrs. Larkspur's seminary down in the town. One of 'em's named Hangelina and the other Seraphina."

"Lovely names too," remarked Harry Merriman, with a smile.

"They're a pair of stunning gals," returned Forks; "not as I thinks they cares a straw about Foggy or Bungbung either, but they thinks they does, which'll answer the same purpose."

"Well?"

"Well, then," Forks went on, with an evident chuckle in his tone, "you must get some of Miss Teachwell's young ladies to write two love letters—two regular strong uns—supposed to come from the Miss Tomkinses, asking the masters to meet 'em at the door in the lane that leads into the back garding. They'll be sure to go like a couple of rats arter a bit of toasted cheese, and when they do, they'll fall into the trap as I'll lay for 'em."

"What trap?" asked the boys.

"I'll put one of the bobbies on the scent, and they'll both be locked up for trespassing," grinned Forks.

This idea was very much relished, and it was agreed that it should be adopted.

Everything now being finally settled, our hero exclaimed—

"Now, then, before we separate, three cheers for luck."

This was readily responded to.

"I'll lead," said Joe, "hip! hip! h——"

Suddenly Jemmy Muddle sprang forward and laid his hand on his companion's arm.

"Hush!" he cried, in a hasty whisper, as he pointed to a portion of the wall that was old, and where the plaster had fallen away.

There was a dead silence instantly.

Everyone looked in the direction of Jemmy's finger.

The bricks appeared loose just at that spot. One especially.

"It moves!" whispered Joe; "there is someone in the playground on the other side, trying either to get it out or push it forward."

"That he may see what's going on inside, I suppose," added Harry Merriman.

"Hush!" returned Joe; "perhaps we may find out who it is."

"I'll bet it's Sneaking Simon," exclaimed Jemmy Muddle. The brick still moved.

Gently but gradually it was forced more and more out of its place. At length it fell.

Joe was on his knees waiting for this.

The removal of the brick left an empty space, in the depths of which the light from the outside revealed a small aperture, through which anyone in the playground might have looked into the coach house.

"Is anyone there?" asked the seven, anxiously, in low tones.

"Not at present; but I expect there will be shortly," returned Joe. "I am waiting patiently."

He had not long to wait, for after a few seconds, the aperture became obscured, and an eye appeared looking through.

"Keep out of sight," whispered our hero; "our prying friend, whoever he is, is making his observations."

"Who is it?" inquired the rest, as they moved away.

"Can't distinguish; the hole's too small," Joe answered; "he can see us better than we can see him."

"Give him something for his trouble."

"I'm going to," replied Joe.

As he spoke he bent down (the aperture being near the ground), and drawing near the cavity, he suddenly applied his mouth and blew with all his strength.

A shower of dust and fine mortar went puffing out, and a stifled exclamation of pain, from the opposite side, proved that the peeper had got more in his eye than he expected.

Forks was instantly dispatched to make his observations, and quickly returned with the information that there was no one to be seen near the spot—no Sneaking Simon cringing about with his handkerchief to his damaged optic.

It was impossible to say who the spy was.

But as nothing resulted from the incident, the seven came to the conclusion that it was a simple piece of mischief on the part of one of the boys, who had been sufficiently paid for peeping.

*   *   *   *   *

It wanted but a week now to the time of breaking up.

The boys had been examined in great form by the principal in the presence of a goodly assembly of paternal and maternal relatives, who lived at or near Whoppington.

It was rather too far for Londoners to travel, however interesting the occasion might be.

The examination had gone off satisfactorily, and the young gentlemen had been pronounced quite up to the mark, both by their preceptor and parents.

This important event over, there was no more work done.

It was on the morning of the 20th of June that Doctor McSwisher, after reading his morning letters, rushed, in a state of joyful excitement, into the apartment where his spouse was preparing breakfast.

Forks had just entered with a plate of toast, and was nearly knocked off his legs by the impetuous principal.

"Arabella!" exclaimed the schoolmaster, "our fame is increasing; the celebrity of our school is spreading far and wide. A lord has written to me, expressing a desire to place his three sons under our fostering care. His three sons, Arabella, only think of that!"

As he spoke, he held up triumphantly a letter which had been carefully concocted by Joe and his companions, copied by Sam Scribble, a lawyer's clerk and friend of Forks, and sent off by our hero to his friend John Bangs, who posted it from London back again to Tickle Toby Hall.

It was written in a fine bold hand, enclosed in a large envelope, and stamped with a grand seal, the device of which was not very distinct.

The doctor, suspecting nothing of the trick, was in ecstasies.

So also was his spouse, whose nose grew several shades redder and more luminous.

"And it is really from a lord, is it, Erasmus." she inquired, eagerly.

"Yes, my love, there's no doubt of it," returned the doctor, exultingly; "look at the coat of arms on the seal."

Mrs. McSwisher looked, but could not distinguish anything particular.

"And what lord is it?" she asked.

"Lord—Lord—a—dear me, the name has slipped my memory, but I know it began with D."

Whilst the doctor and his wife were looking for the name, a suppressed giggle was heard outside.

It was the seven, who had seen the postman deliver the important letter, and, growing bold, under the relaxed state of discipline, had crept to the parlour door to hear what they could.

Forks, also equally anxious to catch the earliest particulars, had remained in the parlour, partly concealed by the window curtains, and was in a position where he could see and be seen by his friends outside. All were in a high state of glee.

"He's got it," telegraphed Joe with his lips, but without making any sound, to Forks behind the curtains.

"All right," Forks telegraphed back, and then pointed to the table where the doctor and his wife were eagerly poring over the epistle.

The seven pushed the parlour door a little more open, so that they could see distinctly through the crevice what passed within.

"Here it is," exclaimed the little principal, vivaciously; "Lord Dolderums."

"Dolderums!" echoed Mrs. McSwisher, reflectively. "Dolderums! — rather a strange name, Erasmus; don't you think so?"

Whatever the doctor might have thought, it was perfectly evident that the seven conspirators regarded it as intensely comic, since they, as well as the actively industrious youth, were doubled up in a convulsed state, that threatened an explosive burst that might have ruined everything.

Jemmy Muddle was writhing on the mat, with his handkerchief crammed into his mouth, in all the agonies of suppressed laughter.

Forks was doing his best to choke himself with the end of one of the window curtains, in order to keep himself within reasonable bounds.

"Be quiet, Jemmy," muttered Harry Merriman, at length, as he inserted his toe between his companion's ribs.

"I can't," gasped the latter, who was black in the face; "I've got the dol—dolde—oh, Lor', I shall burst!"

Jemmy Muddle was obliged to make a hasty rush into the garden, and have his laugh out among the currant bushes, or it is possible he might have ruptured a blood vessel.

"It's a Scotch family, my love," replied the doctor to his wife's remark, not appearing to see anything at all strange in that which so tickled the fancies of his pupils.

But then the doctor was not up to the little joke as they were.

"Yes," continued the principal, profoundly, "Dolderums is decidedly Scotch, and of very ancient origin, I opine."

This was enough to set the whole party off again.

"Hancient horigin!" murmured Forks to himself, as he doubled up and spun round on the tips of his toes, like a cock-chafer on a pin. "Oh, crikey, and we invented Dolderums ourselves, only the day afore yesterday, in the boot house!"

"The idea of his lordship sending us three of his sons," remarked Mrs. McSwisher, proudly; "what an honour."

"Yes, indeed!" assented her spouse, "to say nothing of the increase in our profits, and the prestige it will give us. We must pay the strictest attention to these noble youths!"

Another burst came from the seven and Forks.

"His lordship will recommend us, Arabella," continued the doctor, glowingly, "and we shall have our desks occupied by the heirs of dukes and marquises, and perhaps a prince or two, who knows?"

The matronly Arabella clasped her hands and uttered a snuffling ejaculation.

"But that's not all," the doctor went on; "his lordship wishes to see both of us in town personally, immediately—both of us, my love, and immediately, since he cannot possibly spare the time to pay us a visit here."

"Can we go, Erasmus?" asked Mrs. McSwisher, doubtfully.

"Can we, my love?" exclaimed her spouse, vehemently. "What a question! we must go."

"And leave the young gentlemen to——"

"Certainly. Have we not two assistant masters to look after them?"

"That's true, certainly, Erasmus," rejoined the matron, in a flutter of delight at the prospect of visiting town. "I think we may venture."

"Venture, decidedly! A few days more and the vacation will commence, and it's very hard if Fogem and Bonbon can't manage the pupils without us for that short space."

"I suppose we are to go to his lordship's mansion. Perhaps he may invite us to remain a few days with him," remarked the scholastic lady, arranging her hair and looking at herself in the glass.

"Not at all improbable, my love," returned the doctor.

"Where does Lord Dolderums reside?" asked his wife.

The principal, who, in his excitement, had read the epistle very hastily, was obliged to refer to it for information.

"Ah, here we have it!" he then exclaimed.

"Waggletree Park, Kensington, London."

"And when are we to start?"

"By the very earliest train," returned the principal, consulting his repeater; "there is none now till twelve. We shall therefore have time to finish our breakfasts, and I shall be able to give my instructions to my assistants, before we leave."

The doctor and his wife sat down to their coffee and toast, in the best of tempers.

During which Forks slipped out of the room unperceived, and at once joined the seven.

The entire party were in ecstasies at the result of their scheme, which had proved so triumphant a success.

"We shall be rid of the doctor and his wife at noon," cried Joe, exultingly, "and the pantomime will be performed after all."

"Hurrah!" shouted his companions.

"Ah! but Foggy and Bonbon," exclaimed Harry Merriman, as the assistants crossed his mind, "shall we get rid of them as easily?"

"No doubt of it," replied our hero; "the notes were written on pink scented note paper, and enclosed in pink envelopes, by Fanny Fairchild and Charlotte Berry, and Forks had them to post last night, didn't you, Forks?"

"Of course I did," the youth replied, "and I posted 'em; and they come this mornin', same time as Lord Dolderums'."

"Oh, then the masters have got them!" exclaimed the boys.

"I should rayther say as they had," returned Forks. "Oh, my heye!" continued the small page, grinning all over his face at the recollection, "you should 'ave seen their mugs when I put the billy duxes in their hands. It was enough to make a cat laugh."

"They must have read them long ago, then," remarked Harry Metriman.

"Read 'em, yes, twenty times over, I'll be bound," laughed Forks.

"HE UTTERED A STARTLED EXCLAMATION, AND RECOILED."

"Then they're reading them now for the twenty-first time," exclaimed Joe, as he pointed through the window, "look!"

In an instant all eyes were directed into the playground, at the end of which the two assistants were basking in the morning sun, devouring the contents of the charming little pink love letters.

"Let's go round into the garden," suggested Joe; "we can creep along by the palings behind the shrubs, and get close to where they are standing. I should like to hear what they say."

"Decidedly," assented the rest, eagerly; "let's come!"

The whole party at once made a hasty rush into the garden, and quickly reached the spot.

There were several knots out of the palings, so that the watchers could not only hear the words of the assistants, but observe the expression of their features.

"This is indeed happiness!" gurgled Mr. Fluster Fogem, in a species of rapture, as he held the pink morsel within an inch of his nose, and once more devoured its contents through his spectacles.

"O, mon Dieu, yes!" exclaimed M. Bonbon, taking the cigar he was smoking from between his lips, in order to apostrophise, "it is charmant."

"I had a slight suspicion Angelina was not altogether indifferent to me," continued the English master, in a sepulchral tone, "but I was not prepared for these strong expressions of attachment; oh, no, my wildest dreams could not have imagined it. Oh, Angelina!"

M. Jules Bonbon then went on—

"I did think zat Seraphine like me a leetel, bote I did not hop zat she loaf me so much as zis! Ah, Seraphine! chère Seraph—oh! diable!" he shrieked, suddenly.

In his rapture, he had put the wrong end of the cigar in his mouth.

All this was intensely amusing to the seven, who were unseen spectators.

"We are to be in the lane at the back of the house, at half-past six o'clock," presently remarked Mr. Fogem.

"Yes, at half-past seex!" assented his fellow assistant.

"But how can we get away? The boys don't go to bed till eight."

M. Bonbon curled his moustache, and shrugged his shoulders, in much perplexity.

"It is very hard," he replied.

"It would not do to miss an appointment like this!" exclaimed Fogem.

"Miss it!" cried the Frenchman; "I would not miss it for ze world!"

"But we can't both leave," returned his companion, gloomily.

"It is very hard, it is cruel!" groaned M. Jules, clasping his fat hands and turning up his eyes, with an expression of intense anguish.

"We might appeal to the doctor," suggested Fogem; "tell him important business calls us away."

"Ah, yes, yes," assented the foreigner; "zat vill do; ve must 'peel ze doctair, and he will give us permission."

He clasped his hands once more in a rapture.

"It is my loaf zat calls. O Seraphina adorable!" he exclaimed.

"Oh, amiable Angelina!" murmured Mr. Fluster Fogem, looking uncommonly spoony in his spectacles.

"Lardy dardy! lardy dardy! oh, my!" exclaimed Joe, in a clown's voice, behind the palings.

The assistants started, and hastily thrust their love letters into their coat pockets.

"Vat is zat?" said the Frenchman, apprehensively; "someone say 'lardee dardee.'"

"It must have been someone in the lane, I imagine," returned Mr. Fogem.

Before, however, they had time to make any further investigation, Forks was seen approaching.

"Please, gen'lemen, the doctor wants you immediate."

This summons for the moment put other thoughts out of their heads, and they prepared to obey it.

But as they left the spot, a mocking voice, that came they knew not whence, seemed to follow them and whisper in their ears—

"O Seraphina! O Angelina!"

CHAPTER XXXII.

IN WHICH THE DOCTOR AND HIS WIFE START FOR TOWN, AND THE TWO ASSISTANTS HASTEN TO KEEP THEIR APPOINTMENT—OUR HERO PUBLICLY ANNOUNCES THE PANTOMIME—BOB NAILER, THE CARPENTER, MAKES HIS APPEARANCE.

DOCTOR and Mrs. McSwisher were all ready to start, and the chaise stood at the door ready to take them to the station by ten o'clock.

Just as the hour was striking, the playground bell rang to summon the boys into school.

As soon as they were assembled, the doctor and his spouse entered briskly, ready dressed for travelling.

After running his eye along the desks to be sure no one was absent, the former said—

" Business of vital importance necessitates the immediate departure of myself and Mrs. McSwisher to London."

He paused a moment, and then continued, grandly—

" We have received a pressing invitation from Lord Dolderums, of Waggletree Park, which cannot be set aside; we shall therefore depart by the twelve o'clock express."

The risible muscles of the seven were pretty severely tried as the principal imparted this intelligence in a profoundly important manner.

By dint of strong efforts, however, they contrived not to laugh.

" At some scholastic establishments," the doctor continued, " the absence of the principals might be attended with danger. But it is not so at Tickle Toby Hall.

" The judicious training you have received will lead you to behave in my absence as though I were present.

" I therefore depart with perfect confidence both in my pupils and in the representatives I leave to watch over them. My time has now expired, young gentlemen; I must therefore say farewell until we meet again at the close of the holidays."

The doctor raised his hat grandly,

Mrs. McSwisher bowed her adieux, and the scholastic pair marched out, followed by three hearty cheers by the fifty boys who were delighted to get rid of both.

Six o'clock came—tea was over.

Suddenly the playground bell rang.

Everyone wondered why.

That is, everyone but the seven—they knew.

The fifty pupils came trooping in, and sat down according to custom.

Presently in came the two assistant masters.

Both were dressed in their best things, and both had roses stuck in their coats.

They had evidently gone in—regardless of expense—to create an impression on the Miss Tomkinses.

Watch chains (four and sixpenny ones), depended from their vests.

Studs glistened in their shirt fronts.

Rings (of questionable value) adorned their fingers.

As they walked, the perfume of bear's grease and lavender water, with which their respective heads and pocket handkerchiefs were saturated, filled the air and the noses of the pupils.

There was a good deal of sniffing and whispering, until Mr. Fluster Fogem, ascending the doctor's raised desk, exclaimed—

" Silence, if you please, young gentlemen."

The order was instantly obeyed, and the English master commenced—

" I have sent for you, young gentlemen, to inform you that a melancholy accident has just befallen a mutual friend of myself and my colleague, M. Bonbon."

The Frenchman sighed, turned up his eyes, sobbed slightly, and looked hard at the ceiling.

This information created a considerable sensation among the boys.

"Who is it, Mr. Fogem?" asked half a score of voices eagerly.

The master, who was unprepared for any questions, having no answer, sniffed a few times and applied his scented handkerchief to his face, as though overcome with grief.

"It's poor—dear—old—old—Ta—tid——"

Here his voice became inaudible from sobs, and he murmured some name, convulsively, that sounded to the listeners' ears like Tiddywinks, more than anything else.

M. Bonbon seemed so affected at this that he was compelled to turn away abruptly, and walk towards the fireplace to conceal his emotion.

But the name seemed to take a contrary effect on the boys.

Many smiled, some put their heads in their desks and laughed outright, and one voice exclaimed, in a pathetic tone (it was Jemmy Muddle's)—

"Poor old Tiddywinks; what's happened to him, Mr. Fogem?"

"Down train—four p.m.—collision—poor friend—boiler burst—oh, dear!"

Here the overpowered assistant again dried up, whilst Jemmy kindly undertook to explain to the boys.

"Poor old Thingamyjig's burst his boiler," he said, in a tone so awfully serious that thirty desks out of the fifty instantly opened, and as many heads disappeared into them.

Whether to hide their grief or their laughter was doubtful.

Mr. Fluster Fogem, having somewhat recovered himself, removed his handkerchief, and continued, mournfully—

"Our poor friend has sent a message requesting us to come to him immediately, and under these distressing circumstances, I don't see how we can refuse."

"Certainly not!" exclaimed Joe Muggins, Harry Merriman, and Ben Brisk, altogether. "Go by all means, Mr. Fogem! go at once, or perhaps poor old —a—what's-his-name may be dead before you get to him."

"I may depend upon you, my dear boys, during our absence," said the assistant, who appeared deeply touched by the sympathy evinced by the pupils.

"Oh, yes!" protested the seven; "you may depend on us. We'll take care that everything goes right while you're away."

"Thank you! thank you, young gentlemen, for your kindness," returned Mr. Fogem, evidently much relieved at these assurances. "I will depart at once. Come, Jules."

He descended from the desk, and taking his sorrowing companion by the arm, the affected pair left the schoolroom together.

"Don't hurry back on our account!" cried Joe after them.

"You can stop out all night if you like; we won't tell!" added Jemmy Muddle.

"Good boys! good boys!" returned the masters, from the distance.

No sooner were they gone, than the agile Forks threw a somersault in at the door that opened into the playground.

"'Ere we are!" he cried.

The act was infectious, and immediately the seven went in for an innings at tumbling that lasted several minutes, to the great delight of the spectators.

This done, Joe ascended the desk, and tapping loudly with the ruler, cried—

"Order!"

His schoolmates laughed, but obeyed.

"Now then, my boys, I want to ask you all a question," he said, impressively.

Everyone looked at him eagerly.

"What is it?" cried several.

"Are there any among you who have not seen a pantomime?" continued our hero.

"No, no, no!" cried some forty voices.

"Let all those who have seen a London pantomime hold up their hands," Joe went on.

Forty-two arms went up in the air like so many railway signals.

"Very good; now let all those who like pantomimes put down their hands," repeated Joe.

The forty-two arms dropped immediately.

"Good again!" Joe exclaimed, triumphantly.

Then, flourishing the ruler, he continued—

"Now I've got a secret to tell you all; you're going to see a pantomime!"

"A pantomime!" echoed everyone

"Yes," returned Joe, "a grand comic Christmas pantomime at Midsummer."

"When?" shouted his companions, excitedly.

"To-morrow night."

"Where?" was the next eager question.

"At the Theatre Royal, Tickle Toby House," was the reply; "we've been getting it up all the half year, and now the old Swishers and Foggy and Bonbon are out of the way, we're going to act it to-morrow night."

A shout of intense delight rang through the schoolroom at this joyful intelligence.

The excitement was intense when our hero, taking from his pocket a number of handbills, which the invaluable Forks had had printed, distributed them amongst his schoolmates.

"There!" he cried, as he scattered them hither and hither; "read them; the only correct house-bill of performance."

The bills created an immense sensation.

"Why, they're real bills!" cried the boys.

"I believe you they are too," returned Joe, exultingly.

"Just the same as they have in real theatres!" was the next remark.

"Of course."

The bills certainly were attractive, and read as follows:—

"Theatre Royal, Tickle Toby House. On Thursday Evening will be performed the Grand Comic Pantomime, entitled— 'Harlequin Old Bogey; or, the Brave Boys of Whoppington.'

Characters in the Opening.

The Demon Tingleback (an ugly subject)
    Master H. Merriman.
Baron Bogey (a monster in human form)
    Master Tom Tattler.
Funky Fum (his servant)
    Master J. Muddle.
Jack, the Miller's Son . Master Ben Brisk.
Flourbags, the Miller
    Master C. Dimond.
Goggleeyes (an imp) Master W. Warner.
Pretty Polly, the Fair Maid of Whoppington . . . . Miss F. Fairchild.
Dame Durden (her mamma)
    Master J. Muggins.

Immortals.

Crystal, the Fairy Queen
    Miss Lydia Lester.
Dewdrop   Miss Lucy Sparkle.
Glitter   her   ,, Charlotte Berry.
Spangledrop atten- ,, Alice Lover.
Glow-worm dants ,, Sally Pickles.
Gossamer   ,, Adela Allison.

Scenery and Incidents.

Gloomy abode of Tingleback, in the undiscovered regions of nowhere—Exterior of Baron's Castle—Comic song— 'Funky Fum'—The Old Mill—Pretty Poll and her Suitors—Fairies' Moonlit Retreat—Grand Ballet—All in a Fog— Cleared up by the—

Grand Transformation Scene.

Clown . . . . Master Joe Muggins.
Pantaloon . . . ,, Jemmy Muddle.
Harlequin . . . ,, Ben Brisk.
Columbine . . Miss Fanny Fairchild.
Sprite . . . . Master T. Forks.
Policeman . . . Master H. Merriman.

Fun and Frolic—Butchers, Bakers, and Candlestick Makers—Railway Station—Pawnbroker's and Sausage Shop— Grand Finale."

The above created such a furore as would have made Doctor McSwisher's hair stand on end, if he could have witnessed it.

Leaving the eager crowd to comment upon what they were going to see on the morrow, let us adjourn to the exterior, where the carpenter, Bob Nailer, with his tools and a cart full of timber, waited for admission.

"I thought I had better have him round in good time," said Forks.

"Open the gates!" cried Joe, "and let him in."

In an instant the large gates were unbarred and swung open on their hinges.

Bob led his horse into the yard, and the gates were closed again.

"Well, young gents," he said, with a good-natured smile, "so you wants a stage put up, does you?"

"Yes, yes!" returned the seven, eagerly, "and you must do it, if you sit up all night."

"Wouldn't be the first time as I've done that at pantomime times," Bob replied; "when I used to work at Doory Lane——"

"Were you ever at Drury Lane?" asked the boys, in astonishment.

"I was there five year, off and on, young gentlemen," returned the carpenter. "I know all about tricks and traps and pantomimes."

"Then you're just the man we want," cried the lads, "and the sooner you begin the better."

"The first thing to be done is to get this wood out of the cart," remarked the carpenter, and at once commenced lifting out the planks and poles.

At this juncture Jane the cook and Betsy the housemaid made their appearance.

"Goodness gracious!" they exclaimed, "whatever's all this?"

"Timber," quietly replied Bob Nailer, who was known to them both.

"So it seems," returned the cook, "but what's it for?"

"I'm going to build a stage, my dear!" Bob replied, quietly, as he continued to unload the cart, the youngsters assisting.

"A stage!" cried Betsy; "what stage—a stage coach?"

The seven burst into a laugh.

"No," answered the carpenter, "a theatrical stage."

"Theatrical!" echoed the two domestics, holding up their hands almost aghast; "what do you want with a theatrical stage here?"

Joe advanced and said, blandly—

"We're going to act a pantomime to-morrow night, and you must come and see it."

But Jane and Betsy were perfectly aware of the horror with which their master regarded such amusements, and they looked as aghast as though the house had been about to fall about their ears.

"Lor' bless us, a pantomime!" they exclaimed; "whatever would the doctor and missus say if they was to know it?"

"But they are not here, and so they won't know it," replied the seven, who had gathered round.

"But then there's the masters, they won't allow any performing," said the anxious servants.

"Old Foggy and Bungbung are both gone out, and I don't think they'll hurry themselves home," exclaimed Jemmy Muddle.

"The fact is, Betsy," said Joe, who was on very friendly terms with both cook and housemaid, "we're going to perform a pantomime exactly as they do it in London. It's called 'Harlequin Old Bogey, or the Brave Boys of Whopping-ton.'"

"Oh, my!" exclaimed the domestics, in amazement.

"I'm sure you'll like it," went on Joe; "there's plenty of singing and dancing, and demons and fairies and red fire, and besides," he added, "the young ladies from Miss Teachwell's are coming over to act in it."

At this astounding intelligence the hands and eyes of Jane and Betsy went up in sheer wonder.

"Well, I never!" they each said; but their curiosity was excited, and their horror had diminished in proportion; "and so the young ladies really are coming, are they?"

"They are indeed," the seven assured them, "and the dresses will be splendid."

"I should think they would," exclaimed Betsy, eagerly; "and they'll be fairies, I suppose?"

"Exactly," returned Joe; "you'll say you never saw anything like it before in your life."

"Well, I should like to see you, that I should," said the cook, who was rapidly becoming inoculated with the pantomime mania.

"So you shall, Jane, and so shall you, Betsy," answered our hero, "and," he whispered, "if you've any particular friends you would like to be present, invite them. We'll have plenty of oranges and nuts and ginger wine, and it will be as jolly as being at a real play."

Both the domestics had sweethearts in the town, and it suddenly struck them that it would add greatly to their enjoyment if they were present, and they replied, with a giggle—

"We do know one or two parties, and we'll ask them to come."

"That's right," replied Joe, and added, slyly, "young ladies bringing their sweethearts admitted gratis."

"Oh, Master Joe," they answered, blushing violently, "what a idear."

"A very good idea, I think," joined in Harry Merriman.

"And see here," Joe went on, as he

produced a pair of bright scarlet bows, and presented them; "you must each wear one of these in honour of the occasion."

The domestics received the bows gratefully and made no further objections.

They were now quite as eager for the forthcoming treat as the rest.

CHAPTER XXXIII.

IN WHICH THE SEVEN, ACCOMPANIED BY FORKS, SALLY FORTH TO LOOK AFTER MR. FLUSTER FOGEM AND M. BONBON—WHAT HAPPENED.

BETSY promised our young friends that she would bring forth the pantomime dresses out of the press.

The seven gave three cheers, and walked round the yard on their heads, and then at once turned their attention to the erection of the stage.

Upon consideration the dining-room was decided upon as the most convenient apartment for that purpose, being of considerable length, breadth, and height, and having windows both at the end and on one side, which would afford ventilation, and allow the fumes of the red fire and other combustibles to escape.

Here, then, Bob Nailer commenced his operations.

Joe had dotted down on paper the exact manner in which the stage was to be erected, and the exact size it was to be, and Bob, having received his directions, had only to carry them out.

"You won't want us for an hour or two," said our hero to him.

"Right you are," returned Bob, as he took off his jacket; "I only want to be left alone to my work, and before breakfast-time to-morrow I'll have such a stage ready as you never see in your lives—in a private house, at least."

Accordingly the seven left the carpenter, with a request to Jane and Betsy that they would look after his bodily wants and give him as much bread and cheese and beer as he required.

They then sallied out for the purpose of watching the two assistant masters.

Punctually at seven o'clock Messrs. Fogem and Bonbon, with their roses in their button-holes, and their scented handkerchiefs, strolled past the back door of Mrs. Larkspur's seminary for young ladies.

In order to increase the importance of their approach they both smoked cigars.

The locality into which this back door opened was called Doddy's Lane—probably because someone of that name owned the estate.

There was no thoroughfare through Doddy's Lane, consequently, when the anxious but deluded lovers reached the end, they had to turn back.

Up and down, and down and up, they strolled, and still no signs of the appearance of the fair Tomkinses.

The scholastic gentlemen began to grow impatient.

Mr. Fogem was afflicted with corns, and had on a pair of tight boots, which did not add to the pleasure of his sensations.

"Are they never coming?" he murmured, fretfully.

"Perhaps zey can't get out yet," suggested M. Bonbon; "we must have patience."

There was plenty of room for the exercise of that virtue.

Seven — eight — even nine o'clock struck, and neither the adorable Seraphina nor the amiable Angelina had shown even the tip of one of their graceful noses.

Still the expectant swains persevered.

Up and down, down and up Doddy's Lane they still paced, as the seven cautiously approached. It was now dark, and there was but a young moon.

"There they are," whispered Forks, who was one of the party, and whose quick eyes caught sight of the masters.

"Ha, ha!" laughed Jemmy Muddle, "what a jolly lark; ain't they a pair of spoons? Look at 'em; lardy dardy, lardy dardy dee."

His companions joined in the laugh, and Joe said to Forks—

"Didn't you say you'd made it all right with the bobby to look after them?"

"Yes, Master Joe," returned the youth with the buttons. "I spoke to Police Constable Puncher, 44 X division, and he promised faithful as he'd keep his eye on 'em."

"I don't see anything of him," remarked Harry Merriman, looking around.

"Nor I! Nor I!" echoed his companions.

"Did you tip him the half-crown?" asked Jemmy Muddle.

"Of course I did," returned Forks, rather indignantly, "and if I hadn't, he'd do anything to oblige me, cos he's a relative of mine."

"Oh, that's all right," cried all the boys.

"I'd take the odds he's here already," continued the youth, "propping himself up in some dark corner, and watching the two assistants like a cat would a couple of mice."

"Right you are, Tom," exclaimed a gruff, jovial voice, from some invisible speaker.

"That's him, that's Phil Puncher," cried Forks, enthusiastically.

"Right you are again, my pippin," the voice repeated, and at the same moment, a bright light from the bull's eye of a policeman's lantern flashed in the faces of the party.

"I'm a-looking at you," continued the jolly speaker, facetiously, and at the same moment the portly figure of the constable stepped forward from a doorway in the wall, where he had been concealed.

"Bravo!" cried the boys.

"Three cheers for X 44," exclaimed Jemmy Muddle, rapturously.

"Thank you, young gentlemen, for your good wishes," returned Mr. Puncher, "but I think you'd better owe me the cheer. We don't want to put the parties yonder on the scent, do we?"

"No, no, no! certainly not," admitted the seven.

"Very well, then, the quieter we go about our work the better," remarked X 44.

"Hold hard, they're coming this way," whispered Forks, hastily.

"Suppose we just step round the corner," suggested the constable; "we shall be out of sight then."

Having masked the bull's eye of his lantern, Puncher turned off at the end of the lane and walked away to a short distance.

"He seems a jolly chap, this bobby, doesn't he?" said Joe to his friends, as they followed.

"Capital," they replied.

"He's a first-rate cove, I can tell you," Forks assured them.

"Now then, young gentlemen," said the policeman, as he came to a stop, "what is it you want me to do with these perfessionals?"

"We want you to frighten them almost to death, so that they'll be glad to hide themselves anywhere, and not interfere with us," replied the boys.

"I suppose you wouldn't like me to take 'em into custody, eh? Cos if you would, I can run 'em in easy enough, you know."

The boys consulted together for a moment.

"It wouldn't be half a bad idea to give 'em a night's lodging, would it?" suggested Forks, whose affections were anything but strong towards the assistants.

"I don't quite like the idea myself," returned Joe, "if any other way will do as well."

"Oh, I'll undertake to give 'em such a startler as they never had since they first cut their teeth," said the constable, chuckling; "so suppose you leaves it to me."

"Yes, yes!" exclaimed the party unanimously; "that will be the best way."

"And I suppose you'd like to see a little of the fun, wouldn't you, young gentlemen?" asked Mr. Puncher, with a grin.

"Rather!" the youngsters replied.

"Wait a minute, then," said the policeman, as he walked back to the corner of Doddy's Lane. He appeared to be making his observations, and presently returned smelling very strongly of rum, so it may be supposed he took advantage of his temporary absence to refresh himself from a small bottle he carried in his pocket.

"Come on, my boys, it's all right," he whispered, in a low tone; "they've just been up to the top of the lane and turned back. I think they've come to a stop close by the garden door."

"We're all ready," returned the seven.

"Steady, then," rejoined the constable, "follow me; keep close to the wall, and tread light."

Obeying these injunctions, the party cautiously advanced down the lane till they came within a few yards of Mrs. Larkspur's.

"Hush, hold hard," whispered X 44, as he stopped.

The two assistants, as the latter had said, were halting exactly opposite the door.

They had evidently had enough of marching up and down, and their enthusiasm was rapidly abating.

"How do you feel, Jules?" inquired Mr. Fogem of his companion, rather dolefully.

"Oh, I feel most disappoint," returned the Frenchman, in a tone of despair. "How do you feel yourself, *mon ami?*"

"Almost exhausted, and I have a corn on each of my little toes that troubles me awfully," replied the English assistant.

"It's a case of tight boots and bunions," whispered Jemmy Muddle to Joe.

"Vat can detain ze loavely creatures?" exclaimed M. Bonbon.

"O Seraphina adorable!" he continued, passionately clasping his hands together.

"O amiable Angelina!" groaned Mr. Fluster Fogem, extending his arms despairingly, and giving his colleague a back-handed slap in the dark.

"Oh, my nose!" yelled M. Jules, stamping his feet madly with the pain, and coming down with a crunch on his brother assistant's toes.

"Ah, ugh, my corn!" shrieked Mr. Fogem, and then the two howled together in concert.

"What a jolly row," muttered Forks; "it's enough to frighten all the cats in the neighbourhood into fits."

At length the Frenchman exclaimed, wrathfully—

"Vat for you strike me on my nose, eh, sare?"

"Bother your nose," growled Mr. Fogem.

"Vat! you punch my nose, you ugly Englishman?"

"I would if I could find it, you French frog."

"Bah!"

"Boo!"

All this was intensely delightful to the listeners.

"There'll be a fight in a minute," muttered Harry Merriman.

"Let's get it up if we can," urged Jemmy Muddle, as he stooped down and picked up a piece of dry mould.

Each of his companions did the same.

The pair of irritated lovers were just then in a humour to quarrel, and to take offence at anything.

They were standing in the semi-darkness, growling at each other like a couple of angry poodles.

Jemmy, breaking off a portion of mould, discharged it at a venture.

It took effect on M. Bonbon's right eye.

"Ah! you villain Foggy," he yelled, "you knock my eye out. I shall have your life!"

The podgy little Frenchman clenched his fist, and rushed wildly at his brother assistant for the purpose of annihilating him on the spot.

Mr. Fluster Fogem, who was not remarkable for courage, limped about on one leg, endeavouring to keep out of the way of the irritated Jules.

It being gloomy, neither could see the other's whereabouts distinctly.

They were guided by sound rather than sight.

"*Diable!*" yelled M. Bonbon, "vy don't you come and be kill, you *poltron!* coward!"

"What have I done?" shrieked the English master.

"Vat have you done?" echoed the wrathful Frenchman; "you have knock out vun of my eye. Ah!" he shouted suddenly, as he received a second lump of mould from the hand of Harry Merriman, "now you have knock out ze other. I am kill, I am kill, oh, Seraphina, adorable, oh, oh!" and down he went on the ground.

"I'll take my oath I haven't touched either of your eyes, you mendacious foreigner!" protested Mr. Fogem, vehemently; "if I have, I'll eat my——"

He was about to say "hat," but just at that moment a handful of the Doddy

Lane mould, thrown by the small youth in the buttons, entered his mouth and almost choked him.

"Oh, oh! mur-ur-der!" he gasped, "I'm cho-king. Ugh, you—treacherous —ruffian. Oh, An-ge-li-na, oh, oh, oh!"

Mr. Fluster Fogem, having twirled round several times on one leg, like a tom-tit in a fit, gave way suddenly, and fell heavily upon M. Bonbon's ribs.

There was another yell from the little Frenchman, and then the pair grappled one another, and rolled over and over in the dust and darkness, growling, scratching, and swearing at each other like a pair of infuriated Tom cats, and amidst the suppressed laughter of the seven and Police Constable Puncher.

This interesting performance went on for some time, until our hero, Joe, thought it would be as well to put a stop to it.

So when at length the combatants left off pulling each other's hair and paused an instant to take breath, he murmured, in a counterfeit female voice, that seemed to come from over the wall—"Jules, dearest!"

"Ha!" cried the Frenchman; "some-von call; it is Seraphina."

"Fluster, darling!" whispered Harry Merriman, in a similarly feminine tone.

"Hark!" exclaimed Mr. Fogem; "it is the voice of Angelina."

The assistants hastily scrambled to their feet, and listened intently.

"Are you there, love?" cried Joe again, softly.

"Are you there, ducky?" repeated Harry, both still imitating the voices of the Miss Tomkinses.

"Yes, yes, yes! we are here," eagerly answered the assistants, forgetting their recent animosity in their joy at hearing what they supposed to be their sweethearts' voices. "Where are you?" they asked.

"In the garden," repeated the imaginary fair ones.

"Why don't you come out?" was the next question.

"Alas, we can't get out," was the reply. "Mrs. Larkspur has locked the gate."

"Ze ole cat," muttered M. Bonbon, between his teeth.

"Can't you get over the wall?" sighed the invisible Tomkinses.

This was a brilliant idea, and both the scholastic gentlemen caught at it immediately.

"Ah! yes! we will get over the wall," they exclaimed, eagerly.

They made a simultaneous rush towards it, and there they stopped with their noses against the bricks.

The wall was tolerably high, and neither of the lovers was remarkably good at gymnastic exercises.

They scratched their heads ruefully and looked at each other.

"*Diable!*" muttered Bonbon; "I cannot climb up a straight wall like a cat or a blue bottel."

"No more can I," sighed Mr. Fogem.

"Vat is to be done?" said the Frenchman, reflectively. "I know," he exclaimed, suddenly, turning to his friend, "ve moss help each other."

"Certainly," returned his companion; "what fools we were to quarrel."

"So ve vos; give me your hand."

The assistants shook hands.

"And now what do you propose?" asked the English master.

"I will climb up on to your shoulders to ze top of ze vall, and pull you up after me," answered M. Bonbon; "and zen ve can drop down into ze garden on ze other side."

"Very well," returned Fluster Fogem, as he placed himself in position.

After a good deal of gasping and grunting, the podgy little Frenchman dragged himself to the top, and sat astride on a choice collection of broken glass bottles, placed there to keep off the cats.

"Oh! *diable!*" he groaned; "vot am I sit upon?"

"Help me up," shouted Mr. Fogem, anxiously, from below.

"I can't; it is impossible!" almost shrieked the distressed Jules; "ze top of ze wall is stuck full of pins and needles."

"Psha! it's a paltry excuse," returned his fellow assistant; "you don't want to help me."

What more might have passed it is impossible to say, for just at that moment Mr. Puncher, having possessed himself of the little Frenchman's foot, gave him a sudden hoist, and, with a yell of terror, M. Bonbon descended with startling abruptness into the garden on the opposite side.

Here he lay on his back, threatening vengeance on his companion.

Mr. Fogem, knowing nothing of what had taken place, and feeling the task of scaling the wall hopeless, tried the door.

It was not locked, and opened at the first attempt.

"Ha, ha!" he cried, exultingly, as he entered. "I am inside almost as soon as that traitor Bonbon."

He advanced, and at the first step tumbled over the traitor, who was stretched on the ground right across the path.

Hostilities had nearly broken out again, but prudence restrained them.

Angelina and Seraphina were probably close at hand, and it would not look well for their lovers to be seen fighting, they thought.

They accordingly picked themselves up, and, pocketing their mutual grievances for the time, proceeded to explore the garden.

As soon as they had left the gate, Mr. Puncher looked in cautiously after them.

"All right," he muttered to himself, with a chuckle; then, putting his head out again, he whispered to the seven, "Come on, my lads; gently."

The party entered, and cautiously followed the track of the two dupes.

CHAPTER XXXIV.

IN WHICH MESSRS. FOGEM AND BONBON FAIL TO DISCOVER THE MISS TOM-
KINSES, BUT AROUSE MRS. LARKSPUR INSTEAD—THEIR ARDOUR IS COOLED
BY A SUFFICIENT QUANTITY OF COLD WATER.

MESSRS. FOGEM AND BONBON, treading lightly on the gravel, and occasionally putting their feet in the flower-beds, approached the house.

It was very quiet and gloomy.

"Where are ze lovely creatures?" whispered the little Frenchman.

"I don't see anything answering that description," returned the English master, fretfully; "but that's not surprising, it's so confoundedly dark."

"All ze better, no vun vill see us," remarked M. Jules; "ze young ladees are doubtless waiting for us in the summer house."

"Where the deuce is it, I should like to know?" growled Mr. Fogem, catching his toe against the handle of the garden roller, and plunging forward like a battering ram with his head in the back of his companion, who was a little ahead.

"*Diable!* vot are you about?" shouted M. Bonbon.

"I'll be hanged if I know," returned the startled Fluster. "I can't take a step but I tumble over something."

The adventurers continued their course.

X 44 and his party followed.

"Zey will come soon, I should think," remarked the Frenchman, as they approached the house.

"I hope so," was his companion's reply.

After waiting a little, M. Jules exclaimed, softly—

"Seraphina, my love!"

"Angelina, my angel!" joined in Mr. Fogem.

To which Joe and Harry replied, in muffled tones—

"Jules, my ducky!"

"Fluster, my love!"

"Hark! hush!" exclaimed the expectant pair, excitedly.

"They are coming; we are here!"

"Where?" inquired the invisible charmers, plaintively.

"Here; here, in the dark."

"We can't see you; oh, dear! oh, dear!"

The distressed damsels now began to whimper.

Mr. Fogem and M. Jules strained their eyes till they almost started out of their heads in every direction, but could distinguish nothing of the beautiful Miss Tomkinses.

Their patience was almost exhausted.

"Where the deuce are they?" growled the former; "to be continually hearing the voices of the dear angels close to us, and yet not to be able to catch a glimpse of them, is extremely agonizing."

"'BRAVO!' CRIED THE BOYS, WITH ALL THEIR MIGHT."

"Agonizing!" repeated M. Bonbon, chewing the end of his moustache irritably; "I am in despair. Oh, Seraphina!"

"Oh, Angelina!"

"Lardy dardy! lardy dardy! lardy dardy dee!" murmured Joe, in an exquisitely feminine tone.

"Zere, did you hear zat?" whispered the little Frenchman, laying his hand on his companion's arm; "somevon say 'lardee dardee dee' again. Vot do it mean—'lardee dardee dee?'"

Mr. Fogem scratched his head violently to assist him in explaining the mysterious sounds, but failed to do so.

At this moment, a light appeared shining from a window over their heads, the blind of which was down.

The light attracted the adventurers.

"They must be there," exclaimed the English master, pointing upwards.

"Unable to discover us in the dark, the lovely angels have returned to the house in despair, and are now going to bed."

"Go to bed, an' ve not meet zem after all," wailed M. Bonbon; "oh, it is cruel, it is terrible!"

Both the eyes of the watchers were fixed anxiously upon the blind.

Suddenly a shadow, in profile, appeared reflected on it.

It was a woman's shadow undoubtedly, and though it bore little resemblance (the nose especially) to anything lovely or angelic, it was enough to throw those who gazed upon it, into a fever of excitement.

"It is she."

"It is her," cried the masters, simultaneously.

The shadow went through some awfully expressive pantomime, as though it were making desperate attempts to dislocate its own neck.

Suddenly something seemed to give way, and two shadowy hands appeared grasping a dark mass between them.

"Oh, mon Dieu! she have pull her head off," shrieked M. Jules, in a voice of terror.

But he was mistaken, it was not the head, but the hair that had been detached.

The anxiety of the tantalized pair increased as the indistinct form flitted to and fro between the light and the blind.

M. Bonbon vowed it was his adorable Seraphina.

Mr. Fogem declared it was his amiable Angelina.

How to communicate with them was the question.

Whilst they stood meditating, Phil Puncher and the seven had been arranging the plan which was to bring matters to the crisis they desired.

They had accidentally discovered a garden engine, which was considered by all as a most effective and useful assistant.

This machine had been carried to the end of the path, almost close to the gate.

It was well supplied with water, and could eject a powerful stream to any part of it.

The working of this engine was entrusted to Joe Muggins and Harry Merriman.

The former was to guide the hose, the latter to work the pump.

"You must keep your eyes open, young gentlemen," counselled the police constable, "and let 'em have it strong."

"They shall, you may depend on it," they replied; "we'll give them the best soaking they ever had in their lives."

The assistants had at length hit upon a means of announcing their proximity to their charmers, by throwing up a little fine gravel at the window.

Accordingly they each took up a little.

This was the cue for the boys, who hastily filled their hands with (not a little, but as much as they could hold, of) the same material.

"We must throw it up as gently as possible, or we may break the windows," said Mr. Fogem.

"Oh, yes, very gently," returned his brother professor.

"Oh, yes, very!" murmured Jemmy Muddle, ironically, to his companions, as they crept forward, almost close to the masters; "lardy dardy dee!"

"Now then," whispered the English master, "both together."

They threw up the gravel very circumspectly, so much so that hardly any of it reached the desired spot.

But this was amply compensated for by the seven and Forks, who fired a terrific volley at the same instant, and a violent storm of mould, gravel, and pebbles rattled like hail against the window, accompanied by a flower pot, hurled by X 44, which went crashing against the window sill.

The scholastic gentlemen were quite astounded at the effect they imagined they had produced.

So also was Mrs. Larkspur, whose bedroom it happened to be, and who was about retiring for the night.

Under the impression that the house must be on fire, she threw up the window and looked out.

Messrs. Fogem and Bonbon caught a glimpse of something white (it was Mrs. Larkspur's frilled night-cap), and their fervent imaginations pictured the fair faces of the Misses Tomkins looking down upon them.

"Who is it?" cried Mrs. Larkspur, in ominously gruff tones.

"It is I—me—it is us, your devoted Jules, your affectionate Fogem," exclaimed both lovers, failing in their excitement to notice the harsh voice of the inquirer.

The middle-aged schoolmistress was so shocked at the glowing expressions that she almost fell out of the window, and remained for a moment utterly speechless.

"Come down, dearest Angelina!" cried Mr. Fluster.

"Come down, Seraphina adorable!" echoed M. Bonbon; each extending their arms and making frantic efforts to reach the window by standing on tiptoe.

This daring appeal restored Mrs. Larkspur's power of speech.

"You impertinent fellows, how dare you address me in this manner?—how dare you intrude upon my premises?" she bawled, in a vixenish tone; then, raising her voice several degrees higher, she screamed—"Help! thieves! police!"

"Hollo! hollo! what's the matter?" cried a deep voice from the lane, and the next moment the form of X 44 appeared on the top of the wall.

"Thieves in the garden, Mr. Policeman," bawled the excited lady in the nightcap; "take 'em into custody."

"I'll have 'em, mum, like a shot!" exclaimed the constable, as he dropped from the wall, and, unmasking his lantern, commenced his search.

The horror of the assistants was intense.

There was no escape, for the policeman and his bull's eye were between them and the gate.

Other dark forms too—doubtless attracted by the tumult—seemed to be looming in the distance.

Capture was inevitable—they would be dragged ignominiously to a felon's cell.

In their desperation they clung to one another.

How sincerely they wished the amiable Angelina and the adorable Seraphina at the bottom of the Red Sea—and themselves too—or anywhere else but where they were.

"Oh, miséricorde! vat shall ve do? Ve shall be transport," groaned M. Bonbon.

Just at that moment Mr. Fogem espied the summer house.

Instantly he rushed towards it.

His fellow assistant followed.

In their eagerness to enter they jostled and punched one another.

At length they managed to get inside and closed the door.

There was no lock to the latter, and they could only hope to keep out the enemy by leaning their backs against it.

This they did, and listened with beating hearts for what was coming.

They could hear the heavy tramp, tramp, crunch, crunch, of Police Constable Puncher's heels on the gravel, as he searched about.

Gradually he drew nearer.

He stopped at the summer house.

"The vagabonds can't be fur off; I'm bound to nab 'em!" they heard him exclaim, softly, to himself.

Suddenly the bright light of his lantern flashed upon the darkness.

The policeman hammered at the door of the summer house with his clenched fist, chuckling immensely at the same time.

"Is it locked?" he ejaculated, meditatively, in a tone loud enough for those inside to hear; "yes, it must be; they can't be here."

"Have you caught the wretches yet, policeman?" bawled Mrs. Larkspur from the window at this juncture.

"Not yet, mum," he called back in return. "I'm rayther afraid they've got away somehow."

But Phil Puncher, though he said this, knew very well he had his victims safe under his thumb.

And after replying to the governess, he whispered to Jemmy Muddle and the rest—

"Just give your friends the office to wheel that there garden engine this way. I'm just a-going to give this summer house a slooch out."

Away rushed the boys, and the next moment the machine stood before the door.

"Now then, where's the flexible tube?" he asked.

"Here it is," said Joe, briskly.

X 44 grasped the hose, and quietly inserting the point between the ornamental woodwork in the upper portion of the structure, allowed it to hang as nearly as possible (according to his judgment) over the heads of the culprits.

Then, keeping it steady with his finger and thumb, he whispered to Harry Merriman—

"Now then, pump away like bricks."

Harry went to work with all his might.

Up and down went the handle.

Whizz—fizz—whizz—fizz, poured out the aqueous torrent, as if from an enormous squirt.

Terrific yells from the interior informed the delighted youngsters that X 44 had calculated the position of Messrs. Fogem and Bonbon to a T.

Neither of them dared to move from the door, and there they stood gasping and groaning, with the water pouring down upon their heads till they were drenched to the skin.

"Oh, *mon Dieu!* I am choke," shrieked the Frenchman.

"I shall catch my death of cold!" cried his brother professor, breathlessly.

"Go it, Harry," urged Jemmy Muddle, snapping his fingers in the extremity of his glee. "Let 'em have it; it's better than Tingleback."

There was not the least doubt Harry Merriman did let them have it, and when he was tired Joe relieved him, so that the luckless assistants had more cold water in three minutes than they had ever had in their lives before.

But human endurance has its limits, and the sensations caused by the pumping became at last so unbearable that at last the half-drowned wretches made a hasty bound to another spot.

But here they were no better off than before; the stream followed and squirted over them as vigorously as ever.

Again they changed their place.

But it was no use; the accommodating jet yet came streaming after them, on their heads, in their eyes and ears, down their backs (and fronts), till their very pockets and boots were filled and running over.

Their limbs shivered, their teeth chattered with cold, and they began to feel perfectly desperate.

"*Diable!* if I shall stand zis mosh longer," gasped M. Bonbon. "Let us try to run away."

"I—I—I'm ready," returned Mr. Fogem, in a manner strongly suggestive of a pair of castanets.

"Come on, zen," said his colleague; "give me your arm."

They linked their arms together, and throwing open the door, made a sudden rush out.

Whizz—fizz, came a stream of water full in their faces.

With a loud yell of despair they fell on their backs, and lay full length on the gravel walk.

Police Constable Puncher coolly directed the rays of his bull's eye into their eyes till they were as dazzled and blinded as a pair of owls in the sun, during which the seven had plenty of time to make their escape unseen and unsuspected.

"I've dropped on you at last, you see, my fine fellows," remarked X 44, sarcastically; "knowed I should; there's no getting away from me. When I means nabbing, I nabs."

The luckless pair groaned audibly.

"A pretty disreputable position for two gents as is supposed to be respectable members of society, to be found in, I don't think," continued the policeman, in a tone half of pity at their degraded condition, and half of reproof. "What'll your poor mothers say, eh?"

Another groan was the only answer.

X 44 now put on an air of authority.

"Come, get up," he cried, sternly; "law's law, and duty's duty, and I'm a-going to lock you both up."

At this terrible threat, the drenched

pair sprang to their feet and made a desperate rush towards the gate.

The constable made a great demonstration as if to stop them (which he had no real intention of doing), and after scurrying them up and down, and over Mrs. Larkspur's flower beds for a few minutes, to his own great amusement, he

allowed the frightened professors to reach the gate.

Here he paused, leaning against the wall and laughing immoderately, as he watched Messrs. Fogem and Bonbon flying for dear life up Doddy's Lane, and leaving a stream of water behind them, like two human water carts.

CHAPTER XXXV.

POLICE CONSTABLE PUNCHER GOES ON TO THE STAGE AND PUTS HIS FOOT IN IT—THE RING AT THE BELL—MESSRS. FOGEM AND BONBON RETURN AND TAKE REFUGE FROM OFFENDED JUSTICE IN THE COCKLOFT.

WHEN the seven returned triumphantly to Tickle Toby Hall, they found that Bob Nailer, the carpenter, had not been idle.

He had already got the floor of the stage down, and the four upright poles in their places.

In less than another hour—the boys assisting—the "Theatre Royal" had assumed very much the appearance of the miniature stages sold in the shops, only on a larger scale.

The enthusiastic youngsters gave three ringing cheers as they contemplated the progress of the work, and Bob Nailer was compelled to rest for a few moments and refresh himself with some bread and cheese and ale.

This being despatched, the scenes were hung in their proper places, and pulleys fixed to each, so that anyone standing at the side could raise or lower them by simply hauling at their respective ropes.

After this, the wings were placed in their positions.

Then the sky borders were hoisted, and lastly the proscenium was fastened to the front.

So far as outward appearances went, the stage looked a perfect model of what a stage should be.

Once more a shout of triumph burst from the admiring throng.

"Well, what do you think of it as it looks now?" asked Joe of his companions.

"Splendid! first-rate! wonderful! couldn't be better," were the enthusiastic replies.

Jemmy Muddle declared it ought never to be taken down any more, but left where it stood as a monument of artistic skill.

Jane and Betsy, the housemaid and cook, were summoned to look at it, and their astonishment was of the intensest description.

"Why, I declare, if it ain't exactly like a real theatre," they exclaimed, as they stepped on to the stage.

"Of course it is," returned Joe.

"And scenery too," continued the housemaid, gazing up at the rollers in a kind of paroxysm of surprise. "Well, I never did, and can you let 'em down?" she asked.

"See," cried our hero, as, unfastening the rope that supported them, he slowly allowed it to pass through his hand, and lowered the "Baron's Castle."

"Oh, my!" exclaimed both the domestics, clasping their hands, "that is fine; it ought to be framed, it's so natural."

"And what's on the other side?" asked the housemaid, gliding round the wings, and looking at the back of the scene.

"Nothing," explained Joe; "we don't paint scenes on both sides; there's nothing there but plain canvas."

"Plain canvas?" repeated Betsy, in a tone as though her mind was wandering slightly.

The reason of this was that, staring her in the face, she saw, in large, plain letters printed in marking ink, the well-known characters, "E. McS., Pair No. 12."

"Why, I declare, if they ain't a pair of the missing sheets, as there was such a to-do about. Jane, Jane," she cried, suddenly, "come and look here."

The cook made a hasty rush round behind the scene, and she too fastened her eyes on the back of the "Castle."

"So they are," exclaimed the cook, "and stitched together, too, as neat as possible. Well, if that don't beat anything as ever I see in all my life."

The seven, who were fully prepared for this discovery, and who were listening to the remarks of the domestics, chuckled quietly among themselves.

"They've twigged the sheets," whispered Harry Merriman.

"It's no matter," returned Joe; "it's too late now."

"They'll twig a few more if they go on to the Demon King's Cavern and the Railway Station," said Jemmy Muddle, with a grin.

"Stand clear, Jane; stand clear, Betsy; I'm going to draw it up," cried Joe, as he pulled the rope, and the scene gradually disappeared, discovering the astonished females behind.

"Nice, fine canvas, isn't it?" remarked our hero to them, with a smile.

"Canvas, Master Joe?" they exclaimed, in a tone of indignation; "get along with you; you know better than that; it's missus's sheeting."

"Bravo, bravo!" cried the boys, "so it is; we all said you'd find it out the moment you looked at it."

"And how many pairs have you got?" asked the domestics, in amazement.

"Only four," Joe answered; "we were short of canvas, and so we borrowed that number."

"Well, now, only to think——"

"They'll be just as good as ever after they're washed, you know," Joe continued.

"And what they're boiled in will make capital soup, there's such a lot of size in 'em," suggested Forks.

This savoury idea was too much for Jane and Betsy, and they burst into a laugh.

"Well, really, if you ain't the most audaciousest set of young gentlemen as we ever heard of."

"We can't help it," replied Tom Tattler.

"Oh, no," dropped in Forks, "it's only a way they've got."

"That's it, exactly," added Harry Merriman, "it's not our fault, it's our misfortune."

"Hi, here we are!" cried Joe, suddenly, as he turned several somersaults across the stage, to test its powers of endurance.

"I think it's pretty firm, ain't it?" remarked Bob Nailer, with a self-conscious smile, after watching our hero.

"Firm as a rock, Bob," replied the latter; "I can see you know all about stage building."

The carpenter looked flattered, and said—

"You didn't settle where you'll have the trap cut, Master Joe."

Our hero considered for a moment.

"Let me see," he said, "the Demon's Cave is in the third grooves,* so I think we'll have the demon car to rise in the second."

This point being arranged, Bob Nailer began to saw away in good earnest.

The trap was cut out, and pieces nailed firmly together with cross bars to strengthen them, and then fastened by hinges at the back, so that it could open and shut at pleasure.

While this was being done, Police Constable Puncher, as he went his rounds, casually stopped at the gate of Tickle Toby House.

Some mysterious signal which he made caught Betsy's ear.

"There's the policeman," she whispered to her fellow-servant.

The two domestics then instantly disappeared, but they almost immediately returned, being accompanied by the portly official.

The constable having received an extra half-crown from the seven, over and above that which Forks had handed to him on their account for his services, had replenished his rum bottle, and was altogether in a very genial and festive humour.

"My eyes, young gentlemen," he exclaimed, as the stage burst upon his sight, "why, dash my buttons, if this ain't a regular Theatre Royal, Drury Lane, in miniature, and no mistake."

---

* Behind the third wings, or entrance R. and L.

The constable was heartily welcomed by the boys, who looked upon him as a "brick" of the first water, and who, after giving him a cheer, shouted unanimously—

"Come on to the stage, Mr. Puncher."

Mr. Puncher hesitated. He knew he was a heavy man, and doubted the solidity of the boards he was invited to tread.

"I'm afraid I should put my foot in it," he said, facetiously.

"No fear of that, Phil," remarked Bob Nailer, who was acquainted with the official. "I'll warrant the planks."

"Come on, bobby," repeated the seven; "it's all safe."

Thus assured, the constable stepped up on to the stage, which did not even creak under his weight, although his head almost touched the sky border overhead.

"Well, upon my word, this is about the neatest little fit-up as I ever see," he remarked, after the scenic arrangements had been pointed out to him. "And what are you going to act?—Richard the Third?"

"Oh, no! Pantomime!" cried the boys, with one voice.

"Pantomime, eh?"

"Yes; 'Harlequin Old Bogey!'"

"'Harlequin Old Bogey,'" repeated Mr. Puncher, reflectively; "and a very good title too—capital. I should like to see it. When's it a-coming off?"

"To-morrow night," answered the seven, "and we shall be very happy to see you here."

"I'll be here, trust me," returned X 44. "I'm particklar fond of pantomimes—not as I objects to Shakespeare and the legitimate drammer. I remember seeing Hamlet once; it was very fine, especially where the ghost of Hamlet's grandfather comes up the trap with the blue fire a-shining on his face, which was all over whiting, and looked awful ghastly."

Mr. Puncher became a little excited at this moment, and struck a melodramatic attitude.

"Bravo, Bobby!" cried the seven.

Thus encouraged, Mr. P. drew his staff from his pocket, and after giving it a professional flourish, brought it down to his side, and said—

"This is how the ghost stood when he was a-taking leave of his nevvy."

Here the constable extended his staff majestically.

"And this is what he said," he continued, in a deep voice suited to the solemn occasion—"'Adieu!—(here he took a step back)—adieu!—(another step)—adieu!—(a third step)—remember——'"

Before he could utter the final "me," he trod upon the trap, which had not been secured, and suddenly disappeared.

But only up to his waist, the depth under the stage being limited.

"I knew I should put my foot in it," he remarked, facetiously; "but never mind, there's no bones broke."

Mr. Puncher was speedily extricated from his position and the trap made fast, and the whole incident was looked upon as a capital joke.

"I suppose you ain't seen anything of them two professional gentlemen?" inquired X 44, as he sipped the glass of ale that had been brought for him.

"Not as yet," replied the boys.

"I don't think you will to-night," said the constable, "but if they should make their appearance, you can say as I'm a-searching after them everywhere. They'll be glad enough to keep out of sight without interfering with you."

The seven readily acquiesced in this, and Mr. Puncher departed, promising to be there at eight on the following evening to witness the performance of the pantomime.

Jane and Betsy were once more sent for.

Our hero, Joe, addressed them.

"Of course," he said, in a tone of flattering confidence, "we all look upon you as our friends, and trust to you to give us your assistance, so that everything may go off well."

"We'll do what we can," the domestics replied.

"We feel sure you will," returned Joe; "quite sure."

"But if the doctor and Mrs. McSwish——" Betsy was about to say, apprehensively.

Our hero checked her.

"Never mind them," he said; "they're sure not to come in the way—they're in London, miles off."

"But then," suggested the cook, "there's Mr. Foggy and the French master. They'll never allow any play acting—I'm sure they won't."

"They'll know nothing about it," Joe answered, "and if they did, they wouldn't be able to stop us."

"But they're sure to be back to-night," exclaimed the maids.

"I'm not so sure of that," returned Harry Merriman.

"Nor I," said Joe. "I shouldn't be surprised if they *never* came back," he added, significantly.

Jane and Betsy looked astonished, but before they could ask another question, there came a mild, solitary ring at the bell.

Everybody heard it—everybody looked at everybody else.

"It's *them*, as safe as houses," whispered Forks, hastily, to the seven.

"What's to be done now?" asked several.

"We'll manage it," answered Joe, confidently. "You know what X 44 said—'Let them think they're pursued.'"

This being willingly agreed to, Forks was despatched to open the gate.

The small youth proceeded thither, key in hand.

Outside stood the unhappy professors, shivering and trembling, fancying every instant they heard the pursuing footsteps of the constable.

As soon as the gate was opened, they crept in as quietly as mice.

On entering the door, to their surprise and horror, there stood the seven evidently waiting for them.

The appearance of the assistants was pitiable in the extreme.

They looked as if they had been just fished up from the bottom of a muddy pond.

And not only their clothes, but their hands, faces, and heads were so thoroughly begrimed with dust and dirt that they were scarcely recognisable.

An exclamation of well-counterfeited horror burst from the boys.

"Good gracious!" exclaimed Joe at length, "is it really you, gentlemen? Oh, how glad we are you've returned! We were afraid you'd got locked up."

"Locked up!" gasped the assistants, in a tone of evident trepidation. "Why should you have been afraid of that?" they eagerly inquired.

"Why, because there's been a policeman here after you," Joe informed them.

"A policeman!" they murmured, faintly, their knees knocking together.

"Yes, there has indeed," Joe continued; "he was in a regular fury too; he said you'd been trespassing, and breaking Mrs. Larkspur's windows, and that he's watching to take you into custody."

The terrified assistants turned white under the coat of dirt that covered their faces, and groaned piteously.

"We had an awful deal of bother to get rid of that bobby, too," protested the boys.

"As it was, he said he should come back again in about half an hour," said Joe.

The professors were so overpowered at this intelligence that their legs gave way under them, and they sank down at the foot of the stairs.

"Don't betray us—pray don't!" they exclaimed, imploringly.

"I should think not," returned Joe; "we wouldn't betray you for the world—only if the policeman should come——"

At this juncture Forks gave the wire a terrific jerk, and the gate bell rang furiously.

"Here he is," cried the boys, in assumed alarm. "Hide—hide!"

The assistants sprang to their feet.

"Where?—where?" they shrieked, distractedly.

"Up the chimney, in the coalhole—anywhere," was the hasty reply.

The professors were about to make a frantic rush in three directions at once, when Forks called out—

"Don't go to either of them places, because that's just where the bobby's sure to look first of all."

"Where shall we go then?"

"Up in the cockloft," counselled Forks; "he'd never think of searching there. Lock yourselves in, and don't come out for a week at least. The affair will be blowed over by then."

Away bolted the terrified assistants upstairs, four steps at a time, and never stopped till they reached the loft, in the remotest corner of which they crouched, behind some old lumber.

In the course of half an hour Forks ascended with a heap of blankets and a light, and then tapped gently at the door.

It was some time before they could be induced to open it.

The blankets, however, were highly acceptable, and a tray which the small youth subsequently carried up, containing supper and a bottle of spirits—charitably supplied by the seven — was equally so.

On Forks' assurance that the bobby had been and gone, Messrs. Fogem and Bonbon revived a little.

" You must be sure and not stir out of here till I bring you word it's safe," said the " actively industrious," in an admonitory tone ; " if you do, you're safe to be nicked."

" We won't—we won't !" protested the masters.

" Then you'll be all right," returned Forks, as he locked the door outside, and held up the key with a grin to his friends, who had crept quietly upstairs to see how matters stood.

" Now we're all right," exclaimed Joe; " neither Foggy nor Bonbon can interrupt our pantomime."

CHAPTER XXXVI.

THE MORNING BEFORE THE GRAND NIGHT—ARRIVAL OF THE ROSELIP BALLET —A DISTRESSING DISCOVERY—AN OLD FRIEND APPEARS IN TIME FOR TEA.

THE next day, it will be easily understood, was a busy day—a day of intense excitement, both at Tickle Toby Hall and at Roselip House.

The young ladies who were to take part in the performance were quite as anxious as the pupils at Dr. McSwisher's for the time to arrive.

But our hero Joe had a happy knack of doing things in an orderly manner.

And he had also tact, young as he was, in managing those about him, though they might be older than himself.

In proof of this, after breakfast, he went into the kitchen.

Here he found the cook and housemaid discussing the probable results of the forthcoming performance, and what would infallibly happen if it came to the ears of their master and mistress.

" We shall lose our situations, that's certain," remarked Betsy, as she sipped her tea thoughtfully.

" Not a bit of it," exclaimed Joe, who had overheard her; " before the doctor and Mother Swisher return, the stage will be all cleared away, and everything as it was before."

" I'm sure I hope so," said Betsy.

" And now see here," continued our hero, as he held up a small paper parcel lightly folded together, " I want your opinion of these."

As he spoke, he unfastened the paper and displayed four brilliant bows, such as ladies wear at their necks or on their heads.

" Oh, oh! beautiful," was the exclamation of Jane and Betsy, as they contemplated the articles.

" Do you like them ?" inquired Joe.

" Oh, they're lovely, such brilliant colours."

" Are they for Columbine or the fairies?" asked Betsy, innocently.

" No," returned our hero, emphatically, " they're for your two selves."

" For us !" cried both the domestics, incredulously.

" Yes. Don't you know you're going to sit in a private box," Joe explained, " and when ladies go to the theatre and sit in private boxes, they must of course be tastefully dressed; so I thought I'd buy you these bows to make you look smart and handsome when your sweethearts come."

Jane and Betsy fluttered and giggled and blushed.

" What a one you are, Master Joe," they said at length.

" Yes, I believe I am the only one in the world exactly like myself," he replied, with a laugh.

" But come, now, which do you choose ?" he said; " one must have the scarlet, and the other the blue."

This was soon decided; the housemaid, being fair, chose the latter, the cook, being dark, the former.

The sight of the bows dispelled all the fears of the maids, and they at once fastened them on.

Just as this was accomplished, Joe's friends came in in a body to look after him.

The whole party pretended to be thrown into ecstasies of admiration at Jane and Betsy in their finery.

"Lovely, exquisite," cried Harry Merriman and Tom Tattler, clasping their hands wildly.

"Scrumptious," exclaimed Jemmy Muddle, as he threw his arms round the housemaid's waist, and gave her a kiss.

This example was followed by his companions, and for a few moments there was a regular chevy round the kitchen after the fair ones with the blue and scarlet bows.

Order being restored, Joe said—

"Of course, as we have young ladies coming, we must have something very nice for tea."

"Winkles," suggested Jemmy Muddle, to begin with.

"The idea," cried Tom Tattler, indignantly, "winkles for young ladies! No, thank you, nothing so common."

"Common or not, I like 'em," grumbled Jemmy.

"My idea is this," continued Joe, "we shall want tea and coffee, marmalade, cake, wine and oranges. I think they would be sufficient."

"Let's have some sweetstuff," pleaded Jemmy Muddle; "most young ladies like sweetstuff; especially those little barley sugar drops wrapped up in coloured papers, with a motto in each. They're capital fun; I think they call 'em kisses."

This idea was received favourably.

"Very well, then," said Joe, with a laugh, "suppose we have some kisses."

"I shall, anyhow," chuckled Jemmy to himself, "for if there's none provided I shall find my own."

This being settled, the cook was supplied with money, and dispatched into the town to make the necessary purchases.

The pupils not otherwise employed helped to carry the forms from the schoolroom to the dining room, where the theatre was erected.

There it stood, with the green curtain down, bringing into relief its proscenium, with its strips of coloured foil and its crimson pillars.

No one could see what wonders there were concealed behind.

To go further than the portion railed off for the orchestra was treason.

To the eyes of the boys it looked delightful.

All the more so, from the mysteries in which the green curtain shrouded everything beyond it.

In addition to the forms, several armchairs and a sofa, from the parlour, were placed to answer the purpose of private boxes.

By noon the arrangements for seating the audience were complete.

Our hero, Joe, having surveyed the works, expressed his satisfaction, and having cleared the dining room, locked the door and took possession of the key.

The boys stared at this, not knowing what to make of such an extraordinary proceeding.

Joe Muggins, however, addressed his schoolfellows, and set their minds at rest.

"You know by this time," said he, "that we are going to act a pantomime, and we want to make it as much as possible like the real thing, so don't forget to bring as many oranges and nuts as you can when you come. The more the room smells of orange peel and the more nuts you crack, the more it'll be like a theatre."

The entire school pledged themselves with great alacrity to fulfil these injunctions.

So heartily, too, were they complied with, that old Sally was sold out half a dozen times that afternoon, and had to trot home for more.

And even then the supply was less than the demand.

It was the work of the seven to transport the masks and the properties from Forks' bedroom, where they had so long been treasured up, to the stage.

This was done with due precaution.

Not one of the general public (by which I mean the scholars) caught a glimpse of any of them.

Betsy produced the pantomime dresses and wigs from the press, and placed them in Joe's hands.

They were perfectly dry, and our hero's heart bounded as he gazed once more upon the red and white spots of his own motley garb, and the glittering, snake-like skin that was to encase the limbs of Harlequin.

Forks' rapture as he held the Sprite's dress, with its spiral rings, in his hands was something tremendous.

He could not command his feelings at all until he had thrown at least a dozen somersaults, and walked on his hands across the pit and back again.

Joe Muggins looked round complacently on his companions.

"Everything's right now, I think," he said.

"As right as ninepence," returned Jemmy Muddle, as he popped his head into the pantaloon's wig, and grinned at his companions, who grinned back in reply.

Everything seemed to be perfectly right.

Nothing whatever appeared likely to interfere with or frustrate their plans.

The two masters were in safe hiding, under lock and key, in the cock-loft.

Their meals were carried upstairs by Forks, who took care to keep them in a proper state of alarm, by informing them, every time he paid them a visit, that the constable had been making anxious inquiries after their health.

This was quite sufficient to keep Messrs. Fogem and Bonbon out of sight.

They would not have shown their noses outside the door of the cock-loft on any account.

One circumstance happened, however, just about this time, that created some little surprise and uneasiness.

Betsy the housemaid suddenly entered with considerable consternation depicted on her face.

"Oh, young gentlemen!" she exclaimed, "I think Master Sly's been and gone and run away!"

It was a singular fact that amidst the excitement of all the pantomime preparations, Sneaking Simon had never once been missed, or even thought of, till that moment.

"Run away?" echoed the seven.

"Well, if he hasn't, he ain't to be found anywheres," returned Betsy. "I'd been packing up his box, and wanted to give him the key, but no one seems to know anything of him."

"That's a rum start," remarked Harry Merriman; "he didn't seem like a chap that would bolt."

"No, he hadn't pluck enough," joined in Tom Tattler.

"I'll tell you what I think," said our hero, Joe, coming in with a sudden idea; "I fancy Master Simon thought, as the doctor and his wife were out of the way, that we might pay him out for old scores, and so, as the holidays were so near——"

"He hooked it at once to save his bacon," exclaimed Jemmy Muddle.

"Yes, that's what I think," said our hero, assentingly.

"So do I! So do I! So do all of us!" cried the rest.

This seemed a very satisfactory reason for the disappearance of their sneaking schoolfellow.

Although, as he had never mentioned his intention to a soul, and as no one had seen him depart, his sudden absence looked a little mysterious. But it did not trouble the boys.

"A jolly good riddance to him," they voted unanimously; "he didn't care for pantomimes, or anything else but sneaking and prying, and telling tales of everybody."

In a very short time Sneaking Simon was forgotten, as if no such being existed.

At three in the afternoon a great rattling of wheels and a clattering of horses' hoofs were heard, and the gate bell of Tickle Toby House rang loudly.

"Here are the girls," cried the seven, with chivalrous exultation; "hurrah!"

The door was opened hastily, and out rushed Betsy and Jane, accompanied by the youth in the buttons, to the gate.

The seven followed.

What a joyous sight met their view!

Five broughams stood in the road, containing the young ladies from Rose-lip House.

The gate was thrown open with a clang and a crash.

Fair hands waved from the carriage windows.

The boys had enough to do to hurry up to the different vehicles and pay their welcomes to the pretty guests at the windows.

"JOE ASCENDED THE DESK, AND, TAPPING WITH THE RULER, CRIED 'ORDER!'"

"This is something like a 'grand ballet,' isn't it?" exclaimed Joe, triumphantly to his friends, as vehicle after vehicle deposited its load at the gate.

No small load either, since the whole of Miss Teachwell's pupils had been invited to the breaking-up party, as it was called, and thirty young ladies, with the addition of Miss Finnikin, had contrived to squeeze themselves into the five carriages.

There was also a prodigious number of parcels and band boxes attached to the party.

And the anxiety was great lest any should be left behind.

At length, however, by the united assistance of the domestics, the seven and Forks—whose exertions with the band boxes were almost on a par with the twelve labours of Hercules—everything was pronounced to be quite correct.

"Here we are at last," cried Fanny Fairchild, with her silvery voice, as the door closed at length.

"Hurrah! three cheers for the young ladies of Roselip House!" shouted the gallant pupils of Doctor McSwisher.

The entrance hall was crowded with pretty little fairy forms of various sizes, with their hair done up in curl papers.

It took them a little time to take off their travelling dresses.

And then they all assembled in the doctor's parlour.

As the performance was not to commence till eight in the evening, and it was then only three in the afternoon, there was plenty of time for a nice chat, with the festive additions of cake and wine, and kisses (barley sugar ones, of course, though I daresay there were a few stolen on the sly of another kind) between then and tea.

It would be impossible to imagine a happier or merrier party of juveniles than those assembled.

As for Miss Finnikin, the governess, she quite entered into the fun, and enjoyed herself as much as anybody.

"What a set of guys we all look in our curl papers, don't we?" laughed Fanny Fairchild.

"Perfect frights," cried Charlotte Berry; an opinion in which all her friends coincided.

But the seven would not admit this for a moment.

"You look beautiful," they exclaimed, rapturously.

"You in particular, Sally," whispered Jemmy Muddle, confidentially, to Miss Pickles, by whose side he was seated; "open your mouth."

Sally opened her mouth and received a barley sugar drop for her trouble.

"We thought we'd better not take our curls out of paper till the last thing," explained Fanny, "because we want our hair to look nice on the stage."

"Quite right," returned Joe; "you'll have the doctor's bedroom to dress in. It's very large and comfortable, and there's a nice fire in it."

"Oh, that will be snug," cried the girls; "how jolly we shall be."

"What would old Doctor McSwisher say, if he could see us all at this moment?" exclaimed Lydia Lester, holding up her hands with an assumed expression of alarm in her face.

"Ho! ho!" laughed a dozen musical voices.

"What'd Mother McSwisher say?" said Jemmy Muddle, almost writhing at the ecstasy of the thought; "wouldn't her nose turn a beautiful crimson?"

There was another laugh at this, and Joe replied—

"We shan't have the pleasure of their company. They've gone on a visit to Lord Dolderums, Waggletree Park."

"Oh, my! what funny names," exclaimed the young ladies. "Wherever can that be?"

"It's in the county of Nonsuch Nowhere," returned Joe; "and if they find any such place as that, they'll be clever."

This led to an explanation of the practical joke they had played upon the principal and his spouse.

The fair listeners were almost breathless with astonishment.

"Well, you are daring," they protested.

"If we hadn't been we should never have got up our pantomime, nor should we have had the pleasure of your company," replied Joe and his companions, gallantly.

"And have you got a nice stage for us to act on?" inquired the girls, eagerly.

"I believe you we have, too!" returned Jemmy Muddle, with a burst of enthusiasm.

"It's like a regular theatre," said our
[h]ero, Joe, with conscious pride. "Will
[yo]u come and see it?"

"Oh, yes! yes! we should like to," cried the fair visitors, starting from their seats in a hurry. "Do show us."

Joe led the way to the dining room, followed by the whole party.

A burst of admiration was called forth by the life-like appearance of the mimic stage.

"Oh, it is beautiful!" exclaimed the young ladies.

"I could fancy I was in a London theatre," cried Fanny Fairchild. "And there is a curtain and orchestra, too, I declare."

"And now you must come on the stage," said Joe.

This was reached by a few small steps close to the orchestra.

Expressions of wonder and delight burst every now and then from the lips of the pretty gazers, at the completeness of the arrangements.

"Why, you have scenes, and wings, and borders, just as they do in regular theatres," exclaimed Fanny, her fair young face glowing with animation.

"Yes, dear," whispered Joe. "I told you so."

"Well, it is beautiful," she replied. "And what's this?—a trap?"

"Yes," explained our hero. "That's where the Demon Car is to rise."

"I'm the Demon," called out Harry Merriman, who had put on an awful-looking green mask, with glaring eyes of crimson foil paper, and now popped his head round the wing. "Boo!" he cried.

"Oh! oh!" shrieked the young ladies, with a pretty little affectation of alarm. "What a fright!"

"Pantomime demons generally are," said Joe, "but the effect will be much more imposing at night."

"Will it?" they said.

"Oh, yes," answered Harry Merriman, proudly; "I'm coming up in a blaze of red fire with a blazing torch in my hand, ain't I, Joe?"

Our hero was about to answer in the affirmative, but he stopped suddenly and instead uttered an exclamation of intense disappointment.

"Oh, dear, dear!" he cried.

"What's the matter, old fellow?"

asked his friends and the young ladies, anxiously.

"I thought there was something," he continued, in a tone of great vexation, "and I've just remembered what it is."

"Well, but what is it?" inquired everybody.

"There's neither red fire nor fireworks," Joe cried, despairingly.

"Oh, Joe, oh!" almost groaned the seven; "no red fire? What a sell!"

"No fireworks? The pantomime will be spoilt," exclaimed Jemmy Muddle, with tears in his eyes.

"Of course it will," admitted Joe, gloomily; "but it isn't my fault. I wrote three weeks ago to Johnny Bangs, and ordered lots of blue and red fire, besides crackers, squibs, Roman candles, and Catherine wheels. I can't understand why he hasn't sent them."

"Can't we get any in Whoppington?" asked several, eagerly.

"No, that you can't," replied Forks, who had glided in unperceived; "except just about Guy Fawkes' Day, there ain't no call for such things in this dead-alive place."

This fatal omission quite damped the spirits of the seven.

"They may come down by the afternoon train," said Joe, not willing to give up all hope; "if not, I don't know what we shall do. A pantomime without red fire would be like Christmas without pudding."

"Or a party without cake and wine and kisses," murmured Jemmy Muddle, dolefully.

Very much depressed in spirits, the party returned to the parlour.

To the young ladies it did not seem such a very serious loss, but to the mind of our hero the pantomime had lost more than half its charm.

Tea time came, and they were just about to commence, when Betsy came in and said, mysteriously, to Joe—

"You're wanted, if you please, sir."

"Who is it?" inquired our hero, gloomily.

"I dunno, sir," returned the housemaid. "I only know it's a young gent with a good-sized parcel under his arm."

The word "parcel" was suggestive.

"A parcel?" cried Joe, springing up.

"The red fire and fireworks," exclaimed the rest, dropping their pieces of cake simultaneously.

"I'll go and see," said our hero.

A few seconds of breathless suspense followed, and then Joe's voice was heard shouting, joyously—

"Hurrah, hurrah! they've come!"

The next moment he rushed wildly back into the parlour.

"What's come? Who's come?" was the general inquiry.

"Johnny Bangs and the fireworks," Joe cried, with exultation; "come on, Johnny; you are come just in time for tea."

He dashed the door open, and there entered Joe's old friend Jack, with the brown paper parcel under his arm.

CHAPTER XXXVII.

JOHN BANGS ARRIVES WITH THE FIREWORKS, ETCETERA—THE ACTORS DRESS FOR THEIR CHARACTERS—JOE INSTRUCTS HIS COMPANIONS HOW TO MAKE UP FOR CLOWN—THE CURTAIN RISES AT LAST, AND THE PANTOMIME COMMENCES.

IT is needless to say that Johnny Bangs was heartily welcomed.

Had he been the great Joey Grimaldi himself, he could not have been a more honoured visitor.

The seven sprang upon him at once.

Jemmy Muddle relieved him of his load, whilst the rest embraced him.

The small youth in the buttons, in the warmth of his excitement, not being able to get at anything else, clasped him affectionately by the legs.

At length, the first burst of enthusiasm being over, Jack said—

"We were so busy making fireworks for the Crystal Palace that I couldn't get what you wanted finished until last night, so I thought, sooner than disappoint you, I'd bring them down by train myself."

"Thank you, Jack; you're a brick," cried Joe.

"And so say all of us," echoed his companions.

"You came just at the right moment," our hero went on; "we've got a glorious pantomime, and the only things we wanted to make everything complete were the red fire and etceteras which you've brought."

The young firework maker was then formally introduced to the girls, who received him very graciously.

John Bangs was not, strictly speaking, what might be called a model of youthful beauty.

His eyes were inclined to be what is called goggle, and his mouth had a tendency to extend from ear to ear.

But he was thoroughly good-natured, and entered so heartily into all the plans for the evening's entertainment, that the young ladies, one and all, declared him a very nice, jolly boy indeed.

The gratitude of the seven expressed itself in tremendously large lumps of cake and slices of bread and butter, lavishly spread over with marmalade, which they forced upon the new comer until he was obliged to cry—

"Hold, enough!"

"I'll tell you what I can do," proposed Johnny. "I'll take tickets at the door."

"Good, so you can," assented the boys.

Tea being over, it was time to separate in order to get dressed.

The young ladies who were to take part in the performance adjourned to their dressing room, accompanied by Miss Finnikin, and commenced transforming themselves into the characters they were to represent.

The seven proceeded to their dormitory, where they went through a similar operation.

Both the rooms had fires in them, and looked very cheerful.

Fanny Fairchild, who had often seen her own mother dress herself for the stage, was very useful to her young companions in assisting them to make their stage preparations.

She knew the right method for doing everything.

And so well was she acquainted with the precise way in which fairies wore their wings and wreaths, and did their hair, that her schoolfellows felt almost persuaded she had taken a trip to Fairyland for the express purpose of studying the fashions there.

Nor was our hero, Joe Muggins, less serviceable to his friends.

He helped Harry Merriman into a dress of green calico, striped with foil, with large red wings of the same material, that had a very awful and imposing effect.

His brother pantomimists roared as he put on his mask.

For the latter being made after a model of the features of the principal, he looked like a demoniac kind of Doctor McSwisher.

Next came the Baron Bogey, who was attired like a noble of the middle ages, with enormous boots and gauntlets and a belt round his waist, fastened by a buckle of portentous size, in which his dagger reposed.

The mask of this ferocious personage was an exaggerated likeness of M. Bonbon, the French master, and a shout of laughter burst forth as Tom Tattler thrust his head into the pasteboard head.

By degrees Joe got his *corps pantomimique* all dressed.

"Now then," he called to Jemmy Muddle, who was practising a bit of Funky Fum before the looking-glass, "you'd better let me make you up for the old un."

"I'm ready," cried Jemmy, eagerly.

In a few minutes, by the aid of whiting, Indian ink, and vermilion, Master James Muddle's countenance had undergone a complete transformation.

"Now for your beard," said Joe.

"Here it is," replied Jemmy.

"Pop your chin into it; that's the way; and now let me tie it over the top of your head."

"Is it done?"

"Yes; now the wig."

The wig was put on, and secured by strings under the chin. The effect was perfect.

"How does he look?"

"Splendid! Capital!" cried the seven, as Jemmy stood leaning on his crutched stick and chattering his teeth after the manner of the ancient individual he was going to represent.

Forks, who had been assisting in clearing the tea table, now entered in a state of intense anxiety to get his sprite's dress on his back.

It was not a difficult task, and having inserted himself into the elastic worsted, he had only to be laced up and he was ready, all but his face, which Joe made up with a light red colour, with pieces of crimson foil gummed on his eyebrows and under his eyes, to give him an impish, goblin appearance.

The delight of the small youth was extreme when he found himself at last really converted into a sprite, and he turned somersaults and walked on his hands, and did the splits for fully ten minutes after, just to bring himself down to a proper state of calmness.

Joe dressed himself last.

It was a matter of great amusement to watch him, as he gradually assumed his clown's dress with its red and blue spots, and the red shoes with rosettes.

But the crowning point of interest was the making up of his face, which he assured them he was going to do in the same way as his dad did, and all the great clowns (Joey Grimaldi included) had done before him.

Having arranged his artistic apparatus, which consisted of two little shallow tin pans (one containing lamp black, the other vermillion), a box of bismuth, and two camel's hair pencils, he commenced—

"First of all, my boys, I wash my face clean."

This being done, he continued—

"Then I take a little pomatum in my hands, so; and rub it over my face and neck."

This done, he held up his countenance, glistening with grease, for inspection.

"Now, the next thing I do is to wipe it off."

"What's the use of putting it on if you wipe it off the next moment?" asked Harry Merriman, curiously.

"Oh!" laughed our hero, "enough remains behind to fill up the pores and preserve them from the action of the bismuth, which might else be injurious to the skin."

"Ah, I see," replied Harry, much enlightened.

"The next operation is to apply the bismuth, which I do in this way."

As he spoke, he shook a little of the white powder from the box into the palm of his hand, and then, dipping his fingers into it, proceeded to smear the compound over his face.

This operation he continued until his entire face and neck were covered with a coating as smooth and white as a cast in plaster of Paris.

"There," he said, as he pulled some very pantomimical mugs, "that's what I call laying the foundation."

He then placed the tin pans on the hob for a few seconds, until the colours in them, which were mixed with lard, had been softened by the heat and become liquid.

"Now I am going to paint the half-moons," he said.

To do this required the assistance of a glass, but in the space of a minute this feat had been accomplished with the utmost precision.

Our hero's mouth then underwent sundry additions until it looked about twice its usual size, it being necessary for clowns, who invariably have enormous swallows, to have mouths in proportion.

Having finished with the red paint, it now only remained to apply the black to delineate the eyebrows, and throw up the eyes by sundry little touches at the corners.

"And that's all, my boys," cried Joe, as he laid down his brush and made a grimace that threw them all into convulsions. "Here we are. And now for the wig, and I'm finished."

This last necessary article was soon put on, after which our hero threw a couple of somersaults to refresh himself, after his work.

"There," he exclaimed, "now I'm ready to go on to Drury Lane stage if they wanted me."

"Suppose they did, what should we do without you?" asked Jemmy Muddle, rather ruefully, at the bare idea.

"Why, I shouldn't go, of course," laughed Joe. "I wouldn't miss to-night at the 'Theatre Royal, Tickle Toby Hall,' for fifty Drury Lanes."

Time was now drawing on, and Betsy tapped at the door.

"It's only me," she said.

"Come in, Betsy," called our hero, cheerfully.

The door opened, and the housemaid entered.

"Oh, Lor' a mussy!" she exclaimed, starting back, and almost losing her balance, at the nondescript appearance of the young gentlemen.

"Don't be frightened, Betsy," cried the boys. "We won't eat you."

"Well, I declare, if you don't look orful, you do," she protested.

"Well, if we don't, we ought to," remarked Forks, as he bent himself head and heels together like a hoop. "We've struggled hard for it."

"Have you anything to say particular, Betsy?" asked Joe.

"Oh, yes, sir; I came to tell you the musicianers 'as come," she answered.

"Oh, that's all right," replied Joe. "Give them something to eat and drink, and tell the leader I shall be glad to see him when it's convenient."

The orchestra, which consisted of a cornet, two violins, and a double bass, had been recommended by Bob Nailer, as men who had played at theatres, and who knew the kind of music that was required in a pantomime.

After a short time the leader, having partaken of some bread and cheese and ale, was ushered upstairs into the dressing-room.

"Good evening, gentlemen," said the first violin, as he entered.

"Good evening," returned the seven.

Joe then handed a sheet of music paper to the leader, and said, gravely—

"There are the music cues, Mr. ——I haven't the pleasure of knowing your name."

"Mr. Presto Scrape," returned the musician.

"Mr. Presto Scrape," repeated our hero; "and I shall feel delighted by your letting us have some effective music."

"That you shall, sir," promised the leader, warmly. "I know what you want. Many's the time I've accompanied the great Joey Grimaldi, in Hot Codlins and Tippitywichet."

"That will do, then," responded Joe, graciously. "You'll have to accompany me to-night in the same."

"Very good, sir."

"You'll find all the songs are set to popular tunes."

"Exactly."

"Be kind enough to let the demon music be nice and growling."

"You may depend on that."

"And the fairy music light and lively."

"It shall be especially mellifluous," Mr. Scrape assured our hero.

As they were about to descend, the boys and the young ladies met at the top of the stairs.

The seven in their grotesque panto-mimical disguises, the girls in their gauzy fairy dresses, looking as lovely as so many beings of another world.

There was much smiling and blushing at the compliments the pretty little nymphs received.

At length they got downstairs, and passed between the rows of benches up the steps on to the stage.

The lamps were then lit by Bob Nailer, who kindly offered to make himself useful.

It being now almost time to open the doors, the public (represented by some forty impatient boys) began to be a little boisterous.

Whilst the audience was assembling, however, at the dining room door in the schoolroom, a select number of friends were gradually accumulating in the kitchen.

These consisted of the sweethearts of Jane and Betsy, a young woman who was engaged to Bob Nailer the carpenter, and another blooming damsel of Whopping-ton, who was supposed to be smitten with Police Constable Puncher.

The female portion of the assembly were ushered into the theatre, and seated themselves in the front row of chairs.

In order to keep up the reality of the thing, Phil Puncher, the policeman, stood ready to keep order.

Everything being now ready for start-ing, the doors were opened.

There was a tremendous rush on the part of the forty and odd young gentle-men for seats.

In spite of the entreaties of X 44, who implored them "to take it easy," and assured them "there was plenty of room in all parts of the house," the pupils pushed and fought and jostled one another with all the energy of a Boxing Night audience.

At length all were seated, and nothing was heard but a confused murmur of voices and an incessant cracking of nuts, with the shells of which those in the pit pelted the occupants of the boxes.

"Music!" shouted the most demon-strative.

Some whistled after the fashion of gallery visitors at theatres.

The example was speedily imitated, and in a second or two the whole of the audience joined in, whistling, shouting, and stamping their feet to the great de-light of the actors behind the curtain, it seemed so life-like and natural.

"Bravo, Bobby," cried one or two of the most daring, as their eyes picked out the portly figure of Police Constable Puncher, whom they felt in duty bound to commence clapping forthwith.

"Bravo, Bobby, bra-a-a-a-avo," echoed the rest.

"Play up, fiddlers; me-usic!" rang through the theatre.

Mr. Presto Scrape, with his violin under his arm, turned in his seat, and contemplated the shouting, whistling mass of juveniles with that serene indifference with which leaders as a rule regard the impatient audience, looking at them as much as to say—

"Stamp away, whistle till you're black in the face, shout till you're hoarse. I don't play a note till I hear the prompter's bell."

In a few moments this cheering sound was heard—tinkle, tinkle, from the stage.

This was the signal for an immediate tuning of instruments, and all being in unison, the band commenced the over-ture with an energy perfectly start-ling, considering the smallness of their number.

The fiddles shrieked, the cornet blew, the double bass groaned, in a manner de-lightful to hear.

What they played nobody knew and nobody cared, but everybody seemed perfectly satisfied, and evinced their satisfaction by beating time with their feet.

At length the overture was over.

Loud applause followed from the audience.

"All ready?" inquired Joe, behind the curtain.

"All right, old fellow," returned

Jemmy Muddle, who was standing with the rope in his hand ready to pull up the drop.

"Clear the stage, please," cried our hero to one or two pretty fairies, who still lingered beyond the precincts of the wings.

There was not too much room behind the scenes, but the little nymphs tripped off and joined their sister sprites.

The stage being clear, Joe called out—

"Now then, Jemmy, up with it."

Jemmy's muscles went to work, and the curtain rolled itself up majestically, revealing the gloomy regions behind to the gaze of the delighted audience, amidst awfully growling demoniac music from the orchestra.

The pantomime had commenced, and the very first scene was a triumph.

"Bravo, Joe; bravo, everybody," resounded on all sides.

CHAPTER XXXVIII.

A SLIGHT ACCIDENT OCCURS—THE PANTOMIME CONTINUES ITS COURSE—AN UNEXPECTED ARRIVAL.

TWO imps, Goggle Eyes and Grimgrizzle, are discovered with flaming torches, who, after performing a mysterious incantation, summon their demon master—

"Thy faithful subjects wait thee here ;
Mighty Tingleback, appear."

"Go with the trap," whispered Joe to his friends Jemmy Muddle and Tom Tattler, who had undertaken to wind up the car ; "I'll light the fire."

Away they pulled at the ropes, stormy crescendo from the orchestra, and the demon's car ascends splendidly from the depths, with the fiend king standing in it, torch in hand, and in a blaze of red fire.

Immense applause from the audience and actors as well.

"Isn't it stunning?" exclaims Jemmy Muddle, in ecstasies.

"Couldn't be better," replies Joe, rubbing his hands complacently.

Even as they were speaking a sharp crack is heard.

The rope has snapped, the car topples over, and his demoniac majesty pitches forward on his nose.

Enthusiastic applause from the boys, who pronounce it the best thing they have seen yet.

Bob Nailer rushes round behind the scenes to assist.

The demon's car is at length coaxed off at the wing, and the pantomime continues.

The "Exterior of the Baron's Castle" is next discerned.

Funky Fum, in his grotesque mask, ghastly pale, and with his hair standing bolt upright with terror, lays hold of the affections of the boys at once.

The song is encored vociferously.

The Baron Bogey in his large boots and his fierce-looking helmet — who threatens to consign his trembling servant to the castle dungeon, to be devoured by rats—is also favourably received.

The scene now changes to Old Dame Durden's cottage.

Here Pretty Poll of Whoppington is discovered seated at her spinning wheel.

Great applause from the forty-two juvenile spectators, who all fall in love at once with Fanny Fairchild.

Her sweetheart, Jack, the miller's son, enters, and goes on his knees to her.

Dame Durden comes in in a fury, and knocks him down with a dripping ladle.

Pretty Poll wipes her eye with a corner of her apron.

Expressions of sympathy from the audience.

Old Flour Bags, the miller, hobbles on, and entreats the old dame to smile upon the young folks' suit.

Dame Durden indignantly refuses, and adds insult to injury, by pulling the venerable miller's nose.

Much laughter from the boys.

Jack and his father are about to depart in a state of great mental depression, when the Fairy Crystal enters in disguise, and whispers to the former to "keep his pecker up, for that she is his friend."

Jack accordingly raises his pecker, and having performed a comic dance with his papa, they retire in the highest spirits.

Dame Durden now receives a very extensive letter from the Baron Bogey, brought by Funky Fum, which informs her that, having taken a fancy to her daughter, he intends making her mistress of his heart and home, in other words, Baroness Bogey.

The old lady is dazzled by the offer, and after cutting a few capers, expressive of her joy, is about to enter the cottage, when she runs against Funky Fum, who is amusing himself by catching flies at the porch.

Both go down, and before they can pick themselves up again, the Baron Bogey himself enters.

After kicking his servant and stamping upon his future mother-in-law, he picks the latter up by her bustle, and asks for something to drink.

A jug of ale is brought by Pretty Poll, who evidently acts by compulsion, and scorns the tyrannical Bogey.

The Baron pleads his suit, and asks for a kiss.

Pretty Poll pushes him away indignantly, which causes him to overbalance and sit down very abruptly in a washing tub.

Funky Fum, endeavouring to get his master out, falls in himself.

Loud and continued laughter from the audience.

The youthful miller Jack appears, and declares his intention of defending his love against all comers.

A desperate combat of four now takes place, in which Jack is ultimately victorious, and after knocking the heads of his opponents together, makes his escape, carrying off Pretty Poll.

The scene now changes to the abode of the fairies on the borders of the Silver Lake.

Here the fairy queen appears, surrounded by her nymphs, to the great distraction of the juvenile beholders, who were divided as to their respective merits.

A fairy ballet takes place, at the end of which Jack and his sweetheart enter, pursued by the Baron, Funky Fum, and Dame Durden, who demand the instant restoration of the fugitive lovers.

Queen Crystal refuses to give them up, when the Demon Tingleback suddenly appears, with the intention of destroying the fairy band.

This, however, he finds not quite so easy as he thought, and while he is considering what shall be his next move, the clouds rise at the back, revealing the grand transformation scene, with its revolving star.

Several cases of coloured fires are set going at this crisis, which produce a magnificent effect and a great deal of smoke.

The pantomimical change of characters was about to take place, when suddenly there was heard a very loud and prolonged ringing at the gate bell.

This put a sudden stop to everything, and produced a kind of universal panic.

The fairy queen ceased speaking, the characters on the stage stood mute and motionless.

The audience remained riveted to their seats.

Not a solitary nut was cracked.

Betsy and Jane looked at each other with horror imprinted on their features.

Even the dauntless Puncher turned a shade paler.

The general impression was that it was the doctor and his wife returned.

No wonder everyone looked scared.

"What's to be done if it is the doctor?" asked Joe, at length, of his companions, as they stood on the stage.

The latter shook their heads in their masks hopelessly.

They were at their wits' end.

"Oh, dear! dear!" wailed the pretty fairies, clasping their hands anxiously, and wishing at the moment that their wings had been real, that they might have flown away anywhere.

"Don't be frightened, young ladies," whispered our hero, assuringly.

Then turning to his brother actors, he said, in a decided tone—

"I tell you what, my boys; there's no getting away now, so if it is old McSwisher and his amiable partner, we must meet them as bold as brass."

These determined words inspired the sinking spirits of his comrades.

"So we will, Joe," they replied.

"We must stick together," he continued.

"We will, like bricks!"

"And protect the young ladies?"

"Like heroes!"

"And if the doctor tries to stop the pantomime?"

"We'll all pitch into him at once," exclaimed Jemmy Muddle, in an agony at the bare idea, "and lock him up in the cupboard, and Mother Red Pecker as well!"

This being determined upon, Joe stepped forward to the footlights and said, very gravely—just as if he had been making an apology to a theatrical audience—

"Ladies and gentlemen, we are sorry to be obliged to stop at this very interesting part of the performance, but the gate bell having rung, and as we are not sure that it may not be the doctor and Mrs. McSwisher returned, we shall feel obliged if you'll be quiet and keep your seats until we see who it is."

"Bravo, Joe!" cried his schoolmates in front; "we'll keep quiet."

"That's right," returned our hero, approvingly; then turning to his friends on the stage, he said, boldly, "now then, my boys, come on."

They needed no second invitation, and our hero, descending from the stage in his clown's dress, led the way through the audience, followed by the Demon King, the Baron Bogey, Funky Fum, and the rest of the *corps dramatique*, Bob Nailer accompanying them to lend a hand if needful.

On reaching the door there was a slight consultation who should go out to the gate.

It was rather awkward for anyone of them to answer the summons, attired as they were in their pantomime costumes.

Even Forks, who was usually ready to go to any length of daring enterprise, hung back.

Again the bell rang loudly, and Bob Nailer said—

"I will go."

His offer was instantly accepted.

The door was opened softly, and the carpenter slipped out.

When he reached the gate, instead of the harsh, cracked tones of Dr. McSwisher, or the shrill, shrewish pipe of his spouse, meeting his ear, he was accosted by a round, jovial, hearty voice that said—

"Better late than never. I thought you was all asleep or kicked the bucket, or somethink of that sort."

The visitor was quite a stranger to Bob Nailer, and he said, inquiringly—

"Who is it?"

"It's only *Old* Joe," returned the other, facetiously, "come to look after *Young* Joe."

This was still incomprehensible to the carpenter, until our hero's father (for it was he) said—

"My name's Joseph Muggins, and I've come to see my boy as is at school here."

This was sufficient for Bob Nailer, and he opened the gate at once.

It was more than sufficient for our hero, who had recognised the voice.

"Hurrah!" he shouted, joyously; "it's dear old dad! Come on, all of you, and give him a surprise; he'll be as pleased as Punch."

Out rushed the troop of pantomimists, with young Joe at their head, and met Mr. Muggins, senior, half way between the gate and the door.

"Here we are!" cried his son, as he turned several somersaults, and then threw his arms affectionately round his parent.

The old clown was so utterly astonished at finding himself surrounded by such familiar objects in the very last place where he would have expected to meet them, that he fairly staggered again.

"Lor' bless me, whatever's the matter?" he exclaimed, his eyes and mouth wide open in the intensity of his amazement.

"Nothing's the matter, dad, dear," explained our hero; "it's breaking-up time, and we're having a pantomime, that's all."

That word brought old Joe to his senses in a moment.

"A pantomime?" he repeated; "are you really, though?"

"Yes, we are, indeed, dad, and you've just come in time to see the comic business," his son informed him. "Come on," he whispered; "we're keeping the audience waiting."

"Well, now, the idea of my arriving just at this identical crisis!" exclaimed the old pantomimist, as he walked forward towards the house; "it really seems as if it was done on purpose."

On entering, the door was closed, and Joe briefly introduced his father to his brother actors.

"Very glad to see you, young gents," he exclaimed, heartily, as he shook hands all round; "and now, 'spose we adjourn to the theayter."

The boys gave a shout and conducted Mr. Joseph Muggins in triumph to the interior of the mimic temple, where the transformation scene and the fairies still lingered, waiting for the return of the characters to be transformed.

If the old clown had been surprised at the sight he had encountered in the garden, he was none the less so at the spectacle that now met his gaze.

"Why, I declare." he exclaimed, echoing a former remark of Mr. Puncher's, "if it ain't a reg'lar Doory Lane in miniature."

"Will you see it from the front or come behind, dad?" asked young Joe.

"Oh, I'll stop in front, my boy," returned his parent. "You go on, as the stage is waiting, and don't trouble about me; I'll find a seat somewheres."

"Come on, then, lads!" cried Joe to his friends.

And in a moment the whole party were on the stage again.

Our hero, then advancing once more to the footlights, said to the excited audience—

"Ladies and gentlemen, I am happy to inform you that the bell gave us a false alarm. It was not Doctor McSwisher at the gate, but my dear old dad there, who is the best clown of the present day, and who is going to honour our performance with his presence."

Young Joe pointed as he spoke to where his dad stood, brimful of pride and exultation.

The whole of the boys gave three cheers for Mr. Muggins, senior, which Mr. Muggins, senior, acknowledged with a beaming countenance and a series of bows.

He then found a seat by the side of Police Constable Puncher, who welcomed the great pantomimist warmly, and courteously offered him a pull from his private and confidential rum bottle, which the latter accepted with the utmost heartiness.

After which he prepared himself to enjoy the pantomime.

CHAPTER XXXIX.

THE PANTOMIME GOES ON AND IS BROUGHT TO A SUDDEN TERMINATION BY THE APPEARANCE OF AN APPARITION THROUGH THE WINDOW.

THE performance was taken up again at the precise point where it had stopped.

The transformation of the characters took place.

Harlequin, columbine, pantaloon, and lastly merry clown, at last made their appearance before the delighted spectators.

As our hero's well-known "Hi, here we are!" rang through the theatre, and as he threw a somersault on to the stage, the *furore* was deafening.

As for old Joe, he was as intensely amused at the efforts of the youngsters if he had never seen a pantomime in his life.

The characters having finished the opening rally,* formed a tableau.

The glittering star revolved rapidly, half a dozen squibs fizzed at the wings, more coloured fire, and the scene closed in triumphantly, Mr. Muggins, senior, applauding till his hands ached again.

The comic business having now commenced in earnest, Ben Brisk made a graceful, active harlequin, and Fanny Fairchild a beautiful, charming little columbine.

---

* The business of running under each other's arms, and finally joining hands and swinging round rapidly, invariably gone through by the pantomime characters, immediately after their transformation.

"'THREE CHEERS FOR X 44!' EXCLAIMED JEMMY."

In addition to the usual " trips " of the harlequinade, they went through a variety of character dances in as many different costumes with great success.

Forks made his appearance periodically as sprite, and performed such wonders in the way of contorting his limbs that the audience felt themselves strongly inclined to doubt whether he had any bones or joints at all either in his back or body.

The mass inclined to the opinion that the small youth was all gristle.

Of course the weight of the pantomime rested on the shoulders of our hero, Joe, and his colleague, Jemmy Muddle.

And very manfully they supported the burden.

All they did they did well.

Joe sang " Hot Codlins " and " Tippittywichet," and was encored in both.

Scene after scene went on, and they had got to the last but one, the " Railway Station."

This scene promised to be very amusing, as our hero Joe had at the last moment introduced some incidents that particularly referred to Doctor McSwisher and his wife, and was as follows :—

Enter CLOWN *and* PANTALOON, *evidently out of luck.*

Clown. I say, old un.
Pant. Well, Joey?
Clown. How d'ye feel?
Pant. Very bad indeed.
Clown. You look very bad. What's your complaint?
Pant. (*groaning*). I don't know.
Clown. Where d'ye feel the pain?
Pant. I don't know.
Clown (*feeling his limbs professionally*). Is it here?
Pant. No.
Clown. Is it there? (*continuing his examination*).
Pant. No.
Clown (*opening his mouth and looking down his throat*). Is it there?
Pant. No.
Clown. What an aggravating old fool you are, to be sure! Now, look here! If you say " No " again, I shall hit you. I s'pose you won't like that?
Pant. No.
Clown (*knocking him down*). Take that. I told you what you'd get if you said

" No " again (*picks* PANTALOON *up in the usual pantomime fashion*).
Pant. What a shame to knock a poor old man about that's old enough to be your grandfather.
Clown. Well, then, you shouldn't be so aggravating. I should have done the same if you'd been my grandmother.
Pant. (*dolefully*). I think I know what's the matter with me. I'm sickening for the measles.
Clown (*sarcastically*). You're a nice elderly infant to have the measles, you are. Sit down and let's feel your pulse (*kicks his legs from under him.* PANTALOON *falls with a slap.* CLOWN *catches hold of his foot*).
Pant. Oh! my back.
Clown. Don't make a noise, or I can't count (*takes out watch, looks at it and begins counting*); one, two, three, four! you're in a fev——
Pant. (*interrupting*). That isn't the way to feel anyone's pulse. You ought

Clown (*indignantly*). Will you be quiet, and not aggravate me in this manner? Five, six!
Pant. I was only going to say you ought——
Clown (*starting up fiercely*). If you say " ought " again, I'll dash your brains out with my gold repeater.
Pant. Well, I do say you ought to——
(CLOWN *strikes him on the head with watch.* PANTALOON *rolls over.*)
Pant. Oh, my poor nob.
Clown. Well, then, you shouldn't be so aggravating. I told you what you'd get. Now, let me feel your pulse (*takes hold of* PANTALOON'S *foot again and counts*), one, two, three, four, five, six, seven, eight! Oh, it's clear enough what's the matter with you. You've got the tic doloreux in your big toenail.
Pant. (*alarmed*). Have I? Is it serious?
Clown. Very! If I don't amputate your leg, you'll mortify.
Pant. (*more alarmed*). I object. I won't lose my leg! Besides, I feel better (*gets up*).
Clown. I tell you you're worse. Sit down (*holds him*).
Pant. I tell you I'm better, and I shan't sit down.
Clown. I say you're not, and you shall. Don't contradict.

Pant. But I'm quite well.

Clown. If you aggravate me by telling me you're quite well when I say you're worse, I'll smash you.

Pant. Well, I feel quite——

Clown. Feel that! (*knocks him down and picks him up again*). You needn't apologise; I forgive you if you're sorry, but don't do it again. (*They shake hands and make it up*).

Pant. Times are hard. What shall we do?

Clown. Let's turn railway porters. They lead jolly lives—small wages and nothing to do but work all day long.

Pant. All right. Come on.

[*Exeunt into Station.*

Enter a Doctor and his wife (*their Masks the exact counterpart of* DR. *and* MRS. MCSWISHER). *A shout of recognition and applause from the boys in front.*

Doctor (*looking at his watch*). I wonder what time the train starts, Arabella?

Wife. Can't say, Erasmus. Let's ask one of the railway porters.

Enter CLOWN *and* PANTALOON, *in porters' dress.*

Doctor. My good man, can you inform me when the next train starts?

Pant. At a quarter to twenty-two exactly.

Wife (*astonished*). A quarter to twenty-two! I never heard of such a time.

Pant. My watch is fast.

Doctor (*as* CLOWN *picks his pocket*). So is mine.

Clown. Mine isn't (*looking at* DOCTOR'S *watch*). There's an express to town at half-past forty-one. It's a very rapid one, and reaches town three-quarters of an hour before it gets there.

Wife. That will do for us, my love. We want to get to our journey's end quickly.

Clown. Where are you going?

Doctor. To pay a visit to Lord Dolderums, my dear.

Pant. (*grinning*). He, he, he! Dolderums! What a rum name.

Doctor and Wife (*indignantly*). Rum name, sirrah! What do you mean?

Clown (*aside to* DOCTOR *and* WIFE, *pointing to* PANTALOON). You mustn't mind what he says (*touches his forehead*). He's off his chump.

Doctor (*mollified*). Ah, so I thought. Dolderums is a very ancient family.

Comes from the best Scotch (*is about to take a pinch of snuff*).

Clown (*dipping his fingers in the box*). I always take the very best Scotch snuff myself, sir.

Pant (*dipping in box*). So do I.

(DOCTOR *slaps his knuckles smartly* PANTALOON *wrings his hands.*)

Clown (*grinning*). Mixed with a little rappee (*turns to* DOCTOR). And where does Lord Rumdedols——

Doctor (*correctingly*). Dol-de-rums.

Clown. Ah, yes, Dolderums. Where does he reside?

Doctor and Wife (*grandly*). Waggletree Park, London.

Clown. Good gracious, old un, what a singular coincidence!

Pant. What?

Clown. Why, if my father had been Lord Dolderums' butler, I should have been his lordship's nephew.

Doctor and Wife (*greatly astonished*). Is it possible?

Clown. It's a positive fact.

Doctor. So nearly related and a railway porter!

Pant. Times are hard, sir. Anything now for an honest crust.

Doctor. Can we take any message from you to his lordship?

Clown. Tell him not to forget to send the ten-pound note he owes me.

Pant. Or perhaps the gentleman wouldn't mind advancing the money. His lordship would be sure to pay him when they meet at Waggletree Park.

Doctor (*eagerly*). True, true! I shall be most happy (*taking out his pocket-book*). Anything I can do to oblige a nephew of Lord Dolderums (PANTALOON *doubles up with laughter.* CLOWN *kicks him aside*), I shall consider a privilege. How much was it?

Pant. (*aside*). Say twenty pounds.

Clown. Twenty pounds, if you please.

Doctor (*giving notes*). There are twenty pounds (*puts pocket-book back in pocket, which* CLOWN *skilfully abstracts the next moment.*) And now for the train. Good-bye, my friend (*to* CLOWN).

Clown (*very politely to* WIFE). Good-bye.

(CLOWN *is stealing off,* POLICEMAN *seizes him.* DOCTOR *and* WIFE *advance and seize* PANTALOON, *who has taken the watch*).

Pant. (*alarmed*). It wasn't me that did it; it was him.

Clown (*alarmed*). No, it was him, and it wasn't me.

Doctor. Seize them both; they're a pair of pickpockets, and have robbed me. I am Doctor Erasmus McSwisher, of Tickle Toby Hall.

Wife. And I'm Mrs. Arabella Mc——

At this crisis, the interesting scene was brought to an unexpected close by a well-known voice shrieking out, in accents of violent wrath—

" I'll endure it no longer, you audacious rebels ! Don't hold me, Arabella ; just give me a push up behind, and let me get amongst them !"

At these appalling words, once more a dead silence fell upon the assembly.

There was no mistaking the sounds, and ere anyone had time to move, or even to speak, one of the dining room windows overlooking the garden flew up with a bang and a crash, and Doctor McSwisher plunged in—dashing aside the window blind, and falling head first into the arms of Mr. Augustus Popkins, the dandy hair-dresser of Whoppington (Betsy's sweet-heart), where he lay for a moment to recover his breath.

CHAPTER XL.

DOCTOR MCSWISHER AND HIS WIFE ARRIVE AT LAST, ACCOMPANIED BY SNEAKING SIMON—OLD JOE TURNS CONSPIRATOR AND STICKS UP FOR THE BOYS—A STORMY CONCLUSION TO A MERRY EVENING.

THE domestics shrieked loudly.

" Help me in, Erasmus," also shrieked the doctor's spouse.

" Help yourself, ma'am," growled the incensed principal, springing up, and rushing to the orchestra, where he glared so fiercely at Mr. Presto Scrape that his first string went off at once with a bang, and he himself felt as though he would have liked to creep into his fiddle-case if he could have done so.

Having petrified the conductor with his stony gaze, he next glared at the second fiddle, the cornet, and the double bass, until they shuddered in their seats.

Then he mounted on to one of the chairs, and threw his piercing glances all round the theatre.

Every single one of the forty-two boys was as quiet as a mouse in the presence of the cat.

" Just so ! I see ; yes, yes, ha ! ha !" he muttered, angrily, between his teeth.

" Oh, scissors !" muttered Jemmy Muddle, half inclined to laugh, in spite of all ; " here's a pretty go !"

" I don't mind him," replied our hero, Joe ; " dad's here."

" The doctor won't cane us, will he ?" asked the fairies, apprehensively.

" Cane you ! I should think not," Joe answered, indignantly.

" No, no ; we'll take care of that !" the seven assured them.

Having finished his scrutiny of the pupils that principally composed the audience portion, the fierce principal turned his eyes towards the stage, on which our hero and Jemmy Muddle, in their respective characters of clown and the old un, with the addition of Harry Merriman, who did the policeman, and Tommy Tattler and Charley Dimond, who personated the doctor and his wife, still kept their ground.

Whilst, from the wings, fair girlish faces peered forth occasionally, glancing timidly at the formidable principal, whom they evidently looked upon as some terrible ogre waiting to gobble them up.

" So," he exclaimed at length, in a voice of thunder, " this is the way my strict injunctions are carried out in my absence, is it ?"

No one spoke.

" Where are the masters ?" was the next question.

No answer.

The silence increased the doctor's wrath, and he went on—

" I have been the victim of a vile con-spiracy," he exclaimed, with bitter emphasis.

" We have both been victims, Erasmus," joined in Mrs. McSwisher, who had contrived, somehow, to drag herself through the window, and now joined her husband.

"Yes, both; you are right, Arabella," admitted the doctor. "Both."

The principal extended his arm, and continued, in a tone of strong denunciation—

"We have been sent on a wild-goose chase to town by means of a ridiculous letter, and we might have wandered about the suburbs of the metropolis until Doomsday, looking after a spot that was not to be found, and in search of a person that never existed, but for the noble conduct of Master Simon Sly."

The sneaking youth in question, who had also by this time made his entrance through the window, came creeping forward, looking anything but noble.

"It was he," went on the doctor, "who, having a suspicion of the abominable trick put upon us, followed us to town, and gave us such information as caused us to return by the first train on the following morning."

The seven glared at the high-minded young gentleman alluded to, and vowed internally what they would do to him when they got hold of him.

"And now," exclaimed Doctor McSwisher, with fierce declamation, "I demand to know the author of 'Lord Dolderums, Waggletree Park?'"

Still silence.

"I demand to know how you dare to transform my house into a penny show, and act a pantomime, after my expressly forbidding anything of a pantomimical description?"

No reply.

"I demand to know how you dare to caricature me?" roared the principal, pointing to Tom Tattler, who still wore the doctor's mask and one of the doctor's coats and hats—borrowed for the occasion—and who looked an exact copy of the original.

"And me!" shrieked the portly Arabella, glowing with rage, as she extended her finger towards Charley Dimond, who had on a portion of her wardrobe, stuffed with a couple of pillows to bring him to the proper size and weight of the lady he represented.

Still impenetrable silence reigned.

"And who are those girls?" cried Dr. McSwisher, as he caught sight of the fairies at the wings.

"Girls!" exclaimed his wife; "girls!"

"Yes, girls; I see several in short skirts, with what-you-may-call-'ems on their heads," he shouted.

Miss Finnikin now came forward.

"They are Miss Teachwell's pupils, doctor," she explained, "who were invited to the breaking-up party."

"Breaking-up party!" burst out the doctor, transported beyond himself. "By Heaven! this is too much. Was there ever such atrocity heard of in the world before?

"But there shall be a breaking-up, such a breaking-up as shall be remembered. Every boy in the school shall receive a severe castigation, and those whom I find in anything approaching the dress of a Merry Andrew shall receive treble.

"Arabella, fetch me my cane—no, stop; bring the bundle of canes from the parlour cupboard. Lock the door as you go out. Let none escape."

Away waddled the portly matron, followed by Master Sly, who received several showers of nut shells as he sneaked after her.

Just at that moment the principal's eyes fell upon Mr. Joseph Muggins, who had been an unobserved but very attentive listener to what had transpired.

Seeing the doctor looking at him, old Joe rose.

"How are you, Mr. Swisher?" he said, rather bluntly.

The doctor's eyebrows went up with surprise.

"Eh! What!" he exclaimed. "Is it Mr.—a—Bug——"

"Mug——"

"Ah! yes, yes; so it is—Mr.—a—Muggins," stammered the pedagogue, in his sudden confusion at the sight of the old pantomimist, whom he felt inclined to look upon as an aider and abettor in the conspiracy. "Well, Mr. Muggins, don't you consider this proceeding something —a—a—a—almost diabolical in its atrocity?"

To the horror of the incensed preceptor, Mr. Muggins grinned all over his face as he replied—

"Well, really, if you want my opinion,

I can't see as there's anything at all of a diabolical nature about it, except the Demon King's mask. The fact is, doctor, boys will be boys, all the world over. It comes natural, and they can't help it."

"But they can help being imps of mischief—juvenile ruffians," roared the principal.

"I don't see as they are," returned old Joe; "I don't see as they've done anything to make a noise about, and as to the pantomime, I think it does them a deal of credit. I haven't had such an evening's enjoyment I don't know when."

The doctor staggered back, and glared through his spectacles at the jovial, round face of the speaker like a fiend.

"It's very evident to me, Mr. Muggins, that you defend these disgraceful doings," he exclaimed at length—"doings which would never have occurred if I had not received your son into my establishment. It is at him I must point my finger as the ringleader of all that has happened."

"You've my permission to point your finger at my boy as long as you like," returned old Joe, complacently; "he's one of those conspicuous characters as were made to be pointed at."

"It seems to me you encourage him in his pantomime tomfoolery," remarked the doctor, savagely.

"Encourage him!" burst out Joe Muggins senior, exultingly. "Of course I does. Didn't I teach him everything he knows? Of course I did, and I'm proud of him."

The unpantomimical McSwisher shook his head in deprecation of the benighted condition of the man before him.

At the same moment, the matronly Arabella entered with a bundle of canes, and threw them down before her spouse.

The sight evidently had a cheering effect upon the doctor's wounded spirits, and he was about to swoop down upon them, when the old clown suddenly forestalled him by snatching up the instruments of torture and putting them under his arm.

"What do you mean by that, sir?" shouted the doctor, fiercely. "What do you want with those canes?"

"I was just a-going to ask you the same question, Mr. Licker," responded Joe. "What do you want with them?"

"I've a duty to perform, sir, and I am going to perform it," returned the principal, knitting his brows and grinding his teeth savagely.

"You means to say you're a-going to wallop these young gentlemen all round, cos they've been enjoying themselves and having a happy evening?"

"That is my intention, sir. I don't allow my pupils to have happy evenings in defiance of my authority," exclaimed the doctor, "and I desire you'll instantly deliver up to me those canes."

"Not if I knows it," returned the old clown, grasping the twigs tighter than ever.

"If you'd have joined in with the youngsters, as a master might do at holiday times without hurting hisself, you wouldn't have drove them to act defiant. But, anyhow, you're not a-going to chastise my boy, nor any of the rest either, if I can help it, though you are at Whoppington!"

At this daring and open defiance of his authority, Dr. McSwisher turned almost blue with wrath.

"Give me the canes!" he shouted, as he made a desperate snatch at the implements of flagellation.

"Don't you wish you may get 'em?" responded old Joe, as he threw the entire bundle on the stage, exclaiming, as he did so—

"Help yourselves, boys, and look out for number one."

This the seven immediately did by seizing a cane apiece.

The principal and his wife, quite furious at being thus thwarted, rushed venomously upon the old clown.

But the latter had been in too many comic scenes to look upon the matter in any other light than a good joke.

"Here we are," he cried, as he playfully kicked the doctor's fragile supporters from under him, and laid him on his back on the floor.

Having done this, he very skilfully placed the matronly Arabella in a horizontal position by the side of her husband.

After which, he placed a couple of forms and several armchairs upon them to keep them in their proper positions.

The colloquy between old Joe and the principal had given those on the stage time to arrange a little plan of action.

The descent of the doctor and his wife to the ground was the signal to commence carrying out this plan.

The next moment every light was suddenly extinguished.

The room was enveloped in total darkness.

Form after form was rapidly piled by invisible hands upon the prostrate scholastic couple, till they were completely enclosed in the meshes of a wooden prison.

In vain they struggled, and groped, and shouted, and tried to get out.

There they were obliged to remain.

During this, the forty-two boys who had formed the audience slipped off to bed.

The young ladies were carefully conducted to the parlour.

Master Simon Sly was detected creeping up to his room.

Jemmy Muddle caught sight of him.

"There he goes!" he cried to his companions.

"After him!" they shouted.

Away flew the sneak up the stairs like a hare startled by the hounds.

The seven followed.

Each had his "tingleback" in his hand.

They came up with Master Sly just as he reached his room.

He bolted into it, but had no time to bolt the door—his pursuers were too close upon him.

"Don't hit me!" he howled.

"No, we won't," cried Harry Merriman, "we'll skin you!"

Then the "tinglebacks" went to work.

Whack! whack! whack! Swish! swish! swish! till the sneaking youth yelled for mercy.

This, however, was not granted till he had received a good sound thrashing.

Then, when he was black and blue, and covered with stripes from head to foot, they left him to creep into bed how he could.

But the incidents of the night were not yet over.

The two masters up in the cockloft, hearing the shrieks and confusion, and fancying something terrible had happened, crept downstairs.

The seven watched them and followed.

"Oh, Mister Foggy! Oh, Mounseer Bungbung," whispered Forks, with assumed terror, "for goodness sake get out of sight; there's such a lot of bobbies after you."

The terrified professors rushed from the house.

Forks had given them their hats and scarves, so away they went, only happy to get clear of the house and the "bobbies," of whom the mendacious Forks had spoken.

Doctor and Mrs. McSwisher renewed their outcry.

"Murder! Help!" they shrieked.

Jemmy Muddle crept on to the stage, and having quietly applied a lucifer to the fireworks and red fire, crept quietly out again, locking the door after him.

The effect was almost immediate.

What with the fizzing of the squibs, the bang, bang, bang of the crackers that flew about everywhere, and the glare and sulphurous smoke of the last of these inflammable compounds, the occupants of the room were not only frightened out of their wits, but almost smothered.

They madly struggled to the windows, and threw them open, thinking to get out.

But the shutters were closed, and firmly bolted on the outside.

Getting out was impossible.

The holes in the top allowed the fumes to escape, but nothing else.

Doctor and Mrs. McSwisher were prisoners.

The young ladies took off their stage dresses.

So did the seven, and then they met for a short time in the parlour.

They did not, however, remain longer than was sufficient to take a sandwich and a glass of wine.

This done, the carriages drove up to the door, and took them away amid hearty farewells and mutual regrets at parting.

"We shall meet again some day, I daresay," cried Fanny Fairchild.

"I hope so," answered our hero Joe, as the vehicles rattled away.

Thus ended the performance of the grand pantomime at the Theatre Royal, Tickle Toby House.

It not being considered safe for any of the seven to remain, after what had happened, exposed to the wrath of Doctor McSwisher, old Joe kindly took the entire party—John Bangs and Forks included—with him to the inn where he was staying.

There they had a jolly supper and any quantity of funny stories from the veteran clown, after which they went to bed very tired, but altogether very happy.

The next morning they started to town by the first train, the small youth in the buttons going home with Joe, the idea being to get him an engagement on the stage, for which he was intensely anxious, at the first opportunity.

* * * * *

It was quite an hour after Joe, with his parent and companions, left the school, when Mr. and Mrs. McSwisher found themselves at liberty, the door having been unfastened by cook, who, for her kindness, received a month's notice on the spot.

The other pupils had crept off to bed, and the principal was too fatigued to pursue them.

McSwisher was beginning to revive after a hearty supper, when his wife drew his attention to the fact that both the assistant masters were absent.

Cook was called and questioned, the notice to quit being removed.

" Hain't seen 'em since last night, sir," was her reply.

Housemaid being questioned, gave the same account.

Just as the servants were dismissed, and Mr. McSwisher was about to retire, a noise was heard on the pupils' staircase, which was at the side of the house.

Cook proceeded, candle in hand, to see what it was.

There stood Mr. Fogem !

" Lor', sir ! Where have you been to ?" asked cook.

" Is the doctor in ?"

" Yes, sir. He's bin askin' for you."

The assistant master then proceeded to the principal's room, and a rather stormy interview took place.

At length Mr. Fogem succeeded in persuading Mr. McSwisher that he too had been hoaxed, and peace was restored for the night.

And the next night the school was deserted.

CHAPTER XLI.

IN WHICH YOUNG JOE, BY AN UNEXPECTED CATASTROPHE, IS DEPRIVED OF HIS CHRISTMAS ENGAGEMENT—OLD JOE RECEIVES AN ADVANTAGEOUS OFFER ACROSS THE CHANNEL, WHICH HE ACCEPTS—YOUNG JOE AND FORKS ARE LEFT ALONE.

" MAN proposes ; Heaven disposes," is a proverb universally admitted.

If Joe Muggins, senior, and his adopted son had ever doubted this fact, the truth of it was now to be impressed upon their notice.

On the very next day after their return to London, they read in the morning paper, as they sat at breakfast, the disastrous intelligence that the theatre at which young Joe was engaged for the forthcoming Christmas pantomime had been burnt to the ground on the preceding night.

It was, of course, a great blow to all. Not only in a pecuniary sense, but inasmuch as it would interfere with our hero's professional prospects.

The destruction of the theatre so close upon Christmas left him without the chance of any other engagement.

All the managers had made their engagements long ago, and consequently young Joe found himself at the eleventh hour entirely shut out from all the pantomimes, for this season at least.

A look of blank dismay settled upon his usually lively features at the melancholy catastrophe.

Mrs. Muggins, in the intensity of her disappointment and grief, burst into tears.

Forks, who was with them, almost

choked himself with a crust which the shock caused him to bolt suddenly.

Mr. Muggins, senior, dropped the newspaper, and ejaculated simply—

"Good gracious! who'd have thought it?"

For a few moments there was a silent pause of sheer consternation.

"Well," remarked young Joe at length, in a rueful tone, "there'll be no clowning for me this Christmas, that's certain."

"Nor no sprite for me neither," joined in Forks, dolefully.

"A clear loss of four pounds a week for twelve weeks, certain," sobbed Mrs. Muggins.

"Not forgetting the Ben., which would have come to as much more," supplemented her spouse, with a mournful shake of his head.

"Oh, dear, dear! it don't do to think of—it's too dreadful!" wailed the afflicted female.

"Well, it can't be helped," said old Joe at length, with as much philosophical resignation as he could muster; "I daresay we're not the only people as misfortune's dropped upon, if we only knew it."

"But this is a drop too much, isn't it, dad?" said his son, appealingly.

"Well, yes, Joe; I can't say but what it is," returned the pantomimist, with, however, a twinkle in his eyes that proved he appreciated the little witticism just uttered. "But it ain't no good a-grumbling," he added; "we can only do as the monkey did when he had the toothache."

"What was that, dad?" Joe asked.

"Grin and bear it, my boy," answered the old clown. "That's what I had to do, when my leg was smashed."

This piece of advice did not appear to have the consolatory effect the speaker intended. At least upon Mrs. Muggins.

"I think professionals are always getting 'drops,' of some sort or another, much more than other people," she sobbed.

"They're more exposed to accidents than other people; that's where it is," Sarah," returned her husband.

"But whatever made them burn down the theatre jest at this time?" joined in Forks, in a fretful tone. "They might have waited till after the pantomime."

Old Joe looked at the speaker rather severely.

"What are you talking about, you young donkey?" he replied. "You don't suppose they set it on fire on purpose, do you?"

"I suppose not," admitted the small youth, sulkily. "But it's an orful nuisance anyhow."

"Of course it is," returned the old clown. "It's always a nuisance to be burnt out, though we are not the only ones as feels it. I daresay, now, if you was to see the manager at this minute, he don't look very cheerful."

"No, poor man, I should think not," remarked Mrs. Muggins, sympathetically, as she wiped her eyes. "I feel for him very much, and for all that this fire will throw out of employment."

"Well, mother, it is no use fretting about it," said young Joe, brightening up all of a sudden, and speaking cheerfully, "it can't be helped; and since we can't act on the stage this year, we must have a pantomime in the back kitchen at home."

"Bravo!" exclaimed old Joe, smiling all over his round face at the cheerful idea, "so we will."

This joyous prospect had a most invigorating effect upon everybody.

Our hero threw a couple of somersaults on the hearthrug.

Whilst Forks, in the height of his newly-recovered spirits, did the splits on a couple of chair backs.

Both of these performances seemed to afford Mr. Muggins, senior, the highest gratification.

"It ain't a bit of good fretting about what can't be helped," he remarked cheerfully; "you'll see there'll be summat'll turn up afore long."

The old clown was right.

The very next rat-tat of the postman brought a letter addressed to "Joseph Muggerini, Esq."

"It's business," exclaimed the pantomimist, as he tore open the envelope and devoured the contents.

"Well, there, now, did anyone ever see the likes of that?" he burst out as he concluded.

"Likes of what, Joe?" asked his wife eagerly.

"Why, I'm offered an engagement at

ten pound a week, to manage a pantomime company at Boulogne."

"And do you mean to take it?" asked
Mrs. Muggins.

"I don't see as I should be justified in
refusing it, as it's for a twelvemonth, and
the money's sure," was the old clown's
reply. "I ain't a-growing younger, you
know, and if I can earn ten pound a week,
I feels as I ought to earn it."

"So I think, my dear," returned his
spouse. "When do they want you?"

"As soon as possible; the letter says
directly, if I can."

"What, before Christmas?"

"Yes."

Sarah's countenance fell at this information. She was considerably disappointed.

"Oh, dear," Mrs. Muggins exclaimed,
"that's very awkward. I should have
liked to have spent Christmas at home—
dear Joe's holidays, too."

"It's very awkward, certainly," admitted old Joe, pursing up his lips, and
scratching his head reflectively; "nevertheless, so it is."

"What, do they want you to start at
once, dad?" asked his son.

"Yes, Joe, they does indeed," responded his adopted parent; "but I
really don't like the idea of leaving you,
just at this time, too."

"I don't like the idea either," returned
our hero, taking his father's hand affectionately.

"And, you see, I'm no good without
your mother at my side. She'd have to
go with me."

"And we should be left here alone,
then, shouldn't we?" remarked young
Joe, rather ruefully.

"Yes, it's a moral you would—all
alone, and that's just the point I'm sticking at."

"Oh, well, never mind, dad," said our
hero, at length, in a tone of exhilaration:
"the engagement is too good to throw
up."

"I think so, too," dad replied; it'd be
as good as three hundred pounds in my
pocket."

"And, besides, it's only for a year."

"That's all."

"And a year will soon pass, won't it?"

"Oh, yes, in less than no time."

"Well, then, if I were you, I should
go," said young Joe, emphatically.

"Would you?"

"Yes, I would indeed, dad."

"Then dash my buttons if I don't,"
exclaimed the pantomimist, in a tone of
determination. "It's all settled, Sarah,"
he cried to his wife; "we're off to Boulogne, so you may begin to pack up at
once."

"And the boys?" asked Mrs Muggins, throwing her arms with maternal
fondness round the neck of her adopted
son, and giving him a hearty kiss.

"Oh, we're going to stop and look
after the house, mother," Joe replied;
"we shall be all right."

This being settled, the old clown wrote
off at once, accepting the engagement, and
stating that he should start for Boulogne
on the following day.

The packing went on briskly, and by
tea-time everything was ready, the boxes
tied up and labelled.

They spent a jovial evening in the
snug little parlour, during which old Joe
smoked his pipe, and sipped his grog, and
gave his young listeners all the good advice he could think of.

The next morning Joe's adopted parents
departed in a cab for London Bridge,
whence the packet started.

That night young Joe and his companion sat in the parlour alone.

CHAPTER XLII.

IN WHICH OUR HERO AND FORKS RECEIVE AN UNEXPECTED VISITOR, AND
DETERMINE TO TAKE A TRIP IN THE COUNTRY.

IT was very quiet, and in order to
amuse themselves, they acted a pantomime, on a very limited scale, in the
kitchen.

The audience was also limited, consisting of the domestic and the Tom cat.

But the former of these, a fresh servant, not being pantomimically disposed,

did not laugh nor applaud the slaps and bumps in the slightest.

Whilst the latter, having endured the clatter as long as he possibly could, at length, in a paroxysm of terror, took a flying leap through one of the window panes, and escaped with a crash into the garden.

Under these adverse circumstances, the performance went off in anything but a lively manner, and was not repeated.

Christmas Day came slowly on.

On this festive occasion, our hero and his companion tried to get up a slight sensation by making a plum pudding.

But it was a decided failure.

The amateur cooks forgot, in their excitement, to put any water in the saucepan.

The consequence was the bottom fell out, and the pudding was reduced to a miserable cinder.

Christmas had returned.

So had the weather—very cold—hard and frosty.

And in proportion as the exhilarating effect of the atmosphere braced up our hero's nerves, so did he begin to find the silence and solitude of the lonely house extremely irksome.

"This is very slow work, isn't it, Forks?" he remarked to his companion one morning.

"Awful," returned the small youth, emphatically. "I'd give anything for a good go-in at knife cleaning or boot polishing, but there ain't nothing to do here."

"Nothing," admitted Joe, ruefully; "we can't even act pantomimes without someone to laugh at us."

"That's true; what's to be done?" Forks inquired.

"I don't know just at this moment," Joe replied, "but I feel very much inclined to do something."

"So do I," eagerly assented the small youth. "I'm reg'lar bursting for some sort of excitement. Can't you think of something?"

"I am thinking," answered Joe, reflectively.

Just as he spoke, as if to assist his thoughts, there came a single melancholy tingle at the bell.

"Hullo! what's that?" exclaimed our hero, as the unusual sound caught his ear.

"Somebody coming," cried Forks, vivaciously.

"So it seems. It can't be the baker or the milkman; they don't ring. Who can it be?"

Both the youngsters ran to the window and looked out to where, outside the gate, stood a youth about their own age.

He was rather inclined to be podgy, and his round face (as much as could be seen of it above a red woollen comforter, several yards of which he had wound round his throat) had a good-natured expression in it.

After gazing for an instant, Joe exclaimed, loudly—

"Why, I declare, if it isn't Jemmy Muddle!"

"So it is," ejaculated Forks. "What does he want?"

"I don't know, I'm sure," returned our hero. "But whatever it is, I'm precious glad to see him."

By this time, the servant girl—who belonged to the slow order of beings, was leisurely drifting along the front garden, key in hand, on her way to the gate.

But this did not suit Joe's impatience.

And throwing up the window, he shouted at the top of his voice—

"Hi, Jemmy, old fellow! Here we are!"

Jemmy, who seemed to have been taking a slight nap on the pavement, started from his doze on hearing his name called, and looked up, first at the sky, and then at the chimney pots, and in short everywhere but in the right direction.

At last he found, all of a sudden, a short young woman looking in his face over the garden railings, and asking him rather sharply what he wanted.

"I want to see Master Joe Muggins, if he's at home," responded Jemmy.

"Yes; he's at home, old boy!" shouted our hero, vociferously, from the window. "Open the gate, Susan Jane, and be quick!" he bawled. "It's all right, he's a friend of mine!"

The gate was unlocked, and Jemmy Muddle, still in a fog as to whence the voice he recognised so well proceeded, followed Susan Jane along the path.

www.ingramcontent.com/pod-product-compliance
Lightning Source LLC
Chambersburg PA
CBHW080827250626
47160CB00008B/2869